Philippa Gregory

The Little House

HarperCollins*Publishers*

This novel is entirely a work of fiction. The names, characters and incidents portrayed in it are the work of the author's imagination. Any resemblance to actual persons, living or dead, is entirely coincidental.

HarperCollins*Publishers*
77–85 Fulham Palace Road,
Hammersmith, London w6 8jb

This paperback edition 1998
3 5 7 9 8 6 4

First published in Great Britain by
HarperCollins*Publishers* 1997

Copyright © Philippa Gregory Ltd 1996

The Author asserts the moral right to
be identified as the author of this work

ISBN 0 00 649643 1

Set in Aldus by
Rowland Phototypesetting Ltd,
Bury St Edmunds, Suffolk

Printed and bound by
Caledonian International Book Manufacturing Ltd, Glasgow

The Little House

Philippa Gregory, who went to school in Bristol, has a history degree from the University of Sussex and a PhD in eighteenth-century literature from the University of Edinburgh. She is a fellow of Kingston University. Philippa Gregory lives in Sussex with her family.

By the same author

WIDEACRE
MERIDON
THE FAVOURED CHILD
THE WISE WOMAN
MRS HARTLEY AND THE GROWTH CENTRE
FALLEN SKIES
A RESPECTABLE TRADE
PERFECTLY CORRECT

The Little House

One

ON SUNDAY MORNING, on almost every Sunday morning, Ruth and Patrick Cleary drove from their smart Bristol flat to Patrick's parents' farmhouse outside Bath. They had only been married for four years and Ruth would have preferred to linger in bed, but this Sunday, as almost every Sunday, they had been invited for lunch at one o'clock prompt.

Patrick always enjoyed returning to his home. It had once been a dairy farm, but Patrick's father had sold off the land, retaining only a little wood and circle of fields around the house: an eighteenth-century manor farm of yellow Bath stone. While never being so vulgar as to lie, the Clearys liked to suggest that their family had lived there forever. Patrick's father liked to imply that he came from Somerset yeoman stock and the farm was their ancestral home.

Patrick's mother opened the door as they came up the path. She was always there when they arrived, ready to fling open the door in welcome. Once Ruth had teased Patrick, saying that his mother spent her life peeping through the brass letterbox, so that she could throw open the door as her son arrived, wrap him in her arms, and say, 'Welcome home, darling.' Patrick had looked offended, and had not laughed.

'Welcome home, darling,' his mother said.

Patrick kissed her, and then she turned and kissed Ruth's cheek. 'Hello, dearest, how pale you look. Have you been working too hard?'

Ruth was surprised to find that immediately she felt exhausted. 'No,' she said.

'Freddie, they're here!' Ruth's mother called into the house, and Patrick's father appeared in the hall.

'Hello, old boy,' he said lovingly to Patrick. He dropped an arm briefly on Patrick's shoulder and then turned to Ruth and kissed her. 'Looking lovely, my dear. Patrick – saw you on television last night, the piece on the commuters. Jolly good. They used a bit of it on *News at Ten*. Good show.'

Patrick grimaced. 'It didn't come out how I wanted,' he said. 'I had a new film crew and they all had their own ideas. I might be the reporter, but none of them want to listen to me.'

'Too many chiefs and not enough Indians,' Frederick pronounced.

Ruth looked at him. He often said a sentence, like a little motto, that she had never heard before and that made no sense to her whatsoever. They were a playful family, sometimes quoting family jokes or phrases of Patrick's babytalk that had survived for years. No one ever explained the jokes to Ruth; she was supposed to laugh at them and enjoy them, as if they were self-explanatory.

'That's shoptalk,' Patrick's mother said firmly. 'Not now. I want my assistant in the kitchen!'

It was one of the Sunday rituals that Patrick helped

his mother in the kitchen while Ruth and Frederick chatted in the drawing room. Ruth had tried to join the two in the kitchen once or twice and had glimpsed Patrick's indispensable help. He was perched on one of the kitchen stools, listening to Elizabeth and picking nuts from a bowl of nibbles she had placed before him. When Ruth had interrupted them, they had looked up like two unfriendly children and fallen silent. It was Elizabeth's private time with her son; she did not want Ruth there. Ruth was sent back into the sitting room with the decanter of sherry and instructions to keep Frederick entertained. She learned that she must wait for Patrick to put his head around the door and say, 'Luncheon is served, ladies and gents.' Then Frederick could stop making awkward conversation with her and say, 'I could eat a horse! *Is* it horse again?'

Elizabeth served roast pork with crackling, apple sauce, roast potatoes, boiled potatoes, peas and carrots. Ruth wanted only a little. In Bristol in the canteen of the radio station where she worked as a journalist, she was always hungry. But there was something about the dining room at the farmhouse that made her throat close up. Patrick's father poured red wine and Ruth would drink two or three glasses, but she could not make herself eat.

Patrick ate a good lunch, his plate favoured with the crunchiest potatoes and the best cuts of meat, and always had seconds.

'You'll get fat,' his father warned him. 'Look at me, never gained a pound till I retired from the army and had your mother's home cooking every day.'

'He burns it all up,' Elizabeth defended her son. 'His job is all nerves. He burns it all up with nervous energy.'

They both looked at Ruth, and she managed a small

7

uncomfortable smile. She did not know whether to agree that he would get fat, which would imply an unwifely lack of admiration, or agree that he lived on his nerves, which would indicate that she was not protecting him from stress.

'It's been a devil of a week,' Patrick agreed. 'But I *think* I may be getting somewhere at last.'

There was a little murmur of interest. Ruth looked surprised. She did not know that Patrick had any news from work. She wondered guiltily if her own work, which was demanding and absorbing, had made her neglect his ambition. 'I didn't know,' she said.

He smiled his wide, handsome smile at her. 'I thought I'd wait to tell you until it was shaping up,' he said.

'No point in counting chickens,' his father agreed. 'Spill the beans, old boy.'

'There's talk of a new unit, to do specialist local film documentaries,' Patrick said. 'It'll be headed by a news producer. The best news producer we've got.' He paused, and smiled his professionally modest smile. 'Looks like I'm in line for the job.'

'Good show.'

'Wonderful,' Patrick's mother said.

'What would you do?' Ruth asked.

'Regular hours!' Patrick replied with a little chuckle. 'That's the main thing! I'd still do reports to camera but I wouldn't be on call all the time, and I'd not be running around out of hours. I'd have more control. It's an opportunity for me.'

'Is this a bubble-size celebration?' Patrick's father demanded of Ruth.

She looked at him blankly. She simply had no idea what he meant.

8

'Champagne, darling,' Patrick prompted. 'Do wake up!'

'I suppose it must be.' Ruth stretched her mouth in a smile, trying to be bright and excited. 'How wonderful!'

Patrick's father was already on his way to the kitchen. Elizabeth fetched the special champagne glasses from the sideboard.

'He's got a bottle already chilled,' she said to Patrick. Ruth understood that this was significant.

'Oh ho!' Patrick said as his father came back into the room. 'Chilled already?'

His father gave him a roguish wink and expertly opened the bottle. The champagne splashed into the glasses. Ruth said, 'Only a little please,' but no one heard her. She raised her full glass in a toast to Patrick's success. It was a very dry wine. Ruth knew that dry champagne was the right taste; only inexperienced, ill-educated people liked sweet champagne. If she continued to make herself drink it, then one day she too would like dry champagne and then she would have an educated palate. It was a question of endurance. Ruth took another sip.

'Now I wonder why you were keeping a bottle of champagne on ice?' Patrick prompted his father.

'I have some grounds for celebration – but only if you two are absolutely happy about it. Your mother and I have a little proposition to put to you.'

Ruth tried to look intelligent and interested but the taste of the wine was bitter in her mouth. The taste for champagne, they had assured her, was acquired. Ruth wondered if she would ever like it.

'It's Manor Cottage,' Frederick said. 'On the market at last. Old Miss Fisher died last week and, as you can

9

imagine, I was onto her lawyer pretty quick. She left her estate to some damnfool charity . . . cats or orphans or something . . .' He broke off, suddenly embarrassed, remembering the orphan status of his daughter-in-law. 'Beg pardon, Ruth. No offence.'

Ruth experienced the usual stab of pain at the thought of her lost parents, and smiled her usual bright smile. 'It doesn't matter,' she said. 'It doesn't matter at all.'

'Well, anyway,' said Frederick, 'the house will be sold at once. I've waited for years to get my hands on it. And now, with you getting into more regular hours, it's ideal.'

'And the land?' Patrick asked.

'The garden, and the field, and that copse that joins our bit of wood. It rounds off our land to perfection.'

'Pricey?' Patrick asked.

Frederick laid his finger along his nose to indicate inside knowledge. 'Her lawyer is the executor. And the charity won't be putting it up for auction. They'll want a quick, simple sale. The lawyer will take the first reasonable offer.'

'Who's the lawyer?' Patrick asked.

Frederick grinned – this was the punch line. '*My* lawyer,' he said. 'As it happens. By happy coincidence. Simon Sylvester.'

Patrick chuckled. 'We could sell our flat tomorrow.'

'We should make a handsome profit on it,' his father concurred. 'You could stay here while the cottage is being done up. Couldn't be better.'

'If Ruth agrees,' Elizabeth reminded them.

Both men turned at once to her. 'I don't quite . . .' Ruth said helplessly.

'Manor Cottage is on the market at last,' Patrick said.

'Come on, darling, the little house at the end of the drive. The one I've always had my eye on.'

Ruth looked from one bright impatient face to another. 'You want to buy it?'

'Yes, darling. Yes. Wake up!'

'And sell our flat?'

They nodded.

Ruth could feel that she was being slow, and worse than that, unwilling.

'But how would I get to work? And we like our flat.'

'It was only ever a temporary base,' Frederick said. 'Just a little nest for you two young lovebirds.'

Ruth looked at him, puzzled.

'A good investment is only worth having if you're ready to capitalize,' he said firmly. 'When the time is right.'

'But how would I get to work?'

Elizabeth smiled at her. 'You won't work forever, dearest. You might find that when you have a family-sized house in the country you feel like giving up work altogether. You might have something else to keep you busy!'

Ruth turned to Patrick.

'We might start a family,' he translated.

Frederick gave a shout of laughter. 'Her face! Dear Ruth! Have you never thought about it? We could be talking Chinese!'

Ruth felt her face stiff with stupidity. 'We hadn't planned . . .' she said.

'Well, we couldn't really, could we?' Patrick confirmed. 'Not while we were living in town in a poky little flat, and my hours were all over the place, and you were working so hard. But promotion, and Manor

11

Cottage, well, it all comes together, doesn't it?'

'I've always lived in town,' Ruth said. 'And my job means everything to me. I'm the only woman news producer on the station – it's a real responsibility, and this week I broke a national story –' she glanced at Patrick. 'We scooped you,' she reminded him.

He shrugged. 'Radio is always quicker than telly.'

'We were going to travel . . .' she reminded him. It was an old promise. Ruth was an American child – her father a concert pianist from Boston, her mother an Englishwoman. They had died in the quick brutality of a road accident on a winter visit to England when Ruth was only seven years old. Her mother's English family had taken the orphaned girl in, and she had never seen her home again. When Ruth and Patrick had first met, he had found the brief outline of this story almost unbearably moving and had promised Ruth that they would go back to Boston one day, and find her house. Who knew – her childhood toys, her books, her parents' things might even be in store somewhere, or forgotten in an attic? And part of the chasm of need that Ruth always carried with her might be filled.

'We still can,' he said quickly.

'We'll finish this bottle and then we'll all go down and look at Manor Cottage,' Frederick said firmly. 'Take my word for it, Ruth, you'll fall for it. It's a little peach. Bags of potential.'

'She's not to be bullied,' Elizabeth said firmly. 'We might think it paradise to have the two of you on our doorstep, but if Ruth doesn't want to live so close to us, she is allowed to say "no".'

'Oh, it's not that!' Ruth said quickly, fearful of giving offence.

'It's just the surprise of it,' Patrick answered for her. 'I should have warned her that you've had your eye on that for years and you *always* get your own way.'

'Amen to that!' Frederick said. The father and son clinked glasses.

'But I like our flat,' Ruth said.

Ruth borrowed a pair of Elizabeth's Wellington boots for the walk, and her waxed jacket and her headscarf. She had not come prepared, because the after-lunch walk was always Frederick's time alone with Patrick. Usually Elizabeth and Ruth cleared the lunch table, stacking the plates in the dishwasher, and then sat in the living room with the Sunday papers to read and Mozart on the hi-fi. Ruth had once gone with the men on their walk, but after a few yards she had realized her mistake. They strode along with their hands buried deep in their pockets, shoulder to shoulder in a silent enjoyable communion. She had delayed them at stiles and gates because they had felt bound to hold her hand as she clambered over them, or warn her about mud in gateways. They had kept stopping to ask if they were going too fast for her or if she was tired. Their very generosity to her and concern for her had told her that she was a stranger, and unwelcome. They wasted no politeness on each other. For each other they shared a happy, wordless camaraderie.

The next Sunday Frederick announced: 'Time for my constitutional,' and then he had turned to Ruth: 'Will you come with us again, Ruth? It looks like rain.'

As she had hesitated, Elizabeth said firmly, 'You two run along! I won't have my daughter-in-law dragged around the countryside in the rain! Ruth will stay here with me and we can be cosy. We'll kick our shoes off and gossip.'

After that, the two men always walked alone after lunch and Ruth and Elizabeth waited for them to return. There was no kicking off shoes. Elizabeth was a naturally formal woman, and they had no mutual friends for gossip. Ruth punctiliously asked after Miriam, Patrick's elder sister, who was teaching in Canada. But Miriam was always well. Elizabeth inquired about Ruth's work, which was filled with drama and small triumphs that never sounded interesting when retold, and asked after Ruth's aunt, who had brought her up after the death of her parents. Ruth always said that she was well, but in truth they had lost contact except for Christmas cards and the occasional phone call. Then there was nothing more to say. The two women leafed through the newspapers together until they heard the dog scrabbling at the back door and Elizabeth rose to let him in and put the kettle on for tea.

Ruth knew that Manor Cottage mattered very much to everyone when she was invited on the walk, especially when Elizabeth walked too.

They went across the fields, the men helping the women over the stiles. They could see the Manor Cottage roof from two fields away, nestling in a little valley. The footpath from the farmhouse led to the back gate and into the garden. The drive to the farmhouse ran past the front door. There was a stream that ran through the garden.

'Might get a trout or two,' Frederick observed.

'As long as it's not damp,' Elizabeth said.

Frederick had brought the key. He opened the front

door and stepped back. 'Better carry her over the threshold,' he said to Patrick. 'Just for luck.'

It would have been awkward and ungracious to refuse. Ruth let Patrick pick her up and step over the threshold with her and then put her down gently in the little hall and kiss her, as if it were their new house, and they were newlyweds, moving in.

The old lady's rickety furniture was still in the house and it smelled very faintly of damp and cats' pee. Ruth, with a strong sense of her alien childhood, recognized at once the flavour of a house that the English would call full of character, and that her American father would have called dirty.

'Soon air out,' Frederick said firmly. 'Here, take a look.'

He opened the door on the sitting room, which ran the length of the cottage. At the rear of the cottage were old-fashioned French windows leading to a muddy garden, desolate under the November sky. 'Pretty as a picture in summer,' he said. 'We'd lend you Stephens. He could come over and do the hard digging on Tuesdays. Mow the lawn for you, trim the hedges. You'd probably enjoy doing the light stuff yourself.'

'So relaxing,' Elizabeth said, with a nod to Ruth. 'Very therapeutic for Patrick!'

They turned and went into the opposite room. It was a small dark dining room, which led to the kitchen at the back overlooking the back garden. The back door was half off its hinges, and damp had seeped into the walls. There was a large old-fashioned china sink, with ominous brown stains around the drain hole, and an enormous ash-filled, grease-stained coal-burning range. 'Oh, you'll have such fun with this!' Elizabeth exclaimed.

15

'Ruth, how I envy you! It's the sweetest little room, and you can do so much with it. I can just imagine a real farmhouse kitchen – all pine and stencils!'

A laurel bush slapped waxy green leaves against the kitchen window and dripped water mournfully on the panes. Ruth gave a little shiver against the cold.

'Upstairs is very neat,' Frederick observed, shepherding them out of the kitchen through the dining room and back into the hall. 'Pop on up, Ruth. Go on, Patrick.'

Ruth unwillingly led the way upstairs. The others followed behind her, commenting on the soundness of the stairs and the attractive banister. Ruth hesitated on the landing.

'This is so lovely,' Elizabeth said, throwing open a door. 'The master bedroom, Ruth. See the view!'

The bedroom faced south, down the valley. It was a pretty view of the fields, and in the distance a road and the village.

'Sunny all the day long,' Frederick said.

'And here are two other bedrooms and a bathroom,' Elizabeth said, gesturing to the other doors. She led Ruth to see each of them. 'And this *has* to be a nursery!' she exclaimed. The pretty little room faced over the garden. In the cold autumn light it looked grey and dreary. 'Roses at the window all the summer long,' Elizabeth said. 'Look! I think you can just see our house!'

Ruth obediently looked. 'Yes.'

She turned and led the way downstairs. While the others returned for a second look at the damp kitchen, Ruth went outside and waited in the cold front garden. When they emerged, all smiling at some remark, they looked at her expectantly, as if they were waiting for some pronouncement that would make them all happy, as if she should say that she had passed an exam, or that she had won the lottery. They turned bright, hopeful faces on her, and Ruth had nothing to offer them. She felt her shoulders lift in a little shrug. She did not know what they expected her to say.

'You *do* love it, don't you, darling?' Patrick asked.

'It's very pretty,' she said.

It was the right thing to say. They looked pleased. Frederick closed the front door and locked it with the care of a householder. 'Ideal,' he pronounced.

Patrick slipped his arm around her waist. 'We could go ahead, then,' he said encouragingly. 'Put the flat on the market, make an offer on this place, move house.'

Ruth hesitated. 'I don't think I want . . .'

'Now, stop it, Patrick,' Elizabeth said reasonably. 'You've only just seen it. There's lots to take into account. You have to have a survey done, and you have to have your own flat valued. Ruth needs time to get adjusted to the idea; it's a bigger change for her than anyone!' She smiled at Ruth conspiratorially: the two women in league together. 'You can't rush us and make a decision all in one afternoon! I won't allow it!'

Patrick threw her a mock salute. 'All right! All right!'

'It's a business decision,' Frederick supplemented. 'Not simply somewhere to live. You and Ruth might have fallen in love with it, but you have to be sure it's a good investment too.' He smiled fondly at Ruth and tapped her on the nose with the house key before putting it into his pocket. 'Now don't turn those big eyes on me and tell me you have to have it, little Ruth. I agree, it looks like an excellent bargain for the two of you, but I shall let my head rule my heart on this one.'

'Hark at him!' Elizabeth exclaimed. She slipped her

17

hand in Ruth's arm and led her around the corner of the house to the back garden. 'He's determined to have the place, and he makes it sound like it is us who are rushing him. Come and see the garden! It's just bliss in summer. A real old-fashioned cottage garden. You can't plant borders like this in less than twenty years. They have to mature.'

Ruth trailed after Elizabeth to the back garden and obediently admired the decaying, dripping wallflowers and the seedpods of stocks. At the back of the flower bed were the tall dead spines of delphiniums and before them were bloated pods of last season's love-in-the-mist. The lawn was soggy with moss; the crazy-paved pathway was slick with lichen and overgrown with weeds.

'Best way to see it,' Frederick said. He picked a stick and switched at a nettle head. 'See a property in the worst light and you know it. There's no nasty shocks hidden away. You know what you're getting. If you love it like this, little Ruth, then you'll adore it in summer.'

'I don't think I could really . . .' Ruth started.

'Good gracious, look at the time!' Elizabeth exclaimed. 'I thought I was missing my cup of tea. It's half past four already. Frederick you're very naughty to drag us down here. Ruth and I are faint for tea!'

Frederick looked at his watch and exclaimed in surprise. They turned and left the garden. Ruth plucked at Patrick's sleeve as he went past her. 'I can't get to work from here,' she said swiftly. 'It'd take me hours to get in. And what about when I have to work late? And I like our flat.'

'Hush,' he said. 'Let them have their little plans. It doesn't do any harm, does it? We'll talk about it later. Not now.'

'Here, Patrick!' his father called. 'D'you think this is a legal right of way? Can you remember, when you were a boy, was there a footpath here?'

Patrick gave her a swift, encouraging smile and joined his parents.

Ruth was quiet at tea, and when they finally pulled away from Manor Farm with a homemade quiche and an apple crumble in the usual Sunday box of home-cooked food on the back seat, she still said nothing.

They were in an awkward situation. Like many wealthy parents, Frederick and Elizabeth had given the newlyweds a home as their wedding present. Ruth and Patrick had chosen the flat, but Frederick and Elizabeth had bought it for them. Ruth dimly knew that shares had been sold, and sacrifices made, so that she and Patrick should start their married life in a flat that they could never have afforded, not even on their joint salaries. House prices might be falling after the manic boom of the mid-eighties, but a flat in Clifton would always have been beyond their means. Her gratitude and her sense of guilt showed itself in her sporadic attempts at good housekeeping, and her frenzied efforts to make the place look attractive when Frederick and Elizabeth were due to visit.

She had no investment of her own to balance against their generosity. Her parents had been classical musicians – poorly paid and with no savings. They had left her nothing, not even a home; their furniture had not been worth shipping to the little girl left in England. Patrick's family were her only family, the flat was her first home since she had been a child.

Frederick had never delivered the deeds of the flat to Patrick. No one ever mentioned this: Patrick never asked for them, Frederick never volunteered them. The deeds had stayed with Frederick, and were still in his name. And now he wanted to sell the flat, and buy somewhere else.

'I've loved that cottage ever since I was a boy,' Patrick volunteered, breaking the silence. They were driving down the long sweeping road towards Bristol, the road lined with grey concrete council housing. 'I've always wanted to live there. It's such luck that it should come up now, just when we can take it.'

'How d'you mean?' Ruth asked.

'Well, with my promotion coming up, and better hours for me. More money too. It's as if it was meant. Absolutely meant,' Patrick repeated. 'And d'you know I think we'll make a killing on the flat. We've put a lot of work in, we'll see a return for it. House prices are recovering all the time.'

Ruth tried to speak. She felt so tired, after a day of well-meaning kindness, that she could hardly protest. 'I don't see how it would work,' she said. 'I can't work a late shift and drive in and back from there. If I get called out on a story it's too far to go; it'd take me too long.'

'Oh, rubbish!' Patrick said bracingly. 'When d'you ever get a big story? It's a piddling little job, not half what you could do, and you know it! A girl with your brains and your ability should be streets ahead. You'll never get anywhere on Radio Westerly, Ruth, it's small-time radio! You've got to move on, darling. They don't appreciate you there.'

Ruth hesitated. That part at least was true. 'I've been looking . . .'

'Leave first, and then look,' Patrick counselled. 'You look for a job now and any employer can see what you're doing, and how much you're being paid, and you're typecast at once. Give yourself a break and then start applying and they have to see you fresh. I'll help you put a demo tape together, and a CV. And we could see what openings there are in Bath. That'd be closer to home for you.'

'Home?'

'The cottage, darling. The cottage. You could work in Bath very easily from there. It's the obvious place for us.'

Ruth could feel a dark shadow of a headache sitting between her eyebrows on the bridge of her nose. 'Hang on a minute,' she said. 'I haven't said I want to move.'

'Neither have I,' Patrick said surprisingly. They were at the centre of Bristol. He hesitated at a junction and then put the car into gear and drove up towards Park Street. The great white sweep of the council chamber looked out over a triangle of well-mown grass. Bristol cathedral glowed in pale stone, sparkled with glass. 'I would miss our little flat,' he said. 'It was our first home, after all. We've had some very good times there.'

He was speaking as if they were in the grip of some force of nature that would, resistlessly, sell their flat, which Ruth loved, and place her in the countryside, which she disliked.

'Whether I change my job or not, I don't want to live in the back of beyond,' she said firmly. 'It's OK for you, Patrick, it's your family home and I know you love it. But I like living in town, and I like our flat.'

21

'Sure,' Patrick said warmly. 'We're just playing around with ideas; just castles in the air, darling.'

On Monday morning Ruth was slow to wake. Patrick was showered and dressed before she even sat up in bed.

'Shall I bring you a cup of coffee in bed?' he asked pleasantly.

'No, I'll come down and be with you,' she said, hastily getting out of bed and reaching for her dressing gown.

'I can't stay long,' he said. 'I'm seeing Ian South this morning, about the job.'

'Oh.'

'And I'll ring the estate agent, shall I? See what sort of value they'd put on this place? So we know where we are?'

'Patrick, I really don't want to move . . .'

He shooed her out of the room and down the hallway to the kitchen ahead of him. 'Come on, darling, I can't be late this morning.'

Ruth spooned coffee and switched on the filter machine.

'Instant will do,' Patrick said. 'I really have to rush.'

'Patrick, we must talk about this. I don't want to sell the flat. I don't want to move house. I want to stay here.'

'*I* want to stay here too,' he said at once, as if it were Ruth's plan that they move. 'But if something better comes up we would be stupid not to consider it. I'm not instructing an estate agent to sell, darling. Just getting an idea of the value.'

'Surely we don't want to live down the lane from your parents,' Ruth said. She poured boiling water and added milk and passed Patrick his coffee. 'Toast?'

He shook his head. 'No time.' He stopped abruptly as a thought suddenly struck him. 'You don't imagine that they would interfere, do you?'

'Of course not!' Ruth said quickly. 'But we would be very much on their doorstep.'

'All the better for us,' Patrick said cheerfully. 'Built-in baby-sitters.'

There was a short silence while Ruth absorbed this leap. 'We hadn't even thought about a family,' she said. 'We've never talked about it.'

Patrick had put down his coffee cup and turned to go, but he swung back as a thought suddenly struck him. 'I say, Ruth, you're not against it, are you? I mean, you do *want* to have children one day, don't you?'

'Of course,' she said hastily. 'But not . . .'

'Well, that's all right then.' Patrick gave his most dazzling smile. 'Phew! I suddenly had the most horrid thought that you were going to say that you didn't want children like some ghastly hard-bitten career journalist. Like an awful American career woman with huge shoulder pads!' He laughed at the thought. 'I'm really looking forward to it. You'd be so gorgeous with a baby.'

Ruth had a brief seductive vision of herself in a *broderie anglaise* nightgown with a fair-headed, round-faced, smiling baby nestled against her. 'Yes, but not for a while.' She trailed behind him as he went out to the hall. Patrick shrugged himself into his cream-coloured raincoat.

'Not till we've got the cottage fixed up as we want it and everything, of course,' he said. 'Look, darling, I have to run. We'll talk about it tonight. Don't worry about dinner, I'll take you out. We'll go to the trattoria and eat spaghetti and make plans!'

'I'm working till six,' Ruth said.

'I'll book a table for eight,' Patrick said, dropped a hasty kiss askew her mouth, and went out, banging the door behind him.

Ruth stood on her own in the hall and then shivered a little at the cold draught from the door. It was raining again; it seemed as if it had been raining for weeks.

The letter flap clicked and a handful of letters dropped to the doormat. Four manila envelopes, all bills. Ruth saw that the gas bill showed red print and realized that once again she was late in paying. She would have to write a cheque this morning and post it on her way to work or Patrick would be upset. She picked up the letters and put them on the kitchen counter, and went upstairs for her bath.

The newsroom was unusually subdued when Ruth came in, shook her wet coat, and hung it up on the coatstand. The duty producer glanced up. 'I was just typing the handover note,' he said. 'You'll be short-staffed today, but there's nothing much on. A fire, but it's all over now, and there's a line on the missing girl.'

'Is David skiving?' she asked. 'Where is he?'

The duty producer tipped his head towards the closed door of the news editor's office. 'Getting his cards,' he said in an undertone. 'Bloody disgrace.'

'What's the matter?'

'Cutbacks is what,' he said, typing rapidly with two fingers. 'Not making enough money, not selling enough soap powder, who's the first to go? Editorial staff! After all, any fool can do it, can't they? And all anyone wants is the music anyway. Next thing we know it'll be twenty-

24

four-hour music with not even a DJ – music and adverts, that's all they want.'

'Terry, stop it!' Ruth said. 'Tell me what's going on!'

He pulled the paper irritably out of the typewriter and thrust it into her hands. 'There's your handover note. I'm off shift. I'm going out to buy a newspaper and look for a job. The writing's on the wall for us. They're cutting back the newsroom staff: they want to lose three posts. David's in there now getting the treatment. There are two other posts to go and no one knows who's for the chop. It's all right for you, Ruth, with your glamour-boy husband bringing in a fortune. If I lose my job I don't know what we'll do.'

'I don't exactly work for pocket money, you know,' Ruth said crossly. 'It's not a hobby for me.'

'OK,' he said. 'Sorry. We're all in the same boat. But I'm sick of this place, I can tell you. I'm off shift now and I'm not coming back till Wednesday – *if* I've still got a job then.' He strode over to the coat rack and took his jacket down. '*And* it's still bloody raining,' he said angrily, and stormed out of the newsroom, banging the door behind him.

Ruth looked over to the copy taker and raised her eyebrows. The girl nodded. 'He's been like that all morning,' she said resignedly.

'Oh.' Ruth took the handover note to the desk and started reading through it. The door behind her opened and David came out, the news editor, James Peart, with him. 'Think it over,' James was saying. 'I promise you we'll use you as much as we possibly can. And there are other outlets, remember.' He noticed Ruth at her desk. 'Ruth, when you've got the eleven-o'clock bulletin out of the way could you come and see me?'

'Me?' Ruth asked.

He nodded. 'Yes,' he said and went back into his office and closed the door.

There was a brief, shocked silence. Ruth turned to her oldest friend. 'What did he say to you?' she asked David.

'Blah blah, excellent work, blah blah, frontiers of journalism, blah blah, first-class references, blah blah, a month's pay in lieu of notice and if nothing else turns up why don't you freelance for us?'

'Freelance?'

'The new slimline Radio Westerly,' David said bitterly. 'As few people as possible on the staff, and the journalists all freelance, paying their own tax and their own insurance and their own phone bills. Simple but brilliant.' He paused as a thought struck him. 'Did he say you were to see him?'

'After the eleven-o'clock,' Ruth said glumly. 'D'you think that means that I'm out too?'

David shrugged. 'Well, I doubt it means you've won the Sony Award for investigative journalism. D'you want to meet me for a drink after work? Drown our sorrows?'

'Yes,' Ruth said gratefully. 'But perhaps I won't have sorrows to drown.'

'Then you can drown mine,' David said generously. 'I'd hate to be selfish with them.'

Ruth rewrote the bulletin, one eye on the clock. At the desk behind her David made telephone calls to the police, the fire station, and the ambulance, checking for fresh news. He sounded genuinely interested; he always did. She remembered him from journalism college: when everyone else would groan at a news-gathering exercise, David would dive into little shops, greet shop assistants

26

with enthusiasm, and plunge into the minutiae of local gossip.

'Anything new?' she threw over her shoulder.

'They're mopping up after the fire,' he said. 'There's an update on the conditions from the hospital. Nothing too exciting.'

She took the slip of copy paper he handed to her, and went into the soundproofed peace of the little news studio. The door closed with a soft hiss behind her, Ruth pulled out the chair and sat before the desk to read through the bulletin in a murmured whisper, marking on her copy the words she wanted to emphasize, and practising the pronunciation of difficult words. There had been an earthquake in the Ural Mountains. 'Ural Mountains,' Ruth whispered. 'Ural.'

At two minutes to eleven the disc jockey's voice cut into her rehearsal. 'News coming up! Are you there and conscious, Ruth?'

'Ready to go,' Ruth said.

'Thank the Lord for a happy voice from the newsroom. What's up with you guys today?'

'Nothing,' Ruth said frostily, instantly loyal to her colleagues.

'We hear of massive cutbacks, and journalists out on the streets,' the DJ said cheerfully.

'Do you?'

'So who's got the push?'

'I'm busy now,' she said tightly. 'I'll pop down and spread gloom and anxiety in a minute. Right now I'm trying to read a news bulletin.'

He switched off his talkback button. Ruth had a reputation at the radio station for a quick mind and a frank turn of phrase. Her headphones were filled with the sound of the record – the Carpenters. 'We've only just begun . . .' Ruth felt her temper subside and she smiled. She liked romantic music.

Then the disc jockey said with his carefully learned mid-Atlantic accent: 'Eleven o'clock, time for Radio Westerly news with Ruth Cleary!'

He announced her name as if there should have been a drumroll underneath it. Ruth grinned and then straightened her face and assumed her solemn news-reading voice. She read first the national news, managing the Ural Mountains without a hitch, and then the local news. At the end of the bulletin she read the local weather report and handed back to the DJ. She gathered the papers of the bulletin and sat for one short moment in the quiet. If David had been sacked then it was unlikely that they would be keeping her on. They had joined at the same time from the same college course, but David was probably the better journalist. Ruth straightened her back, opened the swing door, and emerged into the noise of the newsroom. She passed the script of the bulletin to the copy girl for filing and tapped on the news editor's door.

James Peart looked so guilty she knew at once that he would make her redundant. He did.

'This is a horrible job,' James said miserably. 'David and you, and one other. It's a foul thing to have to do. But I have suggested to David that he look at freelancing and I was going to suggest to you that you look at putting together some light documentary programmes. We might have a slot for some local pieces: family inter-est, animals, children, local history, that sort of thing in the afternoon show. Nothing too ambitious, bread-and-butter stuff. But it's the sort of thing you do rather well,

Ruth. If you can't find full-time work, you could do that for us. We'd lend you the recording equipment, and you could come in and use the studio. And you'd get paid a fee and expenses, of course.' He broke off. 'I know it's not much but it would keep your hand in while you're looking round.'

'Bread-and-butter?' Ruth asked. 'Sounds more like slop.'

James grimaced. 'Don't shoot the messenger, Ruth,' he said.

'Who shall I shoot then?' she said. 'Who's responsible for putting me, and David, and someone else out of a job?'

He shrugged. 'Market forces?' he offered.

'This is rubbish,' she said firmly. 'Why didn't you tell them that you couldn't run the newsroom understaffed?'

'Because my job's on the line too,' he said frankly. 'I did tell them that we should keep the staff, but if I make too many waves then I'm out as well. I can't lose my job for a principle, Ruth.'

'So I lose mine for the lack of one?'

He said nothing.

'We should have had a union,' she said stubbornly.

'Yes,' he said. 'Or better contracts, or better management, or more profits. But those days are gone, Ruth. I'm sorry.'

She was silent.

'Look, there's nothing I can do but offer you freelance work,' he said. 'I'll do my best to take everything you do. You're a good journalist, Ruth, you'll make it. If not here, then London. And I'll give you good references. The best.'

Ruth nodded. 'Thanks,' she said shortly.

'Maybe Patrick knows of something in television,' James suggested. 'He might be able to slot you in somewhere. That's where the money is, not radio.'

'He might,' Ruth said.

James got up and held out his hand. 'You'll work till the end of the week, and then take a month's salary,' he said. 'I do wish you luck, Ruth. I really wish this hadn't happened. If things look up at all then you'll be the first person I'd want to see back on the staff.'

Ruth nodded. 'Thank you,' she said.

'If there's anything at all I can do to help . . .' he said showing her towards the door.

Ruth thought of her inability to pay the bills on time and run the flat as it should be run, of Patrick's legitimate desire for a meal when he came home after working all day, of Patrick's pay rise and the ascendancy of his career. Maybe a period of freelance work would be good for them both.

'I'll be fine,' she said. 'Don't worry. It looks like it's all falling into place.'

She rang to leave a message for Patrick that she would meet him at the restaurant, and she ran through the rain to the pub. Although it was barely opening time, David was sitting up at the bar and was smiling and lightly drunk.

'Flying start,' he said genially. 'I took the sensible course of a vodka tea.'

'Gin and tonic,' Ruth said, hitching herself up onto the barstool. 'Double.'

'You got the push too?'

'I did.'

30

'What did he suggest? Freelancing for *Panorama*? Career opportunities on *News at Ten*? Or you could go back to the States and run CNN?'

'It's odd,' Ruth said with mock thoughtfulness. 'He didn't mention any of them. Probably thought they were beneath me.'

David made a face. 'Poor bastard's doing his best,' he said. 'He promised me if I went freelance they'd use my pieces, and I could come into studio to edit for free.'

Ruth nodded. 'He offered me the same. Suggested I do local bread-and-butter stuff for the afternoon programme.'

'It's a great business, the media!' David said with sudden assumed cheeriness. 'You're never out of work. You're either resting or freelancing. But you're never unemployed.'

'Or taking time out to start a family,' Ruth said. She screwed her face up at him in an awful simper. 'I think the first few years are so precious! And I can always come back into it when the baby starts school.'

'Boarding school,' David supplemented. 'Stay home with him until he sets off for boarding school. Just take eleven years off. What's that, after all? It'll pass in a flash.'

'No child of mine is boarding! I think a mother should stay home until the children are grown,' Ruth said earnestly. 'University age at least.'

'First job,' David corrected her. 'Give them a stable start. You can come back to work twenty-one years from now.'

'Oh, but the grandchildren will need me!' Ruth exclaimed.

'Ah, yes, the magic years. So you could come back to

31

work when you're . . . perhaps . . . sixty?'

Ruth looked thoughtful. 'I'd like to do a couple more months before I retire,' she said. 'I really am a career girl, you know.'

They broke off and smiled at each other. 'You're a mate,' David said. 'And you're a good journalist too. They're mad getting rid of you. You're worth two or three of some of them.'

'Last in, first out,' Ruth said. 'You're better than them too.'

He shrugged. 'So what will you do?'

Ruth hesitated. 'The forces are massing a bit,' she said hesitantly. She was not sure how much to tell David. Her powerful loyalty to Patrick usually kept her silent. 'Patrick's parents have a cottage near them that has come up for sale. Patrick's always wanted it. He's getting promoted, which is more money and better hours. And we have been married four, nearly five years. There is a kind of inevitability about what happens next.'

David had never learned tact. 'What d'you mean: what happens next? D'you mean a baby?'

Ruth hesitated. 'Eventually, yes, of course,' she said. 'But not right now. I wanted to work up a bit, you know. I did want to work for the BBC. I even thought about television.'

'You always said you were going to travel,' he reminded her. 'Research your roots. Go back to America and find your missing millionaire relations.'

'If I'm freelance that'll be easier.'

'Not with a baby,' David reminded her.

Ruth was silent.

'I suppose there *is* such a thing as contraception,' David said lightly. 'A woman's right to choose and all that. We are in the nineties. Or did I miss something?'

'Swing back to family values,' Ruth said briskly. 'Women in the home and crime off the streets.'

He chuckled and was about to cap the joke but stopped himself. 'No, hang on a minute,' he said. 'I don't get this. I never thought you were the maternal type, Ruth. You don't really want a baby, do you?'

Ruth was about to agree with him, but again her loyalty to Patrick silenced her. She nodded to the barman to give them another round of drinks and busied herself with paying him. 'You don't understand,' she said. 'Patrick's got this very established conventional sort of family, and he's a very conventional sort of man . . .' She looked to see if David was nodding in agreement. He was not.

'They're very influential,' she said weakly. 'It's very difficult to argue with them. And of course they want us to move house, and of course, sooner or later, they'll expect a baby.'

'Come on,' David said irritably. 'It'll be you that expects it, and you that gives birth. If you don't want to have a baby, you must just say no.'

Ruth was silent. David realized he had been too abrupt. 'Can't you just say no?'

She turned to look at him. 'Oh, David,' she said. 'You know me as well as anybody. I never had any family life worth a damn. When I met Patrick and he took me home, I suddenly saw somewhere I could belong. And they took me in, and now they're my family. I don't want to spoil it. We see them practically every Sunday . . .'

'D'you know what I do on Sunday mornings?' David interrupted. 'I don't get up till eleven. I take the papers

33

back to bed with me and read all the trivial bits – the travel sections and the style sections and the magazines. When the pubs open I walk across the park to The Fountain and I have a drink with some people there. Then I take a curry back home, and I read all the papers, and watch the telly. Then if I feel energetic I go for a jog. And if I feel lazy I do nothing. And in the evening I go round to see someone I like, or people come round and see me. I can't imagine having to be polite all day to someone's mum and dad.'

'They're *my* mum and dad,' she said.

He shook his head. 'No, they're not.'

He saw, as she turned away from him, that he had gone too far. 'Sorry,' he said. He shifted his barstool closer and put his hand on her knee. 'Tell you what, come back to my flat with me,' he said. 'I'll read last Sunday's papers to you.'

Ruth gave him a wan smile, picked up his hand, and dropped it lightly in his lap. 'Married woman,' she said. 'As you well know.'

'Wasted on matrimony,' he said. 'That sexy smile of yours. I should have taken my chance with you when I had it, when you were young and stupid, before you found Prince Charming and got stuck in the castle.'

'Don't be silly,' she said. 'I'm very happy.'

David bit back the response. 'Well, we both are!' he said, lapsing into irony again. 'What with our vivid emotional lives and our glittering careers! Speaking of which – what about our glittering careers? What will you do?'

'I'll look round,' she said. 'And I'll do some local pieces for James. I can keep my hand in and they won't look bad on a CV. What about you?'

'I need a job,' David said. 'I can freelance for a week

or so, but when the money runs out I need a pay cheque. I'll be sweeping the streets, I reckon.'

Ruth giggled suddenly, her face brightening. 'Walking them more like,' she said. 'A tart like you. You could pop down to the docks.'

David smiled back at her. 'I try to keep my self-respect,' he said primly. 'But if you know any rich old women I could be tempted. What about your mother-in-law? Would she fancy a fling with a young gigolo? Is she the toyboy type?'

Ruth snorted into her drink. 'Absolutely,' she said. 'You could pop out on Sunday afternoons and rendez-vous in that bloody cottage!'

Two

RUTH WAS LATE at the restaurant, and her high spirits evaporated when she saw Patrick's sulky face over the large menu.

'Sorry, sorry, sorry,' she said as she slipped onto the bench seat opposite him. 'I went out for a drink with David and I didn't watch the time.'

Patrick's bright blue eyes widened in surprise. 'Well, thanks very much,' he said. 'I hurried here to be with you and then I sit here on my own while you go boozing with some guy from work.'

'He's just been made redundant,' Ruth said. 'And I was too.'

Patrick, who had been about to continue his complaint, was abruptly silenced. 'What?'

'I've been made redundant,' Ruth said. 'Me and David and someone else. We're all out at the end of the week with a month's pay in hand. They offered us freelance work.'

Patrick's face was radiant. 'Well, what a coincidence!' he said. 'Aren't things just working out for us?'

'Not exactly,' Ruth said rather tartly, fired by David and by two double gins. 'I wanted to keep my job; and if I left it I wanted to go somewhere better. I didn't want

36

to get the sack and have a baby as second best.'

Patrick quickly summoned the waiter. 'D'you want spaghetti, darling? And salad?'

'Yes.'

Patrick ordered and poured Ruth a glass of wine. 'You're upset,' he said soothingly. 'Poor darling. How disappointing. Don't feel too bad about it. We'll look round. We'll find you another job. There must be people who would snap you up. You're so bright and a damn fine journalist.'

Ruth's mouth quivered. 'I *liked* it there!' she said miserably. 'And I was doing some really good stories. I even scooped your lot a couple of times.'

'You're an excellent journalist,' he said. 'That's why I'm so confident you'll find work at once somewhere else . . . if you want it.'

As Ruth lifted her head to protest, he held up his hand. 'Not another word!' he said. 'You've had a shock. We won't talk plans tonight. Not a word about jobs or flats or cottages. Not a word! Let me tell you about the interview I did with Clark today – you'll die.'

Patrick told Ruth a story and she laughed politely. Their food came and Patrick continued to lay himself out to please her. He was witty and he could be charming. Ruth, enjoying the mixture of red wine and gin, found herself laughing at his stories and capping them with stories of her own. It was midnight before they left the restaurant, and Patrick put his arm around her as they walked home together.

'I love you,' he said softly in her ear as they opened the front door and went into the warm hall.

They went upstairs together and Ruth turned to embrace him in the bedroom. Patrick held her close and kissed her with warm, seductive kisses. It was so unusual for them to make love during the week that Ruth was slow to respond. She stayed in his arms, content to be kissed, her eyes closed.

'Into bed with you, Mrs Cleary,' Patrick said and gave her a little push towards the bed. Ruth lay back and stretched luxuriously. Patrick dropped his head and nudged sexily at her breasts, his hands pushing up her skirt until he found the waistband of her tights.

'Patrick!' Ruth said. She half sat up. 'Perhaps I had better go to the bathroom!' she said. She meant that she needed to put in her diaphragm, their only contraception.

'I want you,' he said urgently. 'I want you right now.'

Ruth gasped with surprised delight at his urgency. He was stripping down her tights and panties, and kicking off his own shoes. Ruth giggled drunkenly, delightedly.

'I *have* to go,' she protested.

Patrick shucked off his trousers and pants in one swift movement and swarmed up over her, kissing her neck and her ears. His hand reached behind her back and undid her bra, slid his hand under the lace and caressed her breast. Ruth felt her desire rising, felt herself careless, sexy, urgent.

'Come on, Ruth,' he whispered. 'Like when we were first lovers. Let's take a chance. Let's take a sexy chance, Ruth. I want to be right inside you with nothing between us. Come on, darling, I want to.'

His fingers stroked insistently between her legs. Ruth, drunk on wine and drunk with desire, protested inarticulately but could not bring herself to stop. In a small sober part of her mind she was watching him, calculating the days from her last period, fearing the sudden rush of his desire, terrified of pregnancy.

He rolled on top of her, moving steadily and deliciously, Ruth opened her legs and felt her desire rise and rise to match his, but then her caution chilled her. 'Patrick, we shouldn't . . .' she started to say.

With a sudden delighted groan he came inside her.

Ruth's routine changed little after her week's notice expired and she became freelance. She left home at the usual time and she came home, if anything, later than usual. It was as if she were afraid that any slackening would prompt Patrick to exploit her unemployment.

'You could take it easy,' he said on the first Monday.

'Better not,' Ruth said. 'I want to show them I'm serious about getting work.'

Patrick had not pursued his theme – that Ruth could rest, or could tidy the flat, or could visit his mother and see the cottage. He had kissed her and left for work. He was in less of a hurry now in the mornings. He strolled to his car and let the engine warm and the light frost melt from the windscreen before he drove away. He no longer had to be in at the television newsroom first; he now had status. He had a parking slot of his own outside the building and a secretary who had to be in before him to open his post. Patrick's stock had risen dramatically, and his timekeeping could decline. Some mornings in November it was Ruth who was up first and Patrick who lured her back to bed. On at least two mornings they made love without contraception. Patrick had been urgent and seductive and Ruth could not refuse him. She was flattered by his desire and enchanted by its sudden urgency. One morning she was half asleep as he slid inside her and she woke too slowly to resist. One morning she acquiesced with a sleepy smile. Escaping pregnancy the first time, she was becoming reckless.

In mid-December she felt sick in the mornings and felt tired at work. She was trying to persuade the afternoon show producer to commission a series on local Bristol history.

'Something about industry,' she suggested. 'From shipbuilding to building Concorde at Filton. We could call it *Bristol Fashion*.'

'Sounds a bit earnest,' he criticized.

'It could be fun,' she said. 'Some old historical journals. I could read them. And some old people talking about working on the docks and in the aircraft industry before the war. There's loads of stuff at the museum.'

He cocked an eyebrow at her. 'Are you sure? Oh, well, maybe. See what you can dig up. But nothing too dreary, Ruth. Nothing too historical. Bright and snappy. You know the kind of thing.'

She closed his office door quietly behind her and went to the ladies' room. She ran the cold-water tap and splashed cold water on her face and rinsed her mouth.

One of the newsroom copy takers, combing her hair before the mirror, glanced around. 'Are you all right, Ruth? You look as white as a sheet.'

'I feel funny,' Ruth said.

The woman looked at her a little closer. 'How funny?'

'I feel really sick, and dreadfully tired.'

The woman gave her a smiling look, full of meaning. 'Not up the spout, are you?'

Ruth shot her a sudden wide-eyed look. 'No! I can't possibly be.'

'Not overdue?'

'I don't know . . . I'd have to look . . . I'm a bit scatty about it . . .'

The woman, with two children of her own at school, shrugged her shoulders. 'Maybe it's just something you ate,' she said.

'Probably,' Ruth said hastily. 'Probably that's all.'

The woman went out, leaving Ruth alone. She looked at herself in the mirror. Her dark, smooth bobbed hair framed her pale face, her large dark eyes. She looked scared, she looked sickly. Ruth shook her head. She could not see herself as a woman who might be pregnant. She had an image of herself as a girl too young, too unready for a woman's task of pregnancy.

'It's something I ate,' Ruth said to her reflection. 'It's bound to be.'

She bought a pregnancy test kit on the way home from work and locked herself in the bathroom with it. There were two little test tubes and a collecting jar for urine and immensely complicated instructions. Ruth sat on the edge of the bathtub and read them with a sense of growing panic. It seemed to her that since she could not understand the instructions for a pregnancy test then she must, therefore, be totally unfit to be pregnant. She hid the test, tucking it behind the toilet cleaner, secure in the knowledge that Patrick would never have anything to do with cleaning the toilet, and brushed her teeth, splashed water on her face, and pinned on a bright smile for Patrick's arrival home from work.

She woke in the night, in the shadowy bedroom, and found that she was holding her breath, as if she were waiting for something. When she saw the grey-orange

41

of the sky through the crack in the curtains she knew it was morning, and she could do the test. She slipped out of bed, careful not to wake Patrick, and went to the bathroom. She locked the door behind her and took the pregnancy test from its hiding place. She lifted her nightgown and peed in the toilet, clumsily thrusting the collecting jar into the stream of urine for a sample. Then she poured urine and test powder into the little test tube, corked it, shook it, wrapped herself in a bath towel for warmth, and waited.

She had to wait ten minutes before the test was completed. Ruth made herself look away from the tube, fearful that the strength of her wishing would make the results go wrong. She was longing with all her heart for the liquid to stay its innocent pale, pale blue. She did not want to be pregnant, she did not want to have conceived a child. She turned her mind away from Patrick's new insistent lovemaking. She had thought their marriage had taken a sudden turn for the better; she had seen it as a renewal of desire. She had explained his new demanding sexiness as being a relief from the stress of his job as a reporter, a celebration of his new status as a manager. She did not want to think that he had been aiming for this very dawn, for Ruth sitting on the cold floor of the bathroom waiting for the result of a pregnancy test to tell her that she was no longer a free woman with a multitude of choices before her.

She glanced at her watch: eleven minutes had gone by. She looked at the test tube. In the bottom of the tube it had formed a sediment: a bright, strong dark blue. It was unmistakably a positive test. She screwed up her eyes – it made no difference. She took it closer to the light over the mirror. It was the bright blue that meant pregnancy. Ruth folded up the instructions and put the test pack away behind the toilet cleaner again. She was supposed to retest within a week, but she knew she would not bother to do it. She had known this yesterday morning, when the woman in the ladies' room had asked her if she was up the spout. She had recognized the information as soon as it was spoken. She was pregnant. Patrick and his parents had got what they wanted.

She did not tell Patrick of her pregnancy until Boxing Day morning, when he was hungover from his father's best Armagnac, which they had drunk on Christmas afternoon, and liverish with the richness of his mother's Christmas cooking. Some resilient piece of spite made her withhold the information from the assembled family on Christmas Day. She knew that they would have fallen on her with delight; she knew they would have said it was the best Christmas present they had ever had. Ruth did not want them unwrapping her feelings. She did not want them counting on their fingers and predicting the birth. She did not want her own small disaster of an unplanned pregnancy being joyously engulfed by the whole Christmas myth of baby Jesus and the speech by the Queen, who was not her queen, and carols, which were not her carols.

Spitefully, Ruth kept the precious news to herself, refused to spread exuberant delight. Throughout Christmas lunch, when they had skirted around the subject of the cottage and the proposed sale of the flat now that Ruth had nothing to keep her in Bristol, she refused to give them the gilt on the gingerbread of their plans. She ate only a little and drank only one glass of champagne.

43

When the men drank Armagnac and snoozed before the television in the afternoon, Ruth defiantly walked in the cold countryside on her own.

'Pop down and see the cottage,' Elizabeth recommended. 'Get a feel for it without the men breathing down your neck. It's you that needs to fall in love with it, not them.'

Ruth nodded distantly at Elizabeth's conspiratorial whisper. She knew that she could tell Elizabeth that she was pregnant and be rewarded with absolute discreet delight. Elizabeth would tell no one until Ruth gave permission. Elizabeth was always ready to bond with Ruth in an alliance of women against men, but Ruth would not join in. She hugged the small embryo to herself as she hugged the secret. She would not crown their day. The baby was a mistake, but it was her private mistake. She would not have it converted into a Cleary celebration.

Patrick emerged blearily from under the bedcovers. 'God, I feel dreadful,' he said. He sat up in bed, his eyes half closed. 'Could you get me an Alka-Seltzer?' he asked. 'Too much brandy and too much cake.'

Ruth went down to the kitchen and fetched him a glass of water and two tablets. As they foamed she waited. Only at the exact nauseating moment of his first sip did she say, 'I'm pregnant.'

There was a silence. 'What?' Patrick said, turning towards her.

'I'm pregnant,' Ruth repeated.

He reached forward but then recoiled as his head thudded. 'Oh! Damn! Ruth, what a time to tell me! Darling!'

She sat out of arm's reach on the window seat.

44

'Come here!' he said.

She went, slowly, to the bed. Patrick drew her down and wrapped his arms around her. 'That's wonderful news,' he said. 'D'you know you couldn't have given me a better Christmas present! When did you know?'

'Three weeks ago,' Ruth said unhelpfully. 'Then I went to the doctor to make sure. It's true. I'm due in the middle of August.'

'I must phone Mother,' Patrick said. 'Oh, I *wish* you'd told me yesterday. We could have had a real party.'

Ruth disengaged herself from the embrace, which was starting to feel heavy. 'I didn't want a real party,' she said.

He tried to twinkle at her. 'Are you feeling shy, darling?'

'No.'

'Then . . . ?'

'I didn't particularly want a baby,' she said. 'I didn't plan to get pregnant. It's an accident. So I don't feel like celebrating.'

Patrick's indulgent gleam died and was instantly replaced by an expression of tenderness and concern. Gingerly he got out of bed and put his arm around her shoulders, turning her face in to the warmth of his chest. 'Don't,' he said softly, his breath sour on her cheek. 'Don't talk like that, darling. It just happened, that's all. It just happened because that's how it was meant to be. Everything has come right for us, and when you get used to the idea I know you'll be really, really happy. *I'm* really happy,' he said emphatically, as if all she needed to do was to imitate him. 'I'm just delighted, darling. Don't upset yourself.'

Ruth felt a sudden bitterness at the ease with which

45

Patrick greeted the news. Of course he would be happy – it would not be Patrick whose life would totally change. It would not be Patrick who would leave the work he loved, and who would now never travel, and never see his childhood home. For a moment she felt filled with anger, but his arms came around her and his hands stroked her back. Ruth's face was pressed into the warm, soft skin of his chest and held like a little girl's. She could feel herself starting to cry, wetly, emotionally, weakly.

'There!' Patrick said, his voice warm with love and triumph. 'You're bound to feel all jumbled up, my darling. It's well known. It's your hormones. Of course you don't know how you feel yet. There! There!'

'She's very wound up at the moment,' he whispered to his mother on the telephone. Ruth was taking an afternoon nap after a celebration lunch in the pub. 'I didn't dare call you earlier. She didn't want you to know.'

Elizabeth's face was radiant. She nodded confirmation to Frederick as he registered the news and stood close to Elizabeth to overhear their conversation. 'Wait a moment,' Elizabeth said. 'Your father wants a word.'

'Do I hear right? A happy event?' Frederick exclaimed.

Patrick chuckled. 'I have to *whisper*!' he said. 'She's asleep and she swore me to secrecy.'

'Wonderful!' Frederick said. 'Clever girl! And congratulations, old man!'

There was a brief satisfied silence.

'Bring her over,' Frederick said. 'We'll crack a bottle on the baby's head. Can't celebrate over the phone.'

'I can't,' Patrick said again. 'I tell you, I am sworn to

utter secrecy. She doesn't want anyone to know yet. She's all of a state. A bit weepy, a bit unsure. I don't want to rush her.'

'Oh, don't talk to me about weepy!' Frederick said comfortably. 'Your mother cried every day for nine months. I thought she was miserable, but then she told me she was crying for happiness.' He gave a slow, rich, satisfied chuckle. 'Women!' he said.

Patrick beamed into the phone. He very much wanted to be with his father. 'I'll come to see you this evening,' he said. 'I'll make some excuse. I won't bring her, we'll have our celebration drink, and next time we come she can tell you yourself, and you can both be absolutely amazed.'

'I'll put a bottle on ice,' his father said.

'Patrick?' his mother asked as she came back on the phone. 'Ruth is quite all right is she?'

'It's all a bit much for her, that's all,' Patrick said. 'And you know how much her job meant to her. It's a big shock.'

'But she *does* want the baby?' Elizabeth confirmed. 'She is happy about it?'

'She's over the moon,' Patrick said firmly. 'She's happier than she knows.'

As Ruth's pregnancy progressed, she found that Patrick's determination to move from the flat was too powerful to resist. In any case, the flat belonged to his father, and his father wished to sell. There was little Ruth could do but mourn their decision and pack as slowly and unwillingly as possible. Most days she did not go into the radio station, taking calls and preparing work at home. On those days the estate agent might telephone and send potential buyers to look at the flat. Ruth would show them around without enthusiasm. She did not actively draw their attention to the defects – the smallness of the spare bedroom, the inconvenience of the best bathroom being *en suite* with their bedroom – but she did nothing to enhance their view of the flat.

It could not work. They were selling at a time of rising prices and rising expectations, and there were many people prepared to buy. Indeed, by playing one couple off against another Patrick and Frederick managed to get more than the asking price and a couple of months' delay before they had to move out.

'But the cottage isn't even bought yet,' Ruth said. 'Where are we going to live?'

'Why, here of course,' Elizabeth exclaimed. She reached across the Sunday lunch table and patted Ruth's unresponsive hand. 'It's not ideal, my dear, I know. I'm sure you would rather be nest building. But it's the way it has worked out. And at least you can leave the cooking and housework to me and just do as much of your radio work as you want. As you get more tired you might find that a bit of a boon, you know.'

'And she'll eat properly during the day,' Patrick said, smiling lovingly at Ruth. 'When I'm not there to keep an eye on her, and when she doesn't have a canteen to serve up lunch, she just snacks. The doctor has told her, but she just nibbles like a little mouse.'

'I don't feel like eating,' Ruth said. The tide of their goodwill was irresistible. 'And I'm gaining weight fast enough.' Against the waistband of her skirt her expanding belly was gently pressing. At night she would scratch the tight skin of her stomach until she scored it with red marks from her fingernails. It felt as if the baby

48

were stretching and stretching her body, her very life. Soon she would be four months into the pregnancy and would have nothing to wear but maternity clothes. Already the rhythm of trips to the antenatal clinic was becoming more and more important. Her conversations with Patrick were dominated by discussions about her blood pressure, the tests they wanted their baby to have, or, as now, her food. Even her work had taken second place. Only the project about the early industry of Bristol was still interesting. Ruth was reading local history for the first time, and looking at the buildings around her, the beautiful grand buildings of Bristol built on slave-trade money.

'Don't nag her, Patrick,' Elizabeth said. 'No one knows better than Ruth what she wants to eat and what she doesn't want.'

Ruth shot Elizabeth a brief grateful look.

'And you will be absolutely free to come and go as you wish while you stay here,' Elizabeth said. 'So don't be afraid that I will be fussing over you all the time. But a little later on you might be glad of the chance to rest.'

'I do get tired now,' Ruth admitted. 'Especially in the afternoon.'

'I think I slept every afternoon as soon as Patrick was conceived,' Elizabeth remembered. 'Didn't I, Frederick? We were in South Africa then. Frederick was on attachment. All that wonderful sunshine and I used to creep into a darkened room and sleep and sleep.'

'You were in Africa? I never knew.'

'Training,' Frederick said. 'I used to go all over the world training chaps. Sometimes I could take Elizabeth, sometimes they were places where I was better off alone.'

'You were working for the South African government?' Ruth asked.

Frederick smiled at her. 'It was a wonderful country in those days. The blacks had their place, the whites had theirs. Everyone was suited.'

'Except the black homelands were half desert, and the white areas were the towns and the goldmines,' Ruth said.

Frederick looked quite amazed: it was the first time Ruth had ever contradicted him. 'I say,' he said. 'You're becoming a bit of a Red in your condition.'

'Oh, Ruth's full of it,' Patrick volunteered, taking the sting from the conversation. 'She's researching for a programme on early Bristol industry, and she's gone back and back. I told her she'll be at the Garden of Eden soon. She's got her nose in these books from morning till night.'

'Clever girl,' Elizabeth said. 'You'll need a little study when you move in. I could convert the small bedroom for you to work.'

'Thank you,' Ruth said. 'But I will have finished quite soon.'

'And anyway, she should be putting her feet up,' Patrick said. 'She's been reading far too much, and spending half the day in the library.'

'And what about you, old boy?' Frederick asked. 'How's the new post?'

Patrick smiled his charming smile. 'Can't complain,' he said, and started to tell them about his secretary, and his office, his reserved car space and his management-training course. Ruth watched him. She felt as if she were a long way away from him. She watched him smiling and talking: a favourite child of applauding parents,

and as she watched them their faces blurred and their
voices seemed to come from far away. Even Patrick,
beloved, attractive Patrick, seemed a little man with a
little voice crowing over little triumphs.

Three

RUTH AND ELIZABETH were to go down to the cottage together, to measure for curtains and carpets, and discuss colour schemes. The builders had all but finished, the new kitchen had been built, the new bath plumbed in. Elizabeth had tirelessly supervised the workmen, ascertaining Ruth's wishes and chivvying them to do the work right. Nothing would have been done without her, nothing could have been finished as quickly without her. Patrick, absorbed in setting up the documentary unit at work, had been no help to Ruth at all. Without her mother-in-law she would have been exhausted every day by a thousand trivial decisions.

Ruth had planned to walk down to the cottage in the morning, when she felt at her best. But Elizabeth had been busy all morning and the time had slipped away. It was not until after lunch that she said, 'I'm so sorry to have kept you waiting. Shall we go down to the cottage now? Or do you want your nap?'

'We'll go,' Ruth decided. In her fifth month of pregnancy she felt absurdly heavy and tired, and the mid-afternoon was always the worst time.

'Shall I drive us down?' Elizabeth offered.

'I can walk.' Ruth heaved herself out of the low armchair and went out into the hall. She bent uncomfortably to tie the laces of her walking boots. Elizabeth, waiting beside her, seemed as lithe and quick as a young girl.

Tammy, the dog, ran ahead of them, through Elizabeth's rose garden to the garden gate and then down across the fields. Ruth walked slowly, feeling the warmth of the April sunlight on her face. She felt better.

'I should walk every day,' she said. 'This is wonderful!'

'As long as you don't overdo it,' Elizabeth warned. 'What did the doctor say yesterday?'

'He said everything was fine. Nothing to worry about.'

'Did he check your weight?'

'Yes – it's OK.'

'He didn't think you were overweight?'

'He said it didn't matter.'

'And did you tell him how tired you're feeling?'

'He said it was normal.'

Elizabeth pursed her lips and said nothing.

'I'm fine,' Ruth repeated.

Elizabeth smiled at her. 'I know you are,' she said. 'And I'm just fussing over you. But I hate to see you so pale and so heavy. In my day they used to give us iron tablets. You look so anaemic.'

'I'll eat cabbage,' Ruth offered. She climbed awkwardly over the stile into the next field.

'Careful,' Elizabeth warned.

The two women walked for a little while in silence. In the hedge the catkins bobbed. Ruth remembered the springs of her American childhood, more dramatic, more necessary, after longer and sharper winters.

'I forgot to tell you,' Elizabeth said. 'Patrick rang this

morning while you were in the bath. He said he has to go up to London this afternoon for a meeting and it'll probably go on late. He said he'd stay up there.'

Ruth felt a pang of intense disappointment. 'Overnight?' She hated being in Patrick's parents' house without him. She felt always as if she were some unwanted refugee billeted on kindly but unwilling hosts.

'Possibly Tuesday as well,' Elizabeth said. 'You can have a nice early night and a lie-in without him waking you in the morning.'

'I'll ring him when we get home,' Ruth said.

'He's out of touch,' she said. 'In his meeting, and then on the train to London.'

'I wish I'd spoken to him,' Ruth said wistfully.

Elizabeth opened the gate to the garden of the cottage and patted Ruth on the shoulder as she went through. 'Now then,' she said briskly. 'You can live without him for one night.'

'Didn't he ask to speak to me?'

'I said you were in the bath.'

'I would have got out of the bath, if you had called me.'

'I wouldn't dream of disturbing you,' Elizabeth declared. 'Not for a little message that I can take for you, darling. If you want a long chat with him you can save it all up until he comes home the day after tomorrow.'

Ruth nodded.

'There's nothing wrong, is there? Nothing that you need him for?'

'No,' Ruth said shortly.

Elizabeth had the front-door key; she opened the door and stepped back to let Ruth go in. 'Don't cling, dear,' she said gently. 'Men hate women who cling. Especially now.'

Ruth turned abruptly from her mother-in-law and went into the sitting room. Elizabeth was undoubtedly right, which made her advice the more galling. There was still a large patch of damp beside the French windows, which not even the previous summer had dried out.

'Now,' Elizabeth said, throwing off her light jacket with energy. 'You sit down on that little stool and I'll rush round and take all the measurements you want.'

From the pocket of the jacket she pulled a notebook and pen and a measuring tape. Ruth sulkily took the notebook while Elizabeth strode around the room calling out the measurements of the walls and the window frames.

'Fitted carpets, I think, don't you?' she threw over her shoulder. 'So much warmer. And good thick curtains for the winter, and some lighter ones for summer. Perhaps a pale yellow weave for summer, to match the primrose walls.'

'I thought we'd paper it. I want the paper we had in the hall at the flat,' Ruth said.

'Oh, darling!' Elizabeth exclaimed. 'Not William Morris willow again, surely!'

'Didn't you like it?'

'I loved it,' Elizabeth said. 'But don't you remember what Patrick said? He said he kept seeing faces in it. You don't want it in your sitting room, with Patrick seeing faces peeping through the leaves at him every evening.'

Ruth reluctantly chuckled. 'I'll have it in the hall then,' she said.

'And this room primrose yellow,' Elizabeth said

firmly. 'I have some curtain material that will just do these windows, and the French windows too. Old gold they are. Quite lovely.'

Ruth nodded. She knew they would be lovely. Elizabeth's taste was infallible, and she had trunks of beautiful materials saved from her travels around the world. 'But we shouldn't be taking your things, we should be buying new.'

Elizabeth, on her knees before the French windows, scratching critically at the damp plaster, looked up, and smiled radiantly. 'Of course you should have my old things!' she said. 'I can't wait to see my curtains up at your windows and the two of you – no, the three of you – happy and settled here.' She looked back at the damp plaster. 'I shall get someone out to see to this at once,' she said. 'Mr Willis warned me it might be a specialist job.'

They moved to the kitchen, the dining room, and then to the three upstairs bedrooms. Elizabeth carried around the little stool from the sitting room, and insisted on Ruth's sitting in the middle of each room, while she bustled with the tape measure, calling out numbers.

Empty of furniture, but with new kitchen units in pale pine and with a remodelled bathroom upstairs the cottage did look pretty. Ruth felt her spirits rising. 'If they hurry up with the decorating we should get in before the baby's born.'

Elizabeth, stretching across the bedroom window, nodded. 'I'm determined to see that you are,' she said. 'Cream cotton at all the upstairs windows, I think, and then it matches whatever colour walls you choose. But that nice Berber-weave carpet I told you about all through the top floor.'

'In the flat we had varnished boards,' Ruth said. 'I liked them.'

'Weren't they wonderful?' Elizabeth reminisced. 'Georgian pine. And you did have them beautifully done.' She recalled herself to the present. 'So we'll have the biscuit-colour Berber carpet all around the upstairs floor, and pastel walls. We can choose the colours at home. I've got the charts.'

'All right,' Ruth said, surrendering her vision of clean waxed floorboards without an argument. She felt suddenly very weary. 'The sooner we choose it and order it the sooner the house is ready, I suppose.'

'You leave it to me!' Elizabeth said with determination. 'I'll have it ready by August, don't fret. In fact I'll leave you to have your rest when we get home, and I'll zip into Bath and come back with some fabric samples. You can choose them this evening and we can order them tomorrow. I'll order the carpets at the same time.'

'And tiles or vinyl for the kitchen,' Ruth said wearily. 'But I haven't chosen them yet. Patrick was going to take me into town tonight.'

'Would you trust me to choose it for you?' Elizabeth offered. 'I can look when I'm ordering the carpets. They've got a wonderful selection there.'

Ruth got up from the stool. Her back ached and there was a new nagging twinge in the very bones of her pelvis. The walk home over two hilly fields seemed a long, long way.

Elizabeth broke off, instantly attentive. 'Shall I fetch the car, darling?' she asked gently. 'Have you overdone it a bit?'

'I can walk,' Ruth said grimly.

'Or I could run home and fetch the car for you,'

Elizabeth repeated. 'I could be back in a moment. You perch on your little stool and I'll have you home in a flash.'

Ruth resisted for no more than a moment. 'Thank you,' she said gratefully. 'I'd like that.'

Elizabeth threw her a swift smile and slipped down the stairs. Ruth heard the front door bang and her quick footsteps on the path. She sat on her own in the quiet cottage and felt the friendly silence gather around her. 'It'll be all right when we're in here,' she said to herself, hearing her voice in the emptiness of the house. 'As long as we get in here in time for the baby. The last thing in the world that matters is who chooses the wallpaper.'

Elizabeth, half running across the fields, fuelled with energy and a sense of purpose, reached the house and picked up the ringing telephone. It was the builder, calling about Manor Farm cottage and the damp around the French windows.

'Yes,' Elizabeth said. 'My cottage. You must get that damp problem cured at once, Mr Willis. My cottage must be ready by August. I have promised my son and daughter-in-law that I'll have it ready for them by then.'

It was not ready by August. The damp under the French windows was caused by a faulty drain. The flagstones of the path outside had to be cut back and a little gravel-filled trench inserted. None of it seemed very complicated to Ruth, and she wished they would hurry the work; but in the final month of her pregnancy she found a calmness and a serenity she had not known before.

'The work will be finished this week,' Elizabeth said worriedly. 'But then that room will have to dry out and be decorated. I've got the curtains ready to hang, and the carpet fitters will come in at a moment's notice, but if Junior is born on time he'll just have to come home to Patrick's old nursery here.'

'It doesn't matter,' Ruth said calmly.

'Bit of a treat really,' Patrick said. He was eating a late supper. Frederick had already gone up to bed. Elizabeth and Ruth had waited up for Patrick, who had been delayed at work by someone's farewell party. Elizabeth had made him an omelette and he ate it, watched by the two women. 'I like to think of him in my nursery.'

'But I wanted to make the cottage ready for you,' Elizabeth pursued. 'I *am* disappointed.'

'It doesn't matter,' Ruth repeated. She had a curious floating feeling, as if everything was bound to be all right. She smiled at Elizabeth. 'I'll be five days in hospital anyway; maybe it will be finished in time.'

Elizabeth shook her head disapprovingly. 'In my day they kept you in for a fortnight,' she said. 'Especially a new mother who was completely inexperienced.'

'We have to start somewhere,' Patrick said cheerfully. 'And we've done the classes, or at least Ruth has. I'll have on-the-job training.'

'If you so much as touch a nappy I'll be amazed,' Elizabeth said.

'He certainly will,' Ruth replied. 'He's promised.'

Patrick grinned at the two of them. 'I am a new man,' he pronounced, slightly tipsy from the drinks at work and the wine with his supper. 'I'll do it all. Anyway, even if I miss the nappy stage I've already bought him a fishing rod. I'll teach him fishing.'

'And what if it's a girl?' Elizabeth challenged.

'Then I'll teach her too,' Patrick said. 'There will be no sexism in my household.'

Ruth got to her feet; the distant floaty feeling had become stronger. 'I have to go to bed,' she said. 'I'm half asleep here already.'

Patrick pushed his plate to one side and was about to leave the table to go upstairs with Ruth.

'I was just making coffee,' Elizabeth remarked. 'I thought I'd have a coffee and a cognac before bed.'

'Oh, all right,' Patrick said agreeably. 'I'll stay down and have one with you. All right, Ruth?'

She nodded and bent carefully to kiss his cheek.

'I won't disturb you when I come up,' he promised. 'I'll creep in beside you. And I'll be up early in the morning too. I'll slip out without waking you.'

'I won't see you till tomorrow night then,' Ruth said. Despite herself her voice was slightly forlorn.

'Unless tomorrow is the big day and he has to come dashing home,' Elizabeth said cheerfully. 'Patrick, you must leave a number where we can reach you all day, remember.'

'I will,' he said. 'I'll write it down now.'

'On the pad beside the telephone in the sitting room,' Elizabeth instructed.

'Night, darling,' Patrick said cheerfully and went to write down his telephone number as his mother had told him to do.

Ruth lay in her bed. The floating feeling grew stronger as she closed her eyes. The sounds of the countryside in summer breathed in through the half-open windows. They still sounded strange and ominous to Ruth, who was used to the comforting buzz of a city at night. She flinched when she heard the sudden whoop of an owl,

60

and the occasional bark from a fox, trotting along the dark paths under the large white moon.

Ruth slept. Inside her body the baby turned and settled.

Between two and three in the morning, she woke in a pool of wetness, a powerful vice closed on her stomach. 'Oh, my God!' she said. 'Patrick, wake up, the baby's coming.'

He took a moment to hear her, and then he leaped from the bed, as nervous as a father in a comedy film. 'Now?' he demanded. 'Are you sure? Now? Should we go to the hospital? Should we telephone? Oh, my God! I'm low on petrol.'

Ruth hardly heard him; she was timing her contractions.

'I'll get Mother,' Patrick said, and fled from the bedroom and down the corridor.

As soon as Elizabeth appeared in the doorway in her cream corduroy dressing gown she took complete charge. She sent Patrick to get dressed in the bathroom and helped Ruth change from her nightgown into a pair of trousers and a baggy top.

'Everything ready in your suitcase?' she confirmed.

'Yes,' Ruth said.

'I'll phone the hospital and tell them you're on your way,' Elizabeth said.

'No petrol!' Patrick exclaimed, coming in the door, his jumper askew and his hair unbrushed. 'God! I'm a fool! I'm low on petrol!'

'You can take your father's car. Get it out of the garage and bring it round to the front door,' Elizabeth said calmly. 'And don't speed. This is a first baby; you have plenty of time.'

Patrick shot one anxious look at Ruth and dived from the room.

'The suitcase,' Elizabeth reminded him.

'Suitcase,' he repeated, grabbing it and running down the stairs.

The two women exchanged one smiling look. On impulse Elizabeth bent down and kissed Ruth's hot forehead. 'Good luck,' she said. 'It's not that bad, really. Don't be frightened. And there's a beautiful baby at the end of it.'

She helped Ruth to her feet and down the stairs. At the front door the Rover was waiting, Patrick standing at the passenger door. Ruth checked as a pain caught her, and Elizabeth held her arm, and then guided her into the car.

'Drive carefully,' she said to Patrick. 'I mean it. You have plenty of time.'

'Yes, yes,' he said. 'I'll call you.'

She stepped back from the car and waved until it was out of sight. 'Dear little Ruth,' she said lovingly. 'At last.'

She closed the front door and went up the stairs to her bedroom. Frederick was still asleep. Nothing ever woke him. Elizabeth tapped him gently on the shoulder. 'They've gone to the hospital,' she said softly, thinking that the news might penetrate his dreams. 'Dear little Ruth has gone to have our baby.'

The childbirth course which Ruth had completed, and Patrick had attended twice, had laid great emphasis on the bonding nature of birth for the couple. There had been exercises of hand-holding and back rubbing, and little questionnaires to discover each other's preferences and fears about the birth. Patrick, who was not innately a sensual man, had been embarrassed when he was asked to massage Ruth's neck and shoulders in a roomful of people. His touch was light, diffident. The teacher, a willowy ex-hippy, had suggested that he grasp Ruth's hand, arm, shoulder, until he could feel the bones, and massage deeply, to get in touch with the core of Ruth's inner being.

'As if you were making love,' she urged them. 'Deep, sensual touching.'

Patrick, horribly embarrassed, had made gentle patting gestures. Next week there was an urgent meeting at work and he missed the class altogether.

Ruth conscientiously brought home notes and diagrams, and discussed the concept of active birth. She and Patrick were sitting on the sofa while Elizabeth and Frederick watched television. Ruth kept her voice low but Elizabeth, overhearing, had laughed and remarked: 'I only hope he doesn't disappoint you by dropping down in a dead faint. He's always been dreadfully squeamish.'

'In our day fathers were completely banned,' Frederick said. He turned to Elizabeth. 'You wouldn't have wanted me there, would you?'

'Certainly not!' she said. 'I gave birth to two children in two different countries, and never had a class in my life.'

'I want to have a completely natural childbirth,' Ruth said firmly. 'I want to do it all by breathing. That's what the classes are for. And I am counting on Patrick to help me.'

'I'm sure it will be fine,' Elizabeth reassured her. 'And, Patrick, you know all about it, do you?'

'Not a thing!' Patrick said with his charming smile. 'But Ruth has given me a book. I'll bone up on it before the day. I just can't get on with the class, and a roomful of people watching me.'

'I should think not!' Frederick said. 'It's a private business, I should have thought.'

'And it's more difficult for me,' Patrick said, warming to his theme. 'Everyone knows me, they've all seen me on the telly. I could just see them watching me trying to massage Ruth and dying to rush home and telephone their friends and say, "We saw that Patrick Cleary give his wife a massage".'

'I'm sure they wouldn't,' Ruth said. 'They're all much too interested in their own wives and babies. That's what they're there for, not to see you.'

'Don't you believe it,' said Frederick. 'Fame has its disadvantages too.'

'But I'll read the book,' Patrick promised. 'I'll know all about it by the time it happens.'

But Patrick had not read the book. It was in his brief-case on a journey to and from London. But he had bought a newspaper, to look for news stories for the documentary unit, and then there were notes to make, and things to think about, and anyway the journey was quite short. The book, still unread, was in his pocket as he helped Ruth into the maternity unit of the hospital.

As soon as the nurse admitted Ruth it was apparent that something was wrong. She called the registrar and there was a rapid undertone consultation. Then he turned to them. 'I'm afraid we'll have to do a section,' he said. 'Your baby is breeched and his pulse rate is too high. He's rather stressed. I think we want him out of there.' He glanced at Ruth. 'It'll have to be full anaesthesia. We don't have time to wait for Pethidine to work.'

The words were unfamiliar to Patrick, he did not know what was going on, but Ruth's distress was unmistakable. 'Now wait a minute . . .' he said.

'We can't really,' the doctor said. 'We can't wait at all. Do I have your permission?'

Ruth's eyes filled with tears and then she drew in a sharp breath of pain. 'Oh, yes,' she said. 'I suppose so . . . Oh, Patrick!'

'Permission for what?' Patrick asked. 'What's going on?'

The registrar took him by the arm and explained in a quick undertone that the baby was in distress and that they wanted to do a Caesarean section at once. Patrick, out of his depth, appealed to the doctor, 'But they'll both be OK, won't they? They'll both be all right?'

The doctor patted him reassuringly on the back. 'Right as rain,' he said cheerily. 'And no waiting about. I'll zip her down to surgery and in quarter of an hour you'll have your son in your arms. OK?'

'Oh, fine,' Patrick said, reassured. He looked back at Ruth lying on the high hospital bed. She had turned to face the wall; there were tears pouring down her cheeks. She would not look at him.

Patrick patted her back. 'It'll all be over in a minute.'

'I didn't want it to be over in a minute,' Ruth said, muffled. 'I wanted a natural birth.'

The nurse moved swiftly forward and put an injection in Ruth's limp arm. 'That's the pre-med,' she said cheerfully. 'You'll feel better now, and when you wake up you'll have a lovely baby. Won't that be wonderful? You go to sleep like a good girl now. You won't feel a thing.'

Patrick stood back and watched Ruth's dark eyelashes

65

flutter and finally close. 'But I *wanted* to feel . . .' she said sleepily.

They took the bed and wheeled it past him. 'What do I do?' he asked.

The nurse glanced at him briefly. 'There's nothing for you to do,' she said. 'You can watch the operation if you like . . . or I'll bring the baby out to you when it's delivered.'

'I'll wait outside,' Patrick said hastily. 'You can bring it out.'

They went through the double swing doors at the end of the brightly lit corridor. Patrick suddenly felt bereft and very much alone. He felt afraid for Ruth, so little and pale in the high-wheeled bed, with her eyelids red from crying.

He had not kissed her, he suddenly remembered. He had not wished her well. If something went wrong . . . he shied away from the thought, but then it recurred: *if* something went wrong then she would die without him holding her hand. She would die all on her own, and he had not even said, 'Good luck', as they took her away from him. He had not kissed her last night, he had not kissed her this morning, in the sudden panic of waking. Come to think of it, he could not remember the last time he had taken her in his arms and held her.

The book in his pocket nudged his hip. He hadn't gone to her antenatal classes, he hadn't even read her little book. Only two nights ago she had asked him to read a deep-breathing exercise to her when they were in bed, and he had fallen asleep by the third sentence. He had woken in the early hours of the morning with the corner of the book digging into his shoulder, and he had felt irritated with her for being so demanding, for making such absurd requests when everyone knew, when his mother assured him, that having a baby was as natural as shelling peas, that there was nothing to worry about.

And there were other causes for guilt. He had moved her out of the flat she loved and taken her away from Bristol and her friends and her job. He hadn't even got her little house ready for her on time. He hadn't chosen wallpaper or carpets or curtains with her. He had left it to his mother, when he knew Ruth wanted him to plan it with her. He felt deeply, miserably, guilty.

The uncomfortable feeling lasted for several minutes, and then he saw a pay phone and went over to telephone his mother.

She answered on the first ring; she had been lying awake in bed, as he knew she would. 'How are things?' she asked quickly.

'Not well,' he said.

'Oh! My dear!'

'She's got to have a Caesarean section, she's having it now.'

'Shall I come down?'

'I don't know . . . I'm waiting in the corridor . . . I feel at a bit of a loose end . . . It's all a bit bleak.'

'I'll come at once,' Elizabeth said briskly. 'And don't worry, darling, she'll be as right as rain.'

Elizabeth leaped from her bed and pulled on her clothes. She shook Frederick's shoulder. He opened one sleepy eye. 'Ruth's gone to have her baby. I'm going down there,' she said. There was no need for him to know more. Elizabeth never lied but she was often sparing with information. 'I'll telephone you with any news.'

'What's the time?'

'Three in the morning. Go back to sleep, darling,

there's nothing you can do. I'll call you when I know more.'

He nodded and rolled over. Elizabeth sped downstairs and put the kettle on. While it came to the boil she made sandwiches with cold lamb from last night's joint, and prepared a thermos of strong coffee. She put everything in a wicker basket and left the house, closing the front door quietly behind her.

It was a wonderful warm midsummer night; the stars were very bright and close and a harvest moon broad and yellow leaning on the horizon. Elizabeth started her little car and drove down the lane to the hospital at Bath, and to her son.

His face lit up when he saw her. He was sitting on a chair outside the operating theatre, very much alone, looking awkward with his jumper askew over his shirt collar. He looked very young.

'No news yet?' she asked.

'They're operating,' he said. 'It's taking longer than they said it would. But a nurse came out just now and said it was quite routine. She said there was nothing to worry about.'

'I brought you some coffee,' she said. 'And a sandwich.'

'I couldn't eat a thing,' he said fretfully. 'I keep thinking about her ... I didn't even kiss her goodnight, she was asleep by the time I got to bed last night, and I didn't kiss her before she went in.'

Elizabeth nodded and poured him a cup of coffee and added plenty of brown sugar. He took the cup and wrapped his hands around it.

'I didn't go to her classes either,' he said. 'Or read her book.'

'Well, they didn't do much good,' Elizabeth said. 'As things have turned out.'

He brightened at that. 'No,' he said. 'All those breathing exercises and in the end it's full anaesthetic.'

Elizabeth nodded and offered him a sandwich. He bit into it, and she watched the colour come back into his cheeks.

'I suppose she'll be all right?' he said. 'They said it was quite routine.'

'Of course she will be,' Elizabeth said. 'Some women *choose* to have a Caesarean birth. It's much easier for the baby, and no pain at all for the mother. She'll be fine.'

Patrick finished his cup of coffee and handed it back to his mother just as the theatre doors opened. A nurse in a green gown, wearing a ballooning paper hat over her hair and a white paper mask over her nose and mouth, came through the door with a small bundle in a blanket.

'Mr Cleary?' she asked.

Patrick got to his feet. 'Yes?'

'This is your son,' she said. 'And your wife is fine.'

She held the baby out to him and Patrick rubbed his hands on his trousers and reached out. He was awkward with the baby; she had to close his hands around the little bundle. 'Hold him close,' she urged. 'He won't bite!'

Patrick found himself looking into the tiny puckered face of his sleeping son. His mouth was pursed in mild surprise, his eyelids traced with blue. He had a tiny wisp of dark hair on the top of his head and tiny hands clenched into tiny bony fists.

'Is he all right?' Patrick asked. 'Quite all right?'

'He's perfect,' she assured him. 'Seven pounds three ounces. They're just stitching your wife up now and then you can see her in Recovery.'

Elizabeth was at Patrick's shoulder looking into the baby's face. 'He's the very image of you,' she said tenderly. 'Oh, what a poppet.'

The baby stirred and Patrick nervously tightened his grip.

'May I?' Elizabeth asked. Gently she took the baby and settled him against her shoulder. The damp little head nodded against her firm touch.

'Shall I take you in to see your wife?' the nurse asked. 'She'll be coming round in a little while.'

'You go, Patrick,' Elizabeth said. 'I'll look after Cleary Junior here.'

Patrick smiled weakly at her and followed the nurse. He still could not take in the fact that his baby had been born. 'Right,' he said. 'Right.'

Elizabeth had already turned away. She was walking slowly down the length of the corridor, swaying her hips slightly as she walked, rocking the baby with the steady, easy rhythm of her pace. 'And what shall we call you?' she asked the little sleeping head. She put her lips to his ear. It was perfectly formed, like a whorled shell, surprisingly cool. Elizabeth inhaled the addictive scent of newborn baby. 'Little love,' she whispered. 'My little love.'

It was nearly midday before Ruth woke from her sleep and nearly two o'clock before the baby was brought to her. He was no longer the scented damp bundle that

Elizabeth had walked in the corridor. He was washed and dried and powdered and dressed in his little cotton sleep suit. He was not like a newborn baby at all.

'Here he is,' the nurse said, wheeling him into the private room in the little Perspex cot.

Ruth looked at him doubtfully. There was no reason to believe that he was her baby at all; there was nothing to connect him and her except the paper bracelet around his left wrist, which said, 'Cleary 14.8.95.' 'Is it mine?' she asked baldly.

The nurse smiled. 'Of course it's yours,' she said. 'We don't get them mixed up. He's lovely, don't you think?'

Ruth nodded. Tears suddenly coming into her eyes. 'Yes,' she said weakly. She supposed the baby was lovely. But he looked very remote and very isolated in his little plastic box. He looked to her as if he had been assembled in the little box like a puzzle toy, as if he were the property of the hospital and not her baby at all.

'Now what's the matter?' the nurse asked.

'*I* bought that suit for him,' Ruth said tearfully. '*I* bought it.'

'I know you did, dear. We found it in your case and we put it on him as soon as he had his bath. Just as you would have wanted it done.'

Ruth nodded. It was pointless to explain the sense of strangeness and alienation. But she felt as if the little suit had been bought for another baby, not this one. The little suit had been bought for the baby that she had felt inside her, that had walked with her, and slept with her, and been with her for nine long months. It was for the imaginary baby, who had an imaginary birth, where Ruth had breathed away all the pains, where Patrick had massaged her back and held her hand and talked to her engagingly and charmingly through the hours of her labour, and where, after he had been triumphantly born, everyone had praised her for doing so well.

'You want to breast-feed him, don't you?'

Ruth looked at the sleeping baby without much enthusiasm. 'Yes, I did.'

'Well, I'll leave him here with you, and when he wakes up you can ring your bell and I'll come and help you get comfy. After a Caesarean you need a bit of help.'

'All right,' Ruth said.

The nurse gave her a kind smile and left the room. Ruth lay back and looked at the ceiling. Unstoppably the tears filled her eyes and ran out under her eyelids, hot and salty. Beside her, in his goldfish-bowl cot the baby slept.

In half an hour the nurse came back. She had hoped that Ruth would have broken the hospital rules and put the baby in bed beside her, but they were as far apart as ever.

'Now,' she said brightly. 'Let's wake this young man up and give him a feed.'

He was not ready to wake. His delicate eyelids remained stubbornly closed. He did not turn his head to Ruth even when she undid the buttons of her nightgown and pressed her nipple to his cheek.

'He's sleepy,' the nurse said. 'He must have got some of your anaesthetic. We'll give him a little tickle. Wake him up a bit.'

She slipped his little feet out of the sleep suit and tickled his toes. The baby hardly stirred.

'Come along now, come along,' the nurse said encouragingly.

She took him from Ruth and gave him a little gentle jiggle. The baby opened his eyes – they were very dark blue – and then opened his mouth in a wail of protest.

'That's better,' she said. Quickly and efficiently she swooped down on Ruth, propped the little head on Ruth's arm, patted his cheek, turned his face, and pressed Ruth's nipple into his mouth.

He would not suck. Four, five times, they repeated the procedure. He would not latch onto the nipple. Ruth felt herself blushing scarlet with embarrassment and felt the ridiculous easy tears coming again. 'He doesn't want to,' she said. She felt her breasts were disgusting, that the baby was making a wise choice in his rejection.

'He will,' the nurse reassured her. 'We just have to keep at it. But he will, I promise you.'

The baby had dozed off again. His head lolled away from her.

'He just doesn't want to,' Ruth said.

'We'll give it another try later on,' the nurse said reassuringly. 'Shall I leave him in with you for now? Have a little cuddle.'

'I thought he had to go into his cot?'

She smiled. 'We could break the rules just this once.'

Ruth held him out. 'It hurts on my scar,' she said. 'Better put him back.'

Four

PATRICK came at visiting time at four in the afternoon with a big bouquet of flowers. He kissed Ruth and looked into the cot.

'How is he?'

'He won't feed,' Ruth said miserably. 'We can't make him feed.'

'Isn't that bad? Won't he get hungry?'

'I don't know. The nurse said he was sleepy from my anaesthetic.'

'Did she seem worried?'

'How should I know?' Ruth exclaimed.

Patrick saw that she was near to tears. 'Here,' he said. 'Look at your lovely flowers. And dozens of bouquets at home – it looks like a florist's shop. They sent some from my work, and my secretary told Radio Westerly and they sent some.'

Ruth blinked. 'From Westerly?'

'Yes. A big bunch of red roses.'

'That was nice.'

'And your little chum.'

'Who?'

'That David.'

'Oh,' she said. It seemed like years since she had last seen David.

'And how are you, darling?'

'I'm fine,' she said. 'My stitches hurt.'

'Mother said they would. She said that we would all have to look after you especially well when you come home.'

Ruth nodded.

'She said she would come down later if that was all right with you. She didn't want to crowd us this afternoon. But she and the old man will come down this evening if you're not too tired.'

'Perhaps tomorrow?' Ruth suggested.

'They're very keen to see the grandson,' Patrick prompted. 'Dad especially.'

'All right, then.'

'They asked me what we would be calling him. I said that we'd probably stick with Thomas James.'

Ruth glanced towards the cot. She had imagined Thomas James as a fair-haired boy, not this dark-headed little thing. 'I never thought he'd be so small,' she said.

'Tiny, isn't he?' Patrick said. 'Shall I pick him up?'

'Better let him sleep,' Ruth said.

They both gazed at the sleeping baby. 'Tiny hands,' Patrick said again.

'I never thought of him like this,' Ruth said.

'I never really imagined him at all. I always kind of jumped ahead. I thought about teaching him how to fish, and taking him to cricket and things like that. I never thought of a tiny baby.'

'No.'

They were silent.

'He is all right, isn't he?' Patrick asked. 'I mean he

seems terribly quiet. I thought they cried all the time.'

'How should I know?' Ruth exclaimed again.

'Of course, of course,' Patrick said soothingly. 'Don't get upset, darling. Mother will be down this evening and she'll know.'

Ruth nodded and lay back on her pillows. She looked very small and wan. Her dark hair was limp and dirty, her cheeks sallow. There were dark shadows under her eyes.

'You look all in,' Patrick said. 'Shall I go and leave you to have a sleep?'

Ruth nodded. He could see she was near to tears again.

'Everything all right?' he asked.

'Yes,' she whispered.

'See you tonight then.' He bent over the bed and kissed her gently. She did not respond, she did not even turn her face to him. She let him touch her cheek as if she were sulking after some injury. He had a flash of irritation, that he should be behaving so beautifully, with such patience and forbearance, and she should be so limp. In the films he had seen of such situations as these, the young mothers had sat up in bed in pretty beribboned bed jackets, and smiled adoringly at their husbands and gazed devotedly at their babies. Patrick was too intelligent to mistake Hollywood images for reality, but he had expected something more than Ruth's resentful apathy.

He straightened up and turned to the cot. 'See you later, Thomas James,' he said quietly, and went from the room.

Ruth slept for only half an hour. At five o'clock the nurse woke her with dinner. Ruth, hungry and chilled, was confronted with a tray of grapefruit juice, Spam salad with sliced white bread and butter, followed by violently green jelly. As she drew the unappetizing dishes towards her, the baby stirred in his cot and cried.

Ruth's stitches were still too painful to let her move. Shifting the tray and picking up the baby was an impossibility. She dropped a forkful of icy limp salad and rang the bell for the nurse. No one came. The baby's cries went up a notch in volume. He went red in the face, and his little fists flailed against the air.

'Hush, hush,' Ruth said. She rang the bell again. 'Someone will come in a minute,' she said.

It was incredible that a baby so small could make so much noise, and that the noise should be so unbearably penetrating. Ruth could feel her own tension rising as the baby's cries grew louder and more and more desperate.

'Oh, please!' she cried out. 'Please don't cry like that. Someone will come soon! Someone will come soon! Surely someone will come!'

He responded at once to the panic in her voice, and his cry became a scream, an urgent, irresistible shriek.

The door opened and Elizabeth peeped in. She took in the scene in one rapid glance and moved forward. She put down the basket she was carrying, picked up the baby, and put him firmly against her shoulder, resting her cheek on his hot little head. His agonized cries checked at once at the new sensation of being picked up and firmly held.

'There, there,' Elizabeth said gently. 'Master Cleary! What a state you're in.'

She looked over his head to Ruth, tearstained in the

bed. 'Don't worry, darling,' she said gently. 'The first days are always the worst. You finish your dinner and I'll walk him till you're ready to feed him.'

'It's disgusting,' Ruth whispered. 'I can't eat it.'

'I brought you a quiche and one of my little apple pies,' Elizabeth offered. 'I didn't know what the food would be like in here, and after I had Patrick I was simply starving.'

'Oh! That would be lovely.'

Holding the baby against her neck with one casual hand, Elizabeth whipped a red-and-white-checked cloth off the top of the basket with the other, and spread it on Ruth's counterpane, followed by the quiche in its own little china dish. It was still warm from the oven, the middle moist and savoury, the pastry crisp. Ruth took the miniature silver picnic cutlery from the basket and ate every crumb, while Elizabeth wandered around the room humming lullabies in the baby's ear. She smiled when she saw the empty plate.

'Apple pie?'

'Please.'

Elizabeth produced a little individual apple pie and a small punnet of thick cream. Ruth ate. The apple was tart and sharp, the pastry sweet.

'Better now?' Elizabeth asked.

Ruth sighed. 'Thank you. I was really hungry, and *so* miserable.'

'The quicker we get you home and into a routine the better,' Elizabeth said. 'D'you think you could feed him now? I think he's awake and hungry.'

'I'll try,' Ruth said uncertainly.

Elizabeth passed the little bundle to her. As Ruth leaned forward to take him, her stitches pulled and she cried out with pain. At the sharp sound of her voice and the loss of the rocking and humming, Thomas opened his eyes in alarm and shrieked.

'There,' Elizabeth said, hurrying forward. 'Now tuck him in tight to you.' Expertly she pressed the baby against Ruth. 'I'll pop a pillow under here to hold him close. You lie back and make yourself comfortable.' She arranged the baby, head towards Ruth, but Thomas cried and cried. Ruth, half-naked, pushed her breast towards his face, but he would not feed.

'It's no good!' Ruth was near tears. 'He just won't! I can't make him! And he'll be getting so hungry!'

'Why not give him a bottle just for now?' Elizabeth suggested. 'And feed him yourself later on when you feel better?'

'Because they say you *have* to feed at once, as soon after the birth as possible,' Ruth said over a storm of Thomas's cries. The baby, more and more distressed, was kicking against her and crying. 'If he doesn't take to it now he'll never learn.'

'But a bottle . . .'

'No!' Ruth cried out, her voice drowned out by Thomas's anguished wails.

The door opened and the nurse came in. 'I'm sorry I couldn't get down before,' she said. 'Are you all right in here?'

'I think the baby should have a bottle,' Elizabeth said smoothly. 'He's not taking to the breast.'

The nurse responded at once to Elizabeth's calm authority. 'Certainly, but I thought that Mother . . .'

Ruth lay back on her pillows, the baby's insistent cry half deafening her.

'Shall I take him?' Elizabeth asked.

79

'Take him,' Ruth whispered.

'And give him a bottle, get him fed, darling, and settled?'

Miserably Ruth nodded. 'All right! All right!' she said with weak anger. 'Just do what you want!'

Elizabeth took the baby from her. 'You have a nice rest,' she said. 'I'll get him sorted out.'

The nurse stepped back. 'Aren't you lucky to have your mum to help you?'

'Yes,' Ruth said quietly, thinking of her own mother, so long dead, and distant and unhelpfully gone.

Three weeks later Ruth and Thomas came home. Ruth had been proved right in one respect. Thomas, offered the bottle by Elizabeth and then dandled on Frederick's knee, never breast-fed. Despite Ruth's intentions, despite all the books, the good advice, and her resolutions, her baby had been born by Caesarean section and was fed from the start on powdered milk. He was a potent symbol of her failure to complete successfully the job she had not wanted to take on. Ruth had not expected to be a good mother; but she had set herself the task of learning how to do it. Conscientious and intelligent, she had done her absolute best to master theories of childbirth and child raising. But Thomas was a law to himself. She felt that he had been born without her – simply taken from her unconscious body. She felt that he preferred to feed without her. Anyone could hold him while he had his bottle. He appeared to have no preferences. Anyone could comfort him when he cried. As long as he was picked up and walked, he would stop crying. But Ruth, exhausted and still in pain from the operation, was the only one who could not easily pick him up and walk with him.

It was Elizabeth who cared for him most of the time. It was Elizabeth who knew the knack of wrapping him tightly in his white wool shawl, his little arms criss-crossed over his stomach, so he slept. It was Elizabeth who could hold him casually in the crook of her arm while she cooked one-handed, and it was Elizabeth's serene face that his deep blue eyes watched, intently gazing at her as she worked, and her smile that he saw when she glanced down at him.

While Ruth slept upstairs in the spare bedroom of the farmhouse, Elizabeth rocked Thomas in Patrick's old pram in the warm midsummer sun of the walled garden. While Ruth rested, it was Elizabeth who loaded Thomas into her car in his expensive reclining baby seat and drove to the shops. Elizabeth was never daunted at the prospect of taking Thomas with her. 'I'm glad to help,' she told Patrick. 'Besides, it makes me feel young again.'

The health visitor came in the first week that Thomas and Ruth were home. 'Aren't you lucky to have a live-in nanny!' she exclaimed facetiously to Ruth, but in her notes she scribbled a memo that Mother and child did not seem to have bonded, and that Mother seemed depressed. On her second visit she found Ruth surrounded by suitcases and languidly packing while Elizabeth was changing Thomas's nappy in the nursery.

'We're moving to our house,' Ruth said. 'The builders have finished at last. I'm just packing the last of my clothes.'

The health visitor nodded. 'You'll miss having your family around you,' she said diplomatically, thinking that at last mother and baby would have some privacy.

81

'Is your new house far away? I shall have to have the address. Is it still in my area?'

'Oh yes, it's just at the end of the drive,' Ruth said. 'The little cottage on the right, Manor Farm Cottage. We're within walking distance.'

'Oh,' the health visitor hesitated. 'Nice to have your family nearby, especially when you've got a new baby, isn't it?'

Ruth's pale face was expressionless. 'Yes,' she said.

They moved in the third week in September. Elizabeth had organized the arrival of their furniture from the store, and placed it where she thought best. Elizabeth had hung the curtains and they looked very well. She and Patrick went down to the cottage with the suitcases and unpacked the clothes and hung them in the new fitted wardrobe in the bedroom. Patrick had planned to make up the bed and prepare Thomas's cot, but the new telephone rang just as they arrived in the house, with a crisis at work, and he stood in the hall, taking notes on the little French writing desk, which Elizabeth had put there, while his mother got the bedrooms ready and made the cot in the nursery with freshly ironed warm sheets.

The gardener had started work, and the grass was cut and the flower beds nearest the house were tidy. Elizabeth picked a couple of roses and put them in a little vase by the double bed. The cottage was as lovely as she had planned.

Patrick put the telephone down. 'I *am* sorry,' he said. 'I didn't mean you to do all this. I promised Ruth I would do it.'

'You know I enjoy it,' she said easily. 'And anyway, I don't like to see a man making beds. Men always look so forlorn doing housework.'

'You spoil us,' Patrick said, his mind on his work. 'Will you go up to the house and fetch Ruth?'

'I should really go in to work. There's a bit of a flap on – a rumour that some Japanese high-tech company is coming in to Bristol. We had half a documentary about their work practices in the can, but if the rumour's confirmed we should really edit it and run it as it is. I need to get in and see what's going on.'

Elizabeth was about to offer to fetch Ruth for him, but she hesitated. 'I think you should make the time to bring her and Thomas down here, all the same,' she said. 'I'm sure she's feeling a bit neglected.'

He nodded. 'Oh, all right. Look. Run me back home and I'll dash in, pick her up, whiz them down here, and settle them in, and then I'll go in to the studio.'

Elizabeth led the way to her car, and they drove the mile and a half up to the farmhouse.

Ruth was rocking Thomas's pram in the garden, her face incongruously grim in the late-summer sunshine, with the roses still in lingering bloom behind her. 'Ssssh,' she said peremptorily. 'He's only this minute gone off. I've been rocking and rocking and rocking. I must have been here for an hour.'

'I was going to take you both down to the cottage. It's all ready,' Patrick whispered.

Ruth looked despairing. 'Well, I'm not waking him up. He's only just gone. I can't bear to wake him.'

'Oh, come on,' Patrick said. 'He'll probably drop off again if we just transfer him into his carry cot.'

Ruth thought for a moment. 'We could walk down, and push the pram down with us.'

Patrick instinctively shrank from the thought of walking down the road, even his own parents' private drive, pushing a pram. There was something so trammelled and domestic about the image. There was something very poverty-stricken about it too, as if they could not afford a car.

'No,' he said quickly. 'Anyway, I don't have the time. I have to go in to work. I wanted to drop the two of you off.'

'Not work again . . .'

'It's a crisis . . .'

'It's always a crisis . . .'

'Why don't the two of you go?' Elizabeth interposed. 'And leave Thomas here. Ruth can settle in, have a little wander around, have a bit of peace and quiet. I'll keep Thomas here until you want him brought down. You can phone me when you're ready. The phone's working.'

'That's very kind of you,' Ruth said, 'but . . .'

'It's no trouble to me at all,' Elizabeth assured her. 'I have nothing to do this afternoon except a spot of shopping, and Thomas can come with me. He loves the supermarket. I'll wait till he wakes and then take him out.'

Ruth hesitated, tempted by the thought of an afternoon in her new house.

'If I get away early I'll come home in time for tea,' Patrick offered. 'We could have a bit of time together before we collect Thomas.'

Elizabeth nodded encouragingly. 'Enjoy your new house together,' she said. 'Thomas can stay with me as long as you like. I can even give him his bottle and bath him here.'

Ruth looked directly at Patrick. 'But I thought we were moving into our house, all together, this afternoon.' She let the demand hang in the air.

Elizabeth smiled faintly and moved discreetly out of earshot. Patrick slipped his arm around Ruth's waist and led her away from the pram. 'Why don't you go down to our little house, run yourself a bath, have a little rest, and I'll bring home a pizza or a curry or something and we'll have dinner, just the two of us, and christen that bedroom?'

Ruth hesitated. She and Patrick had not made love since the birth of Thomas. She felt a half-forgotten desire stir inside her. Then she remembered the pain of her stitches, and the disagreeable fatness of her belly. 'I can't,' she said coldly. 'It's too soon.'

'Then we'll have a gentle snog,' Patrick said agreeably. 'Come on, Ruth, let's take advantage of a good offer. Let's have our first night on our own and fetch Thomas tomorrow. Mother will have him overnight for us; he's got his cot here and all the things he needs. And they love to have him. Why not?'

'All right,' Ruth said, seduced despite herself. 'All right.'

Ruth had longed to be in her own house, and to settle into a routine with her own baby. But nothing was as she had planned. Thomas did not seem to like his new nursery. He would not settle in his cot. Every evening, as Patrick returned Ruth's cooling dinner to the oven, Ruth went back upstairs, rocked Thomas to sleep again, and put him into his cot. They rarely ate dinner together; one of them was always rocking the baby.

During the day, Thomas slept well. Ruth could put him in the pram and wheel it out into the little back garden.

'That's when you should sleep,' Elizabeth reminded her. 'Sleep when the baby sleeps, catch forty winks.'

But Ruth could never sleep during Thomas's daytime naps. She was always listening for his cry, she was always alert.

'Leave him to cry,' Elizabeth said robustly. 'If he's safe in his cot or in his pram he'll just drop off again.'

Ruth shot her a reproachful glance. 'I wouldn't dream of it,' she said.

'But if you're overtired and need the sleep . . .' Elizabeth said gently.

'She's determined,' Patrick said. 'It's in the book.'

'Oh, the book,' Elizabeth said and exchanged a small hidden smile with Patrick.

Ruth stuck to the book, which said that the baby should be fed on demand and never left to cry, even though it meant that she could never settle to anything during the day, and never slept at night for more than a couple of hours at a time. She saw many dawns break at the nursery window before Thomas finally dozed off to sleep and she could creep back into bed beside Patrick's somnolent warmth. Then it seemed to be only moments before the alarm clock rang out, and Patrick yawned noisily, stretched, and got out of bed.

'Be quiet!' Ruth spat at him. She was near to tears. 'He's only just gone off to sleep. For Christ's sake, Patrick, do you have to make so much noise?'

Patrick, who had done nothing more than rattle the clothes hangers in the wardrobe while taking his shirt, spun around, shocked at the tone of her voice. Ruth had never spoken to him like that before.

'What?'

'I said, for Christ's sake do you have to make so much noise? I've been up all night with him. He's only this minute gone off.'

'No, you weren't,' Patrick said reasonably. 'I heard him cry out at about four, and I listened for him. I was going to get up, but he went back to sleep again.'

'He was awake at one, for an hour, and then again at three. He *didn't* go back to sleep at four, it was you that went back to sleep at four. *He* woke up and I had to change him and give him another bottle, and I was up with him till six, and I can't *bear* him to wake again.'

Patrick looked sceptical. 'I'm sure I would have woken if you had been up that often,' he said. 'You probably dreamed it.'

Ruth gave a little shriek and clapped her hand over her mouth. Above her own gagging hand, her eyes glared at Patrick. 'I couldn't have dreamed it.' She was near to tears. 'How could I have dreamed anything? I've been awake nearly all night! There was no time to dream anything, because I've hardly ever slept!'

Patrick pulled on his shirt and then crossed the room and sat on the edge of the bed, touching her gently on the shoulder. 'Calm down, darling,' he said. 'Calm down. I'm sorry. I didn't know you'd had a bad night. Shall I call Mother?'

'I don't *want* your mother,' Ruth said fretfully. 'I want you to be quiet in the mornings so you don't wake him again. I want you to get up without waking *me*.

And I want *you* to come home early so you have him this afternoon and I can sleep then.'

Patrick got up and briskly pulled on his trousers. He hated demanding women, having had no experience of them. 'No can do, I'm afraid. I've got a meeting at six. I was going to be late home anyway. I'll call Mother as I go out. You get your head down and get some sleep. She'll be down straightaway and she can get Thomas up and dressed and take him up home for the day.'

'I don't want your mother,' Ruth insisted. 'I want you to look after Thomas. Not her. He's your son, not hers.'

Patrick smoothed the lapels of his jacket down over his chest and glanced at the pleasing reflection in the mirror. 'I can't be in two places at once,' he said. 'Be reasonable, Ruth. I'm doing my best, and I'm working all the hours God sends to make a go of this documentary unit. If I get the pay rise I've been promised we could get some help, perhaps a girl to come in and look after Thomas a couple of mornings a week.'

'I don't want a girl,' Ruth said. 'I want *us* to look after our son. Not a girl, not your mother: you and me.'

Patrick said nothing. The silence seemed to be on his side.

'So I'll call Mother, shall I?' he asked, as if she had not spoken.

The temptation of a morning's sleep was too much for Ruth.

'All right,' she said ungraciously. 'I suppose so.'

Five

'IT'S RUTH,' Patrick said without preamble when his mother answered the phone. 'She's not up to managing Thomas this morning, and I have to go to work. Can you have him?'

'Of course,' Elizabeth said easily. 'You know how I love him.'

'Weren't you doing something today? Isn't it your day at the church for flowers or something?' Patrick asked with belated politeness.

'Yes, but Thomas can come too. He's so good. He's no trouble at all.'

Patrick felt himself relax. The sense of permanent crisis that eddied around the little house was calmed by his mother's competence. 'I wish you could teach Ruth how to handle him,' he said suddenly. 'We don't seem to be getting on at all.'

There was a diplomatic silence from his mother.

'She can't seem to settle him at night, and then she's tired all day. She wanted me to come home early from work and I simply can't.' Patrick realized he was sounding aggrieved and at once adjusted his tone. 'I suppose we're beginners at this,' he said, the good humour back in his voice. 'Apprentices.'

'There's nothing wrong, is there?' Elizabeth asked. 'Apart from her being tired?'

'What d'you mean?'

'I don't know. I just wondered if she was perhaps a little depressed. Baby blues or something?'

Patrick thought for a moment. If he had been honest he would have known that Ruth had been unhappy from the moment the pregnancy had been confirmed, from the moment she gave up her job. She had been unhappy at the move to the little house, she had been unhappy at living so close to his parents. And now she was unhappy with being left alone all day, every day, with a new restless baby.

'She seems to be making very heavy weather of it all,' he said eventually. 'I don't know if she's depressed. She's certainly making a meal of it.'

'I'll come down at once,' Elizabeth said. 'See what I can do.'

'Thank you,' Patrick said with real gratitude. Then he put the receiver down, picked up his car keys, and drove to work with the agreeable sense of having done all that a man could be expected to do for his wife and child.

Elizabeth tapped on the front door very gently, and when there was no reply let herself in with her own key. In the kitchen Patrick's morning cup of coffee was cooling on the table. Someone had forgotten to switch on the dishwasher the night before and the plates were still dirty. The kitchen curtains were closed, and the room looked shadowy and hungover. Elizabeth drew the curtains back and fastened them with their tiebacks. She moved around, easily, confidently, clearing up and wiping the worktops, admiring the colour scheme, which she had chosen. The sitting room was reasonably tidy, but it had the neglected appearance of a room that was seldom used. Elizabeth picked up the evening paper and put it in the log basket for lighting the fire, put the *Radio Times* tidily beside the television. She plumped up the cushions on the sofa and moved the coffee table into place. There were no flowers in the room, just a dying African violet in a pot with browning leaves and dry petals. Elizabeth frowned slightly, fetched a glass of water and dribbled it onto the thirsty soil.

She heard a movement and a little cry from the nursery upstairs and went soft-footed up the stairs. The Berber-twist carpet she had chosen went well with the William Morris wallpaper, which Ruth had insisted on using. Elizabeth took it all in with the pleasure of a house owner.

The cry from the nursery grew louder as Thomas woke.

'Coming! I'm coming!' There was an exasperated yell from the bedroom, and then the bedroom door was flung open and the two women suddenly faced each other.

Ruth was in a dingy maternity nightgown, her body, still fat with the weight of pregnancy, only partly masked by its folds. Her feet were bare, her hair limp, her face a mask of tiredness, dark shadows deeply etched under her eyes. She looked exhausted and unhappy. Elizabeth was trim in grey wool slacks with a pale cashmere jumper. She had a light-coloured scarf pinned at her neck by a small expensive brooch; she wore the lightest of makeup. Her perfume, as usual, was Chanel No 15.

'Oh,' Ruth said blankly.

'Patrick phoned me to come. He said you wanted to sleep.'

The wails from the nursery grew louder. Both women checked a move to go, deferring to each other with careful courtesy.

'I was up all night,' Ruth said. To her own ears she sounded as if she were making excuses to a strict teacher.

'Of course, my dear, and I love to have him.'

'I wanted Patrick to come home early . . .'

'Well, men have to work.' Elizabeth stated an inarguable fact. 'And I'm just up the road doing nothing. Let me get him up and give him his bottle and get him dressed, and I'll take him up to the farm with me. And when you've had a good sleep, and a bath' (and washed your hair, she mentally added) 'then you can come up to the farm and fetch him, or I'll bring him back.'

'I don't like to impose,' Ruth said awkwardly.

'Nonsense. If it were your mother within walking distance, she would be caring for you both.'

At the mention of her absent mother Ruth's face changed at once. Her eyes filled with ready tears. 'Yes,' she said miserably.

'So let me. At least Thomas has one granny. And Frederick can take him out for a walk in the pram this afternoon. The exercise and the fresh air will do them both good.'

Ruth nodded.

Elizabeth turned for the nursery and went in. The room smelled sickly sweet from the bin of dirty nappies. Thomas, rosy-cheeked and bawling, was kicking in his cot. His nappy, sleep suit, even his bedding were soaked through with urine.

'What a little terror!' Elizabeth exclaimed. She took a

towel from the changing table and wrapped him as she picked him up. Thomas, feeling the security of being held firmly and confidently, settled down to a little whimper of hunger. Elizabeth held him close to her neck, and he snuffled against her warm skin and familiar perfume.

'You go back to sleep,' Elizabeth said kindly to Ruth. 'You look all in. Shall I bring you up a cup of tea and some breakfast?'

'No!' Ruth said, repelled at the thought of Elizabeth in her bedroom. 'I'll get something, it's all right.'

'I'll sort out this young man and take him up to the house, then,' Elizabeth said. 'He can come into the garden while I pick some flowers and then we'll go down to the church. It's my day for the flowers.'

'Oh no!' Ruth suddenly remembered. 'It's clinic day. He has to go to be weighed.'

Elizabeth smiled. 'They surely can't think he needs weighing every week,' she said. 'He eats like a horse.'

'He *has* to go,' Ruth said. 'They fill in his weight chart to make sure he gains steadily. He has to go every week.'

Elizabeth suppressed her opinion of clinics and weight charts when anyone holding this armful of wet kicking baby could know that they had a perfectly fit child in their arms. 'I'll take him, then,' she said.

'I have to,' Ruth said. She was looking increasingly anxious. 'I have to go with him.'

'Nonsense,' Elizabeth said firmly. 'What do they do – weigh him? and write up his chart? I can take him on my way in to church.'

The thought of someone dropping in to the baby clinic while en route for somewhere else quite stunned Ruth. To her it was a target to aim for all morning. The clinic, with the other screaming babies and the frighteningly competent staff, the brisk unfriendliness of the nurse, and the cliquish circle of other mothers, was a place she dreaded. Thomas had to be weighed naked, so she had the task of undressing him and then dressing him again, while the other mothers watched her incompetent fumblings. He screamed all the time as she struggled with the intricate fastenings, and she thought that the staff despised her for her inability to care for her child. Other mothers had toddlers in tow as well, and they managed to control both babies and small children while Ruth was obviously defeated by just one.

'It's awfully hard,' she said. 'You have to undress him to be weighed, and they fill in the card, and then you have to dress him again.'

'I should think I could manage that,' Elizabeth said.

Ruth looked at her curiously. Elizabeth was smiling gently, humorously, as if the task were genuinely an easy one. It was obvious to Ruth that Elizabeth found the nightmarishly difficult task of caring for Thomas both natural and enjoyable. She felt her throat tighten; she turned to go to her bedroom before Elizabeth saw her cry. 'All right then,' she said.

'Will you come to the house when you are ready?' Elizabeth asked the closing door.

'Yes,' Ruth said, her voice muffled. The door clicked shut.

Elizabeth faced the closed door, Thomas snug against her shoulder. 'I'll look after him till you come then,' she said, contentedly.

The clinic was held in the health centre in the Babies Room. When Elizabeth tapped on the door and walked in with Thomas strapped into his plastic carrier, the noise hit her like a wall of sound. Half a dozen babies were crying and the mothers were shouting comments and gossip over the noise. The health visitor on duty and the one clinic clerk wore expressions of stolid patience. Elizabeth went up to the desk.

'Thomas James Cleary,' she said.

The clerk found the form. 'Undress over there,' she said. 'The health visitor will call you.'

Elizabeth looked at the cold plastic changing mat on the high narrow shelf with disfavour. Instead she sat on one of the low chairs and undressed Thomas on her knee, wrapping him in a shawl when he was naked.

'Thomas Cleary,' the health visitor said. 'Oh! It's Thomas's grandma, isn't it?'

Elizabeth rose. 'Yes,' she said. 'I am Mrs Cleary.'

'Mother not well?' the health visitor asked as they watched the red arrow of the scales tip over at sixteen pounds.

'Overtired,' Elizabeth said.

The health visitor nodded. 'Moved into her new house, then? I should have called in, really. Doing all right is she?'

Elizabeth allowed a shadow of doubt. 'It's very hard work,' she said. 'Coping with everything. Especially with a first child.'

The health visitor passed the form to the clinic clerk, who entered the weight carefully in the appropriate column. Elizabeth, who had raised two healthy children without benefit of scales or health visitors, tried to look appropriately respectful. Unseen, the health visitor flipped through her notes. She remembered Ruth when she found the note she had written about the mother and baby failing to bond, and now here was the grandmother turning up at the clinic.

'Let's have a little sitdown and a chat,' she invited.

Elizabeth sat in the chair and started to put a new nappy on Thomas. The health visitor noted her easy competence with him. 'None of my mothers can do that,' she said. 'They all dress them on changing mats.'

'We didn't have changing mats in my day,' Elizabeth said. 'I always feel safer with him on my knee.'

'Is Mother all right?'

Elizabeth hesitated. 'She's very overtired.'

'Bit depressed?' the health visitor offered.

Elizabeth shrugged. 'I try not to interfere. I'm only here today because my son asked me to have Thomas for the morning.'

'And do you have him often?'

'Whenever I am asked.'

The health visitor felt a certain unease at Elizabeth's patrician reserve. She was not confiding. It was hard to know how to ask the next question.

'Are mother and baby on good terms?' she asked clumsily. 'Getting to know each other? Lots of play and tickling?'

Elizabeth shot her a guarded look, which spoke volumes. 'I think so.'

The health visitor looked at her notes. Thomas was well-dressed and clean; he was gaining weight; there was no reason to fear that there might be anything wrong at home. But she remembered Ruth's sleepy uninterest in the baby at the farmhouse and how every time she had called, the baby had been with his grandmother. Now the grandmother was bringing him to the clinic. When Ruth had come she had looked stressed and anxious, roughly pulling the baby's clothes over his head, bundling him into his carry cot. She had forgotten to bring a spare nappy on one visit and she had been near tears. The child should not be at risk, with this extended family around him, and yet . . . and yet . . .

'D'you think it's a bit too much for her?' she asked. 'New baby, new house, and her husband must work all hours, doesn't he?'

Elizabeth warmed at the mention of Patrick's fame. 'He's terribly busy.'

'Does Mother need a bit more support perhaps?'

'Well, we do all we can,' Elizabeth said, a slight edge to her voice. 'Every time I'm asked I have Thomas for her. She knows she only has to pick up the phone.'

'So what's the problem?' the health visitor asked boldly.

Elizabeth slid her a swift sideways glance as she straightened Thomas's tiny socks. 'Not the maternal type,' she whispered. It was like admitting a crime.

'Not?'

'Not.'

The two women sat in conspiratorial silence for a moment. 'I thought not,' the health visitor said. 'She just didn't seem to take to him.'

'He was a Caesarean, and she couldn't feed him. She didn't stick at it so it never happened, and now she just seems quite incapable of getting up to him in the night or waking up in the morning.'

'Is she depressed?'

Elizabeth checked an impatient response. 'I don't know,' she said carefully. 'I wouldn't know. We've never had any depression in our family, or anything like that.'

'Perhaps the doctor should see her, have a word.'

Elizabeth shrugged. 'We can always care for Thomas,' she said. 'I'm free all day, and he can come with me for all my little chores. We're going to do the church flowers now, I've got a car full of Michaelmas daisies.'

'Lovely,' the health visitor said. 'Will you make an appointment for your daughter to see the doctor then?'

Elizabeth hesitated. 'She's my daughter-*in-law*,' she emphasized. 'It makes it a little difficult.'

The health visitor nodded, thinking. 'What about her mother?'

'Both her parents are dead,' Elizabeth said. 'And there's no family to speak of. She's very alone in the world. It's a mercy we are here to care for her.'

The health visitor hesitated. Her first impression of a young mother struggling to cope with a new baby and to deal with continual interference was changing. In the light of Elizabeth's discreet emphasis, she thought now that Ruth was sliding into depression despite the help of her family.

'Could your son bring her in to see the doctor?'

Elizabeth shook her head. 'It would look so strange. She would wonder what was going on.'

'I know,' the health visitor said. 'Tell her that the doctor wants to see her and Baby for an eight-week check. Absolutely routine, and I'll see that Dr Mac-Fadden knows that we are concerned.'

'I'm not *concerned*,' Elizabeth said carefully. 'Not exactly *concerned*.'

'Well, I am,' the health visitor said baldly. 'And I want her to see the doctor.'

*　　*　　*

Ruth ate breakfast cereal on her own in the quiet kitchen. Elizabeth had been right in seeing the potential of the cottage. In the autumn morning sunshine the little house glowed. Ruth looked around the new kitchen fittings and the bright pale walls as if they were the walls of a prison. She ate spoonful after spoonful of muesli and tasted nothing. She drank a cup of instant coffee, then she put her head down on the kitchen table and crouched quite still.

She nearly dozed off, sliding from despair into sleep, but she roused herself and went up the stairs, her bare feet warmed by the thick carpet that Elizabeth had chosen. Their bedroom was untidy with cast-off clothes. Ruth walked to the bed, seeing neither the mess nor the pretty view from the bedroom window, which looked over the little garden up the hill to the farmhouse. She climbed into bed and pulled the duvet over her shoulders and closed her eyes. She was asleep in moments.

It was three o'clock in the afternoon when she jerked awake with a gasp of terror. There had been a dream in which Thomas had been missing. She had been looking for him and looking for him. She had been searching the path all the way from the little house to Manor Farm House, and everywhere she looked she could hear his cry, just ahead of her. At Manor Farm, Elizabeth had been in the garden, pruning shears in hand. She had paused in pruning the roses and asked Ruth what was wrong. Ruth had been weeping with distress, but when Elizabeth asked her what she was searching for, she could not remember Thomas's name. She knew she was looking for her baby, but the name had completely gone. She just stared at Elizabeth, speechless with anxiety, knowing that Thomas was missing and she could not remember how to call him back to her.

Ruth gave a little gasp at the shock of the dream and then looked around her bedroom in surprise. The light was wrong for early morning, Patrick was not there, then slowly she remembered that Elizabeth was caring for Thomas, and that she had promised to fetch him from the farmhouse.

'Oh, no,' she said softly and jumped out of bed, reaching for the bedside telephone. She dialled the number from memory and waited anxiously.

'Manor Farm.' It was Frederick's voice.

'Oh! It's me!' Ruth said. 'I overslept, I'm so sorry. I'll come up straightaway.'

'Hold tight,' he said. Elizabeth had told him that the health visitor thought that Ruth was depressed. He was not surprised, believing that all women were prone to anger and tears and unexplained grief. 'Steady the Buffs.'

'But I said I would come up . . . I thought I'd be with you before lunch . . .'

'So when you weren't I took him out for a little walk, he had his sleep, and now he's out shopping with Elizabeth,' Frederick said. 'Nothing to worry about at all.'

Ruth found that she was gasping with anxiety. 'I just feel so awful . . .'

'Steady the Buffs,' he repeated. 'We've had a lovely day with him. Elizabeth adores him. We'll pop him down to you when they come home. No trouble at all.'

'Thank you,' Ruth said weakly. 'I was so tired I just slept and slept . . .'

'Good thing too,' he said kindly. 'Best medicine in all the world.'

'Thank you,' Ruth said again. She could feel her eyes

watering at the kindness in his tone. 'I'll wait for them to come home.'

'You do that,' Frederick said, and put down the telephone.

As he did so, Elizabeth's car drew up outside the front door, and he went out to help her with the shopping.

'Ruth called,' he said. 'Apparently she's only just woken.'

Elizabeth paused, about to lift Thomas from his seat. 'Shall I take Thomas down there? How did she sound?'

Frederick hesitated. 'A bit fraught,' he said.

Elizabeth unbuckled Thomas from his car seat. 'I'll take him down later,' she said. 'At bedtime. There's simply no point in Ruth having him if she can't cope.'

Frederick held out his arms for his grandson. 'Hello, young chap,' he said lovingly. 'Here for the duration, eh?'

Ruth made the appointment to see the doctor, thinking that it was a routine check-up for Thomas, as the health visitor had advised. Elizabeth insisted that Patrick drive Ruth to the health centre and go in with her. After a cursory look at Thomas, Dr MacFadden suggested that Patrick take Thomas outside – 'while I have a word with Mum.'

Ruth flinched slightly at being called 'Mum', but she let Patrick and Thomas go.

Dr MacFadden glanced at his notes. He was a young man, newly married and childless. He had endured sleepless nights himself when he was a young doctor on attachment to a busy hospital, but he did not think that dreary blending of night and day, that sea of fatigue in which all colours became grey and all emotions melted into weariness, was similar to the experience of caring for a small sleepless baby. After all, one was work and directed to a goal while the other was part of a natural process. He knew that women with new babies were always tired. He did not think of them as being sick with lack of sleep. He looked for another cause for Ruth's white face and dark-ringed eyes.

'And how are you?' he asked gently.

Ruth felt her face quiver. 'I'm fine,' she said stubbornly. 'Tired.'

He glanced down at his notes. He had not seen her during pregnancy, she had gone to the hospital for her antenatal care. He had seen her and Thomas only once before, at their six-week check-up, and had thought then that she looked ill and depressed.

'Feeling a bit down?' he suggested.

'A bit,' Ruth said unwillingly.

'Are you sleeping all right?'

She looked at him as if he were insane. 'Sleeping?' she repeated. 'I never sleep. It feels as if I just never sleep at all.'

'Baby keeping you up all night?'

'I never get more than a couple of hours together.'

'A lively one,' Dr MacFadden said cheerfully. 'Does Father take a turn with you?'

'No,' Ruth said. 'He's very busy at work . . .'

He nodded.

'Are you a bit weepy?'

She turned her face away. 'I'm miserable,' she said flatly.

'I think we can do something to help with that,' he

said. 'I expect you feel a bit distant from the baby, do you? It's perfectly normal.'

Ruth turned her face back to him, questioning. 'Is it? I just keep thinking how *unnatural* it is.'

'No, no, lots of mothers can't bond with their babies straightaway. It takes a bit of time.'

'He just seems . . .' Ruth broke off at the impossibility of explaining how Thomas – who had been born on his own and preferred to feed without her, and who now crowed and gurgled at the sight of his grandmother or his grandfather, or his father, without apparent preference – seemed so utterly independent of her and remote from her. 'It's as if he weren't my baby at all,' she said very quietly. 'As if he belonged to someone else but I'm . . .' she paused '. . . I'm stuck with him.'

Dr MacFadden nodded as if none of this was so very dreadful. 'I expect you resent having to care for him?'

Ruth nodded. 'Sometimes,' she whispered. 'At the start of the day when Patrick goes, and Thomas is awake and I look ahead and it just goes on and on forever. I never know whether he'll go to sleep or not. And if he *does* sleep during the day I can't rest. I'm always listening for him to wake up. And sometimes he only sleeps for a few moments anyway, so just when I've gone back to bed and I'm dozing off he wakes up and I have to get up again, and then he cries and cries and cries,' her voice rose. 'And there are times when I could just *murder* him!' She clapped her hand to her mouth and looked aghast. 'I didn't mean that. I didn't mean to say that. I'd never hurt him. Never!'

'A lot of mothers feel like this,' Dr MacFadden said gently, retaining a sympathetic smile and holding his voice steady. 'It's perfectly normal, and it's very good to acknowledge it. You'd be surprised how many mothers I see who feel just as you do, and when they've had a bit of sleep and a bit of help they bring up perfectly happy children.'

'I wouldn't hurt him . . .' Ruth repeated.

Dr MacFadden nodded and wrote a note. It said: '? baby at risk?' 'I'm sure you wouldn't,' he said. 'But you're obviously a bit overwrought just now. Have you ever shaken him or smacked him at all?'

'No! No, of course not.'

'That's good,' he said soothingly. 'No baby was ever hurt by a thought, you know.'

Ruth nodded. 'I wouldn't hurt him,' she said. She sounded less and less certain.

'No,' he said. 'Now I'm going to write you a prescription that will help you feel more relaxed, and will make things a bit easier. I want you to take one in the morning and two at night, and come back and see me in a week.'

'What are they?'

'Amitriptyline,' he said. 'Just to get you on your feet, to help you through a difficult patch. All right?'

'Yes,' Ruth said.

'Start with two at night, and then one every morning, for a week,' he said. 'And come back and see me next week.'

Ruth nodded and rose slowly from her chair.

'I'll have a word with Dad about getting you some more help,' Dr MacFadden said. 'Sometimes us men can be a bit insensitive. We don't always understand or make allowances. And a new baby in the house is a bit like a bomb going off, you have to take time to let the dust settle.'

Ruth nodded, still saying nothing, and went out to

the waiting room. Thomas was asleep in his carry cot, Patrick was leafing through a magazine. Ruth thought it was obvious to any casual observer that this was an easy baby to manage. Anything that was going wrong between her and Thomas must be her fault. Ruth sat down and looked at Thomas's rosy, angelic sleeping face. Dr MacFadden nodded to Patrick from the door of his office and Patrick went reluctantly in.

'She's under a lot of strain,' the doctor said frankly. 'I'm glad we spotted it now. I'll have the health visitor pop in every week, and I've put her on Amitriptyline to try and make life a little easier. Do you have help at home?'

'My mother lives just up the road,' Patrick said. 'She'll have Thomas any time we want, but she doesn't want to interfere.'

The young doctor shook his head. 'Don't worry about interfering just now,' he said. 'What Mum needs is as much help as she can get. Tell your mother not to be shy about chipping in. All help gratefully received. Mum needs a proper break and a couple of nights' sleep.'

Patrick nodded, only partly convinced. 'I don't see why she can't cope,' he said, and then corrected himself. 'I'm concerned of course . . .'

'Some women have the knack and others have to learn it,' Dr MacFadden said airily. 'This mum is taking it hard. She'll settle down in a little while, if we give her the help now. Can you get home a bit more? Give her a bit more support?'

Patrick shook his head, refusing. 'I'll try,' he said.

'Sounds like the best bet is Grandma then,' the doctor said. 'And thank heavens you've got a good grandma on the spot.'

Six

THE PILLS were innocuous-looking, friendly little pebbles. Ruth took two at bedtime and within moments felt a dreamy sense of release and calmness, as if she had just gulped down a schooner of sherry. She chuckled at the thought of it, and Patrick, getting undressed for bed, stared at the unfamiliar sound of Ruth's sexy giggle.

'Are you all right?'

'Happy pills,' Ruth said. 'Now I know I'm a depressed housewife.'

'Well, I haven't seen you smile in months,' Patrick commented. He got into bed beside her and pulled the covers over on his side.

'I feel better,' she said. 'And your mother is coming early in the morning so I don't have to get up. Heaven.'

'How would you ever have managed without her?'

Ruth felt as if she were floating in a warm bath. 'How would you?' she retorted, but her tongue felt slow, and nothing could threaten her good humour. 'I don't see you ironing your own shirts.'

'Well, you should be doing them really,' Patrick pointed out. 'It's not as if you're working now.'

Ruth chuckled again. 'I'll swap you,' she said. 'Eight hours a day, and half of those in meetings or chatting to people, against twenty-four hours a day on call with Thomas.'

Patrick turned over and turned off the light. 'Well, you've got tomorrow morning off,' he said, 'and every morning that you want, so you've not got much to complain about.'

The pleasant drunken feeling was growing stronger. 'I'll complain if I want,' Ruth said stubbornly, and then giggled at her own intransigence. 'I bloody will if I bloody want to,' she said.

She slept for only an hour before Thomas's loud wail echoed through the house. She got up and staggered down the stairs to where the bottles were ready in the fridge. She ran the hot tap and shook the bottle under the stream of hot water until the milk was warmed through, then she trudged up the stairs again to the nursery.

Thomas was thrashing in his cot, arms and legs flailing, desperate with hunger and distress.

Ruth did not feel her usual tide of panic at his cries. 'Oh, hush,' she said calmly. She picked him up: he was wet. 'Oh, never mind,' she said. She wrapped him in a blanket and sat with him in the rocking chair. The rocking rhythm soothed them both. Ruth hummed quietly to Thomas. He sucked greedily and then more and more slowly, then his eyes closed and his head lolled away from the bottle. Ruth took it from his mouth and transferred him gently to her shoulder. She patted his back. Thomas burped richly but did not wake. Slowly, carefully, she transferred him back into his cot, putting him down as if he were a basket of fragile eggs, taking her hands away only when his full weight was on the mattress, first one hand, and then another.

Only then did she remember that she had not changed his nappy. 'Oh, damn,' she said carelessly. 'Never mind.' She left him, wrapped in the damp blanket, and went back to her bed and fell asleep.

Two hours later Thomas woke again. Ruth, dreaming of some strange street far away from Thomas and Patrick, with white clapboard houses and wide fresh lawns, got out of bed unwillingly. It was colder now: the little house had lost its overnight heat. Through the landing window a white moon sailed in a yellow aura of frosty clouds. Ruth trailed downstairs again, warmed a bottle, and trudged back up the stairs.

Thomas was wet through, sodden nappy, sleep suit, blanket. Even his bedding was wet, his little duvet and his sheets. Ruth put him down on the cold changing mat and stripped off his clothes. He kicked and screamed in distress as she pulled the poppers apart and tore off the disposable nappy. His bottom was bright pink as if he had been scalded. She wiped it quickly with the cold, wet baby wipes and patted it dry and then smeared on some cream. He wriggled and she could not fasten the nappy properly. In the end she got it on his writhing body, and pushed his hands and feet into the arm and leg holes of the sleep suit. She did up the poppers and found they were wrongly fastened when she had two extra at the top.

There was nothing she could do to the cot bedding, she thought. She settled back into the rocking chair. Thomas was too distressed to take his bottle. 'Hush,' Ruth said tiredly. She gave him a little shake to make him stop crying. 'Be quiet, Thomas, your bottle is here.'

It seemed to work. The baby clutched at her with frightened hands and latched onto the bottle. Ruth rocked in the chair, enjoying the silence after the painful crying. 'Hush,' she said.

When Thomas fell asleep again, she remembered that the cot was damp. She took a clean blanket and wrapped it around him, leaving the wet duvet spread out on the landing to dry.

In the bedroom Patrick had moved diagonally across the bed; there was no room for Ruth. She slipped in beside him and pushed him gently. He did not move. Ruth curled up in the small space available and went instantly to sleep.

Thomas slept for an hour and a half and then woke, thirsty, irritable, and sweating in the tight swaddling of the blanket. Ruth went downstairs to the kitchen again, heated up a bottle, and trudged back up. Thomas was damp with sweat, his dark hair stuck to his head, his neck and face moist. He cried desperately, irritable with the heat. Ruth lifted him up and unwrapped him. The chill air of the cold room hit him and he started to shiver. His loud, angry cries turned to despairing wails of discomfort. She cuddled him up to her warmth and pushed the bottle into his mouth. Thomas whimpered but then started to suck, and went quickly to sleep.

This time she could not get him to go back into his cot. Every time she put him gently on the damp mattress he turned and cried again, and she had to pick him up, offer him his bottle, and rock him to sleep once more. Four or five times Ruth rocked him to sleep and then gently, carefully, put him down in his cot, and four or five times he started awake, and had to be picked up and rocked again.

It was half past five before Ruth got back to bed. This time Patrick had moved over, taking the duvet with him, and there was a wide space of cold sheet. Ruth got in beside him and gently tugged a corner of duvet to cover her. She lay wakeful, her feet were cold, she was certain Thomas would wake again and cry. She lay, waiting for him to cry, knowing that she would have to get up, staring blankly at the ceiling. She knew she should sleep, she knew that she was tired. But she could not make herself sleep. She was certain that the moment she fell asleep Thomas would wake, and she thought she could not bear to be woken again. It was almost better to be awake, to stay awake all night, if needs be, than to suffer that terrible disappointment of being dragged from warmth and dreams.

At half past six Ruth took her pill and at once felt the easy floating sense of release, and fell asleep. She did not even wake when Patrick's alarm clock went off, and he got out of bed at half past seven. He went downstairs and made himself a cup of coffee. At a quarter to eight his mother's car drew up outside and she came quietly up the path. He opened the front door to her.

'They're both of them sound asleep,' he said. 'I don't know what we're making such a fuss about.'

'You go off to work,' his mother said. 'Have you had breakfast?'

'I had a cup of coffee, I didn't want anything else.'

She shook her head. 'D'you have time for a boiled egg?' she said. 'I can have it on the table with some toast in five minutes?'

He hesitated. 'All right.'

Elizabeth moved quickly around the kitchen while Patrick sat at the table, waiting for his breakfast. Within the promised time it was before him: lightly boiled egg, lightly browned toast, and a fresh pot of tea.

'Does she seem better?' Elizabeth asked.

'The pills certainly seem to be doing her some good,' he said. 'She was quite cheerful last night, and she was only up once in the night.'

'They'll soon settle down,' Elizabeth said. 'I was very tense with Miriam. First babies are always difficult.'

'Well, bless you for coming in.' Patrick wiped his mouth on a piece of paper towel. Elizabeth made a mental note to buy some linen napkins. 'I don't know what we'd have done without you. The doctor practically prescribed you.'

'You know how much I love Thomas,' Elizabeth said lightly. 'I'd have him all day every day if it was any help.'

Patrick gave her a kiss on her cheek, and went to the door. 'When the Sleeping Princess awakes, you might tell her that I'll be home late tonight,' he said. 'I've a late meeting at work and a working dinner after. Tell her not to wait up.'

Elizabeth nodded. 'Then I'll have Thomas for another spell this afternoon, if you're not coming home,' she said. 'I don't think Ruth can manage all day without a break.'

'Bless you,' Patrick said absently, and left.

Elizabeth waited a few minutes as the noise of his car died away, and then tidied up the kitchen. She unpacked the dishwasher and loaded it with Patrick's breakfast things. She threw the egg shells in the flip-top bin and caught sight of the rubbish from last night's dinner. The packet from a frozen pie, the empty bag of frozen chips, and an empty bag of frozen peas. Elizabeth frowned and then rearranged her face into an expression of determined neutrality. She reminded herself that there was no innate virtue in homemade food. Patrick had never tasted a frozen ingredient until he had left home, but it was not fair to expect Ruth to show the same dedication to high domestic standards as Elizabeth. 'A different generation,' she said quietly to herself.

She opened the fridge door to see what was for dinner. The fridge was virtually empty except for a pint of milk, a box of eggs (which should be kept in the larder and not in the fridge), and cheese. The cheese was out of date.

A little cry from upstairs prevented her from exploring the larder cupboard. She hurried up the stairs and picked Thomas up just as Ruth's bedroom door opened.

'Oh! Is it morning already?'

Elizabeth took in the untidy nursery, the discarded sleep suit, the row of empty bottles, and the stained duvet drying on the banister.

'Yes, dear, but it's still quite early. I'll take care of Thomas, you go back to bed.'

'I didn't realize you were here.' Ruth's speech was slow, slightly slurred.

'I'll take over now,' Elizabeth said reassuringly. 'You can leave it all to me.'

'I didn't hear Patrick get up.'

'He'd have crept out. We were trying to get you some more sleep.'

'I couldn't sleep,' Ruth said. 'When I got back to bed and it was light, I couldn't sleep for ages.'

'I'll get this young man a bottle and you go back to bed,' Elizabeth said. 'When shall I bring him home? Lunchtime?'

'Yes, please,' Ruth said slowly.

'Patrick said to tell you that he would be home late

tonight; he's out to dinner. He said not to wait up.'

Ruth's shoulders, her whole body, slumped. 'He's out all evening?'

'Shall I come round? Or would you like to come up to the farm for dinner?'

Ruth shook her head slowly. 'No, no,' she said. 'I'll be all right here.'

Elizabeth scanned her with a keen glance. 'I'll bring Thomas back at midday, and I'll pop down again in the middle of the afternoon, to see if you want a hand,' she said. 'It's no fun trying to cope on your own.'

'No,' Ruth said dully. She did not even look at Thomas in his grandmother's arms. She turned and went back into her bedroom, as if she did not want to see him, to see them together. The little bottle of pills was beside her bed. She knew she had to take one in the morning. She took one and let it rest on her tongue. It tasted strange: it spread a numb tingling through her mouth, it had an acrid bitter taste, a powerful taste. She swallowed it and felt the ease and relief seep through her. Thomas, Elizabeth, even Patrick seemed a long way away and no longer her responsibility. She closed her eyes and slid into sleep.

Elizabeth gave Thomas a little of his bottle and then took him downstairs to the kitchen. She made up a couple of spoonfuls of baby rice with the warmed milk and spooned them competently into Thomas's milky smile. She took him back upstairs to the bathroom and stripped off his damp nightwear. His bottom was sore, the skin was puckered and nearly blistered. Elizabeth folded her mouth in a hard line. She laid him on his back on his

113

changing mat while she ran a bath for him, and after his bath let him kick free of his clothes and nappy, so that the air could get to his sore skin. The marks were fading quickly, but Elizabeth still looked grim. Leaving him safe on his mat, on the floor, she went into the nursery. The mattress was still damp and was starting to smell. The bedding had obviously been wet all night. Elizabeth stripped the bed, wiped the mattress cover with disinfectant, took the mattress to the airing cupboard to dry, and piled the damp clothes and duvet in the laundry basket.

She went back to Thomas and dressed him in his day clothes, tickling and stroking him, playing peekaboo over the towel. Then she put him into his carry cot, bundled all the washing into a large bag, and drove baby and laundry up the drive to the big house.

Frederick was waiting for them. 'How's the young Master Thomas?' he asked, coming down the shallow flight of steps and opening the rear door of the car.

Elizabeth made a small grimace, but did not say a word until they were in the house with the door shut. Not even the blackbird on the lawn should hear her criticizing her daughter-in-law. 'His cot was soaked, his bedding flung all round the house. He has a nappy rash. It looks to me as if she just shut the door on him and didn't go to him all night.'

Frederick had Thomas on his knee, gently bouncing him up and down, holding his little clenched hands. 'I thought she was up all hours with him?'

'There's no evidence of it, except for half a dozen dirty bottles. She clearly isn't changing his nappy or changing his bedding,' Elizabeth said. 'Patrick said that she was up only once in the night, but she looked like death this morning. They had frozen food for dinner last night – I saw the packets, and Patrick was dashing out of the house this morning with nothing but a cup of coffee inside him.'

'It won't do,' Frederick said firmly. He turned his attention to Thomas. 'It won't do, will it?' he demanded. 'Won't do at all. Someone will have to take your mummy in hand. And *we* know the woman to do it!'

'No no,' Elizabeth said, smiling. 'I can't go barging in there and take over, much as I long to. The sitting room! And the state of the kitchen already! But it's Ruth's home and she must have it as she likes.'

'But what does Thomas like?' Frederick asked the baby's bright face. 'Thomas doesn't want a damp cot, does he? Perhaps he'd better come here for a few days.'

'I can hardly suggest . . .' Elizabeth said.

Frederick looked up. 'If she can't cope with the baby, if she's not getting up to him in the night, and if he's being neglected, then it's your duty,' he said bluntly. 'No suggest, no ifs and buts. If the child needs care and he's not getting it, then you tell Patrick that Thomas is to come here until Ruth pulls herself together.'

'She looks awfully ill.'

'What does the doctor say?'

'Overtired, that she needs more support.'

'Well, give her more support,' Frederick ordered. '*We* don't mind having Master Cleary to stay, do we? And Master Cleary won't be going into a damp bed with Granny to look after him, will he?'

'Oh, *don't* call me Granny,' Elizabeth exclaimed. 'You sound just like that dreadful health visitor.'

Frederick chuckled. 'Granny Cleary did a spell and

they all lived happily ever after,' he said to Thomas. 'Happily ever after.'

The phone woke Ruth at eleven in the morning.

'Did you think I was dead?' David asked.

'Oh, my God!' Ruth said delightedly, incredulously. 'No! I thought I was. Dead and gone to hell.'

'I sent you flowers.'

'I know. I kept it. A little violet in a pot.'

'And I thought about you a lot. But I didn't know whether I should call or not. They said you had a rough time. I didn't want to intrude.'

Ruth gave a little breathless chuckle. 'Oh, if you *knew* how lovely it is to hear your voice! Someone who isn't completely obsessed with babies! I expect you even read a book or a newspaper sometimes!'

'Man of the world,' David said promptly. 'Urbane, elegant, unemployed.'

'Still no work?'

'Freelance, I call it. You got out while the going was good.'

'I didn't exactly get out,' Ruth reminded him.

'Well, after your departure and mine there were three other people laid off, and a whole load of journalists sacked off the evening paper too. Bristol is knee-deep in unemployed hacks, all falling over each other trying to get to a story first.'

'Are you doing shifts at Westerly?'

'I am the midnight man,' David said impressively. 'Nine till midnight most nights. None of the staff want to work those hours, but it keeps a bit of money coming in, and I can steal pens and paper, and watch telly in the warmth for free. These things matter when you're a bum.'

'What about features?'

'I am a creative powerhouse,' he said with mock dignity. 'I generate a feature a minute. And I sell quite a few. But it's a brutish and short existence. You are well out of it. What's it like being a professional wife and mother?'

Ruth tried to say something lighthearted in reply. She found her throat too tight to speak. 'I . . .'

'Too blissful for words?'

Soundlessly she shook her head.

'Are you OK?' David asked, suddenly serious. 'I didn't mean to be cheap. Are you OK, Ruth?'

'Yes,' she said very quietly. 'It's just that . . . Oh, David, I didn't know . . .'

'Know what?'

'I didn't know what it was like,' she said eventually. 'I am so tired all the time, and it's so lonely. Thomas is lovely, of course, but there's so much *washing* to do. And I spend my days wiping down work surfaces so they're clean enough. And at night . . .' she broke off.

'What about night?'

'He just never sleeps,' she said in a little strained voice. 'It doesn't sound like much when it's someone else's baby, everyone says that babies don't sleep . . . but when it's your own . . . David I just doze and wake, and doze, and get up again, all night long.'

'It sounds like hell.'

'Oh, no,' Ruth said quickly. 'Because the house is so nice, and Thomas is so lovely, and Patrick helps all that he can . . . it's just . . .'

'Can I come round and see you?' David asked. 'One afternoon, this afternoon?'

'Oh, yes,' Ruth said, thinking of the long afternoon and evening ahead of her. 'Oh, that would be lovely. But – you mustn't mind . . .'

'Mind what?'

'I don't look the same at all,' Ruth confessed. 'I'm miles overweight. I look dreadful.'

'I won't mind,' David said reassuringly. 'The more of you the better as far as I'm concerned.'

Seven

WHEN SHE opened the door to him he nearly recoiled in shock. She was overweight, as she had warned him, but it was her face that shocked him. She was white, an almost candlewax white. Her eyes were ringed with shadows, black as mascara, and her face was hard and sharp, with lines of fatigue and sadness that he had never seen before.

He stepped forward and put his arms around her and held her close. She didn't feel the same: she was carrying more weight and her breasts were bigger. He sensed the extra weight – she was softer, whereas before she had been light to the touch. He thought she might be breast-feeding the baby and felt himself shrink back, for fear of hurting her or even touching her in some way that was now no longer allowed. Her hair, which used to be so smooth and glossy, was tired and lank, and she smelled different: of indoors, of baby talcum powder, of small rooms.

'So this is the palace,' he said with forced brightness. 'And where is His Highness the baby?'

'In the sitting room,' she said. She led the way in. There was a small log fire burning in the grate. On a towel before the fire Thomas was kicking his legs and looking at the ceiling.

David regarded him from a cautious distance. 'He looks nice,' he said. 'Here,' he dived in his pocket. 'I brought this for him. I didn't quite know what he would like.'

It was a small yellow plastic duck.

Ruth felt her eyes fill with tears. 'Thank you,' she said. 'Oh, David! Thank you!'

'Here!' he reached out for her but then remembered the embarrassment of the doorstep embrace. 'Don't cry. What's the matter?'

She sank onto the sofa and pulled a handkerchief out of the pocket of her baggy maternity jeans. She still could not get into her ordinary clothes, and her maternity clothes were worn and shabby. 'I'm sorry,' she said miserably. 'It's nothing. It's everything. Sorry.'

He waited for a moment, looking at Thomas, who stared with unfocused blue eyes at the space before him.

'Is it Patrick?' David asked.

Ruth shook her head and crushed her handkerchief back into her pocket again. 'There's nothing *wrong*,' she said. 'It's just that I'm so tired, and everything seems such an effort, and the least thing makes me cry.'

David felt completely lost with this new, weepy Ruth.

'Is this – er – what-d'you-call-it? – postnatal depression?' he asked.

'*I* don't know,' she said abruptly. 'No. I told you. I'm just tired.'

'Well, can't someone else have him at night?' David glanced down again at Thomas, who looked completely innocent of any desire to disturb anyone.

'Well, Patrick can't, he's working too hard. And

his grandmother could, but I don't like to ask her.'

'But you need help,' David said reasonably.

'Oh, stop!' she said with a sudden flare of temper. 'Don't come in here with a load of questions and solutions, David. I'm perfectly all right except for the fact that I'm running all the time on a couple of hours' sleep. If you were as tired as me you'd hang yourself.'

'OK,' he said quickly. 'OK. I won't say another word.'

She gave him a brief watery grin. 'And they do help out,' she said, 'Patrick's family. She started coming in in the mornings so that I can sleep. And I've seen the doctor. So I'm OK. Really.'

David nodded, still unconvinced.

'Tell me the gossip,' Ruth commanded, trying to distract them both. She went down on the floor and waved a rattle in front of Thomas. He put his hands up to reach for it, and she waved it again.

David dredged up some small scandals from work and then, warming to the theme, told Ruth how the station had been restructured and how the few competent journalists left were running around and working twice as hard, and all applying for other jobs.

'It sounds like chaos,' she said.

'It is. And the place is always packed with people freelancing or coming in to sell ideas or tapes. James couldn't bring himself to sack anyone outright, so everyone who should have been sent home is now working there for free. The telephone bill must have doubled, and of course we're all selling pieces all around the country so the studios are always booked. I doubt they've saved any money at all.'

Ruth nodded. 'Patrick's place is cutting back too,' she said. 'He's really worried. They've only had the new

121

documentary unit up and running for a few months and they're already reconsidering.'

David nodded, suppressing his prejudiced belief that Patrick's egotistical direction of the unit was the greatest problem it faced.

'D'you want a cup of tea?' Ruth asked.

David nodded.

At once she looked strained.

'What's the matter? Shall I make it for you?'

'I know it sounds silly,' she said. 'But since he's happy here I don't really want to disturb him. If I pick him up and he starts crying it's really difficult to make him stop. I know it sounds stupid . . .'

'Not stupid to me,' David said stoutly. 'I don't want him to start crying. Shall I make the tea while you watch him?'

She hesitated. 'I know it's crazy,' she said in a sudden rush. 'And everyone else just picks him up and lugs him about. My mother-in-law takes him to the shops with her, and out in the car, and everywhere she goes. But I just can't face it . . . I just can't face him crying and crying, and I don't know how to make him stop.'

David patted her hand feebly. 'I bet everyone feels like that.'

She looked at him, scanning his face to see if he was sincere. 'D'you think so?'

'Lots of them,' David said. 'But people don't talk about it.'

She turned her head away from him and looked at the fire. 'Sometimes I'm not sure if I love him at all,' she said very quietly. 'I don't enjoy being with him much, and I'm so tired . . .'

She fell silent.

'I'll make the tea,' he repeated. 'Would you like that?'

'Yes,' she said. 'Everything is in the cupboard above the kettle. The milk is in the fridge.'

David nodded and went to the kitchen. When Ruth heard him filling the kettle and switching it on, she quietly took the bottle of pills from her pocket and took one. Within moments she could feel her anxiety melting away. She leaned over Thomas and smiled down at him. She blew into his little face and watched him pucker in surprise at the sensation. When David came in with the tea she was rosy and smiling.

'I can't stay long,' he said. 'I've got a shift.' He handed her a mug.

'What's going to happen about your work?' she asked.

He was pleased to see her taking an interest and looking more like the old Ruth. 'I'll get somewhere,' he said. 'I've got an interview in London next week. Something will come up, and I'm staying in practice and my voice is heard. Something'll come up.'

'I hope so,' she said. 'Don't go missing on me, will you? Don't go without giving me your address. I don't want to lose touch.'

He nodded, getting to his feet. He thought that in all the years that he had known her Ruth had never invited his attention. He had always been pursuing her, and she had always been casually indifferent as to whether he was there or not. Now it seemed that she needed him, and he was guiltily aware that this tearful, plump, white-faced housewife was not the woman he had desired.

'Of course,' he said. 'Give me a ring when you're free and we'll go out to lunch.'

'Yes,' she said, but she knew that she would not dare to ask Elizabeth to baby-sit while she went out to lunch with a man. Patrick obviously would not baby-sit under those circumstances, and naturally enough, with a mother-in-law next door, Ruth had no other baby-sitters. 'It's a bit tricky to get out while Thomas is so young,' she said. The Amitriptyline had steadied her: she did not feel like crying, she managed a smile. 'In a couple of years I'll be out dancing every night.'

He patted her on the shoulder in farewell. He did not want a closer embrace. 'I'll see myself out,' he said. 'You stay there with him. He's a lovely baby.'

'I know he's lovely,' she said. She sounded uncertain. 'I know he is.'

David let himself out and closed the front door behind him. The air was sharp and cold. He felt a sense of release and an elated awareness of his own youth and freedom. He was deeply glad that he was not Ruth, trapped in the little house, waiting for Patrick to come home, seeing no one but a baby. He was even glad that he was not Patrick, coming home every night to a plump, white-faced woman who cried for nothing, and a baby that never slept. He went quickly down the garden path, as if he were afraid that Ruth might call him back and he would see her crying again.

As he was unlocking the door of his car, an Austin Rover pulled in and parked in front of him. The woman driver, an elegant, attractive woman, gave him a friendly smile.

'Are you going? Have I left you enough space?' she asked.

The mother-in-law, David thought. And me creeping off like a clandestine lover. 'That's fine,' he said boldly. 'I've just been visiting Ruth Cleary.'

'Oh! I'm Mrs Cleary,' the woman sounded convincingly surprised, as if it had not occurred to her that he might have come from the cottage. 'How nice for Ruth to have some company.'

'I'm David Harrison. I used to work with her, at Radio Westerly.'

'I'm sure she misses her work a lot,' Elizabeth said. 'She'll have enjoyed hearing about it. Are you still working there?'

'Yes,' David said. 'She seemed a bit tired.'

Elizabeth smiled. 'A new baby can be absolutely exhausting,' she said. 'I've brought her down some supper, and I'll take Thomas back home with me to give her a little break.'

David brightened. 'I'm sure that's a good idea,' he said. 'She doesn't seem to be getting much sleep.'

Elizabeth's charming smile never wavered. 'Actually,' she said, lowering her voice, 'I've been rather worried about her. I was afraid she was getting depressed.'

'She seemed very weepy,' David said.

Elizabeth nodded. 'Exactly,' she said. 'And she's on anti-depressants, but they don't seem to do her much good.'

'Ruth is taking anti-depressants?' He was shocked.

Elizabeth nodded sadly. 'It's her choice. And I can hardly interfere.'

David shook his head incredulously. 'I don't believe it!'

'I'm afraid she's very low.'

'I wouldn't have thought she was the type . . .' David was adjusting his view of Ruth from the confident, bright journalist, the quickest, most able worker in the newsroom, to the sad housewife on pills. 'They can be addictive, can't they?'

'The doctor prescribed it,' Elizabeth said doubtfully. 'He must be aware of the situation.'

'But Ruth!'

'I know, it hardly seems possible does it? She's just finding motherhood terribly hard going.'

David thought for a moment. 'Is it the baby? Is there anything wrong with him?'

'No, that's the absurd thing. He's an absolute peach. He sleeps well and he eats well and he's no trouble at all. I think she may be one of those women that simply never take to motherhood.'

'Well, it's not as if she planned it . . .' David said indiscreetly.

Elizabeth's face gave nothing away as she registered this crucial piece of information. 'No,' she said. 'But she was quite happy about it, wasn't she?'

David grimaced. 'I never thought so. It couldn't have come at a worse time, and she's a natural journalist . . .'

Elizabeth nodded. 'Oh.'

'Is there anything I can do?' David asked.

Elizabeth hesitated for a moment 'How kind of you to offer,' she said coolly. 'But I'm sure we can manage.'

David heard the snub, and opened the door of his car.

'It's been so nice meeting you,' Elizabeth said. Her smile was warm. 'I hope to see you again.'

'Thank you, Mrs Cleary,' David said. 'I'd like to keep in touch with Ruth – and with Patrick too, of course.'

'Oh, but you must!' she said earnestly. 'Poor Ruth needs all the friends she can get.'

David blinked. He had never thought of Ruth as 'poor Ruth' before. 'Thank you very much, Mrs Cleary.'

'Call me Elizabeth! Please!'

'Well, thank you, Elizabeth. Good-bye.'

Elizabeth watched him pull away and then went into the cottage.

There was no one in the sitting room but there were wails of distress coming from the upstairs bathroom. The sitting room smelled of vomit.

'Oh, dear,' Elizabeth said softly, and went up the stairs.

Ruth was trying to undress Thomas, who was liberally covered in regurgitated milk. Ruth's hair and shoulder and the front of her shirt and trousers were sodden.

'He just threw up!' she said desperately. 'He was drinking well, a whole bottle, and then the whole lot suddenly came up. Is he ill?'

'No,' Elizabeth said reassuringly. 'He's fine. He just probably overdid it a bit.'

In her haste Ruth had not undone all the buttons on Thomas's shirt. Pulling it over his head, she had got his head stuck. He was shrieking piercingly from inside the garment.

'Oh, God!' Ruth cried above the noise.

'Shall I?' Elizabeth asked.

Ruth shot a desperate look at her.

'You go and get changed out of those dirty clothes,' Elizabeth commanded kindly. 'And leave Master Thomas here to me. I'll bath him and change him and take him up to the farm. When you're ready there's supper for you downstairs in the warming oven. Patrick can collect Thomas on his way home. You have a quiet evening on your own for a change.' She moved forward and took Thomas – vomit and all – onto her lap.

Ruth hesitated, glancing at Elizabeth's immaculate slacks and cashmere sweater. 'Are you sure you don't mind?'

'Mind?' Elizabeth laughed. 'Ruth dearest, I have nothing else to do and it is my greatest treat. He'll be fine once he's clean and dry again, and his grandfather will play with him all evening. Just relax and leave it to me.'

She slid her fingers inside the narrow neckband of the shirt and undid the buttons. Thomas, suddenly released, came out red-faced and tearful.

Ruth slipped from the bathroom as Elizabeth stripped off the rest of the wet, foul-smelling clothes, wrapped Thomas in a warm towel, and started to run a bath.

When he was washed and changed and sweet-smelling and sweet-tempered, she put him in her car and drove up to the farm. Frederick looked up as she carried the baby seat into the drawing room.

'Hello, my dear! Hello, Master Thomas! All right?'

'She was practically in hysterics because he had brought up his feed,' Elizabeth said. 'She really can't cope at all.'

Frederick unbuckled Thomas from his baby seat. 'Well, that's no good,' he said, speaking half to the baby.

'She'd had a friend call for tea,' Elizabeth said. 'David Harrison from Radio Westerly. Very charming, rather attractive.'

Frederick turned his attention to his wife and raised his eyebrows. 'Not quite the thing, is it?'

'I'm sure there's no harm in it,' Elizabeth said. 'And she's terribly lonely.'

'Better mention it to Patrick all the same.'

'I don't like to tell tales . . .'

Frederick turned back to Thomas. 'Us chaps must stick together,' he informed him. '*I* shall tell Patrick.'

*   *   *

Ruth was asleep when Patrick came in, and he did not disturb her. But in the night she woke, half listening even in sleep for a cry from the nursery. The house was silent; Patrick was breathing noisily at her side. The pillow and his hair smelled slightly of cigarette smoke. Ruth moved away. She glanced at the illuminated dial of her bedside clock. It was four in the morning. Thomas had never slept through till four in the morning before. She lay back smiling. Perhaps everything was working out at last. Thomas sleeping through the night, David calling to see her, perhaps life was returning to normal. She closed her eyes and dozed off again.

She woke with a start. It was half past four. Thomas still had made no sound. A superstitious fear made her sit suddenly upright. She thought of cot death, suffocation, kidnapping, any one of the fears that new mothers carry with them all the time, wherever they are. She slipped out of bed and tiptoed along the dark landing. She listened at the door of Thomas's room. She could not hear him. Usually in sleep he made little snuffling noises, or stirred. She could hear nothing.

Careful not to wake him, she gently touched the door, pushing it open one silent millimetre at a time. The carpet under the door made a soft hushing noise as the foot of the door brushed against the new pile; but still Thomas did not wake.

She crept forward so that she could see over the side of the cot. His little duvet was folded at the foot of the bed. Thomas was not there. The cot was empty.

Ruth screamed. 'Thomas!' and scrabbled for the light switch. Frantically she looked around the room as if he could have crawled out of bed and hidden. The nursery was empty. She ran across the landing to the bedroom. Patrick was sitting up in bed, blear-eyed.

'What the . . .'

'Thomas! It's Thomas! He's gone! Oh, God, Patrick! He's gone!'

'No . . .' Patrick shook his head.

Ruth was unstoppable. 'Christ, someone has taken him! Patrick, get up, call the police! He's gone. I just woke up and thought he was quiet and went to his room and his cot is empty!'

She could feel hot tears pouring down her cheeks and hear her voice getting louder and higher in panic. 'I thought it was funny that he hadn't cried but then I went . . .'

'Ruth, get a grip!' Patrick shouted over the tide of her hysteria. 'He's quite all right. He's at home. He's with Mother. I left him up there! We thought you'd like the break.'

Ruth was screaming but the words slowly penetrated. She fell silent, she stared at Patrick, but oddly the tears did not stop, they still poured down her cheeks. 'He's where? Where?'

'He's at home,' Patrick said. 'With Mother. In my old nursery, in my old cot. Safe and sound.'

Ruth whimpered, a soft animal sound. 'I thought he'd been taken . . .'

'I know. I should have woken you and told you. But you were asleep and I thought you needed your sleep.'

'I thought he was gone.'

'I'm sorry. We thought it was the best thing to do.'

Ruth's dark eyes were huge. 'It's worse than that,' she said.

'Shush,' Patrick got out of bed and put his hands on

her shoulders, drawing her back to bed. 'Settle down, Ruth, I'll make you a cup of tea. Have one of your pills.'

'I thought he was gone,' she said again.

Patrick looked around for Ruth's bottle of Amitriptyline and shook two of the little pills into his hand. 'Take this,' he said. 'Calm down, Ruth.'

He offered her a glass of water and her teeth clanked on the glass; her hands were trembling so much she nearly spilled it. She took the pills and sipped the water. He thought that she looked old and haggard. He had never seen her less attractive. He had a headache from the wine at his dinner and he was deeply tired. He had a weary sense of one crisis following another, and everything left to him.

'Come on, darling,' he said. 'Lie down. Go to sleep again. It's all right now.'

She looked at him with her enormous tragic eyes. 'It's worse than that,' she repeated.

'Worse than what?'

'Worse than thinking he was gone.'

'Shush shush,' he said. He slipped into bed beside her and drew the covers up.

Ruth felt the pills beginning to weave their sleepy magic around her. Already her terror felt as if it had happened to someone else, as if it were another woman who had woken in the night to find her baby's cot empty, and her baby stolen away.

'It's worse than that . . .'

'What is worse?' he asked wearily.

'I was glad,' Ruth said with bleak simplicity. 'I thought, Oh, good, he's gone, and at last I'll be able to get some sleep.' She smiled her misty, uncertain smile at Patrick, her eyes unfocused. 'I told you it was worse,' she said. 'I thought he was kidnapped and I thought, At least I'll be able to get some sleep now. That's really bad, isn't it?'

'Shush,' Patrick said automatically. 'Not to worry, shush, Ruth.'

Ruth nodded, her eyes slowly closed, she slept.

For more than an hour Patrick lay, with his head thudding and his eyes open, looking at the darkness and hearing over and over again in his mind Ruth's slurred confession, and wondering what it meant.

Patrick left for work at the usual time, leaving Ruth asleep and a note for her on the pillow. It said:

THOMAS IS WITH MOTHER AT THE FARM. PHONE THEM WHEN YOU ARE READY TO HAVE HIM BACK. MOTHER SAYS SHE CAN HAVE HIM ALL DAY IF YOU WOULD LIKE A REST. I WILL BE HOME AT THE USUAL TIME, AND I WILL SHOP FOR SUPPER. TAKE IT EASY, DARLING. SEE YOU AT 6.

He had written it in black felt tip, in printed capital letters, as if he could not trust her to read script.

But Patrick did not go to work; he drove up to the farm and let himself in with his front-door key. His mother was in the kitchen in her embroidered pale-blue silk housecoat. Thomas was sitting, padded with a pillow, in Patrick's old wooden high chair, watching her with quiet approval. Elizabeth was making toast for herself and baby rice for Thomas.

'Good morning, darling,' she said over her shoulder as Patrick came in. 'Come for breakfast?' Then she saw his face, and turned quickly around. 'What's wrong?'

'Ruth,' Patrick said the one word as if it would explain everything.

'Sit down,' she said automatically. 'I'll make you some breakfast. Tea? A couple of boiled eggs?'

'Yes, please,' he said. 'I have to phone work. I have to tell them I'll be late.'

She heard him go into the hall and telephone his office. Swiftly and efficiently she put on the kettle, set a couple of eggs to boil, and sliced bread for toast. Then she sat before Thomas and spooned baby rice and milk for him. When Patrick came back into the kitchen it smelled warm with the familiar smell of breakfast. His son turned a wobbly head and looked at him.

'Where's Dad?'

'He went out with his gun to get some rabbits, early,' his mother said. 'He should be back soon. D'you want to talk to him?'

'To you both,' Patrick said.

She nodded and wiped Thomas's face with a square of soft muslin. She set the table before Patrick and poured his tea. The last of the sand fell silently through the egg timer, and she brought two eggs out of the saucepan. She put them in the egg cups of his childhood, a set of little friendly-faced china animals. Patrick managed a wan smile.

'Thomas will enjoy these when he's a little older,' she said. 'He likes it here.'

'Sleeps well in my cot?' Patrick asked.

'He only woke once,' she said. 'And then he went straight down again.'

Patrick nodded and ate his toast and boiled eggs. She watched him chewing and carefully swallowing, and she felt her throat tighten in sympathy.

'You never really let go,' she said looking from her son to her grandson. 'You never stop loving if you are a mother.'

Patrick glanced up at her, and she was shocked at the strain in his face. 'Really?' he said doubtfully.

She nodded and put her hand gently on his shoulder. 'Well, *I* never will.'

The back door opened, and they heard Frederick ordering the dog to his basket, shucking off his boots, racking his gun, and locking the case. He padded into the kitchen in his shooting breeches and thick socks. 'Hello, old man,' he said. 'Come for a bite to eat?'

Patrick nodded. 'Did you get anything?'

'Couple of rabbits. We'll have pie tonight, shall we, my dear?'

'If you skin them,' Elizabeth said.

Frederick chuckled. 'I will.'

'Do you want any breakfast?'

'I'll take a cup of tea,' he said. 'I went out with a roll of bread and cheese. I did very well, thank you, my dear.'

Elizabeth poured the tea. 'Patrick wants to talk with us,' she said.

Thomas let out a little squeak and Elizabeth drew up her chair beside him and gave him a wooden honey scoop to hold, her eyes on her son.

'Trouble?' Frederick asked.

Patrick nodded. 'It's Ruth,' he said. He paused, hardly knowing what to say. 'She woke in the night and went to look for Thomas. I didn't wake her when I got in; I thought I should leave her to sleep.' He looked at his mother. 'She was sound asleep; I thought I should leave her.'

'Quite right,' Elizabeth said briskly. 'She was desperately tired yesterday.'

'So when she woke she didn't know where Thomas was.'

'She must have known,' Frederick interrupted. 'She knew he was with us. If he wasn't at your home, then clearly he was still with us.'

'She panicked,' Patrick said. 'I woke up to hear her screaming like an express train in the nursery. She thought he was kidnapped. She was screaming and crying. She couldn't even hear me when I told her that everything was all right.'

Frederick exchanged a glance with Elizabeth.

'I had to shout her down,' Patrick said. 'She wouldn't hear me, she went on screaming and screaming. When she was finally quiet I gave her two of her pills and she went all soft and sleepy. But she kept saying there was something worse, there was something worse.'

Thomas reached for the honey scoop where Elizabeth had placed it on the wooden table of the high chair. Elizabeth guided his little hand to it.

'She was half asleep but I think she meant it,' Patrick said. 'She said that she wished that he had been kidnapped so that she wouldn't have to look after him any more. So that she could get some sleep.'

Elizabeth drew in her breath sharply. Frederick rose to his feet and stood, looking out of the kitchen window, his back to the room.

'I see,' he said quietly.

'I didn't know how seriously I should take it . . .' Patrick began. 'I thought I should talk it over with you.'

Elizabeth nodded. 'Quite right,' she said. She glanced at Frederick's back. 'Do you think she meant it, Patrick?'

Patrick shrugged. 'I can't tell,' he said. 'We should perhaps talk to the doctor, but I didn't want to take this any further without talking it over.'

Elizabeth hesitated, glanced towards Frederick again. 'Did she ever want him?' she asked. 'Did she ever want to be a mother?'

Patrick shook his head in silence.

Frederick turned back from the window. 'I think we have a serious problem,' he said. 'And we've both seen it coming, Patrick. Your mother has been worried sick about Ruth's care for the baby. When she collects him in the morning he's been neglected all night. When she returns him in the afternoon, Ruth never seems to want him back. Frankly I think she's rejected him. This comes as no surprise to me at all.'

Patrick looked at his mother. 'You never said...'

She shook her head. 'How could I? It's not my place to criticize my daughter-in-law. And besides I kept hoping that she would get better. She started on the pills and I thought she would be less depressed. I made sure she could sleep during the day. I thought that things would improve. Short of taking Thomas away from her all day and all night I didn't see how I could do more.'

There was a brief silence.

'She needs help,' Patrick said. 'Do I start with the GP?'

Elizabeth said nothing.

'He's not been up to much so far,' Frederick said. 'Anti-depressants indeed!'

Both men turned to Elizabeth. Still she said nothing.

'I think we need something a bit more decisive,' Frederick went on. 'Get this sorted out once and for all. We've been worried sick, Patrick, I can tell you. We knew she wasn't pulling her weight, but we didn't know what more we could do.'

Patrick shrugged. 'But I don't know what to do,' he said. 'I suppose she should see a counsellor. Get some help. I could ask the doctor, and the health visitor was good, wasn't she?'

Elizabeth slowly shook her head. 'I'm not sure that we want the health centre to know all about this.'

'Why not?' Patrick asked.

'If we call them in – the doctor and the health visitor and the social workers, all of them – we can't control what happens. What if they say that Ruth has to go to hospital for a couple of months? What if they say she has to have treatment?'

'We could manage,' Frederick said easily.

'Yes, but what if they won't let us manage? What if they say she has to take him with her? Or what if they say that he has to be put into care, that we're too old to have him? Once you call these people in, they can do what they want. What if they say Ruth has been neglecting him or abusing him and they take him away from us?'

The two men looked blankly horrified. 'They couldn't say that!' Frederick exclaimed.

'The authorities these days have tremendous powers,' Elizabeth reminded him. 'If they think that Ruth has endangered Thomas, they can take him right away from us all and we might never see him again. Once you ask them in, you give them the power to do what they want.'

'But they couldn't think that Ruth . . .' Patrick broke off.

Elizabeth looked steadily at him. 'She has neglected him since the day he was born,' she said calmly. 'From the first days in the hospital when she wouldn't feed him, till now when she says she wishes he was kidnapped. She never wanted him, did she? He was conceived by accident.'

Patrick nodded. 'It was my fault,' he confessed. 'I wanted a baby.'

'Nothing wrong in that,' Frederick said stoutly.

'Nothing at all,' Elizabeth said. 'It's not you in the wrong, Patrick, it's her. She should have learned to love him. If the health visitor knew the half of it, I think she'd call in social services, and once they start, anything can happen.'

Frederick looked absolutely stunned. 'I've had no experience of this sort of thing . . .'

'How should we have any experience?' Elizabeth demanded, an edge of disdain in her voice. 'No one in our family has ever been mentally ill. No one has ever needed health visitors and doctors and drugs and psychiatric treatment.'

Patrick looked at her as if he were a naughty little boy but she might give him a note to excuse him from detention. 'This is awful,' he said.

Her face softened. 'It's not your fault,' she said gently. 'It's not your fault, darling, I know how hard you've tried. And it's not little Thomas's fault either – a sweeter, easier baby never lived.' She glanced out of the kitchen window across the fields to where the roof of the little house was just visible. 'It's Ruth,' she said simply. 'She's just not up to it.'

Patrick breathed slowly out and put his head in his hands. Frederick looked at his wife's stern, beautiful face. 'You're right,' he said unwillingly. 'What d'you suggest, my dear?'

'I think Thomas and Patrick should move in here, so that we can look after them. Patrick can have some regular meals and regular hours for a change, and Thomas can be properly cared for. This running up and down from one house to another is no good for him at all.'

Frederick nodded.

'And Ruth can come and live here or go to stay with her aunt. She needs a complete break.'

'She hardly ever speaks to her,' Patrick protested. 'And she lives miles away.'

'Are there no American relatives at all? Where she could go for a long visit?' Elizabeth asked.

'No, she's almost completely alone in the world.'

Elizabeth nodded. 'Then it's up to us,' she said. 'We're her only family; no one is even going to inquire. We could send her to a convalescent home to have a good rest, get away from it all. Or she can stay on her own in the cottage. And when she feels strong enough she can come back, and take up her life with Patrick and Thomas again.'

Thomas knocked the honey scoop to the floor. Elizabeth bent down and picked it up, rinsed it under the tap, and handed it back to him.

'It's a nightmare,' Patrick said unbelievingly. 'I would never have dreamed this could happen to us.'

Elizabeth put her hand gently on the nape of his neck. The skin was as soft under her fingers as it had been when he had been just a little boy, bent over his homework. She felt a great rush of tenderness for him, and for his little son.

'You come home, darling,' she said gently. 'You and Thomas come home and leave it to Mother. I'll sort it all out for you.'

Eight

IN THE LITTLE HOUSE Ruth stirred and woke. The brilliant autumn sun was streaming in the window, the white light blindingly bright in the white bedroom. On her pillow was Patrick's note written in large printed capitals. Ruth read it carefully, smiled at the instruction to take it easy – touched by his consideration. Her bottle of pills was at her bedside. She knew she had to take one in the morning but she thought she had forgotten to take one at bedtime. She took two, letting the warm sleepy drunkenness spread through her. She had forgotten the empty cot and her panic of the night before. She had a vague, distant memory of some awful fright – like the shadow of a nightmare.

She lay back on the pillows. The little digital clock said 10:32. Ruth closed her eyes and slept again.

She woke at one o'clock with an anxious start. She had been dreaming that Thomas was crying, but then she saw Patrick's note again and realized that the house was empty. She read it, as if for the first time, and took her morning pill. She felt as if she were floating. Slowly, luxuriously, she got out of bed and went, a little unsteadily, to the bathroom. The walls undulated comfortably around her. She ran a bath and poured a long stream of bath oil into the hot water. She slipped off her nightgown and sank into the hot, scented water. She lay back and closed her eyes. Far away she heard the telephone ring but she could not be bothered to answer it. She thought for a brief moment that it might be Elizabeth, that something might be wrong with Thomas.

'No point asking me,' she said into the steam-filled room. 'I'm the last person to ask. I haven't a clue.'

When the water grew cold, she heaved herself out of the bath, wrapped herself in a large towel, and lay on the bed. She felt too deliciously idle to move. When the telephone rang on the bedside table beside her, she could hardly be bothered to pick it up.

'Ruth?' It was David.

'Oh, hello.'

'You sound funny.'

'I've just woken up.'

'But it's half past two!'

'I know. Bliss, isn't it?'

'Where's Thomas?'

For a moment Ruth could not remember. 'Oh, he's with Elizabeth,' she said. 'She knows how to look after him.'

'I'm just down the road from you,' David said. 'I had to cover a council meeting in Bath. I've done my report and I'm on my way home. I wondered if you'd like to come out for a drink.'

'All right,' Ruth said.

'I'm at the Green Man, on the Radstock Road, very close,'

'I know it,' she said. 'I'll come at once.'

'See you in a minute then.'

The phone clicked and he was gone. Slowly and

thoughtfully Ruth began to dress. Choosing her clothes seemed a tremendously difficult task. She tried and discarded three or four skirts before pulling on a pair of black leggings and a black embroidered smock top. Most of her clothes were still too tight at the waistband, but she had a superstitious fear of buying anything the next size up. She thought that if she went into a bigger size she would never be thin again. In the meantime she had a wardrobe full of smart clothes, all the wrong size, and an increasingly shabby selection of maternity clothes, which she was tired of seeing. She brushed her hair and peered at her pale face in the mirror. 'Oh, well,' she said. 'It's only David.'

The loss of her looks, of her slim figure seemed unimportant. Ruth was cocooned in a warm, drugged haze, far away from everything. As she turned to leave she remembered that she usually took her morning Amitriptyline as she dressed. She took one, and then, guiltily, took another. She slipped the bottle into her pocket, to take one later. The feeling of drunken sensual relaxation was too enjoyable. She did not want it to wear off.

She drove unsteadily to the pub. The road seemed distant and far away, the car sluggish. She felt as if she were driving some immensely slow ocean liner on a great sea. When she came to the pub, she missed the wide turning into the parking lot and had to reverse back up the road. A van, rounding the corner, pulled out around the wildly zigzagging car and hooted loudly. Ruth waved pleasantly at the driver.

When she walked into the pub she could not at first see David. It was as if he materialized out of darkness. She blinked and smiled at him.

'Hi,' he said. 'What d'you want?'

'I'll have a gin and tonic,' she said.

He glanced at her, and then gave the order to the barman. Ruth went to a seat in the corner and sat down, with her back to the window.

'Are you OK?' he asked, as he brought the drinks over and sat opposite her.

'Perfectly,' she said. Her lips felt thick and unwilling; she took her time over the word, and said it with care.

He looked at her narrowly. 'Have you been boozing?' he asked. 'On the cooking sherry, Ruth? Housewife's temptation, you know.'

She shook her head. 'No,' she said. 'Just sleeping. I'm addicted to sleep. I could sleep forever, I think.'

'Are you taking drugs?' he asked blankly.

She widened her eyes to emphasize her innocence. He saw that the pupils were dilated. Her dark eyes were all black. 'Of course not,' she said. 'We don't get an awful lot of dealers up at Manor Farm, you know.'

'I meant anti-depressants.'

She sipped her drink and turned her face away from him. 'Why on earth should you think I'm taking anti-depressants?'

He thought of admitting that Elizabeth had told him, but shrank from the appearance of a conspiracy against her. 'I thought you were a bit down. If you've been to the doctor, it's the obvious conclusion.'

'Not me,' she said firmly.

He sighed. He did not think she had ever lied to him before. At college together, at long boring events when they had waited together for an interview, she had never avoided a question or glossed an answer. It was not that they had sworn mutual honesty, it was the comfortable consequence of having nothing to hide. There was nothing in his life that he was ashamed of, there was nothing that Ruth could not tell him. He had thought that her baby would make a difference to their relationship. But he could never have predicted this.

'Jesus, Ruth . . .' he said unhappily.

Ruth turned to look at him. He seemed very distant; his distress was very unimportant.

'Oh, what does it matter?' she said idly. She took another gulp. 'What does it matter either way?'

'It matters to me,' he said. 'I don't mind what you take or what you do. You know that. I've never tried to muscle in on your life, or tell you what I think. But you've always told me what you were feeling about things, and I've always been frank with you. It's strange – you being so distant. It feels awful. It feels like hell.'

She nodded. 'I do feel distant,' she said, her speech slightly slurred. 'I *like* feeling distant,' she said. 'D'you know I think this is how Patrick feels all the time. I think Amitriptyline just makes women feel like men. It fits you for a man's world. I love Patrick, and I love Thomas, and I'd lay down my life for them. But if you asked me whether I'd rather go home and care for them, or go to work right now, I'd far rather go and do the job I'm good at with people who like me for what I am and not because I'm married to them, or gave birth to them . . . or married their son,' she added.

'But that's because you miss your work,' David suggested.

She shook her head. 'It's the pills,' she said. 'It's how men are all the time. Most men would rather go to work than spend time at home, you know that. Men are detached and distant. Even Patrick is. Amitriptyline just makes us equal. I feel detached and distant too.'

145

'*I'm* not detached,' he said passionately. 'It's not true of all men.'

'You're not now,' she said, as if it hardly mattered to her. 'But once you're married and the novelty has worn off, you will be.'

He downed his pint. 'It's a dismal, dismal prospect,' he said fiercely.

'Isn't it?' she said calmly. 'Get us another drink; do.' She handed him a five-pound note. David took it and went up to the bar. As the barman fetched their drinks, he watched her in the smoked mirror behind the bottles. She took something from her pocket and put it in her mouth.

'You've just taken one,' he said flatly as he came back and put her drink before her. 'I saw you.'

She gave him her familiar mischievous smile. 'Oh, sod off, David,' she said. 'I've seen you pissed often enough. I am taking Amitriptyline and it makes me feel equal to Patrick. It makes me feel relaxed with Thomas, and then I can look after him better, and I don't mind when Patrick works all hours. It makes me unwind. You should be pleased for me.'

'It doesn't seem right,' he said stubbornly. 'Your life should be better for you. You shouldn't need it.'

'Well, it isn't, and I do,' she said easily. 'It's just while Thomas is so small. When he's a bit older, and sleeping through the night, when Patrick's job is more secure . . . oh, lots of things will change. This is just a rough patch I have to get through somehow.'

He nodded. Her speech was getting worse; she sounded drunk.

'I'm sure you shouldn't be mixing them with gin,' he said.

She chuckled. 'You're an old woman,' she said. 'Now shut up and tell me the gossip. What story were you covering, and how much did you have to do? Is the Bath studio still in the bottom of the council cellar? Is the mad caretaker still there who won't let you in unless you show your driving licence?'

David nodded. 'Yes, *she's* still there. I've been there three times in the last fortnight and she pretends not to recognize me. I say, "Hello, Mrs Armitage," and she says, "Name?" just like that, and I have to sign in. It was a vote about selling a school playing field to a supermarket. I did a nice package for Westerly and I've sold it.'

She smiled. She felt as if he were far away, a charming, once-beloved friend. 'And what were you doing before – on the other three times in the studio?'

'Planning inquiry – a new bypass. And a Farmers Union meeting. Ruth –'

Her eyelids were drooping. 'Yes?'

'You look half asleep.'

'It's the baby,' she said drowsily. 'Every time I fall asleep he wakes up. I think he knows it. When he's up at the farm he sleeps all the time. But when he's with me he does it in half-hour shifts.'

'It's not the baby,' he said. 'You're completely out of it.'

She giggled sleepily. 'I wish I was,' she said. 'Completely out of it. Completely. Out. It.'

Her head was dropping towards the table.

'Ruth . . .' he said urgently.

'Your round,' she said. She folded her arms on the table, and to his horror she slumped lower and lower until her head was resting on her forearms. 'Nighty night,' she said. Her smile, half hidden by the sleeve of her smock, was her old mischievous smile. 'Sorry, David, I'm a complete goner.'

He went to shake her but she was already asleep. For a moment he looked at her with tenderness, and then he realized that she was stranded in the pub with him, with no way of getting home.

'Ruth!' he said urgently, and shook her shoulder.

She slumped to one side. She was clearly not going to wake. He glanced uncomfortably to the bar; the barman was watching him.

It suddenly occurred to David that she might be seriously ill. He did not know how many Amitriptyline she had taken, nor if she had taken more than the two gins he had seen her drink. 'Christ!' he said.

He shook her again, more urgently. She was completely limp. He let her fall gently towards the table and went up to the bar. There was nothing to do but face the music.

'Watch her,' he said flatly to the barman. 'I'm getting my car up to the door and I'll drive her home.'

'Pissed?' the barman asked.

'She's ill,' David said loftily. 'She's on antibiotics and she shouldn't have mixed them with drinks. I'll take her home.'

The barman raised an eyebrow. 'She won't remember a thing then,' he said suggestively.

'Christ,' David said again miserably, and went out to fetch his car.

The barman had to help him lift Ruth into the front seat. Her legs had completely gone. David thought that in all their times of comradely drinking he had never seen her completely out of control. He missed, with a brief passionate pang of nostalgia, Ruth's giggly drunkenness, he remembered her howling with laughter and clinging to his arm.

'Christ,' he said again and started the car.

He knew he had to take her home, and he dreaded meeting Patrick. He drove to the cottage in a mood of stoical dread, but when he drew up outside the little house and saw the drive empty of cars and the door shut he realized that it would be worse than that – he would have to take her to her mother-in-law's house.

'This is a fucking nightmare,' he said precisely to the windscreen. He shook her gently. 'Ruth, Ruth!'

Her head dropped back, her jaw dropped open. Again he was afraid. He thought that for all he knew she might be sliding into a coma caused by a drug overdose. He thought of Elizabeth's air of calm competence and he felt a great longing to hand over the whole problem to her. Besides, she was baby-sitting Thomas, and she would have to know that Ruth could not collect him. He gritted his teeth and turned down the drive towards Manor Farm.

It was worse than he could have predicted, for when Elizabeth opened the dark front door he saw Patrick in the hall behind her.

'I'm dreadfully sorry,' he said. 'Ruth is with me, and I think she's ill.'

Patrick exclaimed and came quickly past his mother out to the car.

'We were at the Green Man,' David said to Elizabeth. Her steady gaze never wavered. 'She had two gins, and I know she took at least one Amitriptyline. I think she'd had some before she came out. I'm afraid she's ill.

Perhaps you should call a doctor.' He spoke precisely; he felt quite sick with embarrassment.

Patrick came up the shallow steps with Ruth in his arms. David shrank back.

'Put her in the yellow bedroom. I'll come up in a moment.'

Patrick nodded grimly and climbed the stairs. He ignored David completely.

Elizabeth's face was full of sympathy. 'Thank you for bringing her home,' she said. 'We've been worried. We didn't know where she'd gone or what she was doing.'

'She was quite safe,' David said awkwardly.

Elizabeth came out with him to his car. 'Does she often drink to excess?' she asked gently.

'Never!' David exclaimed.

'You've never seen her drunk before?'

'Well . . . we've been friends a long time,' he said. 'We were at college together. We all used to drink then . . . and in the old days, when we were working, we might have a drink after work, we used to drink a bit then . . . but everyone did . . . after work you know . . . after a tough day . . .' he sounded as if he were making excuses.

She nodded gravely. 'So this is nothing new.'

'I'm terribly sorry,' David said. 'But it's not how it looks.'

Her silence was worse than an interrogation.

'We're just friends,' David said. 'Very good friends. I'm very fond of her. But that's all. She's always been in love, madly in love, with Patrick.'

Elizabeth nodded. 'Is she still?'

David was about to swear that nothing had changed,

but then he remembered Ruth in the pub saying that men were like women on Amitriptyline – cut off from life, insensate.

'I don't know,' he said honestly. 'She's not like herself at all.'

Elizabeth lowered her voice; David leaned closer to hear.

'We are thinking that she needs a complete rest,' she said. 'A complete break.'

David felt an intense sense of relief that someone else would deal with the problem.

'Do you think that would be a good idea?' Elizabeth asked him. Her anxious scrutiny of his face assured him that his opinion was of material importance. 'Do you think that would be the best thing for her?'

'Yes,' David said. 'Yes, I think so. She can't go on like this.'

Elizabeth nodded. 'I'll see if I can find somewhere that she can go, and get her booked in at once then,' she said. 'But if she calls you – or writes –' she paused.

David waited.

'You wouldn't take her away, or visit without telling us, would you? Even if she asked you. If she has a drink problem or a drug problem she must stick it out. You will help her stay there, won't you? Even if she calls you and wants to leave?'

'Jesus,' David said miserably.

Elizabeth touched his hand. 'I am sorry to have to ask for your help,' she said. 'But you are her only friend. If she were to turn to you we have to know that you would do the best for her – which isn't always the easiest thing to do.'

David nodded. 'If she calls me, or writes, I'll let you

know,' he said. 'I wouldn't want to interrupt her treatment. She has to get well again.'

Elizabeth nodded. 'That's what we all want.'

He swung into the car seat and then hesitated. 'But if she gets better, and wants to go back to work, or – I don't know – change everything – I'd always be on her side.'

Elizabeth's smile was understanding. 'You're *her* friend,' she said. 'I understand that. And she comes first for you. That's as it should be.'

David nodded and she stood back and let him slam the door. She waved as he drove away, and he glanced in his rear-view mirror at the elegant figure receding into the distance. He thought she was a beautiful and intelligent woman, he thought she would care for Ruth and manage the whole family with skill and sensitivity. He had another contradictory feeling – which he ignored – that he had betrayed Ruth, and betrayed their long friendship, and that he should have done anything with her but drive her home to that woman.

Frederick was consulting Sylvesters, his lawyers.

'Small problem,' he said in his usual shorthand. 'Just a brief inquiry.'

'Yes, Colonel Cleary,' Simon Sylvester said.

'Domestic sort of thing.' Frederick cleared his throat. 'Daughter-in-law. Not up to caring for the new baby. Rather a poor show.'

Simon Sylvester drew a notepad towards him and scribbled the Cleary name on top.

'Drinking,' Frederick said shortly. 'And drugs. We're concerned for her, of course, but mainly for the well-being of the child. Any idea where we stand?'

Simon Sylvester thought quickly. 'The child's well-being comes under the Children Act, so any action would have to ensure that his interests are paramount.'

Frederick nodded. 'Goes without saying,' he said. 'Where do we stand with the mother?'

'In what way?' Simon Sylvester asked cautiously.

'Getting her sorted out,' Frederick said with frank brutality. 'Locked up, dried out, that sort of thing.'

'If she's a danger to herself and to others, you can get her committed under the Mental Health Act,' Sylvester said. 'But it's rather drastic.'

'How d'you do it?'

'You have to have a warrant from her doctor and next of kin to say that she must be hospitalized. You can keep her inside for a period of assessment, and that can be renewed or challenged.'

'One relation and a doctor?' Frederick confirmed. 'And how long does she get locked up for?'

'Twenty-eight days,' Sylvester said. 'Renewable. That's for assessment. It's a rather drastic piece of legislation, actually. There's no appeal. No way out. If you can get her GP to say she needs treatment, she can be inside for six months.'

'And the child? Would they want to take him into care?'

'I think he would stay with the father. Father can cope, can he?'

'We can cope,' Frederick said.

'Then you want a residence order. Father goes before a magistrate and explains the situation. Magistrate rules where the child is to live.'

'There'd be no problem with that,' Frederick said.

His lawyer smiled. Frederick Cleary was a magistrate himself and on first-name terms with every member of the bench in the county.

'Thanks for your advice,' he said. 'Very useful. I may call again.'

'It's a measure of the last resort,' his lawyer cautioned him. 'I imagine that she would resent it very bitterly. It would be hard to restore a proper family atmosphere after such an action.'

Frederick nodded. 'Point taken,' he said briskly. 'But I like to know what I've got up my sleeve.'

Dr MacFadden came as soon as Elizabeth called him and examined Ruth as she lay asleep in the yellow guest bedroom. When he came downstairs, Elizabeth, Frederick, and Patrick were all waiting to see him in the hall.

'She can sleep it off,' he said. 'She'll probably sleep the rest of today and wake up tomorrow with a headache. No harm done.'

'Not this time,' Elizabeth said. 'Fortunately she was with a friend who brought her home to us. If she had been at home with the baby, or tried to drive somewhere, it could have been very serious.'

Dr MacFadden nodded. He was fighting with a sense of guilt. He thought he should have spotted that Ruth was unstable enough to overdose. He had a strong sense that Ruth had let him down by misusing the medicine he had given her.

'The thing is,' Frederick said firmly, 'that the time has come for a more permanent solution. We can't go on like this.'

Dr MacFadden responded at once to the voice of authority. 'Yes,' he said.

'We're thinking of sending her on a little holiday,' Frederick said. 'Give her a complete break, away from it all. How does that sound to you?'

'Good idea,' the doctor said. 'A very good idea.'

'That's agreed then,' said Frederick. 'We want no repetition of this.'

'Where will you go?' Dr MacFadden asked Patrick.

'She'll go alone,' Elizabeth said smoothly. 'My son cannot leave his work at present. I shall care for Thomas while she's away.'

'Oh. Fine.'

Dr MacFadden headed for the door. Frederick went with him to his car. 'The thing is,' Frederick said confidentially, 'that I'm not sure she's entirely well. We might have to consider some sort of mental treatment. She's a bit unstable, there's a family history – very artistic people – and she's completely failed to care for the baby, and now drinking and taking drugs . . .'

Dr MacFadden's sense that Ruth had been irresponsible with her prescription gave him a sense of grievance, and he liked and respected Frederick and Elizabeth. 'Whatever you want . . .'

'Hope we won't have to call on you,' Frederick said.

Uncertainly Dr MacFadden nodded. He did not know quite what Frederick meant, nor what he was promising. 'Anything I can do . . .'

'Hope it won't be necessary,' Frederick said. He stood back from the car as the doctor drove away.

Elizabeth made them a lunch of salad and omelettes, denoting a sense of urgency. Patrick pushed the food around his plate and ate little. His mother watched him even while she rocked Thomas with her foot resting against his little bouncing chair.

'I think we had better make up our minds that something needs to be done,' Frederick said, when they had finished eating. 'We can't have a repetition of this.'

Elizabeth nodded, watching Patrick.

'What can we do?' he asked his father. 'What can we do?'

'I think she needs to go away, a complete break, and get dried out,' his father said frankly. 'She's no good to anyone if she's drinking and taking drugs like this.'

'She's not an alcoholic . . .' Patrick demurred.

'Of course not,' Elizabeth agreed with him. 'But she needs help.'

'Where could she go?'

'Celia Fine's daughter went to a marvellous man in Sussex,' Elizabeth said. 'I'll call her and get the number.'

'Celia's daughter was on heroin!' Patrick exclaimed.

Elizabeth shrugged. 'Well, she's a starting point.'

'The thing is that I think we might be overreacting,' Patrick said. 'Ruth's been through a rough time and I haven't been really aware . . . if I can get home more, and we keep an eye on her . . .'

Both his parents were silent.

'I don't think we can take the risk,' Elizabeth said. 'Not with a new baby.'

'Let's bite the bullet and get it sorted out,' Frederick said. 'Once and for all.'

Patrick was nearly convinced. He looked at his mother. 'I just wish I knew I was doing the right thing.'

She put out her hand and touched his fingers. 'I know,' she said. 'Leave it to me.'

As the doctor had predicted, Ruth slept all afternoon

and all night. When she woke in the morning her mouth was dry and tasted foul, her head thudded. She did not at first recognize the room, and then she could not remember how she had got to the farm. She could remember nothing of the previous day at all. She felt anxious about Thomas; she could not remember when she had last seen him.

The door opened and Elizabeth came in with a beautifully laid breakfast tray.

'Oh, you're awake!' she said with evident pleasure. 'I am glad. And how are you feeling?'

'I'm OK,' Ruth said. 'Well – headachy and foul. But fine. But I can't remember coming here. And where's Thomas?'

Elizabeth put the tray on Ruth's knees, anchoring her to the bed. 'We have Thomas,' she said. 'I collected him the day before yesterday – d'you remember? And he stayed overnight last night, and the night before.'

'Is he all right?'

'Of course.'

Ruth shook her head. At once the pain in her head and neck thudded. She closed her eyes for a moment. 'I don't remember,' she said.

'You're not very well,' Elizabeth said gently. 'You're not very well at all, Ruth. Better take two of your pills.'

Ruth looked at her. The light seemed very bright. Elizabeth's shirt in cream and her grey tailored skirt seemed to shimmer with excess light. The bottle of pills was on the breakfast tray. Ruth took two.

'What's happened?' Ruth asked.

'We think you have a problem caring for Thomas.'

'I'm fine,' Ruth said. Her voice was thin and faraway.

'You know you're not,' Elizabeth said calmly. 'There's

157

a doctor coming in half an hour to see you, and if he thinks he can help you then we want you to go with him, to his centre, where he can treat you.'

'What for?'

'Depression,' Elizabeth said.

'I'm not depressed,' Ruth said. 'I'm just tired. I never sleep. There's nothing wrong but that.'

Elizabeth smiled. 'So go with this doctor and have a good long rest. You've been through so much, Ruth. You need a rest.'

'But what about Thomas?'

'He can stay here with us.'

'What does Patrick say?'

'He agrees.'

Ruth lay back on the pillows. 'Where *is* Patrick?' she asked at length.

'He's dressing Thomas in the nursery. He'll come and see you in a minute, when you're freshened up.'

'How long do I have to go away for?'

Elizabeth did not show that she had heard the defeated acquiescence in Ruth's voice. 'Not long,' she said reassuringly. 'And you can come home whenever you wish. But we all want to see you rested and well again.'

'What *did* happen yesterday? How did I get here?'

'You took too many of your pills, and you met David at the pub, and you drank too much. You passed out and he brought you here. You left the keys in your car and it was stolen overnight. We had to put you to bed. You slept all afternoon and all night.'

Ruth felt a deep corrosive sense of shame. 'David brought me?'

'He had to carry you out of the pub.'

'And Patrick was here?'

'He had come for Thomas. None of us knew where you were. You just walked out of the little house; you left it unlocked.'

Ruth dropped her head, her hair tumbled forward hiding the deep red of her cheeks. 'My car . . .'

'We've reported it missing. It may just have been taken by joyriders, it may turn up.' Elizabeth hesitated. 'It won't be insured since you left the keys in it. I'm afraid you may have lost it.'

Ruth pushed the tray to one side, Elizabeth put the bottle of pills on the bedside table, and took the tray away. 'Be brave, darling,' she said gently. 'Dr Fairley is coming at ten. If he thinks he can help you, he has a wonderful house in Sussex where they can give you lots of rest, and make you well again. You can come back to Patrick and Thomas and make a fresh start.'

Ruth turned her head away.

'Unless you'd rather not . . .' Elizabeth suggested.

Ruth turned back. 'Rather not what?'

'Unless you'd rather start again somewhere else?' Elizabeth said gently. 'Your career is so promising . . . you could start a new life . . .'

'Move away?'

'If you wanted.'

'With Patrick and Thomas?'

Elizabeth met her eyes. The two women looked at each other. Elizabeth was serene and powerful, Ruth looked sick. 'No, Patrick and Thomas will stay here,' Elizabeth said firmly.

Ruth nodded. 'I see.'

She said nothing more. It was as if Elizabeth's calm assurance had set the tone of the whole day. Ruth hardly said a word to Patrick when he came in to see her, and answered the doctor in monosyllables. She did not ask for Thomas, who was, in any case, out for a long walk with his grandfather. Dr Fairley had come in his large comfortable car, and offered to drive her to Springfield Hall at once. Patrick produced a suitcase already packed, and put it in the boot. Elizabeth gave Dr Fairley an envelope containing a cheque with the fees for the first month. Ruth, wrapped in one of Elizabeth's pale camel-hair coats, walked to the car and got in. She saw her feet going down the steps but she had no awareness of the hardness of the paving stones.

'See you soon, darling,' Patrick said, bending down to the car. 'I'll come down and see you at the weekend. And you can phone me.'

'Will you be at home?' she asked, meaning the little house.

'Yes, I'll stay here,' he said, meaning the farmhouse. 'It'll be easier, and I'll see more of Thomas.'

She nodded.

'When you're better I'll bring him down to see you,' Patrick promised. 'And soon you'll be home.'

'I don't know what's wrong with me,' Ruth said dully.

'Dr Fairley can deal with all of that,' Patrick said reassuringly.

'But if I don't know what's wrong with me,' Ruth's brain was working slowly but stubbornly, through the haze of hangover and Amitriptyline, 'if I don't know what's wrong, then how can I get better?'

Patrick leaned forward and kissed her cheek. 'Trust Dr Fairley,' he urged. 'He's had a lot of experience. Mother says he's the best in his field. Mother and Father are paying a packet for you to stay there. He'll make you well again.'

The doctor got into the car beside Ruth, and started the engine. Patrick stepped back and carefully shut the door. 'I'll call tonight,' he said. 'And every night. See you at the weekend!'

Ruth stared past him, unseeing.

The doctor put the car in gear and they moved smoothly off, down the drive. Ruth could just see, at the side of the house, Frederick pushing the pram around and around the garden, rocking Thomas to sleep and waiting for her to be gone. They had not wanted her to see her baby, in case she made a scene. Ruth lay back against the comfortable headrest and closed her eyes. She would never have been able to make a scene in Elizabeth's house, she thought.

'All right?' Dr Fairley asked. He glanced sideways at her and saw that her eyes were shut but that tears were trickling from under her closed eyelids and running down her cheeks.

'I don't know,' she said. 'I don't know anything any more.'

Nine

AT NINE WEEKS, Thomas was too young to cry for his mother, but Elizabeth thought that he had noticed her absence. He was placid and happy, quick to laugh or coo with pleasure, but his brightest vitality seemed to drain away during the month that his mother was away.

Elizabeth tried to ignore it, and she never mentioned it to either Frederick or Patrick. But she could not deny that – though he slept through the night, and ate well – Thomas was quieter and less joyful than when his mother had been, however incompetently, taking care of him. Elizabeth found herself strangely offended by his loyalty. She would have preferred him to forget Ruth as soon as he ceased to see her. But there was something loving and stubborn about little Thomas, and Elizabeth could see that when a door opened and he turned his head to the noise, a light died from his face when someone else came in, when it was not his mother.

Elizabeth felt, rather resentfully, that she was being haunted by Ruth. Her daughter-in-law remained a worry. Patrick telephoned her every evening at seven o'clock, and drove cross-country to Sussex every Saturday morning to spend the day with her.

He came back from these trips tired and silent, and

his father made a habit of sitting with him late on Saturday night, with a bottle of malt whisky and a jug of still spring water between the two of them in companionable silence.

On Sunday morning they all went to church and came back to Elizabeth's Sunday roast, then in the afternoon they took Thomas for a walk. Elizabeth had bought a backpack for Thomas; Patrick would put it on, and Elizabeth lift Thomas onto his father's back. With the dog at their heels they would walk across the fields and up to the hills, Frederick, Elizabeth, Patrick, and little Thomas, his head bobbing with every step.

He often fell asleep on these walks, and would sometimes sleep all the way home, not stirring even when the pack was carefully set down on the sofa while Elizabeth made tea. Then they would read the Sunday papers – the *Sunday Telegraph* for Frederick, who mistrusted the sports coverage in any other paper, and the *Sunday Times* for Elizabeth and Patrick.

When Thomas had slept for an hour, Elizabeth would wake him for his supper. He was no longer given jars of baby food or powdered mixes. Elizabeth had painstakingly cooked, puréed, and frozen a wide selection of adult meals to make tiny dinners just for him. Patrick always bathed him on a Sunday night, and put him to bed. When Patrick came downstairs, leaving Thomas asleep, Elizabeth would have a large gin and tonic ready for him, in a crystal goblet packed with sliced lime and ice.

Patrick felt as if he had never left home, never married, but had somehow been miraculously joined by the next son and heir. He enjoyed being a father to Thomas in a way that he had not experienced before. Under Ruth's care Thomas had been a problem, his sleeping – or lack of it – was a continual unspoken area of conflict between them. His clothes, his feeding, his nappy changes were all areas where Ruth silently and resentfully pressed Patrick to do more, and which Patrick silently and skilfully avoided.

But with Elizabeth running the nursery Patrick need do no more on a weekday than kiss his son's milky face at breakfast time in the morning as he left for work, and play with him for half an hour before bed in the evening. He never saw Thomas except washed and clean and ready for play. He never wiped his face, sponged his hands, changed his nappy, or struggled to get his vest over his little head. It was the fatherhood that Frederick had enjoyed: in which a father returns from the outside world at predictable intervals, volunteers a period of enjoyable and bonding play, and disappears again when the chores of babyhood are to be done. Father and child meet only at their best moments. The tantrums, the washing, the feeding, all take place miraculously out of sight. It is the fatherhood still enjoyed by men who employ either professional nannies or devoted wives. It is not the way fatherhood is usually practised in the 1990s, when men and women are working towards equality of work and mutuality of experience. Patrick much preferred it.

He liked the way Thomas's little face lit up when he came into the room. He liked the way his presence was a treat and not a duty. He liked the way he could open the front door and hear his mother say to his son, in the tones of absolute delight, 'Here's Daddy home!' and Thomas, cued by her enthusiasm, would kick his feet and wave his hands and beam.

They all spoke of Ruth with tenderness and concern,

but within a fortnight there was an unavoidable sense that this lifestyle – this comfortable, affectionate, orderly lifestyle – was better than anything any of them had experienced before. Patrick went to work in the morning with a well-cooked breakfast inside him, and a sense of order and solid well-being. He came home at night knowing that no domestic crisis would have broken out, and that his home would be tranquil and welcoming. His work became easier, no longer interrupted by desperate phone calls from home, and his attitude to his staff became more relaxed and tolerant. The documentary unit produced a couple of good ideas and one very good film, which was short-listed for a minor award. Patrick's style: confident, well-dressed, and relaxed, fostered the impression that he was a brilliant young man, doing well in a competitive business.

He had never looked more handsome. His clear, regular features were enhanced by the immaculate cleanness of his shirts and the pressing of his suits. His shoes shone with loving attention. Even his briefcase was polished.

Frederick enjoyed the company of his grandson. He developed his own little rituals with him: taking him for a walk in the afternoon, rocking him to sleep in his pram. Frederick played with him for an hour in the morning, while Elizabeth prepared lunch and supervised the work of the daily cleaning woman. Thomas was settled and quiet with his grandfather. Sometimes Elizabeth would put her head around the door and see Frederick solemnly reading paragraphs from the *Telegraph* aloud while Thomas lay in his bouncy chair, his wide, serious eyes fixed on his grandfather, as if the English touring cricket team was the most entrancing story.

'This is the life,' Frederick said to her one lunchtime,

as he poured a glass of sherry. Thomas had eaten earlier and was asleep in his pram in the conservatory.

'Don't get too attached to it,' Elizabeth warned. 'It will all change when Ruth comes home.'

'Yes,' Frederick said thoughtfully. 'It seems almost a shame. I can hardly bear to think of Thomas leaving us. He's so happy here, and Patrick looks so much better too.'

Elizabeth nodded. 'I'm afraid we have no choice really,' she said. 'It's not as if she left him; it's not as if there was a problem with the marriage. She just couldn't cope with a new baby. It's not as if they were separated or divorced.'

Frederick nodded. 'I suppose everything *was* all right for them,' he said. 'It was just Ruth getting overtired? It couldn't have been something more?'

Elizabeth gave a small shrug. 'He's never said anything to me,' she said. 'But if they were having difficulties I wouldn't be surprised. Patrick's not a man to wait for a woman forever. And Ruth was seeing that other young man – from the radio station.'

Frederick shook his head. 'It doesn't seem right,' he said, dissatisfied. 'We're all so happy now, and she could come home at any moment, and we'll be back to square one again.'

'No,' Elizabeth agreed. 'I don't think Thomas should go back to her until she's completely better. Even if she comes home, I don't think Thomas and Patrick should go back to the little house until we are all confident that she's completely well again.'

There was a brief silence.

'Patrick doesn't seem to see much of a change in her,' Frederick volunteered. 'He said she hardly spoke to him last time he was there. Didn't look at the flowers we sent. Hadn't read her book. Very quiet.'

'Maybe it'll be longer than a month then.'

'Maybe.' He hesitated, finding the truth. 'I can't say I'll be sorry.'

Elizabeth shot him a small half-hidden smile.

At Springfield House in Sussex Ruth's days passed in structured activities. She was called at eight o'clock and she showered and was down to breakfast at nine. She was making a tapestry and she worked on the large frame from half past nine until eleven. At eleven they all stopped for coffee, and her group – five men and five women – went to the meeting room for their session of group therapy. Ruth said nothing during the first four meetings. She barely listened. There was a young woman addicted to drugs, and one in deep depression; there was a woman recovering from alcoholism and one woman being treated for anorexia. The men, Ruth had not observed at all. She sat in the circle on the soft, comfortable chairs and observed her feet. They were not allowed to wear shoes in the group-therapy room. Ruth had a pair of pink socks; she moved her toes gently inside them and felt the soft wool caress her insteps. As much as possible she made herself deaf to the low-toned murmur of the group.

The walls of the room were an encouraging yellow-tinged cream. There was a large reproduction of an Impressionist picture hung on one wall, and a large picture window overlooking the well-kept garden. Ruth looked at the picture, at the millions of little dots of paints, at the illusion of solid flesh and sunlit river water.

She did not want to see the garden in its wintry, sodden bareness. It reminded her of home, of the little house set amid the cold fields and the drive leading up to the farm.

She missed Thomas and she put the pain away from her mind every waking moment. She thought of her Caesarean scar and the strange loss in her belly after he had been born. She thought of the sense of weightlessness and the loss of the curve of her stomach. She felt that she had lost him at birth, when someone had put her to sleep and taken him from her, and that she had been a fool to let them do that – to steal her baby out of her own body. And now she had let it happen again. She had put herself to sleep and let them steal her baby from her.

She could think of nothing to do but to stay asleep. She turned her head to study the picture again. She admired the bright sugar-almond pink of her socks. She decided that she would not think about Thomas, who was too young to care whether or not she was there. She would not miss Thomas, who would be cooing in his grandmother's arms. She would not acknowledge this dreadful pain – a pain as deep and as agonized as an amputation. She would not even think of the little house, the boredom and claustrophobia of her relationship with Patrick, the wet fields and the dominating, imposing presence of the farm, and the gradual, irresistible theft of her baby.

After lunch they lay down on their beds, or chatted in the common room. Ruth liked an afternoon rest. She lay on her bed, watching the ceiling, not thinking about Thomas, not thinking about Patrick, not thinking about the little house.

Sometimes people walked past her door. Sometimes one of the other women from her group came in and tried to talk to her. Ruth turned a blank, pale face to their inquiries.

'I'm sorry. I'm very tired,' she said politely. And they would go away.

Someone raised his voice in the group, Ruth turned her attention to the picture, trying to block out the sound. Then Agnes, the recovering alcoholic, suddenly turned on her. 'Why d'you never talk?' she asked abruptly.

Ruth slowly turned her blank, uninterested gaze.

'Why d'you never talk?' Agnes demanded. 'You've sat in that same seat for a week, looking at nothing and saying nothing. In recreation time you lie on your bed. You're like a sleepwalker. You're half dead.'

Ruth looked towards the group leader, George. He was a young man in a crisp white jacket, the duty nurse. She expected him to tell Agnes that Ruth must be left alone. He said nothing.

'I want an answer!' Agnes said.

Ruth looked to George, the nurse. Still he said nothing.

'Say something!' Agnes pressed. 'Say anything! You sit like you're dumb, like you're deaf and dumb.'

George nodded, waiting like the rest of the group.

'I've got nothing to say,' Ruth said unwillingly.

Agnes leaped to her feet and came towards her. Ruth recoiled. 'Why not?' she demanded. 'Why nothing?'

Ruth shook her head.

George leaned forward; the whole of the group were watching this exchange. Agnes looked around. 'Isn't she half dead?' she demanded.

A couple of the men nodded, and one of the women. Ruth felt anger flare inside her.

'Do I have to listen to this?' she asked George. She expected him to take her part, to tell Agnes to sit down.

He smiled gently, saying nothing.

Ruth looked into Agnes's angry face. She was flushed, her face shiny with sweat. Her black curly hair was greasy and uncombed. Ruth pulled her feet up, out of Agnes's way; she sat holding her toes like a scolded child.

'I want you to answer me,' Agnes said determinedly. 'You say nothing and you do nothing. I want you to tell me what it is that is keeping you so quiet.'

'Nothing,' Ruth said unwillingly. Against her pulled-up legs she could feel her heart pounding. 'It's nothing. I'm sorry.'

'Sorry for what?' one of the women demanded.

'Nothing,' Ruth said. 'I just want to be left alone.'

'But I don't want to leave you alone,' Agnes said. 'Why do you never speak to anyone?'

Ruth looked to George again. He was leaning forward, waiting for her answer.

'I'm not well,' Ruth said.

'Why do you cut yourself off?' Agnes demanded.

'I'm overtired,' Ruth said. 'I need to sleep . . .'

'You've been sleeping ever since you got here!' Agnes exclaimed. Other people nodded. It was like a steady, insistent tow, bringing Ruth out of the depths of her despair into a bright, interrogating light. 'Why d'you never say anything? Why do you even try not to listen?'

'I don't . . .' Ruth said desperately.

'You do,' one of the men said. His voice was gentle. Ruth turned to him, hoping he would rescue her from this attack. 'You do try not to listen, and you look at the picture any time someone raises their voice.'

'It's just . . .' Ruth started and then broke off.

They were all waiting. She looked up at the picture and then out the window over the wet fields. The view reminded her, inescapably, of the little house and the dreadful, dreadful loss of Thomas. She could feel panic building inside her at the thought of his absence, and then she found it bursting out of her mouth, in a high childlike voice, which she did not even recognize. She thought she was going to cry for Thomas, but instead she said: 'I miss my mother!' in a voice that was not her own but a child's voice ringing with grief. 'I miss my mummy! She's dead and I can't bear it! And I don't know what will happen to me! And I miss her! And I miss her! And I miss her!'

She was screaming as she cried, and she felt her face hot and wet with an unstoppable stream of tears. No one moved towards her, no one enfolded her in their arms, no one even touched her. Ruth hugged herself while the dreadful racking sobs went on, and rocked her own body back and forth, and felt the horror of being a little girl, weeping in deep grief, with no one at hand. Only when the hoarse, horrified sobs quietened a little did George the nurse cross the floor towards her and put his arms around her and draw her head onto his shoulder as if she were a very small girl.

'I see you miss her,' he said gently. Ruth could hear his voice coming from deep in his chest. 'I think that was the most awful thing to happen to a little girl.'

Ruth felt her energy stream through her, from her toes to the very top of the head, as if her tears had somehow burst through a blockage that had cut her in half, kept her half dead, half cold, half turned to stone for all her life since the death of her mother. 'It was,' she said with certainty. 'And everyone told me not to mind, and that everything would be all right.'

George pulled back so he could see her face. For the first time since she had been in the group she looked directly at him, her cheeks were flushed, her eyes were red-rimmed but bright. She looked alive for the first time since he had seen her. '*Was* everything all right?' he asked.

Ruth drew a breath that seemed to resonate through her very bones. 'No,' she said with a simple certainty. 'I did mind, though I never told anyone how much. And everything was *not* all right. And everything has been wrong ever since.'

That afternoon Ruth slept without dreaming, a deep, easy sleep as if she had been at hard manual work all day. When she woke it was time for tea, and she went down to the refectory and saw Agnes and one of the men from the group at a table together. When they saw her they turned and smiled, and Ruth took her tea tray over to their table and joined them. Nobody said very much, but Ruth knew that she was among people who had witnessed her deep and agonized grief, and had not turned away.

That evening Patrick telephoned from work to speak to his mother.

'There's a new producer here, at a bit of a loose end,' he said. 'I was wondering if we could stretch to another place at dinner?'

'Of course,' Elizabeth said agreeably. In the background Patrick could hear his son cooing.

'I can hear Thomas,' he said with pleasure.

'Yes, he's just finishing his tea,' his mother said. 'Of course you can bring someone home, darling.'

'About eight o'clock then,' Patrick said. 'She's new to the area so I'll drive her out and home again after dinner.'

Elizabeth noted in silence that he had asked if he could invite a guest before explaining that it was a woman. 'Of course,' Elizabeth said.

'About eight then,' Patrick said again.

Elizabeth put down the telephone and turned back to Thomas's tea. Frederick was proffering a spoonful of strained blackberries at arm's length. Thomas waved sticky hands. His face, his hair, his arms to his elbows were plastered in dark juice.

'A guest for dinner,' Elizabeth said neutrally.

'That'll be nice,' Frederick said. 'Anyone we know?'

'A lady producer,' Elizabeth said, her tone carefully level.

'Oh,' Frederick said.

There was a brief silence. Thomas reached out, took the spoon, and put it to his cheek, his nose, and finally his mouth.

'I wonder if that's quite cricket?' Frederick said thoughtfully. 'With Ruth in a convalescent home, and all. You know if she were in hospital with a broken leg we'd be visiting her every day, and there would be no guests at dinner.'

Elizabeth rinsed a warm flannel at the sink to wipe Thomas's face and hands. 'Exactly,' she said.

Frederick waited for an explanation.

'If she were in hospital with a broken leg, then we would know that she was happily married to Patrick, and a good wife and mother, and that she had suffered an unfortunate accident and was coming home soon.'

She wiped Thomas's mouth with careful efficiency, undid the straps on the high chair, and lifted him out.

'Instead she had a breakdown and could not cope with motherhood or married life, and we don't know if she will ever come home, or what sort of state she'll be in when she does come home.'

'Still married,' Frederick said softly.

'I don't see Patrick as tied to a sick woman for the rest of his life,' Elizabeth said. She held Thomas against her shoulder and patted him gently on the back, waiting for him to burp. 'I don't see that he should sacrifice his life, with all his prospects, just because she can't cope.'

Frederick nodded but was unconvinced.

'Besides,' Elizabeth said, 'what matters most is Thomas, and making sure that Thomas is safe and happy.'

Frederick nodded. 'Here with us,' he said.

'Yes.'

Despite the warmth of Elizabeth's welcome and Frederick's unfailing courtesy, the evening did not go well. The visiting producer, Emma, had thought that when Patrick invited her to dinner he would be taking her to a restaurant, and she had worn a rather low-cut black dress. In the sitting room, on the chintz-covered sofa, she looked overdressed and tarty. Elizabeth, sitting beside her in a smart woollen suit with her pearls, could not put her at ease.

'Do you all live together?' Emma asked curiously.

'My daughter, Miriam, lives in Canada,' Elizabeth said, carefully misunderstanding. 'She's got the travel bug. She's just like her father. She did two years voluntary service in Africa and now she teaches disadvantaged children in Canada. She's just outside Toronto.'

At dinner Emma announced that she was a strict vegetarian. Elizabeth's smile never wavered. She left Frederick carving the joint of beef and went to the kitchen, reappearing with a vegetable quiche and a green salad.

'I would have said,' Emma remarked. 'But I thought Patrick was taking me out for dinner.'

'I do admire you,' Elizabeth replied. 'I couldn't bear to give up meat.'

Emma did not want any dessert. Emma took tea instead of coffee after dinner. She did not drink brandy or port, which she was offered. She asked for another gin and tonic instead, which was usually served only as an apéritif.

'Of course,' Frederick said pleasantly. 'Will you have it with your cup of tea or after?'

Fortunately, Patrick had a report from his documentary unit on television that evening, and so they watched it in silence.

'Excellent,' Frederick said as he switched off the set at the end of the programme, and after they had admired Patrick's large billing as executive producer.

'I thought you went rather soft on the police,' Emma remarked. 'Someone should have put the civil-liberties angle.'

'It wasn't that sort of programme,' Patrick explained.

'I understand that – that's my problem with it,' Emma

insisted. 'It's soft-focus news. I think you'd get more viewers if you were harder.'

Elizabeth and Frederick exchanged a brief look. They had never heard Patrick contradicted – it was a strange and unpleasant experience to have this badly dressed stranger take him to task in their own drawing room.

'It seemed right at the time.' Patrick did not reveal that hers was exactly the same comment made by the Head of News. 'The right tone for the piece.'

'But all your pieces have this tone,' she said. 'Kind of daytime television, comfy viewing. I thought you'd go for more bite.'

'Maybe,' Patrick said equably. 'Look! Is that the time? Would you like a nightcap, Mother? Emma? Father?'

'Not for me,' she said briskly. 'I'll call a taxi.'

'I'll drive you back,' Patrick said, getting to his feet. He had rather assumed that he would run her back to her hotel in Bristol, and that she would invite him up to her room for a nightcap and that they would have sex.

'Not all the way to Bristol at this time of night!' she said. 'I made a note of the number.'

Briskly she went out to the hall and telephoned for a taxi. Frederick and Elizabeth tidied the cups and glasses and went into the kitchen and tactfully closed the door.

'I was rather looking forward to driving you back to Bristol,' Patrick said engagingly. He smiled his charming television smile.

'I was rather looking forward to dinner in a quiet restaurant and walking back to my hotel,' she said smartly.

'Sorry.' Until now it had not occurred to him that he was being snubbed, that she had disliked spending the evening with his parents. He was so accustomed to Ruth's complaisance that this woman's rejection of him, of his parents, even of his mother's cooking did not make sense. He thought he was bestowing on her a great privilege – inviting her to his home. 'Perhaps we got off to a bad start . . . you see . . .' he paused and played for her sympathy . . . 'my mother is caring for my son, so I like to be here in the evening, in case he wakes. My wife is away, she's ill, and my son needs me. He's only a baby.'

'I know, I've heard all about it at the studio.'

Patrick uncomfortably wondered what exactly she might have heard. 'She's in a convalescent home, a sort of health farm. She's unstable.'

'I have children too,' Emma said surprisingly.

'You do?'

'Yes. Two, actually. I'm divorced. Their father has them when I have to go away.'

'I had no idea . . .'

'I never discuss them at work,' she said smartly. 'People patronize a woman if they know she's a mother and managing on her own.'

Patrick felt obscurely that his sympathy card had been soundly trumped. He managed a game smile. 'It's hard work bringing them up on your own. I'm only just learning the ropes.'

'I'd certainly like the live-in staff you have,' Emma said acidly. 'Does your mother get up to him at night, as well as having him all day?'

'He goes through the night now,' Patrick lied. 'Thank God!'

Emma raised her arched eyebrows.

Patrick heard the taxi draw up outside and went to the door. He slipped Emma's coat around her shoulders and just brushed the bare nape of her neck.

'See you tomorrow,' he said softly. 'And maybe we'll find that quiet restaurant later in the week.'

'Maybe,' she said. 'But perhaps you had better stay at home with your mother.'

Ruth slowly started to talk in the group. She told them of the death of her mother and father and how her aunt had tried to protect her from feeling grief, from the bereavement itself. They had buried her parents without telling her, she had never been able to say good-bye; and whenever her aunt, or her husband, Ruth's Uncle Stephen, had found the little girl in tears, at bedtime, or bathtime, or walking slowly home from school, they had said bracingly to her, 'Don't cry now! What have you got to cry about? A big girl like you!' And Ruth – not understanding that they were thinking of the orphanage where she could have gone, if they had not agreed to take her – could only look at them and wonder if they had forgotten already.

She told the group about the long years of loneliness and silent grief, that she had been teased for talking 'funny' at school, and for not knowing the English children's stories. She told them that in the end she had decided to erase her American childhood from her mind, smooth out the American twang from her speech, pass as an English girl in an English home. Not until she met Patrick – and especially Patrick's family – had she found a complete solution to the emptiness, and to the question of where she belonged. Elizabeth and Frederick and the beautiful house, the warmth of their welcome, and the ease with which they called her 'daughter' made her feel as if she were not lonely and sad and missing her parents, and a foreigner in a strange country, but were instead pampered and loved and wanted.

She tried to describe the farmhouse and Elizabeth's hospitality and her kindness, but the people in the group did not smile and nod as if they understood.

'It's like a perfect house,' she said. 'A perfect house, and they are just perfect parents.'

There was a brief silence. Ruth wondered why she sounded so unconvincing. Then Agnes spoke.

'I think they've done you over,' she said.

'What?'

'I think they've done you over.'

Ruth checked her reply, swallowed the words, started again, almost choked. 'What d'you mean?'

'I think they saw you coming,' Agnes said. 'Lonely, all on your own, no parents, and no guardians who cared that much for you, and I think they thought they could make you fit in. You'd spent all your childhood trying to fit in. You would learn to fit with them. They wanted you because you wouldn't rock the boat. They could keep their darling son, and you wouldn't be able to take him away. You didn't have anywhere to take him away to.'

Ruth was about to exclaim that Agnes was talking complete nonsense, but she saw that other people were nodding, as if they agreed.

'It's not like that at all,' she said swiftly. 'They're very loving people. They are wonderful in-laws! Why, when I was so tired with Thomas, Elizabeth would have him all day, every day. She's got him now so Patrick can go to work. She's been completely wonderful. She's been like a mother to me.'

Agnes shook her head stubbornly. 'Or else she liked you because she knew you'd never have the balls to take Patrick away from her, and then she took your son from you.'

The enormity of the lie filled Ruth's head like a rushing wind. 'That's a dreadful thing to say! That's a wicked thing to say! She loves me, and of course she loves her son and her grandson, and she would do anything to make us all happy. Anything!'

'Yes,' Agnes said. 'But what if what makes Patrick happy and Thomas happy is to get rid of you?'

Ruth went white and turned to George. 'Tell her to shut up,' she said sharply.

George leaned forward. 'Why is it such a bad suggestion?' he asked. 'If it's not true, it doesn't matter what she says. Does it?'

Agnes looked triumphant, like a bully in a playground. 'They've done you over,' she said again. 'And they've nearly won. They got you into such a state that you were hardly there at all. You've lost your baby and you've lost your husband and you're in the loony bin. You're a loony, and they did it to you. Don't tell *me* that they love you.'

'No,' Ruth screamed. She jumped and ran at Agnes to push her ugly gloating face away. George moved like lightning and grabbed her from behind. He wrestled her to the ground and held her still. Ruth struggled and swore, words that she had never used. Words that Elizabeth had never heard.

'No physical contact,' George said in her ear. He

sounded perfectly calm. 'Those are the rules. No physical contact.'

'I'll kill her!' Ruth gasped. 'I'll kill the bitch!'

'No physical contact,' George said again.

In the distance, Ruth heard a bell ring and heard the noise of running feet. Then George's weight was lifted from her and she lunged towards Agnes again. At once she was enveloped in a tight fold of material, like a white sheet. She bucked and struggled, but they had her fast. They slung her, like a rolled carpet, onto a trolley and wheeled her out of the room, to her bedroom. They humped her onto the bed without unwrapping her; if anything the bindings were pulled tighter. All Ruth could see was the ceiling, and all she could feel was the firm, gentle handling. 'I'll kill her,' she said again.

'No physical contact,' one of the nurses said. 'Now you have a little sleep, and next time you see her, you tell her what you think of her.'

There was a slight prick in the skin of her inner arm and then Ruth felt the delicious languor spreading all over her. 'It's not true, what she said,' she whispered.

'Well, you tell her that,' the nurse recommended. 'No point in killing her. But you could tell her that she's wrong.'

'She is wrong,' Ruth asserted. 'They love me like a daughter. I know they do.'

'Good,' the nurse said soothingly.

Ruth started to drift into sleep. 'They do ... they do ...' she whispered. 'I know they do.'

* * *

When she woke it was early evening. She stirred and found that someone had undone her bindings and she was free to get up. She stumbled to the bathroom, her feet were still cramped, and then she went cautiously to the dayroom. Half a dozen people were watching television. It was Thursday evening; they were watching *Top of the Pops*. Ruth blinked at the strange lunatic costumes and joyless erratic dancing on the programme, and the orderly silence of the inmates.

One of the men from her group glanced around and saw her. 'OK now?' he asked.

Ruth nodded, feeling embarrassed.

'You're doing really well,' he said.

She puzzled over that for a moment. He spoke as if her grief and her rage were somehow signs of material progress.

'Are you being funny?'

He shook his head with a smile and then turned back to the television screen. 'It's bottling it all up that is crazy,' he said. 'Letting it out is sane.'

'Do you mean . . .' she started.

He shook his head again. 'Don't ask me, I'm a schizophrenic,' he said cheerfully. 'I'm as crazy as you can get.'

Ruth took the chair beside him. 'Have you been here long?'

He nodded without taking his eyes from the screen. 'Long and often. In and out. I go out when I get straight, and then I come back in again when I start flying, or hearing voices, or chatting to God.'

'You do that?'

He nodded. 'That's the best times.'

'I've always been frightened of mad people,' Ruth observed.

182

He was not interested.

'I've always been frightened of people who talk in the street. They always seem to come and talk to me.'

'Well, I wouldn't,' he said with sudden energy. 'I wouldn't talk to you because you're always trying to be nice. I'd rather talk to someone who was really there. Real and nasty. Someone who had a bit of substance. Not a pink jelly.'

Ruth recoiled at the unexpected attack. 'I'm not a pink jelly!'

He clicked his tongue as if he had been guilty of some minor social solecism. 'Tell me in group,' he said; and he watched the television, and would not speak to her again.

Ten

ON MONDAY MORNING Patrick went in late to work. He wanted to telephone Ruth's convalescent home, and he did not want the call overheard by his staff.

Elizabeth, leisurely polishing the banister in the hall, while Frederick rocked Thomas's pram in the garden, was able to hear most of the conversation without appearing to listen.

'Dr Fairley? It's Patrick Cleary.'

Dr Fairley drew Ruth's notes towards him. 'Ah, Mr Cleary. Good to hear from you. Your wife is making excellent progress,' he said.

'She wouldn't speak to me on the telephone, and she didn't want to see me this weekend. I thought something must be wrong.'

'No,' Dr Fairley said calmly. 'She is getting in touch with her feelings. We have to be patient with her. She is experiencing anger and grief. She is doing very well.'

'Anger?' Patrick asked blankly. 'What does she have to be angry about?'

Dr Fairley hesitated. 'This is therapeutic work,' he said tactfully. 'Sometimes a patient goes back almost to babyhood. Sometimes it is recent or recurrent grief. But your wife is confronting her difficulties well and is making good progress.'

'What d'you mean – therapeutic work?' Patrick demanded. 'What has she got to be angry about? She's had everything she wanted all her life, and especially since we were married. If she says that she's been badly treated it's just not true.'

'I do not attend her group sessions,' Dr Fairley said gently. 'So I do not know the details. Even if I did, then the confidentiality of the patient would mean that I could not discuss such things with you. But I can say – in the broadest of terms – that she is getting in touch with her feelings, and expressing them.'

'When I phoned the other night they said she could not come to the telephone because she was "in treatment",' Patrick said, his voice very tight.

Dr Fairley turned back a page and sighed a small silent sigh. 'Yes, that was the case. She was under restraint,' he said gently.

'Under restraint?' Patrick demanded.

'Yes.'

'You had her in a padded cell? In some kind of strait-jacket?'

'Please, Mr Cleary, don't distress yourself with these anxieties,' Dr Fairley said gently. 'There was an incident in her group between herself and another patient, and she was sedated and returned to her bedroom. She woke at – let me see – just after seven o'clock and watched television with the other patients. She behaved perfectly normally at supper, and took part in all the activities the following day.'

'Are you telling me that she was fighting with

someone, that you knocked her out and then she got up and watched television?'

'Yes, that is what seems to have taken place. As I say, I am not her group leader, so I was not there myself.'

'Is she mad?' Patrick demanded, outraged.

'No, most certainly not.'

'Then what is going on?'

Dr Fairley sighed gently. 'Mr Cleary, you must be patient with her, and even with yourself. She was deeply wounded as a child by the death of her parents, and she has got to come to terms with that loss and with her grief and anger. Her inability to care for her own son no doubt springs from that early trauma, and of course, on top of that, she feels the natural anxiety of the young and inexperienced mother. She is doing wonderfully well in coming to terms with all of this, and she is making good progress.'

Patrick was silent for a moment, trying to take it all in.

'When will she come home?' he asked.

Dr Fairley thought of Ruth as he had seen her that morning. Her step was more confident; she had acknowledged him in the corridor. 'I think she should be the one to decide,' he said. 'But I would think within a fortnight. Then I would recommend a therapist near to you, so that she can go on with her therapeutic work. But she will know what she needs. She will be the best person to decide.'

'Even though she's the mad one?' Patrick asked rudely. 'Are the lunatics running the asylum?'

Dr Fairley observed the rise of his own temper until he had it under control and out of his voice. 'Your wife is not mad, Mr Cleary,' he said politely. 'She was a sad and angry little girl and she has had difficulties in adult life. But she is as sane as I am, or as you are. And indeed there are many therapeutic communities that are self-run.'

Patrick bit back a retort. 'I'll visit her on Saturday unless I hear to the contrary,' he said shortly.

'I will give her your message,' Dr Fairley said with courtesy. He put down the receiver. 'And she is certainly more pleasant than you,' he said roundly to the absent Patrick. 'Better mannered, less selfish, more loving, and generally a nicer person to be with. She is growing to be an honest and mature woman while you are just a bossy little boy!' Then, with his temper relieved, Dr Fairley pulled on his jacket and went to do his rounds.

Patrick sat in silence for a moment, and then the sitting-room door opened and his mother brought in a tray with freshly made coffee.

'Thank you,' he said heavily.

She poured him a cup in silence and handed it to him. 'Bad news?'

He made a face. 'I can hardly tell. The doctor says that he thinks she'll be home within a fortnight. But after that she'll need to see some local chap.' He looked at his mother in bewilderment. 'She was violent,' he said wonderingly. 'She attacked a patient and had to be sedated, and tied up, or something.'

Elizabeth sank to the sofa. 'Oh! my dear!'

'I can't imagine it!' Patrick said. 'Little Ruth! Why, until we had Thomas, I don't think I ever heard her say a cross word. She never once even raised her voice to me. What can have happened?'

'Didn't he explain?'

Patrick shrugged. 'He said he was bound by patient confidentiality – but he didn't seem too concerned. He made me feel as if I were making a bit of a fuss over nothing.'

Elizabeth nodded. 'I suppose he sees worse every day,' she said, 'in his work. It must be dreadful.'

'But Ruth . . .'

'Did he say what we should do when she comes home?' Elizabeth demanded.

Patrick shook his head. 'I didn't ask . . . what d'you mean . . . what we should do?'

Elizabeth's look was open and concerned. 'To protect Thomas,' she said.

Patrick was astounded. 'Protect him?'

'If she is violent, and she is with Thomas, on her own . . .'

Patrick gave an abrupt exclamation, put down his cup of coffee and went to the window. In the garden outside Frederick was rocking the pram, the rhythm of the movements slowing as Thomas fell asleep, and then stilled. Frederick bent down and carefully put on the brake, adjusted the hood of the pram against the bright wintry sunlight, and checked that Thomas's little hands were warm in their knitted mittens. He turned and came towards the house.

'She can never be alone with Thomas,' Patrick said as if the words were forced out of him. 'I'll have to check with Dr Fairley and make sure they are aware . . . but for our own peace of mind we'll have to watch her all the time.'

Elizabeth nodded, her face full of pity. 'Oh, Patrick,' she said softly.

He turned to her and managed a little smile. 'I'm all

right,' he said. 'Thank God I've got you and the old man.'

She nodded. 'You'll always have us,' she assured him. 'For you and little Thomas. We'll always be here for you both.'

In the group session Ruth and Agnes sat facing each other, as wary as fighting cocks. George said his usual gentle introduction: 'Who would like to start?' and Ruth said quickly: 'I would.'

'Last time I was carried out of here,' she said bitterly. 'George, you held me, and you called some other nurses, and you carried me out and stuffed me full of some drugs.'

George nodded.

'I was angry,' Ruth said. She was breathless with nervousness at speaking to the whole group, but she was determined to finish. 'I was angry but I wasn't mad. I'm not insane. There was no need to take me out like that. It frightened me.'

'Um . . . I don't believe that.' It was the man from the television room.

Ruth turned to him.

'I don't believe you were frightened,' he said. 'You didn't look frightened. But you looked really mad.'

'I'm not mad,' Ruth said quickly.

'Slip of the tongue,' he said easily. 'Freudian slip. You looked angry. I'm just saying I don't believe you were frightened.'

Ruth took a breath. 'Yes,' she said. 'I was angry.'

The man smiled at her. 'Well, that's what I thought,' he said.

'Ruth, we have a no-physical-violence rule for group work and all our therapeutic work, you know that,' George said gently. 'You can embrace someone or hold their hand, but you must not hit or threaten them with any physical violence at all. You agreed to that when you started with this group, and you have to hold to that agreement.'

He paused, waiting for Ruth's reply.

She nodded.

'I have to know that you agree.'

'I nodded.'

'I have to hear you *say* that you agree that there will be no physical violence to yourself or to others.'

'I agree to no physical violence to myself or to others,' Ruth said sullenly.

'OK,' George said. He settled back in his seat and smiled at her. 'Now, go on with what you were saying.'

Ruth felt temporarily deflated. 'I was saying I was angry,' she repeated.

George nodded. 'Was there any special reason?'

'I was really angry with Agnes.'

'Then tell her,' George advised.

Ruth turned to Agnes. 'I was really angry with you.'

It was a bad day for Agnes. She was shrouded in a huge man's cardigan. The leather patches on the elbows were down at her wrists. She was folded up in her chair, her knees under her chin, her face moody.

'Oh, yes,' she said without interest.

'You said some things about my family that are unforgivable,' Ruth said, 'and untrue. You said that they had done me over. I don't begin to know what you mean. But I do know that they have loved me and cared for me, they took me into their family when I never had anyone to care for me before. They bought us our first flat, and I loved it there and I was really happy there. Then when we had our baby they bought us a beautiful cottage in the country. My mother-in-law is wonderful with the baby. They have both been wonderful to me.'

Agnes nodded listlessly.

'It is not how you said,' Ruth said urgently. She badly wanted Agnes to respond. 'What you said wasn't true. They have been wonderful to me, and I really appreciate it.'

'OK,' Agnes said wearily. 'OK.'

'They love me,' Ruth said. 'They do all they can for me. Why, at this very moment they are looking after Thomas so I can be here!'

Agnes shrugged and looked away.

'To suggest anything else is a lie,' Ruth made herself continue. 'Elizabeth loves me as if I were her own daughter, and she adores Thomas. She furnished our house for us, with her own lovely things. She thinks about us all the time. She's a wonderful woman.'

'They bought your house and she furnished it?' the man from the television room asked Ruth.

'Yes! Yes! Why on earth not?'

He smiled his shy smile at her. 'It's just a bit odd,' he said quietly. 'Usually people choose their own houses and furniture.'

Ruth looked at him with dislike. 'I was pregnant,' she said. 'She did everything for me; she was quite wonderful.'

'So is it her house or yours?'

'Mine!' Ruth exclaimed. 'Of course it's mine!'

He nodded as if in agreement. 'You pay the mortgage?' he suggested.

Ruth suddenly flushed and turned to George the nurse. 'Do you want the details of my bank account?' she asked. 'Is this what we're supposed to be doing here? Discussing my personal finances?'

'You wanted to go first,' one of the women said sulkily. 'So get on with it.'

'I just wanted to say one thing to Agnes!' Ruth protested.

'Well, now someone has asked you something,' the woman said. 'So do you pay the mortgage on your house or not? Let's just get on with it!'

'But what has that got to do with anything?'

George smiled his patient smile. 'Perhaps nothing,' he said equably. 'But is there a reason why you don't want to tell us?'

'There's no reason,' Ruth said, 'because there's no mortgage. They bought the house and gave it to us outright.' She threw an angry look at the quiet man. 'I hope you're satisfied,' she said.

He nodded and would have stopped, but George intervened. 'What were you thinking about, Peter,' he asked gently, 'when you asked about the mortgage?'

The man spoke to him alone. 'I was just thinking that maybe they *hadn't* given Ruth her home at all, but just let her live in one of their houses, and then furnished it how they liked. I just wondered how much it is her house, and how much it belongs to her husband's parents.'

George nodded. 'I was wondering that too,' he said companionably. He turned back to Ruth. 'I think we were all wondering that,' he said gently.

Ruth slumped back in her seat. 'I'm tired of this,' she said. She felt a small pleasure at refusing to speak to them. 'I'm tired. I've said all I had to say.'

The thin woman leaned forward. 'So answer the question, and let's move on,' she said. 'Is it her house – your mother-in-law's house – or is it yours?'

'Of course it's mine,' Ruth said. 'I live there, don't I?'

'But she owns it?'

'Yes.'

'And she furnished it?'

'Yes.'

'And you have no lease and you pay no rent?'

Ruth shrugged. 'Yes. So what?'

The thin woman shrugged back, mirroring Ruth's weary contempt. 'Then it's not your house,' she said. 'And actually you've got no rights at all. You're not even a tenant. You're a squatter. They can evict you any time they like.'

'I'm their daughter-in-law, for God's sake!' Ruth suddenly yelled.

The woman nodded. 'All that means is that you are married to her son,' she said. 'You haven't got a home or a family at all.'

Ruth gasped at that as if she had been hit. She turned to George and he saw her face was white. 'That's a dreadful thing to say,' she whispered. He saw her face crumple like a little child's. 'That's a dreadful thing to say to someone – that they have no home or family.'

· He nodded, his face was tender. 'It is a dreadful thing,' he said, repeating the words she had used. 'And especially hard for you, Ruth.'

She nodded. He could see that her eyes were filling with tears, her face looked stricken. He thought it was how she would have looked when she learned she had lost both parents and her home. And now she had learned that she had not been able to replace them.

'It's a dreadful thing to say to *anyone*,' she said, still pushing the truth away.

'But worse for you,' he suggested again. 'Because you know what that loss is like.'

'I can hardly remember . . .'

He shook his head. 'I think you know what that loss is like,' he said again, and watched in pity as her expression dissolved and she turned in her chair, buried her face in the soft back, and wept. 'I can't remember,' she insisted. 'I was too young to remember.'

His face was tender with pity. 'I think you *do* remember, Ruth.'

They all heard the catch in her throat, and then the deeper grief as she wept. George stepped across the circle and held her in his arms. His embrace was comforting, professionally sexless. Ruth – far away in memories, deep in grief – felt only the relief of arms around her, holding her allowing her to cry.

In the farmhouse Thomas stirred in his pram. He opened his eyes and saw the comforting canopy of the pram and the little dancing toys that Elizabeth had strung from one handle of the hood to another. He made a shape with his mouth and moved his lips. A sound was coming, slowly, he could make a sound. 'Ma,' he said. 'Ma.'

That evening Ruth sat between Agnes and Peter when they ate their supper in companionable silence. When she turned towards her room, Peter said quietly: 'You did well today,' and Agnes looked up and smiled.

'It's hard,' Agnes said. 'But Pete's right. You did do well today. In the end.'

Ruth was aching with tiredness. 'I've never felt so bad in my life,' she said.

Agnes nodded. 'Oh, yes,' she said. 'You've got to get all the bad stuff out before you feel better. Don't you feel better at all?'

Ruth paused and thought. Somewhere there was a sense that a lie had been challenged, that a truth had been told. She thought of the pleasure she used to have as a journalist on the rare occasions when she had caught someone out in a deception. She felt as if she liked knowing the truth, and that for most of her marriage with Patrick she had been lying about herself, and that others had been lying too.

'Yes,' she said honestly. 'I do feel better. I'll do some more tomorrow.'

'Good,' Pete said.

Another woman started the session the next day. Ruth watched and listened as another person's pain unfolded before her, and saw how George and the group gently encouraged her to speak. She was the daughter of a wealthy family; she was addicted to drugs. She trembled with desire for the comfort of drugs even as she spoke of the damage they had done to her. Ruth thought of her own longing for the easy sleep given to her by Amitriptyline and shivered. When the other woman dissolved into tears and then wrapped her arms around her own thin body, shivered a little, and said, 'I'm done,' Ruth spoke.

'You were right yesterday,' she said to them generally.

'The little house is not my home, it belongs to Frederick and Elizabeth.' She took a breath. 'And Patrick is my husband, but he was their son before he ever met me, and he is more their son than he is my husband.' She looked round. 'I'm not doing this very well,' she said with a new humility. 'I don't know how to be honest about this.'

'You're being honest,' George said.

'He's theirs,' Ruth said. 'He likes being in their house best. He likes being with them more than he likes being with me.' It was a sharp, bitter truth she was telling. 'It's her. She makes him comfortable in a way that I don't know how to. It's not just cooking and furniture. He acts like he belongs there. At our home he acts like he is on a visit.' She thought for a moment. 'A working visit,' she said. 'It's not a very nice place to stay.'

She choked on the words for a moment, recognizing the little house in that damning phrase. 'They don't love me particularly,' she said. She had a strange sense like diving into completely unknown deep water, which might wash her in any direction at all. 'They love me because Patrick brought me to them and said he wanted me. If he had brought someone else it would have been her. Up to a point, it could have been anyone. If we were to separate,' her voice shook slightly, 'if he found someone else, they would like her just as much.' She paused. 'Possibly more. They hardly see me. In all the time I have known them, they only really saw me when I was pregnant. They cared for me then because it was important that Patrick's child was well. It wasn't me they cared about. It never has been.'

She could hear the words spilling out as if it were someone else talking from far away, saying things that reversed her life like a negative instead of a print, when everything that should be white is black, and everything that should be black is white. But she recognized what the voice was saying, and there was a clear, clean honesty at last in what the voice was describing. And everything that had puzzled Ruth and hurt her in the past – Patrick's 'helping' in his mother's kitchen before Sunday lunch, Patrick's private walk with his father after lunch – all made sense now. These were the techniques they were forced to use to share the joy of their son's presence, and divide the task of entertaining his wife. Each of them wanted time alone with him, each of them had to pay for that pleasure by spending time alone with her.

'I am a real burden to them,' she said brutally. 'What they want is Patrick – and now Thomas too. But they had to have me. They found all sorts of ways of managing me. But I never really fitted in.'

There was a silence.

'And is this a new way?' Peter asked.

George shot him a bright, acute look. 'What d'you mean?'

'Is this a new way to manage you? Put you in a loony bin?'

She recoiled. 'They didn't do it,' she said positively.

Peter raised an eyebrow. 'Who pays?'

'You always ask that!' she said impatiently. 'Who pays! Who pays! There are other things more important than money, you know! It doesn't always matter who pays!'

He nodded. 'But it tells you a lot,' he observed. 'Who is paying for you to be here?'

'Who's paying for you?' she retorted like a child.

'My company,' he said easily. 'They know that the way they work drove me crazy. They know that if they

197

had worked well I wouldn't have had a breakdown. They know they did it. So they're putting it right. Is that what's happening for you?'

Ruth was about to deny it but she paused. She thought of the little house, which she had never wanted, and the baby, which she had conceived and carried against her will. She thought of the remorseless good nature of Elizabeth and Frederick and their view of life, which accepted no argument, or even dissent. She thought that she could never have fitted into the mould of their daughter-in-law, that in the end something had to crack. The distance between the flat in Bristol and the farmhouse outside Bath had preserved their mutual privacy, but once Ruth was on the doorstep she was bound to be scrutinized, and once she was scrutinized they would have to see that she did not do things as Elizabeth did them, and that if they were not done as Elizabeth did them then they would be bound to be wrong. And anyone persisting in being wrong would be crazy to behave in such a way – crazy, mad, insane.

'Yes,' Ruth said quietly. 'They did it to me. They didn't mean to do it to me, and there was the birth, and being really tired, and all the hormones jumbled up as well, and Thomas not sleeping – but yes, living next door to them has driven me completely insane, and now they are trying to put it right.'

'So you're a loony, in the loony bin,' Peter said cheerfully.

The rest of the group smiled. It was like some form of initiation. 'Yes,' Ruth said, joining at last. 'I am a loony in a loony bin, and I am going to get sane and get out.'

* * *

Patrick arrived at the clinic on Saturday night looking tired. Ruth normally met him at the door and they went to her bedroom. This Saturday she was not waiting at the door, and he had to make his own way down the hall to her room. A woman came out of a door and stared at him without smiling. Patrick recoiled. He was accustomed to the curious gaze of the audience upon a minor celebrity, but there was nothing of that sycophantic half-smile from the woman. She gazed at him in quite a different manner. As if he were not important, as if she did not like him.

'Evening,' Patrick said pleasantly. He could not comprehend dislike at all.

She looked through him and beyond him. She did not want to see him, and by very little effort she could make him transparent.

'Evening,' Patrick said again, but with less certainty, and dived into the relative safety of Ruth's bedroom.

He was surprised to find it was empty. At other visits Ruth had waited for him at the front door, and when he was ready to go he had left her lying, weeping silently, on the bed. He had thought that there was nowhere else for her to be but waiting at the door for him, or lying on the bed and grieving for his absence. He had not seen the dayroom, or the group room, or the garden, or the handicrafts room. He sat in the chair, waiting for her, and then he strolled around the room, looking at the bed, the wardrobe, the chest of drawers, the curtained window. He glanced at himself in the mirror and smoothed his hair. His good-looking reflection reminded him of the woman who had looked through him in the corridor. 'Barmy cow,' he said. He showed his even teeth in his charming smile. 'Barmy cow,' he said again.

'You said it,' Ruth said, coming in behind him.

He whirled around. 'Hello, darling!' he said. 'Feeling better?'

'Much worse actually,' she said precisely. 'How is Thomas?'

'He's fine. Completely fine. Mother said to tell you that she thinks he's cutting a tooth. But he's completely fine. Everything under control.'

Ruth closed her eyes briefly at the thought of her son cutting a tooth, and her not knowing.

'And how are *you*?' said Patrick, putting emphasis on the 'you' and making his voice warm.

'Worse, as I said. But *how* are *you*?' Ruth inquired in an exact parody.

Patrick hesitated. He was not sure how to deal with Ruth, who looked the same, rather better actually: the same dark-eyed, petite, kissable little thing, still a little plump, but now unrecognizably difficult. She was tense, he decided. He would reassure her. 'I'm fine. Missing you all the time.'

'Eating well?' Ruth asked. There was something not quite caring about her tone.

Patrick made a little downturned mouth. 'Homecooking,' he said dismissively.

'Sleeping well? No crying babies at night?'

He scanned her face. 'Thomas is sleeping quite well,' he said. 'And Mother gets up to him. You knew that.'

'Oh, yes,' Ruth said viciously. 'I know that your mother gets up to see to my baby. I know that I left him with her, not with you – his own father. I know that the last trump wouldn't wake you after one of her dinners and a couple of your father's best bottles of claret and a couple of nightcaps.'

He recoiled. 'Steady on.'

'You sound just like your father addressing the natives in Poona,' she said mercilessly. 'You're something like a hundred years out of date. All of you.'

'Ruth . . .'

'Patrick . . .' she mimicked his reproachful tone.

'I don't know what's wrong with you . . .' he started.

'If you don't know what's wrong with me then why did you put me away?' she demanded.

'I hardly put you away,' he said, stung. 'You were knocking back pills and boozing on top of it. You weren't fit to care for Thomas. It's all very well to get self-righteous about it now, Ruth, but you were a danger to Thomas and to yourself. What did you expect us to do?'

She was instantly deflated. 'Oh.'

'"Oh," what? Mother was worried sick that you would hurt yourself, or hurt Thomas. They couldn't keep supervising you and him at long distance. I couldn't be home all the time. What did you want us to do? Are you saying you shouldn't have come here? Are you saying you want to come home?'

Ruth put her hands out, as if to halt him. 'Patrick . . .'

'It's all very well sitting here and thinking about everything and blaming us, but we're just doing the best we can in a completely impossible situation. People at work keep asking me how you are and I keep saying that you're fine. People in the village keep asking why you're not looking after Thomas, and Mother keeps having to say that you're resting. You've put us in an impossible situation, and now you're trying to blame us.'

She was white-faced. 'I'm sorry,' she said weakly. 'I know a lot of it was my fault.'

'I'd have thought all of it was your fault,' Patrick said powerfully. 'Your choice, all along the line.'

'I didn't want to move out of Bristol . . .' Ruth started.

'Oh, you can keep harking back forever,' Patrick said impatiently.

'I didn't want to live there, right next door to them . . .'

'It was an excellent choice of house, a wonderful investment, and we would have been mad to turn it down.'

'But it's not *my* house . . .'

'Why not?'

'Elizabeth decorated it, she chose almost everything . . .'

Patrick turned towards the door and then spun around. 'Mother did everything she could to make you comfortable and to spare you worry, and now you're making her out to be some sort of harridan,' he said. 'It's so unfair, Ruth. You're being so unfair to everyone. She did everything she could to make it easy for you and now you're accusing her of interfering.'

Ruth's lips were white. 'I'm not,' she said weakly.

'Well, it sounds like that.'

'I just thought . . . I've been thinking and thinking, Patrick.'

'Well, stop thinking disloyal and unfair thoughts and start thinking how you're going to pull yourself together and come home,' he said brusquely. 'Your child is being cared for by my mother, your house is being run by her. She's looking after me, and she's doing all her own usual work. And you're in here – at *their* expense, I might remind you, because we could never afford the bills – you're in here, and all you're doing is lying around on your bed imagining how badly you've been treated.'

'I'm not! I'm not!' Ruth cried. She pitched forward into his arms, and Patrick felt his satisfaction mix with desire at the warm, desperate closeness of her. 'I'm sorry, Patrick, you don't know what it's like here. We chew over everything, over and over, and at the end you don't know what to think.'

He stroked her hair and stepped to one side a little, pressing her slight body closer to his. He glanced at the bed and wondered if he shut the door whether anyone would come in. It was not as if it were a hospital, after all. It was a private nursing home and his parents were footing the bill and it was his own wife . . .

Ruth was sobbing, her body shaking with grief. He patted her back. 'There,' he said, absentmindedly. If the door had a bolt on it he had a good mind to shut it and to have Ruth on her little narrow hospital bed. Female despair had always stimulated Patrick, and it had been a long time since he and Ruth had made love. Emma's rejection had shaken him; he wanted Ruth's grateful response.

'There,' he said again. Ruth was still crying.

Patrick reached behind him and flicked the door shut with his spare hand. Ruth looked up, her face tearstained and sore.

'The doors have to stay open,' she said.

'Not during visiting time, surely . . .'

She shook her head. 'All the time.'

'I thought we might be together. Ruth, together.'

She shook her head. 'The doors have to stay open.'

He felt sexually frustrated and angry with her. 'For God's sake, Ruth, I'm paying for this!'

She stepped back from him; her face was still young and blotched with her tears but she looked different, she looked wiser, and she looked at him as the woman in the corridor had looked, not as if she were arrested by his handsome face but as if she could see into his very soul – and it was completely transparent, there was nothing there at all. She looked as if she could see completely through him. 'No,' she said slowly. 'No, Patrick. I think *I* am the one who is paying. You are benefiting.'

Eleven

THOMAS was in his cot. Slowly into his line of vision his clenched fist swam forward, and then backwards again. He observed it with careful concentration. Just when he was starting to make the connection between the sensation of movement and the phenomenon of vision he was completely surprised by another hand, which approached from the other side.

He opened his mouth in amazement. 'Ma,' he said. 'Ma-ma.'

'He's saying "Grandma",' Elizabeth said with wonderment. 'Frederick – come and listen! Thomas is saying "grandma".'

Her smiling face swam into Thomas's line of vision. 'What a clever boy!' she said. 'What a clever boy.'

Somewhere in Thomas's memory cells was the fading image of another face. It was not smiling, it was pale and tired-looking, but she smelled right, and she was infinitely dearer. His lip trembled. 'Ma-ma,' he said. But they would not hear him.

Ruth was getting ready to leave the convalescent home, having her farewell interview with Dr Fairley.

'So tell me,' he said agreeably. 'What differences have you been able to make in your life since being with us?'

Ruth looked across his desk. 'I've stopped using tranx,' she said, and then she corrected herself with a rueful grin at him. 'Tranquillizers, I should say.'

'Yes,' he said. 'I'm glad of that. They seem as if they're helping but they don't get you very far.'

She shook her head. 'No,' she said shortly. 'I should never have been offered them, and I should never have used them.'

He nodded. 'You could still consult the doctor for other illnesses,' he said. 'He might be a very good GP for broken legs. Postpartum depression is very hard to treat.'

'Yes,' Ruth said. 'And he was under pressure from my family, I'm sure.'

'Ah, your family . . .'

Ruth smiled. 'I've thought a lot about them too, these last few weeks.'

'Yes?'

'They're not all bad,' she said. 'I wanted more from them than they could ever have given. Patrick's not a bad man – he's vain and he's been spoiled, but I love him, and he's the father of my child, and I've got every reason in the world to go home and to try and make it work with him.'

'Oh,' Dr Fairley said, neutrally.

Ruth nodded. 'I'll see what we can do,' she said. 'He's very attractive, and he's brilliant at his job. In many ways I'm lucky to have him. I don't think he's God's gift to women any more, but I do know that many women would want to be in my position. And I want to make it work. We've got a lot going for us – a lovely home, a wonderful baby, plenty of money, and he's got a great career – we should be able to make it work. I'm going to try.'

Dr Fairley, thinking of the several difficult phone calls with Patrick, nodded and reserved his opinion.

'His parents adore him,' Ruth said simply. 'And of course they will never love me like that. It was unfair to them and unfair to myself to hope for more. I was playing happy families in my head. I wanted them to fill all the spaces of my childhood – I know that now, but I didn't know it then. I wanted my own parents back so badly . . .'

She broke off and reached for a tissue from the box on his desk, wiped her eyes and blew her nose, without apology for the show of emotion. 'They're good people, and they love Patrick and they love Thomas and they love me too – up to a point – I'm going to go back and accept that limitation.' She gave him a small brave smile. 'And in time, when they see that I care for Patrick and I care for Thomas, they'll respect me,' she said. 'They'll see that I'm a good wife, and a good mother, and they'll respect that.'

'Good,' Dr Fairley said with careful neutrality.

Ruth nodded. He let a little silence fall on her good intentions.

'And what about you,' he said. 'As an individual?'

She spread her fingers out on her lap. 'I'll look after Thomas while he's little, and I'll do some freelance work,' she said. 'I might write, if I can't get back into radio work. I might write magazine articles; I could do that. And when Thomas is older and goes to school then I'll go back to radio work again.'

He nodded. 'And how will you keep from being depressed, at home on your own with a small demanding baby?' he asked.

She smiled her urchin smile. 'I shall see the consultant that you have referred me to,' she said, ticking off the tasks on her fingers. 'I shall *not* ever take tranx or uppers or downers or anything again. I shall make a relationship with Patrick that is a real relationship between adults based on love and self-respect. I shall learn to enjoy being with Thomas. I shall ask Elizabeth for advice and help but I shall stop her invading my life, and I shall try to become friends with Frederick, and to see him as a real person, and to make him see me as a real person and not just as an adjunct of Patrick. I shall see my friends from Radio Westerly, and I shall find friends in the village, women who have babies like Thomas, and I shall spend time with them and talk about babies and child care with them.'

He nodded again. 'That all sounds very practical and workable,' he said. 'And how will you know that it is working for you? How will other people know?'

She nodded at the lesson that George and the others in her group had taught her. 'Oh, yes! I will know that I am OK because I will not feel the need for any kind of drug, and I will not be sleepy all the time. I will enjoy things like food and talk and jokes. I will feel joy and sadness. And I will start to love Thomas.' She suddenly looked up, and her eyes were filled with unshed tears. 'I want to love Thomas,' she said suddenly. 'I feel as if I have only given birth to him now, as if all the days before were just part of a hard pregnancy. I'm ready to love him now, and I want to see him and hold him and smell him and bath him and kiss him.'

Dr Fairley smiled for the first time since she had come into the room. 'I think you will make an excellent mother,' he said. 'Thomas is a lucky boy to have such a loving mother, who has come through so much to be with him.'

She nodded. 'I have,' she said simply. 'And I want to be his mother now, and I never did before.'

'I think you have worked very hard,' he said. 'You've come through a great shadow on your life, and you will never be so alone and so unhappy again.'

She looked at him with hope. 'Can you promise that?'

He nodded. 'Yes. Not because I'm a magician, but because the loss of a parent for a little child is perhaps one of the worst things that can happen. And you were never allowed to acknowledge that loss until now. You've faced it now and started to deal with it, and it's unlikely that you will ever have to face anything worse.'

She nodded. 'I feel as if I've been crying non-stop ever since I arrived.'

'Maybe you will cry some more,' he suggested. 'And there is nothing wrong with crying.'

She reached for the tissues again. 'I cry all the time.'

He smiled gently. 'Newly exposed emotions can be very sensitive,' he said. 'When I first did my therapy I went around weeping for months. I felt completely out of control and completely wonderful. Everyone else thought I was miserable, but it was a different feeling from sadness.'

She was silent for a moment.

'Anything else?' he asked, trying to read her face and the relaxed set of her shoulders.

She looked up and he saw she was smiling through her tears. 'No,' she said. 'I think I've finished. But I do thank you for having me here, and for all that you and everyone has done for me.'

He made a little gesture with his hands. 'It is my job,' he said. 'And you have a right to the best treatment we can give.' He hesitated. 'If you ever need us, we will still be here,' he said. 'Don't feel that this was like school that you have to leave and can never go back.'

'I don't think I'll need to come back,' she said. 'Things are going to be different at home. I'm going to be straight and honest and adult with them, and things will be very different.'

Dr Fairley thought of the remorseless niceness of Elizabeth, and of Patrick's little-boy charm. 'I wish you the very best of luck,' he said simply.

Patrick came to collect Ruth and was relieved to find her waiting in the hall with her small suitcase at her feet. There was no one to see her off. When she saw the car draw up outside, she rose and carried her suitcase down the shallow flight of steps. Patrick took it from her, feeling that she should not be carrying heavy weights, that she was ill. He put it in the boot and held the car door for her. Ruth got in and he slammed the door carefully. He remembered bringing her home from the hospital when Thomas was born and felt the same irritable concern, as if Ruth had just played a master stroke, which would ensure that all the attention was focused on her instead of him.

'Thank God I don't have to spend another minute in that place,' he said abruptly as they drove through the tall gates.

'Yes,' Ruth said neutrally. 'How are things at home?'

'Fine.'

'And Thomas?'

'Fine.'

'What's he doing?'

'How d'you mean: "what's he doing?"'

'I mean, how does he look, what is he eating, how is he behaving?'

'He looks just the same,' Patrick said. He did not mean to be unhelpful, but the differences in Thomas's development were too slight to be noticed by him. 'Mother will tell you,' he said.

'Was it a tooth coming through?'

'No, he was just a bit pink-cheeked and restless.'

Ruth nodded and looked out of the window. The easy tears threatened to come at the thought of Thomas's being pink-cheeked and restless and her not there to comfort him.

'So that's that, is it?' Patrick asked after a while.

'What is?'

'You don't have to go back again?'

She shook her head. 'I'll see a therapist in Bath for a while,' she said. 'But I don't plan to go back to Dr Fairley.'

'Does he say you're completely OK?'

Ruth threw him a swift smile. 'I don't think he quite deals in those sorts of judgments,' she said, amused. 'I don't think he would recognize the concept of completely OK.'

'Well, he says you're normal?'

'I was always normal.'

'Well, you're better then?'

'Better than normal?'

Patrick clicked his tongue. 'Look, Ruth, it's been a long worrying time for me, and I had to go in to work at seven this morning to get something out of the way so I could collect you today. I've driven two hours here and I'm driving two hours back, and I'm not in the mood for clever games. I'm asking you if you're OK now. Can you tell me that?'

Ruth belatedly remembered her resolution to be straight and clear with Patrick and his family. 'I'm sorry,' she said. 'What was wrong with me was a form of post-natal depression, which took me back to the loss of my parents.' She could feel the tears coming and she swallowed and took a deep breath. 'I have spent a lot of time grieving for them, and now I feel ready to take up my life again. I am really sorry that things went so bad with Thomas, and I want to start all over again with him. And I'm really pleased that, however bad it's been, it's happened now, and it's over and done with now. He and I can start our relationship again. Agnes says . . .'

'Who's Agnes?'

'One of the patients – Agnes says that her children were really wonderful from about six months, so I want . . .'

'I hardly think her opinions would be very helpful.'

Ruth recoiled. 'What?'

'Well, what's wrong with her?'

'Nothing. Nothing's wrong with her?'

'What was she in there for?'

'She has an addiction. But . . .'

Patrick snorted. 'Well, I hardly think we need take some druggie's opinion on child care, need we?'

Ruth paused for a moment before carefully replying. 'She is a rather wonderful person, who is very brave, and who was very kind to me. I liked her a lot, and I'm going to stay in touch with her.'

'In touch with her?'

'Yes.'

'You mean write to her?'

'Yes, and when she comes out I'll visit her and I'll ask her to visit us. I want her to see Thomas, and I want to meet her children.'

Patrick shook his head, but said nothing.

'You don't approve,' Ruth said flatly.

He shook his head again; he was smiling.

'You don't want me to see her?'

Patrick was imperturbable. He watched the road with his level blue eyes.

'Patrick, please speak to me,' Ruth said, trying to keep her rising temper out of her voice. 'Agnes is a friend of mine. Of course I shall want to see her, and of course I shall write to her.'

'Fine,' Patrick said flatly. 'Fine. Whatever you like, Ruth, and I hope it makes you happy and helps you, and makes her happy and helps her. *I* don't want to meet her, and I won't meet her. And I don't want her to see Thomas either. But you have every right to do whatever you like, pursue your new friends and life.'

Ruth felt an uneasy sensation of tumbling, as if her return to her stable marriage and life were a mirage, and that she had never been more insecure. 'It's not a new life,' she said. 'My life is with you and Thomas. I'm coming home to my old life, that's what I want. But Agnes was a good friend to me, and I want to stay in touch with her. That's all.' Her voice was plaintive and she checked herself. 'Come on, Patrick. We're not even home yet. I don't want to quarrel with you.'

He shook his head. 'Of course not,' he said. 'There's no quarrel. I said that you can have the friends that you want. But I don't have to meet them, do I?'

'No.'

'And my family certainly won't meet them,' he said. He leaned forward and switched on the radio, drowning out any further conversation. 'D'you mind if I catch the news?'

Elizabeth was listening for the car, waiting for the scrunch of the wheels on the gravel. She had kept Thomas from his morning sleep so that he would be certain to be asleep when his mother came home, to give them all time to assess Ruth before she saw her son. She saw Patrick's car from the nursery window; in the antique wooden cot below the window Thomas was soundly asleep. She closed the nursery door behind her and ran down the stairs to open the front door as Patrick drew up and Ruth got out.

Elizabeth noticed at once that they had been listening to the radio rather than talking together, that Patrick looked strained and sulky. Then she looked at her daughter-in-law. Ruth was looking wonderfully well. The tired, strained look had quite gone from her face, her eyes were bright again, her hair clean, her face young and optimistic. It was how she had looked when Patrick first brought her home and Elizabeth had realized, with a feeling of dread, that this would be the girl who would be her daughter-in-law, that this was the one he would marry.

'Darling!' she exclaimed and hurried down the steps and put her arms around Ruth and held her tight.

Ruth had lost weight in the four weeks she had been away from home; Elizabeth could feel the bones in her shoulders and her hips as they embraced.

'It's so good to have you home,' she said. 'It's wonderful. Come in, I've got lunch ready for you.'

'Where's Thomas?' Ruth said as she went into the hall.

'Upstairs having a sleep. I've just this minute put him down.'

Ruth started for the stairs and did not see the swift exchange of looks between Patrick and his mother.

'I'll come up too,' Patrick said and followed Ruth up the stairs.

She tiptoed into the nursery and leaned over the side of the cot. Thomas was asleep on his back, his eyelashes curled on his pink plump cheeks. His downy hair was close around his perfectly round skull; his mouth was a tiny rosebud. One hand was outflung above his head, the fingers curled into the palm. The other was thrown sideways as if the baby were quite abandoned into sleep. Ruth drank in the sight of him, as if she had been thirsty for him for months. 'Oh, God, he's so lovely,' she whispered.

Patrick leaned against the doorpost.

Ruth reached down and put her finger on the little wrist. There was a small crease where the plump arm met the plump hand; Ruth stroked it. Thomas stirred slightly in his sleep and turned his head. Ruth bent low over the cot and inhaled the warm scent of his breath. He smelled of warm skin, of baby shampoo, and of milk.

'Let's go down,' Patrick said. 'Mother won't want him woken up if she's just put him down.'

'You can go,' Ruth whispered.

He did not move.

Ruth leaned into the cot and let her lips and nose brush Thomas's fine hair, inhaling the scent of him, sensing the warm sweetness of him. She felt like some animal – a mother lion – reclaiming a lost cub. She wanted to strip him of his little romper suit and sniff him all over, she wanted to lick him, she wanted his naked warm skin against her own. With a sharp pang she realized that she had lost her chance to breast-feed him, and that only now was she ready for that intimacy.

'Come on,' Patrick said from the doorway.

Ruth glanced behind her. 'You go on down,' she said. She had forgotten he was there. 'I just want to see him for a moment. I'll be down in a minute.'

'I'll wait,' Patrick said.

'No, go on,' she said.

He did not move. Ruth kissed Thomas gently on his warm rounded skull but she felt Patrick's scrutiny on her back. She straightened up and tiptoed towards the door. 'He's so vulnerable,' she said. 'I had forgotten all about that. When I was ill I felt as if he were a little monster, draining the life out of me. Now that I can see him properly I can see what a delicate little thing he is. Completely defenceless.'

She slipped her hand in his arm and leaned against him. 'I'm so glad to be home,' she said. 'Thank you for being so patient, darling, you've been wonderful. I'm so glad to be home.'

Patrick kissed the top of her head and led the way from the nursery and down the stairs.

Elizabeth and Frederick were waiting for them in the sitting room with the decanter of sherry and glasses. There was a jug of fresh orange juice on the tray as well.

Frederick came forward and kissed Ruth with a word of greeting.

'Sherry, darling? Orange juice, Ruth?' Elizabeth asked.

Ruth hesitated. 'I can drink sherry,' she said awkwardly.

Elizabeth shot a quick look at Patrick.

'We thought you'd have to be on the wagon,' he said. 'We assumed you'd prefer juice.'

'I'd like an orange juice,' Ruth said. 'But I can drink alcohol if I want.'

Frederick poured the drinks with care and handed Ruth her juice and then sherry to Elizabeth and Patrick. 'Never does to mix them,' he observed to nobody in particular. 'Drugs and drink, never do mix.'

'I'm not taking any drugs,' Ruth said.

Again Elizabeth and Patrick exchanged that swift intimate glance.

'I thought you'd be on something, until you get to see the Bath therapist,' Patrick said.

Ruth shook her head. 'The whole point of going there was to get off the drugs,' she said. 'And it was only Amitriptyline, I wasn't a complete crackhead. And now I'm clean.'

Elizabeth's face was a study of polite interest. 'I'm very glad to hear it,' she said, ignoring the drug jargon as she would have ignored an obscenity.

Frederick glanced uncomfortably at her, uncertain as to how they should handle this glimpse into a world they could usually ignore.

'I wanted to say something to you, to you all,' Ruth started. She was reminded with a surprising rush of nostalgia how she would sometimes start talking in her group. She looked at the anxious faces around her – Frederick's distinguished craggy scowl, Patrick's handsome half-smile, Elizabeth's unaffected charm. 'I wanted to say that things were very bad for me from the moment Thomas was born – even before. And I'm really sorry that they turned out like that. I've thought through what was wrong and it will never be that bad again. I want to start afresh with you.' She looked at Patrick and then she looked from him to his mother and his father. 'I want you to give me another chance,' she said. 'You've been generous and kind and helpful to me and now I want to come to you as an equal and start again.'

There was a silence. Frederick cleared his throat. 'Fair enough,' he said. 'Everyone has a right to one mistake.'

Ruth's face lightened with sudden joy. 'Frederick, you're *so* straight!' she exclaimed with pleasure. 'Thank you.'

Elizabeth recoiled slightly at Ruth's easy use of his Christian name. 'Of course, my dear,' she said. 'You know we wanted to help you with Thomas and we've been glad to do everything we can. I'm so pleased that you are home and completely cured.'

Ruth hesitated at the word 'cured' with its implication of illness and a suffering patient, but she let it go. She was learning quickly that the outside world had retained its own codes and language even while she had been changing.

'I'll be a good mother to Thomas, and a good wife to Patrick,' she promised. 'And a good daughter-in-law to you.' She looked from Frederick to Elizabeth.

'Well, I'll drink to that,' Frederick said, robustly closing the conversation. He raised his glass. 'Here's to little

Ruth coming home and looking like our pretty girl again.'

The others raised their glasses to her, and Ruth – blushing slightly and smiling at the compliment – did not detect that she had been silenced.

'Lunch is served,' Elizabeth said, seeing Frederick had finished his sherry. 'Only a casserole, I'm afraid. I didn't know how long the journey would take you.'

'Lovely,' Ruth said.

They ate in the dining room. The weather had turned wintry, and halfway through the meal Elizabeth put on the lights. The sky outside the windows was dark and brooding, and there was a sudden scud of rain on the panes.

'I wanted to walk home,' Ruth said in disappointment. 'We'll have to drive.'

A sharp look of complicity passed between Elizabeth and her son. But neither of them spoke.

'When will Thomas wake?' Ruth asked. 'I so want to see him.'

Elizabeth glanced at her little gold watch. 'In about half an hour,' she said. 'If he doesn't wake, you can pick him up. He sleeps for about an hour and a half morning and afternoon now. Any more than that and he doesn't go off at night.'

'You'll have to take me through his day,' Ruth said. 'I'm completely out of practice. And Patrick said you thought he might have had a tooth coming! I couldn't believe it.'

'It was a false alarm,' Elizabeth said. 'I don't know how I came to mistake it. But one little cheek was scarlet

219

and so hot! It must have been a little fever he had. It was all over within the day.'

'Did you call the doctor?'

Elizabeth smiled. 'There was no need. I just gave him plenty to drink and kept an extra-special eye on him.'

Ruth nodded. 'And what's his weight?'

Elizabeth was vague. 'Oh! I haven't taken him to the clinic,' she said. 'Not since you went away.'

'But you're supposed to!' Ruth exclaimed. 'Every week!'

Elizabeth's smile was a little fixed. 'They only weigh them and measure them,' she said. 'I could see myself that he was thriving.'

'But they're supposed to see him . . .'

'It's not so important after six weeks,' Elizabeth said soothingly. 'I'd have taken him if he'd gone off his food or anything. But he was obviously so well . . .'

'I took him *every* week,' Ruth exclaimed.

Elizabeth had flushed slightly; she glanced at Patrick.

'Well, Mother didn't,' he said flatly. 'You can start again, now that you're back.'

Ruth looked from one to another, trying to read their expressions. 'I don't understand why not?' she said, looking at Elizabeth. 'Why didn't you take him?'

'I think I have explained,' Elizabeth said. Her voice was slightly higher with irritation.

'I don't understand,' Ruth said again stubbornly.

'I was embarrassed,' Elizabeth said, forced into honesty. 'I thought they would ask where his mother was, and I didn't want to say that she was mentally ill, that she was in a home. I thought it would go down in his records if I said that, and he would be branded, for the rest of his life, as a boy whose mother was mad.'

Ruth gasped. Frederick turned his attention to the rim of his water glass, and examined it minutely.

'They wouldn't write such a thing,' Ruth stammered. 'And I was not mad ... and in any case, it's *in* the notes, in my notes. I had postpartum depression, there's nothing shameful in it ...'

'It's in *your* notes,' Elizabeth said. 'But I saw no reason for it to be in Thomas's notes too. I saw no reason for him to have that mark against him. I didn't want them to know unless it was absolutely essential. And it was not absolutely essential. I didn't want the nurse to know, or the health visitor, or any passing social worker. I believe that private things should be kept private.'

'So where does everyone think I have been?' Ruth demanded.

'On holiday,' Elizabeth replied concisely. 'Brighton. A health farm.'

Ruth gasped. 'But surely no one would believe such nonsense! I'm not the sort of woman who goes for a month to a health farm!'

Elizabeth shrugged and glanced at Patrick, handing the whole difficult conversation over to him.

'What did you want us to say?' he asked. 'With my position, the press would have been onto me, wanting to know about you, and about Thomas. The social workers might have wanted to take Thomas into care. We had to think all this through, and we did the best we could. It's a bit rich coming back, all full of good intentions, and then telling us we've done everything wrong.'

Ruth recoiled at once from his anger. 'Yes, I'm sorry. I didn't mean to be critical.'

'Well, you were critical,' Patrick said. 'And to Mother who has worked to make Thomas happy night and day since you went off, and keep the family together.'

Ruth nodded. 'I'm sorry,' she said again.

'And it's all very well saying it should all have been done differently,' Patrick continued, his voice rising. 'But we might as well say that you shouldn't have given in to it. If you felt ill you should have told us. Taking handfuls of Amitriptyline and going out and getting drunk wasn't quite the way to cope with it.'

Ruth could feel her heart beating faster, and tears coming to her eyes. She had forgotten about the pub, about her car abandoned in the parking lot, about being drunk and drugged in front of her in-laws. She looked down at her hands clenched tight in her lap and felt her cheeks burn.

'If there's going to be any criticism . . .' Patrick started ominously.

'Steady the Buffs,' Frederick said simply. 'Water under the bridge, I think. Spilt milk.' He looked at Elizabeth. 'What about some coffee, darling?'

She rose automatically and started clearing the plates. Ruth got up too. 'Let me help.'

'Certainly not,' Elizabeth said coldly. She cleared the plates in silence and took them to the kitchen. Ruth sat at the table like a naughty child, her eyes downcast.

'You'll never believe the weather we've had,' Frederick said kindly. 'I think it's rained every day since the middle of November. All my late roses were completely washed out, and the river has flooded further down the valley.'

Ruth took a sip of water. 'Really?'

'The lane was running with water last Wednesday,' Frederick said. 'I warned them, when they wanted to build that new estate on the lower levels – you can work with Nature but you can't beat her. They bricked in the riverbank, and now it's completely overflowed and there will be water all through the ground floors of those new houses if it doesn't stop raining soon.'

'What a shame,' Ruth said automatically. She pressed her lips together to restrain the sobs, holding in her anger and her pain.

Elizabeth came in with the coffee and put a cup precisely before each of them, cream and brown sugar in the centre of the table.

'Yes, you can work with Nature but she always gets her own way in the end,' Frederick said into the continuing frosty silence. 'Still, it's a black cloud that has no silver lining – the floods have done my willow trees no end of good. You should take a stroll down and see them, my dear. They're very pretty, standing in the water. When the light is right you can see their reflection – rather picturesque.' He nodded at Patrick. 'You might take a snap of it. It might look rather well.'

'Coffee?' Elizabeth asked distantly.

Mutely Ruth passed her cup and held it while Elizabeth poured with a steady hand.

'I'm sorry, Elizabeth,' she said in a little voice.

Elizabeth hesitated. 'I would much rather you called me Mother, as you did before,' she said. 'Or does that have to change too?'

Twelve

THERE WAS a little cry from the nursery. Ruth leaped to her feet. 'I'll go!' Patrick wearily put down his cup and followed her. When he got to the nursery she was lifting Thomas from his cot, her hand under his firm little head, her arm around his compact body.

'Oh, Thomas!' she said. The ready tears were pouring down her face as she held his head to her cheek and inhaled the scent of him. His cry stilled as he was picked up, and he sensed the new feeling of being held by his mother, and the smell of her, and the gentle brush of her hair against his head.

'My baby,' she said.

Patrick softened at the sight of them, at the tenderness in Ruth's face, at the tiny movement as Thomas snuggled closer into her arms. In his first spontaneous gesture since she had come home, he stepped towards her and put his arms around them both. Ruth leaned back against him and tipped her head back against his shoulder. Patrick bent down and kissed her cheek, salty-tasting from her tears.

'I love him,' she said. 'I really love him, Patrick, whatever it looked like when I was ill. The love was all there, just waiting to come out.'

'I know,' he said. 'I'm glad you're back.'

They heard Elizabeth coming up the stairs, and Patrick immediately released her and stepped away.

'I just wanted to make sure you had everything you need,' Elizabeth said pleasantly. 'Patrick knows where everything is, I think. There are his clean nappies there, and a clean romper suit there,' she gestured to the chest of drawers. 'He's generally wet through and needs to be changed at once.'

Ruth looked around for a changing mat to put him down. There was none.

'Oh! Of course!' Elizabeth exclaimed. 'I sit on the chair and change him on my knee. I'm so old-fashioned!'

Ruth smiled in relief at the warmer tone. 'I've never learned to do it,' she said. 'I'll have to put him on the floor.'

'Oh no!' Elizabeth said. 'Too draughty with this miserable weather. Give him here, and I'll get him dressed in a moment and bring him down to you.' She took Thomas from his mother's arms and sat on the rocking chair in the corner of the nursery. Competently, she stripped him of his damp romper suit, and unpinned the towelling nappy. Ruth did not leave, as she had been told to do, but stayed to watch.

'A towelling nappy?'

'I can't bear the disposable kind,' Elizabeth said. 'I think it's so unhygienic!'

'Unhygienic?' Ruth protested. 'I don't know anyone who uses real nappies these days!'

Elizabeth, with the baby securely on her lap, looked up and laughed. 'I just do it the way I always have done,' she said. 'In the old days we put the nappies in to soak and washed them through at the end of the day, and the

225

baby had clean, warm, dry towelling nappies every time he needed them. You never run out when the shops are shut, you're not putting chemicals against the baby's skin, and you're not polluting the environment with all that paper waste!'

She wrapped the clean nappy around Thomas and pinned it skilfully with one pin at the front, and then tied a waterproof cover on top. Before he could protest, she had pulled a clean romper suit over his head and thrust his little hands and legs into the holes and fastened him up.

'There!' she said with satisfaction. 'Now you're ready to go to your mummy.' She handed Thomas back to Ruth and busied herself with picking up the wet suit and clearing away the wet nappy. Ruth took Thomas back into her arms but he smelled different. There was the pleasing aroma of clean towelling and ironed laundry, but he smelled slightly of Elizabeth's washing powder, and his head and hands smelled pleasantly of Elizabeth's perfume. By taking him and changing his clothes, she had somehow made him her baby again; Ruth felt like an intruder.

She turned and went slowly downstairs with Thomas held to her shoulder. 'That's a sight for sore eyes!' Frederick exclaimed, and drew her into the sitting room. 'Let's hope he's not forgotten you!'

For a moment Ruth looked stricken, and then she cuddled Thomas a little closer. 'Well, we'll just have to start from the beginning again,' she said. She sat on the chair and laid the baby along her knees so that she could look into his open clear face. 'Hello, Thomas,' she said lovingly. 'Hello.'

Elizabeth came in and smiled at the two of them. 'I

think we should light the fire, Frederick,' she said. 'It's so dark and cold.'

Frederick stepped forward and bent over the grate and started to lay the fire with kindling and small pieces of coal.

'Perhaps you should have a rest, Ruth?' Elizabeth offered. 'I can have Thomas if you would like a lie-down. You'll find all your things in your bedroom.'

Ruth glanced at Patrick, who had followed his mother into the room. 'I thought we'd be getting home,' she said uncertainly.

His quick glance to his mother should have warned her, but Ruth had spent four weeks with people who were committed to clarity and frankness, and she had lost the skill of decoding silences. 'I want to take Thomas home,' she said, after a moment.

Elizabeth said nothing; she waited for Patrick to speak.

'I thought we'd stay here for a while,' he said. 'The heating has been off at home, and the place needs to be warmed through and aired before we can take Thomas back, anyway. And there's nothing to eat in the house. We've been living here. I just shut up the cottage.'

'I've kept an eye on it, don't fret,' Frederick assured her. 'When I take Thomas out on a walk we often stroll down that way. It's safe and sound.'

'Well, I'll go down there now and put the heating on,' Ruth said. She still had not understood. 'It should be warmed up by this evening. We can go home at Thomas's bedtime.'

Patrick cleared his throat. 'I thought we'd stay here for a while,' he said again.

Ruth looked from Patrick to Elizabeth to Frederick as

227

she realized a decision had been made. 'How long for?' she asked simply.

'A couple of weeks.'

'Weeks?'

'Yes.'

Ruth had the strange sense of the ground falling away underneath her feet again. 'What d'you mean, Patrick? Why can't we go home?'

At the sound of the alarm in her voice Thomas's face puckered up and he let out a little wail. Elizabeth started forward at his cry and then checked the movement. Deliberately, she went and sat in a chair at the fireside and looked at the flames, which were curling around the kindling in the cold grate. Frederick sat back on his heels and looked at the fire.

'Don't upset Thomas,' Patrick said. 'Let's leave it for now.'

Ruth took a breath. 'I won't upset Thomas,' she said quietly. 'I want to go to our home. Is there something wrong, something you're not telling me?'

Patrick glanced at his mother.

'We were just thinking what was best for you, Ruth,' she said gently. 'You've only come out of hospital this morning. You don't want to overdo things in your first week.'

'We thought you'd want a bit of help,' Patrick agreed. 'And Thomas is used to being here. A bit of continuity is what he needs, and I would feel much happier at going off to work and leaving you if I knew you were here.'

Ruth nodded slowly. 'I see that,' she said. 'But I am quite better now. I wasn't in hospital because I had a broken leg, or a physical illness. I don't need to rest.

I was unhappy, but I understand it now. I feel quite different.'

'Well, you may feel different, but we feel the same,' Patrick said bluntly. 'We saw that you couldn't cope with Thomas, and it got worse and worse and none of us knew what to do. We don't want that happening again.'

'Neither do I,' Ruth said quickly. 'It won't.'

'So it would suit everyone if we stayed here for a while, until we see how things are going. To reassure ourselves.' He glanced at Elizabeth for confirmation. She made an infinitesimal nod. 'Keep things under control,' he said.

Ruth thought of the lessons of her group. 'And how will we know that everything is all right?' she asked.

Patrick glanced at his mother. 'We'll know,' she said with a little smile. 'We'll all know that things have turned out perfectly, Ruth. We'll just know it.'

'Then how will we know if things are *not* going well?' Ruth persisted.

'Oh, I hope that won't arise!'

'But if it does arise?'

'If you are ill again?'

Ruth shook her head. 'I won't be ill again. But how will we know that things are not going well enough for us to go back to the little house? Who is to decide? And on what basis?'

Elizabeth shrugged. 'I don't even want to think about it,' she said. 'You tell me that you're well now, and that's enough for me, Ruth dear. You'll be the one that decides. Let's take it one day at a time and see how it goes.'

Ruth paused for a moment, and then the warmth of Thomas against her shoulder gave her renewed strength.

'The thing is,' she said slowly, 'that I don't want to live here. I know you've been wonderful –' she looked from Frederick to Elizabeth – 'but we have our own home and our own lives to lead, and I want to go to our own home, and start again.'

'And so you shall!' Elizabeth said firmly. 'As soon as you are completely well, you'll start life again in your new home, and we'll be the first to congratulate you.'

Ruth hesitated, looking from Elizabeth's smiling face to Patrick's determined one. 'I really have to make this clear. I am not living here permanently.'

'Of course not,' Elizabeth said pleasantly. 'You have your own life to lead – why, we've even replaced your car!'

'My car?'

Frederick rose from his place before the fire. 'Your old car never turned up, I'm afraid. Whoever took it from the pub car park probably had it resprayed and resold within the week. And your insurance didn't cover you for theft since the keys were left in it.'

Ruth flushed scarlet with shame at the memory.

'Bought you another,' Frederick said gruffly. 'Little runabout. Welcome-home present. Show of support.'

'Because we know you need your freedom,' Elizabeth supplemented sweetly.

Ruth felt the easy tears rise into her eyes again. 'You're so good to me!' The words were wrenched out of her by their generosity. 'Thank you.'

Elizabeth came forward and took Thomas from her. 'We just want you to be happy,' she said gently. 'Let's all be happy, now.'

* * *

Ruth bathed Thomas in the yellow bathroom that night and Elizabeth tidied the linen cupboard on the landing outside the bathroom so that she could listen at the door and make sure that Thomas was safe.

When Ruth came down with Thomas all pink and smiling and clean, his grandfather held him while Ruth made his bottle, and then handed him back with a good-night kiss.

'He likes to be rocked while he has his bottle, and then when he has finished his bottle, you put him up on your shoulder and rock him like that,' Elizabeth instructed. 'You'll feel him go all limp and his breathing deepen when he has fallen asleep, and then you can put him in his cot. I leave the night-light on, and he has his duvet cover just up to his tummy.'

Ruth nodded and took her son up the stairs to the nursery.

'You go,' Elizabeth said in an undertone to Frederick. 'You can read the newspaper in our bedroom and just keep an ear open. Just in case.'

He nodded obediently, and folded his paper under his arm and followed Ruth and his grandson up the stairs.

'She's bound to notice after a while,' Patrick said to his mother. He followed her out into the kitchen and poured them both a gin and tonic while she sliced vegetables for the evening meal.

'I think we can be tactful,' she said. 'There are three of us; we can take it in turns. I think we can always have someone within earshot.'

'We won't go back to the little house until I am confident that Thomas is safe with her,' Patrick said firmly. 'Whether she likes it or not.'

She glanced at her son. 'That must be your first duty,' she said. 'Your first duty must be to our boy.'

Ruth's days took on a new routine, living at the farmhouse with Patrick and his parents. If Thomas woke in the night she went to him and rocked him to sleep again. Then he would often sleep until eight o'clock, so Patrick got up and left for work without disturbing her. Elizabeth and Frederick were always up from seven, Elizabeth to cook Patrick's breakfast and see him off to work, Frederick to eat breakfast and go out for his morning stroll with the dog around the fields.

When Thomas woke, he and Ruth would go downstairs for breakfast, Ruth in her dressing gown and Thomas in his sleep suit. Elizabeth would have Ruth's toast and coffee ready, and she would feed Thomas while Ruth ate, and then take him upstairs to dress him while Ruth had a shower.

If the day was sunny and bright, Ruth would wrap Thomas warmly and put him in the pram for Frederick to push him a little way down the lane until he fell asleep. Then he would come home and draw the pram into the house, through the French windows of his gunroom, where Thomas could sleep undisturbed by the noise of housework in the rest of the house. Frederick would potter at his workbench or his desk, tying flies for the fishing season, or writing letters while Thomas slept in his pram in the corner of the room.

Ruth had nothing to do. Elizabeth would not accept any help in the house; she said she had her own way of doing things and there were no chores to do. Instead, Ruth started walking down the lane to her own house, the little house, vacuuming and dusting the cold rooms, cleaning the windows, and tidying the cupboards, and then locking it all up and walking back to the farmhouse in time for lunch.

Ruth always picked Thomas up after his morning sleep, changed his nappy and played with him before lunch. Obediently, she dressed him in the bulky towelling nappies that Elizabeth preferred, and fed him with Elizabeth's freshly puréed dinners. In the afternoon Ruth would play with Thomas in the living room, or in her own bedroom. She did not notice that someone was always with them. If they were in the living room together, playing on the mat before the fire, then Frederick would be in his chair, behind the *Daily Telegraph*. If they were in her bedroom or in the nursery, then Elizabeth would be cleaning the bath, or doing the flowers on the landing, or dusting the picture frames. Ruth, absorbed in finding a new and valuable intimacy with her baby, simply did not notice that she was constantly supervised.

Patrick, secure in the knowledge that his child was safe, came home in time for dinner at seven-thirty, sometimes only just in time to kiss Thomas goodnight.

'You hardly see him,' Ruth complained.

'I see him at the weekends,' he said. 'And besides, when you were away I saw him all the time. He needs his mother now.'

Elizabeth cooked an impressive dinner every night, with either a starter, entrée and cheeseboard, or with a main course and a homemade pudding. After dinner they watched television in the sitting room, the nine-o'clock news followed by whatever programme was on BBC1 or BBC2. If Frederick wanted to watch something different, he went to his gunroom. If Patrick wanted to watch either of the independent channels, he went upstairs to their bedroom and watched it on the small television up there. It was an unwritten and unchallenged rule that they watched only the BBC in the sitting room. The only time the rule was broken was when one of Patrick's documentaries was on, and then it was watched and videotaped in solemn silence. Some evenings Patrick took Ruth out for a drink, once to the cinema. But Patrick's work was still so demanding that during the week he preferred to go to bed early, and he slept heavily.

At the weekend Patrick and Ruth took Thomas to the park, or out for a walk, or for a stroll around the city centre, window-shopping. On Saturday night they generally left him with Elizabeth and went out for dinner. On Sunday morning they slept in, and Elizabeth had him all to herself until eleven o'clock, when they all went to church. After Sunday lunch they went for a walk. It was all as it had been when Patrick and Ruth used to visit on Sundays, except now the visit had been prolonged indefinitely, and sometimes Ruth feared that she would never get home.

On Thursday afternoon, in the second week, Elizabeth had Thomas all afternoon when Ruth went in to see the Bath therapist – a woman called Clare Leesome. She had consulting rooms on the ground floor of her house, a solid Victorian house, on the outskirts of Bath. Ruth rang the doorbell and Clare showed her into a room furnished with soft chairs and large floor cushions. Clare Leesome sat on one chair, Ruth sat on another. The house was very quiet. Clare asked Ruth a few questions and then sat very still, letting her slowly reveal more and more.

She started with the clinic, and the discovery of her grief at her parents' death. Clare Leesome nodded; she took no notes. Ruth cried as she spoke of the death of her mother, and the therapist watched her cry as if tears were a sign of health, an appropriate expression, and not a symptom of illness that should be apologetically mopped up. They agreed that they would meet weekly for Ruth to talk through the loss of her parents. It was to be an open-ended arrangement, to last as long as Ruth wished.

'I don't want to be one of these people with an analyst for the rest of my life,' Ruth said.

Clare smiled. 'No,' she said. 'I don't work like that either. But you have been through a difficult time; there are bound to be things that will come up for you that you will want to talk over.'

'And will I be happy?' Ruth demanded. 'Will I stop crying and crying and feel steadily happy?'

'If your life gives you cause to feel happy,' Clare replied. 'If you have a sad and troublesome daily life, then you will feel sad and troubled. But if you have a happy and fulfilling life, then you will feel happy and fulfilled. All we can do is to make sure that you feel the emotion that is relevant – so that you're not unhappy when everything is going well. It will be up to you – when you are in touch with your feelings and can make the judgments – to decide whether your life needs to change or not.'

Ruth telephoned David at Radio Westerly at the end of the second week. For some reason, which she did not choose to examine, she used the telephone in the little house, when she was visiting one morning.

'Hello.'

'Ruth! God! How wonderful to hear from you! Are you out?'

'No, I drove my motorbike and jumped over the wire, what d'you think?'

'I think you're out.'

'I am.'

'And – are you all right?'

'Yes. Look, I'm so sorry that you were stuck in the middle. I can hardly remember the pub, but they tell me you had to bring me home. I imagine it was dreadful.'

He chuckled. 'God, Ruth, you will never know. They were all frightfully British and restrained about it. I should think Patrick wanted to murder me.'

'How awful. I *am* sorry, David.'

'Think nothing of it,' he said grandly. 'I only wish I had known what to do. I did feel that I had abandoned you, and then I heard you'd gone off for a – er – a rest.'

'You did the right thing,' she assured him. 'And they found me an excellent residential therapy centre. I wasn't locked up screaming, you know. It was an excellent place and I'm really well now.'

'Want to come and get drunk then?' he offered mis-chievously.

She giggled. 'Sounds good to me.'

'Lunch?'

'Elizabeth baby-sits for me on Thursdays. I go into Bath to see a therapist. I could have lunch with you first.'

'Twelve o'clock at the Black Bull?'

'OK,' she said. 'If there's any problem you can phone me. I'll give you the number.'

'I've got the number.'

There was a little pause. 'I'm not at home. We're at Patrick's parents' house.'

He was instantly alert. 'Oh. Why's that?'

'They wanted us to stay until we are all settled down again. I think they wanted to know I was going to be all right.'

'So when do you go back home?'

'It was supposed to be this weekend. But Patrick has to go away overnight, and they don't want me on my own in the little house, so it'll be the middle of next week.'

He thought for a moment. 'I'll see you for lunch, anyway.' He thought about wishing her luck. For an odd superstitious moment he had a sense of her as facing obstacles that were almost too great for her. 'Without fail,' he said, as if he could will her through the days. 'Is Thomas OK?'

'He's fine.'

'And Patrick?'

'Fine.'

'See you on Thursday then,' he said.

When the phone clicked and she was gone he felt as if he had lost her to the Cleary family all over again.

The decision that Ruth should stay at the farmhouse while Patrick was away was made almost by default. Ruth had thought that they would move out on Friday, but then the meeting in London came up, and Patrick would not be home until Sunday. He said he could not face the packing and the disruption and the moving of all Thomas's toys and things when he had just got home;

he said he would do it in the following week. Thus the third week of the visit started.

'I could move us,' Ruth said brightly at dinner on Tuesday night. 'You don't need to do anything, Patrick. I could do it all.'

'I want to help,' Patrick said. 'I just can't do it for a couple of days. There's no problem, is there? We can move into the little house at the weekend.'

'I just feel that we're rather in the way ...' Ruth started.

'Oh, no,' Elizabeth said swiftly. 'You know we love having you here. Don't feel that, Ruth! We'll be quite lost without you.'

'Give it another week,' Frederick advised. 'Then you can go back in time for Christmas.'

'Thomas's first Christmas,' Elizabeth said, smiling. 'What are you going to get him?'

'Is he too small for one of those bouncy things?' Patrick asked. 'Those bouncy things that you hang on doorways?'

'I always worry that they'll collapse!' Elizabeth said.

'Not if it's properly hung,' Frederick advised. 'I could put you up a good solid butcher's hook in the kitchen ceiling, if you wanted. Screw it into the beams. He'd have to bring the whole house down with him to get it down.'

'Chap at work says his daughter spends half the day in hers,' Patrick said. 'He says she loves it.'

'But when shall we go home?' Ruth asked abruptly.

Patrick leaned over and patted her hand. 'It's lovely to see you so well and anxious to get back,' he said affectionately. 'But I don't want to rush back.'

'And you're more than welcome here, Ruth,' Elizabeth

said. 'I should hate to see you getting overtired again.'

'I wasn't overtired,' Ruth said carefully. 'I was depressed. I was suffering from the mental illness of depression. But now I have recovered, and I am continuing with therapy to make sure that I stay well. We'll have to go back sooner or later; I'd like to get back and get on with our lives.'

There was a brief silence. 'What does your therapist say?' Patrick asked.

'Nothing . . .' Ruth replied, surprised. 'That is, I haven't asked her. She hasn't said anything about where we live. It hasn't come up.'

'She doesn't know that you want to move back to living on your own, without any support?' Patrick asked heavily.

Ruth was lost for words. 'No,' she said. 'We've not discussed it.'

'Perhaps you should see what she thinks,' Elizabeth said gently, a glance at Patrick. 'When you go on Thursday. Talk it over with her.'

'Two heads are better than one,' Frederick added. 'Ask the experts.'

'It's not really anything to do with her,' Ruth said. 'We talk about my feelings, not my living accommodation.'

'But she'd have an opinion,' Patrick urged. 'Ask her what she thinks. Then we'll have something to go on.'

Ruth felt absurdly blocked, as if she had been driven into a cul de sac. 'All right,' she said grudgingly. 'I'll ask her on Thursday afternoon.'

* * *

On Wednesday morning Patrick telephoned Clare Lee-some and left a message on her answering machine. On Wednesday afternoon she called him back. When she said her name he got up and shut the door to his office, with elaborate caution. 'Thank you for calling back,' he said.

'Certainly.'

'It's about my wife, Ruth Cleary.'

'Yes?'

'As you may know, we're living at home with my parents. When she went into the clinic it was the only way we could manage with the baby, and it seemed a good thing that she should have the continued support when she came out.'

Clare Leesome wondered at the smoothness of Patrick's sentences, and thought it was a prepared speech.

'She now wants to move back into our own house, and we have suggested that she take your advice.'

'Oh,' Clare said unhelpfully.

'Our feeling is that she needs the support of our family,' Patrick said confidingly. 'The baby is a very active, wakeful child, and with her history . . .' he tailed off but she did not interrupt him. 'She was violent in the clinic with another patient, and she was short-tempered with Thomas . . .' Still Clare Leesome held her irritating silence. 'We feel that she should stay living with my family until we can be sure that she has completely recovered.'

There was a complete and unhelpful silence.

'I wanted your advice,' Patrick said.

'Concerning what?' Clare asked, as if Patrick's lengthy preamble had never been said.

Patrick curbed his temper. 'I wanted you to advise me

that we are doing the right thing in keeping her at home with all of us,' he said.

She said nothing for a moment. 'I'm not sure,' she said eventually. 'I don't have enough facts to make a judgment.'

'The facts are as I have described them,' Patrick said tightly. 'And she has this history of not being able to care for Thomas . . .'

'I wouldn't call it a history exactly,' Clare said thoughtfully. 'I'd call it an episode.'

'Well, what more do you need to know? History, episode, the facts are that she was incapable of caring for a newborn baby on her own.'

'Oh, yes,' Clare said pleasantly. 'As are most people . . .'

'So I want to know that you agree that it is best for her to live with my family until we are sure she is better.'

'As I say,' Clare repeated, 'I couldn't judge.'

'Surely you must have an opinion!'

Clare noted Patrick's rising tone. 'It depends on so many things,' she said. 'Her relationship with you, with your mother, with your father. The family dynamic. Her contact with the child, issues about privacy, issues about sharing. I cannot say what Ruth thinks. I think, if it were me, I would rather live in my own house.'

Patrick wanted to shout at her. He held the telephone away from his ear for a few moments and took a couple of deep breaths. 'But we are talking about a disturbed woman,' he said.

'Oh, no,' Clare said briskly. 'If you mean psychotic – she's certainly not that!'

'I don't know the jargon!'

241

'No,' Clare agreed.

'I'm saying she's unstable!'

'If you mean neurotic – she's not that either.'

'She needs help,' Patrick insisted.

'I think she is getting help,' Clare said mildly. 'Regular therapeutic help.'

'She needs more than that,' Patrick said. 'She needs supervision. I want you to tell her that she would be best looked after at home with our family.'

'No,' Clare said decidedly. 'I cannot tell her any such thing.'

'But I just explained . . .'

'You explained why *you* think she should be looked after at home by your family. But I don't have enough facts to judge.' She paused for a moment. 'Indeed, on what I have seen of your wife, and on what you have told me, I think she would do better to live in her own house.'

Patrick felt his temper flare. 'I have told you she would do better to stay where she is! But you won't listen!'

There was a complete silence.

'I'm sorry,' Patrick said. 'I'm under terrible stress. I must ask you to overlook that. I can't tell you how worried and unhappy I have been about her . . . and it has been months of worry.'

'Of course,' Clare said pleasantly.

'I just want to know that she and the baby are safe,' Patrick said in his gentlest, most engaging voice, 'while I am at work and cannot keep an eye on them.'

'I am certain that she is perfectly safe with the baby,' Clare said. 'I am convinced that she can look after him perfectly well. And if there were to be any trouble at all, then you would have plenty of warning, and time to

242

devise strategies for coping with any emerging problem.'

'I would feel easier if she were being cared for by my mother,' Patrick said.

Clare nodded. 'Perhaps you would,' she said. 'But that is not the issue, as I understand it.'

'I would prefer it if she stayed with my parents,' Patrick said again, as if emphasis could achieve his wishes.

'I think you should follow her preference in this,' Clare said levelly. 'Has she said what she would like to do?'

'No,' Patrick lied quickly. 'No. Not at all.'

Clare heard the lie at once. 'Then I suggest you ask her,' she said simply.

'Will you advise her to stay with my parents, if she asks you tomorrow?'

'No,' Clare said firmly. 'I will advise her to do what she wants to do. I think her best interests lie in determining her own life.'

'Thank you for talking to me then, Ms Leesome,' Patrick said. He emphasized the 'Ms' slightly; it made him feel better. It named her as an eccentric, as a feminist, as a troublemaker. 'I assume that this conversation has all been in confidence?'

'Very well,' she said.

'Thank you,' Patrick said. 'Good-bye.' He waited until he heard the click of the telephone before he crashed the handset down into the receiver. 'Snotty bitch,' he said aloud. 'Snotty know-all bitch.'

Thirteen

DAVID WAS LATE at the Black Bull pub, and when he arrived Ruth was sitting at a corner table with a mineral water before her. He waved to her, bought himself a pint of lager, and then threaded his way through the tables, which were busy with shoppers and businessmen eating sandwiches.

'You look fabulous!' he said. 'I can't tell you how good it is to see you.' He sat down beside her and scanned her face. 'Lost weight,' he commented. 'Pink cheeks, bright eyes – looks like a good place, your clinic.'

'Health farm,' Ruth said promptly. 'Cold showers and cucumber face masks. Actually, that's what they're telling everyone.'

David looked puzzled. 'What?'

'Patrick's family – well, his mother mostly – when anyone asked after me she told them I had gone to a health farm to recuperate from the effort of childbirth. Just as well for her that I've come back looking well.'

'Why does she tell people that?'

Ruth giggled, and it was her old reckless giggle. 'The *shame*, darling! She seems to think that I was completely bonkers and we must make sure the neighbours don't know.'

David nodded. 'The stigma of mental illness,' he said pompously. 'I shall do a programme on it.'

'It's a real problem for her,' Ruth said more seriously. 'And it's funny because she was the one to see that things were going badly, and she did the most to help. But when it comes to naming names she'd rather look the other way. According to her I was overtired, and now I am nicely rested.'

David nodded. 'She was really concerned about you when I met her.'

Ruth nodded. 'She is nice,' she said. 'And she's all-of-a-piece, you know? In the way that modern women aren't. She knows her job – which is home and support and child care – and she does it really well. She has no ideas about feminism or freedom or career or any of that stuff. And it makes her very powerful. The home is completely hers, and it is run without a hitch. She aims at perfection and she gets very close.'

David nodded. 'The sort of woman a successful man needs to have behind him. Would she marry me?'

She took a sip and shook her head. 'Oh, no! Women like her are very careful with their choices. They know that they are choosing a career as well as a husband. They choose a successful man, and then they get behind him. I can't see you getting the gold-spoon treatment in the same way.'

'And what about her husband? Your father-in-law?'

Ruth smiled. 'He's rather a sweetie,' she said. 'He's very quiet compared to her. But he's solid, you know? He's dependable. I could tell you what he thinks about every single thing. You know where you are with him.'

'And where are you with him?'

A shadow crossed her face. 'Well, I was Patrick's girlfriend, which made me a pretty young thing . . .' almost unconsciously she had mimicked Frederick's staccato speech. David grinned, hearing it. 'And then I was his wife, so I became the daughter-in-law, outside comment, above reproach. And then I had Thomas, so I was a lovely girl, and a wonderful mother. And then I had my breakdown, so I was a jolly poor show. And now I'm better, and I think I'm becoming a plucky little thing.'

David laughed aloud. 'A plucky little thing?'

She grinned at him. 'Yes. But you can see why I like him so much. You don't have to do much to earn his approval. You just have to stay inside a boundary of good behaviour – and it's quite a wide boundary.'

'But what if you crossed it?' David asked curiously. 'What if you did drugs, or had an affair, or abandoned the baby and Patrick? What would happen then?'

'Oh I'd drop off the edge of the world!' she said gaily. 'I'd become a *jolly* poor show, and he'd never talk about me ever again.'

David nodded. 'Wow,' he said. 'It's a world I know nothing about. My family don't have that sort of confidence.' He thought for a moment and then he smiled. 'And we bear grudges,' he said. 'Nobody drops out of our world for bad behaviour; we resurrect them every Christmas and have the quarrel all over again.'

She chuckled. A waiter came to the table and they ordered two rounds of sandwiches.

'So what are you doing today, without Thomas and all?' David asked.

'I see a therapist on Thursdays,' Ruth said. He liked how she told him without hesitation. She had caught none of her mother-in-law's shame. 'She's just round the corner from here.'

'What d'you do?'

'Nothing really. From the outside it looks completely boring. I talk, and she listens, and every now and then she says something. And it's completely illuminating, and I see things in a quite different way.'

He shifted uneasily. 'I'd hate you to change.'

She shook her head. 'I'm changing already,' she said. 'There were always two of me – the confident one at work, and the dependent baby-me at home.'

'I didn't know that,' he said. 'I only knew the one at work. I like her.'

'You may not have seen the baby one, but you saw the consequences,' she said swiftly. 'You saw how I wouldn't stand up to Patrick, how whatever he wanted – we did. You saw me lose my job without a fight and move house and even have Thomas because that was what Patrick wanted.'

David felt a quiver of apprehension at her plain speaking. 'Are you saying you didn't want any of that?'

'You know I didn't,' she said simply.

'How could he make you do it?'

She shrugged. 'I couldn't bear to contradict him, I suppose,' she said. 'I wanted him to love me more than anything else. I couldn't ever make myself stand up to him.' She glanced at him and laughed aloud. 'You look astounded,' she said.

He took a gulp of beer. 'I *am* astounded! I did see a lot of that, and I couldn't quite understand how at work you could be so – I don't know – assertive –'

'Bossy,' she interpolated.

'Bossy,' he agreed. 'Bossy in the newsroom, and then rush home at six o'clock frightened that you'd be late in cooking supper for him.'

She nodded. 'I think a lot of women are like that anyway,' she said fairly. 'And I did think he was rather a catch, you know. I did think I was lucky to get him, and that I'd better make an effort to hold on to him. And also . . . I was completely besotted with him. I would have done anything for him. I felt completely grateful and delighted that he loved me. And I loved it when he was pleased with me.' She stopped and gave a little laugh. 'It sounds absurd now,' she said. 'But I felt like I was a not very attractive kid, and that if I tried really hard, he might let me tag along.'

David made a face of distaste, and took another swallow of beer. 'I see,' he said.

She nodded. 'A bit pitiful, wasn't it? If I'd had parents who loved me I'd never have been so dependent. Or if I'd been older when I first met him . . .' she shrugged. 'Anyway, that's how it was. I met him when I was very young and very alone, and very impressionable. And when he loved me I was tremendously grateful.'

'And now?' David asked.

To his relief she looked suddenly radiant. 'Now we start all over again!' she said. 'Now we have to make a marriage between equals, rather than between the wonderful Patrick and the little drip: me. It's a real opportunity. It's a real challenge!'

He took up his sandwich and bit into it. 'I thought you might leave him,' he said bluntly.

She shook her head. She was very certain. 'No,' she said. 'Because none of it is his fault. I love him, and he's my husband, and the father of my son . . . and he's done nothing wrong. He accepted the relationship I offered, and when it all went wrong for me he did the very best

248

he could to get it right again. You can't fault him.'

David thought for a moment of Patrick's charming selfishness. 'I wouldn't call him exactly faultless. It suited him too,' he observed.

She was eating, and she nodded with her mouth full. She swallowed and said, 'Yes, but he didn't force me into anything. He made it clear it was what he wanted, and then I went along with everything. As soon as I have the strength to make my own choices, we'll have to share the decision making. We'll be equal.'

David was quiet for a moment – wondering how far he could go. Then he decided to speak out. 'No, you won't,' he said finally. 'You'll never be equal.'

'Why not?'

'Because the set-up is weighted against you. He's got a good career and you have a baby. He earns money, and gives you some of it. He controls an office with a budget and half a dozen staff, and you control a little house. He's a man, and you're a woman, and most of all – when you count his family on your doorstep – there are three of them and only one of you.'

He was afraid that he had said too much because the brightness had drained from her face, and she pushed her plate to one side. She nodded.

'I'm sorry,' he said. 'I'm a big mouth. Sorry, Ruth. I spoke out of turn.'

She put her hand out to him and touched the back of his hand. 'It's OK,' she said. 'It's OK. And anyway . . . you're right.' She took her glass and sipped her water. 'I'll have to take it slowly,' she said thoughtfully. 'And I have to get it right this time.'

*   *   *

'And what did Ms Leesome have to say today?' Patrick demanded at dinner that night.

'Why d'you call her that?' Ruth asked.

'What?'

'Ms Leesome. She's single. You can call her Miss. Or you can call her Clare.'

'I thought that was how she was to be addressed.'

'Absolute nonsense,' Frederick said loyally from the foot of the table. 'Much better to do it as they do in France. If you're under thirty, you're *Mademoiselle*; if you're over, you're *Madame*. Then everyone knows where they are. I can't bear this *Ms Ms* business.'

'It *is* a very ugly sound,' Elizabeth agreed. 'Like the word *miserable*. Patrick used to say it when he was ill, when he was a little boy. He used to say: "I feel a bit mis."'

Ruth smiled. 'Did he?'

'All right,' Patrick said. 'How was Miss, Mrs, or Clare Leesome today?'

'She was fine,' Ruth said. 'I did ask her about whether we should stay here, and she said it was completely my decision. I asked her whether she thought I would be OK on my own with Thomas while you were out at work, and she said that only I could be the judge of that and that it must be our decision: yours and mine.'

'Oh,' Patrick said. 'Did she express no opinion at all?'

'She said it should be our own decision,' Ruth said.

'And so it should,' Frederick said fairly. 'Provided the medics are happy, you two can do as you wish.' He nodded kindly at Ruth. 'But you're always welcome here, my dear, for as long as you like.'

'I would rather stay a little longer,' Patrick said thoughtfully. 'I've got rather a busy time coming up, and the little house is so cold and dark in winter.'

'Certainly,' his mother said. 'Ruth, do keep us company for another week or two, and you and I can go down and get your house ready for you to move back. You could go back over Christmas, when Patrick has some time off.'

'But it's only 8 December now,' Ruth protested. 'And we were supposed to go home last weekend.'

'Let me sort out the Christmas holiday time,' Patrick offered. 'I'll take some extra days off and we can go down to the house together, get everything ready, and move together over the Christmas holiday.'

'There's hardly anything to do,' Ruth protested.

'Oh, there's all Thomas's toys, and most of his clothes. There's all Patrick's clothes and books and a lot of your things,' Elizabeth protested. 'And I think the chimneys need sweeping, and it would be nice to have the windows cleaned outside and in before you go back. Why don't we take the opportunity for a little spring cleaning, and then you can go back and make a fresh start?'

'I just thought we could put the heating on, and go back,' Ruth protested.

Frederick smiled at her and put his warm hand over her own. 'I think you're outnumbered,' he said gently. 'Retreat gracefully, that's my advice, little Ruth! Live to fight another day.'

For a moment she did not think of the kindness of his advice or the roguish smile on his face. She thought of her situation as she had described it to David, and his certainty that she would never win against the Cleary family because it would always be three against one.

'I'll retreat then,' she said with a weak smile. 'But

we are agreed – aren't we – that we'll be home for Christmas?'

'It's a promise,' Patrick said easily, and smiled at his mother.

They were not. When Ruth and Elizabeth left Thomas with Frederick and went down the drive to the little house to put on the heating and check that the chimneys had been properly swept, the place was icy cold, the heating had not come on. There was a problem with the thermostat. Elizabeth telephoned the heating contractor, while Ruth prowled unhappily around the cold bedrooms, but it was the week before Christmas and he was very busy.

'You would have spent Christmas Day with us anyway,' Elizabeth said consolingly as Ruth came slowly downstairs. 'So it's only an extra couple of nights.'

Ruth looked so disappointed Elizabeth thought she might cry.

'Don't look so desolate, darling!'

'But I wanted to put up decorations in my own home. I wanted Thomas in his nursery on Christmas morning!'

Elizabeth's smile was understanding. 'Of course,' she said. 'And it's such a shame that it hasn't worked out like that. But perhaps you'll do our decorations at home? I have a wonderful box of things, some bells and scarves from India, and some from Africa. I have a whole box of Victorian decorations from my mother. You might like to look through them, and you can pick out what you like and take them home with you for next year. This year you can be with us, and next year we can come to you. You've got a lot of Christmases ahead of you, Ruth dear. It's not just this one.'

'I wanted to spend Christmas here,' Ruth said stubbornly.

Elizabeth nodded. 'Next year,' she assured her. 'And anyway, you wouldn't have anything prepared for this year, surely?'

Ruth did not understand her. 'Prepared?'

'Your Christmas pudding? Your Christmas cake? Your dried flowers?'

Ruth looked completely blank.

'Don't you make your own?' Elizabeth asked.

Ruth thought back to all the Christmases she had spent with the Cleary family since her marriage. The pudding was the pinnacle of a delicious dinner. She had never thought whether it was homemade or bought, she merely registered that it tasted better than anything she had ever had before.

'I make it in September,' Elizabeth said. 'So that it has time to mature. And I make my Christmas cake in November, and ice it in December. And when my hydrangeas flower in summer, I pick them and dry them for the Christmas decorations. When the holly berries come out in November, I put bags over them to stop the birds getting them so they are fresh and red for the table decorations and the hall. I buy a crate of Cox's Pippins in October, when they're just in season and store them in the spare garage and then polish them and put them in the apple pyramid in the hall in the middle of December. And I freeze a summer fruit pudding in July for us to have on Boxing Day. Surely you remember!'

'I remember,' Ruth said awkwardly. 'I just didn't realize that you planned so far ahead.'

Elizabeth laughed gently. 'How else could everything be ready for the day?' she asked. 'It's no good dashing around a week before, hoping to get things in time. There are seasons to good housekeeping. You have to think about autumn in midsummer, and you have to think about Christmas in midautumn.'

Ruth felt hopelessly superficial. 'I haven't even bought presents yet,' she said.

Elizabeth laughed, ushered Ruth out of the hall, and closed the front door behind them. 'Then thank heavens you don't have to worry about the house as well as everything else,' she said. 'I'll have Thomas every afternoon this week and you can go in to Bath and shop. I hope it's not too crowded.'

Ruth watched Elizabeth drop the key to the front door of the little house in her camel-hair-coat pocket. 'When did the heating man say he could come?'

Elizabeth made a face. 'You know what they're like,' she said. 'Not until after the New Year holiday. I think everything just shuts down between Christmas Day and New Year's Day. Still, you can go home the first week in January, and then you can start afresh in the New Year.'

Ruth turned and trudged up the lane to the farmhouse, Elizabeth followed her, a little way behind. She nodded to Frederick's Labrador dog, who ran between the two of them and stopped to sniff at a gatepost. 'So that's all right,' she said quietly. 'We've got another month.'

Ruth and Patrick were in bed, Thomas asleep in the nursery next door, Elizabeth and Frederick in the bedroom further down the landing. Ruth had been with Clare Leesome in the afternoon, and she was alert and excited. Patrick had been up early, and had spent an arduous day in the editing room with a producer who had misunderstood what was wanted from the very first day of filming. Huge reels of film would be wasted; some parts would have to be reshot. The documentary was way over budget, and Patrick was so confused between the initial brief, the producer's interpretation, and his own second thoughts that he felt quite incapable of patching together a film that would make any sense at all.

He spent a long time in the bathroom, sitting on the toilet and reading *Broadcast* magazine. He did not acknowledge it, even to himself, but he was rather hoping that Ruth would be asleep by the time he finally emerged. He undressed and put on some pyjamas. Before they had moved into the farmhouse Patrick had slept naked, or wearing only a pair of boxer shorts. But under his mother's roof he wore crisp cotton pyjamas, which he changed twice a week and which she washed and ironed. He came to bed smelling pleasantly of fabric conditioner and clean cotton, but Ruth missed the caress of bare skin and the natural scent of his body. On the infrequent occasions that they had made love since her return from the clinic, she found herself irritated by the pyjamas. Patrick's fumbling with the trousers and his laziness in leaving on the jacket were a powerful antidote to sexual desire.

Patrick looked at himself in the bathroom mirror. He had put on weight since living back at home, and his jawline was fatter than it used to be. He stretched up his chin and watched the skin recede. He looked at himself critically. He feared he was losing his looks and that his young, glossy handsomeness would not develop into his father's craggy, attractive face, but would blur into plumpness and indistinction.

'I should get fit,' he said thoughtfully to himself. 'Do some training, join a gym.'

He did not mean it. The hours that he worked and the demands of his home life made any extra activity too much of an effort to be pleasurable. He shook his head at his reflection. 'No time,' he said. 'Never a damn moment.'

He shook his head again, feeling harassed and unfairly treated. He splashed water on his face and brushed his teeth and rubbed his face briskly in the warm towel. The touch of the fleecy cotton on his skin cheered him at once. At least he was now living in a well-run home, he thought. The towels in the little house had been unreliable, and often he had to use a damp one.

He went quietly across the landing, noting the line of light under his parents' bedroom door, and thought of them placidly reading their books in their big double bed. He had a vague sense that marriage should be like that: secure, mutually dependent, at peace.

Ruth was waiting for him, sitting up in bed, turning the pages of a magazine.

'You've been ages,' she said with a smile. 'I nearly came to find you.'

'I thought you'd be asleep,' he said. He turned back the duvet and got in beside her. At once she held out her arms and he slid into her embrace. The thought of making love to her surfaced in his mind and he instantly dismissed it. He would have to get up early in the morning, and he needed his sleep. If Thomas happened to wake then, Ruth might expect him to go to the nursery. After lovemaking Ruth generally went to the bathroom,

256

and that would disturb his parents, and – more than anything else – Patrick was rarely aroused under his mother's roof. There was something deeply inhibiting about the family home. His mother changed their sheets twice a week, and would know if they had made love. He could not bear the thought of them hearing the squeaking of the bed, or Ruth's breathy cries or, worst of all, his own groan at climax. The thought of his parents hearing his lovemaking, or even worse, deliberately listening and then perhaps exchanging a smile, froze his desire before he was even conscious of it.

'Let's have a cuddle,' Ruth said invitingly.

Patrick stretched out and put out the bedroom light and cuddled her up against his shoulder as he lay on his back. There then ensued a dance as formal as if it had been choreographed. Ruth wriggled up the line of his body to kiss his neck, just below his ear, and spread her thigh across his groin, pressing against his penis. Patrick wriggled up also, to tuck her down to his shoulder again, pushing her down in the bed, so she was not sprawled across him. She raised herself up a little and reached across to kiss him on the lips; he felt her breasts press against his pyjama jacket, warm and heavy against his chest. He kissed her with tenderness and then took her head in his hands and firmly placed it on his shoulder.

'I love sleeping cuddled up with you,' he said, and then pushed her gently so she rolled over on her side and he cuddled up behind her.

Ruth moved slightly backwards, so that her buttocks were pressing against his penis. Despite himself, Patrick found that he was getting aroused. Ruth moved a little away, and then back again. Patrick put his hand down and held her hipbone to push her gently away.

'Enough of that!' he said, in a warm, caressing tone. 'I have to sleep.' As soon as he spoke he knew he had made a mistake in making his refusal explicit. She moved away from him at once, rolled onto her front, and raised her head so she could see his face in the half-light from the window.

'It's been ages,' she said.

He sighed. He hated any analysis of personal life, and since she had been seeing Clare Leesome her desire to talk and talk and talk was even worse.

'I'm just very tired tonight,' he said. 'And you must be exhausted too. Was the traffic terrible coming out of Bath? It's late-night shopping now, isn't it?'

She would not be diverted.

'We haven't made love for ten days,' she said. 'And before that, it was a fortnight.'

He forced himself to chuckle in a soft, confident tone, and drew her back towards him. 'I know,' he said. 'It's difficult at the moment. I'm incredibly busy at work and I feel really stressed, Ruthie darling. Wait till my Christmas days off and we'll make up for lost time.'

'You can't,' she said flatly. 'You can't ever make up for lost time.'

He thought how much he hated these conversations, which could go from the most basic practicalities – such as the last date that they had made love – to the most fanciful of philosophies – such as whether you can make up for lost time.

'I know,' he said. 'And it's as bad for me as it is for you. Let's sleep now, and have an early night tomorrow. Mother can baby-sit and we can go out for something to eat. How would that be?'

He stroked her hair, willing her to feel sleepy.

'It's being here that puts you off, isn't it?' she asked. 'In your parents' house?' She had a strong sense of how his mother's care, his mother's roof, made him regress to the little spoilt boy he must have been.

'Not at all,' he said firmly. 'I've told you what it is, and it's very simple and very boring. It's being overworked, darling. Nothing complicated and psychological at all. Now can we go to sleep?'

She was silent for a little while, and he thought that he had got away with it. But then he knew by the tautness in her body that she was crying, and keeping her tears silent.

For a moment he thought he would take her in his arms and kiss the tears off her silly pretty face. But he knew that if he held her he would want to make love to her, and the thought of his parents awake, and hearing everything, was too much for him. He pretended to hear nothing, to know nothing, and shut his eyes, and waited for sleep.

Fourteen

CHRISTMAS DAY was organized into a state of domestic perfection by Elizabeth. They woke in time for church, and as Ruth went downstairs, carrying Thomas dressed in his smart new navy jumper and trouser set, she smelled the warm, appetizing scent of cooking turkey from the kitchen. Frederick drove them all to church, and they sat near the crib so that Thomas could see the stable scene with his wide, interested eyes.

When they came home Frederick produced a bottle of champagne and they opened their Christmas presents. Frederick and Elizabeth had been generous to Ruth. They had bought her an expensive set of bath oils, gels, and shampoo, and a wide-cut swing jacket in a soft russet tweed. Ruth felt its soft warmth as she spread it out.

'If you don't like it, I can take it back,' Elizabeth said, watching her face. 'But I thought it was such a lovely colour! And such wonderful material.'

'I love it,' Ruth said honestly.

Patrick had bought her a water-colour painting of Princes' Crescent, where they used to live. When he saw her face as she recognized the clean curved line of the building, he thought he had been rather tactless. For a moment she looked as if she might weep.

'I thought it would remind us . . .' he said weakly.

She glanced up at him with a speaking look. 'I don't ever forget. It was our first home . . .' The fact that the little house at the end of the drive had never been a proper home, and was even now cold and empty, did not need saying.

'And what has Thomas got from Mummy and Daddy?' Elizabeth asked brightly.

They could not persuade him to pull at the paper, so Patrick and Ruth unwrapped the big box. They had bought him a baby bouncer. Frederick let out a little cheer. 'You know, it crossed my mind that you might get him that. I put up a hook in the kitchen last night. We can try him out in it now.'

'Last night!' Patrick exclaimed.

'While I was stuffing the turkey,' Elizabeth said, smiling. 'So don't blame *me* if there's plaster in the chestnut stuffing!'

They took the harness and the elastic strap through to the kitchen and adjusted it carefully. Then Ruth put Thomas into the seat and clapped her hands in delight as he put his toes cautiously down to the ground, and then ecstatically kicked off, again and again. 'He loves it!' she said.

'He can watch me serve lunch,' Elizabeth said.

'Can I do anything?' Ruth asked, knowing what the answer would be.

'You go and have another glass of champagne with Frederick,' Elizabeth said warmly. 'Patrick can help me, and Thomas can tell us what to do.'

Ruth smiled, and she and Frederick left the kitchen. At the doorway she glanced back. Patrick, his mother, and his child made a pretty picture of domestic contentment. There was a unity about the three of them, as if they were parents and child, as if Thomas belonged to them alone. As if she and Frederick were visitors to this family, welcomed in the drawing room, but banned from the intimacy of the kitchen and the natural love that flowed between the other three.

In the drawing room Frederick poured her another glass of champagne. 'You have no objection to us going back to the little house, have you?' she asked frankly. It was rare that they were alone together, and even rarer that they should speak of matters of importance.

He bent over and fiddled with the neck of the bottle. 'I know Mother was worried that you wouldn't be able to cope,' he said.

'She must see that I can manage now.'

He did not meet her eyes. 'And Patrick wanted to know that you were all right during the day, when he couldn't be with you.'

She nodded. 'But I am fine.'

He looked her in the face for the first time. 'I've no axe to grind,' he said simply. 'If you are well and Thomas is well and Patrick is happy, then anything else is your own business. And it shouldn't be me that you're speaking to . . .'

She thought he was giving her some kind of clue. She waited.

He nodded in the direction of the kitchen. 'Patrick. Your husband. It's his job to provide you with a home, and his job to see that you're happily settled in it.' He paused for a powerful moment. 'And his job to make sure that you get on with your own lives.'

*   *   *

After Christmas lunch, following the annual tradition, they telephoned Miriam in Canada. The phone rang for a while at the other end, and when it was answered it was a man's voice. He called Miriam to the phone.

'Hello, darling,' Elizabeth said. 'Who was that?'

She listened intently. 'Oh. So how long has he been living with you? Two months! Why didn't you . . . ?'

Ruth could hear the tantalizing sound of speech but not distinguish the words. She thought she had never seen Elizabeth so rattled.

'I'm not prying!' Elizabeth exclaimed. 'I'm trying to wish you a Happy Christmas, darling!'

The telephone squawked indignantly. Ruth realized she was grinning and straightened her face.

'I am absolutely not trying to interfere . . .' Elizabeth said. She broke off and held the telephone away. Even Ruth, on the other side of the room, could hear Miriam's anger.

Elizabeth exchanged a look with Frederick. 'She really is quite impossible,' she said. She put the telephone back to her ear. 'Your father wants to say hello.' Elizabeth beckoned to Frederick.

'Hello, Mimi,' he said affectionately. 'Happy Christmas.'

Ruth watched Elizabeth following the one-sided conversation. Frederick told his daughter that they had been to church and eaten Christmas dinner; he told her that they were missing her. Ruth noticed that there was no mention of Patrick and Ruth's living at the farmhouse, and that the reference to Thomas did not mention his mother's health.

'She wants to talk to you.' Frederick passed the receiver to Patrick.

'Did she say who he was?' Elizabeth whispered.

Frederick shook his head. 'I wasn't going to ask,' he replied. 'She'll tell us soon enough, if she wants to.'

'It's been two months and she's never so much as mentioned a boyfriend,' Elizabeth exclaimed.

Frederick smiled and patted her hand. 'She's thirty-six,' he said. 'I don't think she'd call him a boyfriend. And she can run her own life.'

'I just like to know!'

He smiled. 'I know you do. But that little bird has definitely fled the nest. She'll tell you when she's ready.'

Patrick, finishing his conversation with his sister, said, 'Good-bye, Happy Christmas,' in his most charming voice, and put down the phone.

'That's done,' he said.

'Fancy Miriam living with a man,' Elizabeth said to her son: her youngest child, her favourite.

Patrick chuckled. 'Brave man,' he said.

'But fancy her never saying!' Elizabeth wondered. 'She must know that I would want to know. It's so eccentric of her to try and cut us off like this.'

Patrick shrugged. Ruth had a sense of quite scandalous nosiness. 'Surely she's had boyfriends before,' she said.

'Never one that passed muster,' Frederick said tactfully.

'Completely awful people,' Elizabeth said roundly. 'One young man who lived in a tent and travelled around the country trying to stop people building bypasses.'

'An ecologist,' Frederick supplemented.

'Shall I phone back?' Elizabeth hesitated. 'Now she's had a chance to cool down. So we can have a proper chat?'

'Leave it,' Frederick counselled her. 'She'll tell us all we need to know in her own time.'

They went through to the drawing room, and when Thomas became fretful and sleepy Patrick took him upstairs to his cot. Elizabeth sat on the sofa and looked at the gardening book that Ruth and Patrick had given her. Ruth sat in domestic peace and silence and felt the afternoon stretch unendingly before her.

'Let's go for a walk,' she suggested.

Patrick, who had been settling down for a doze, was reluctant.

'Do you good,' said his father unsympathetically. 'Work some of that weight off your middle!'

'And there's Christmas cake for tea, remember!' Elizabeth warned. 'Go on, both of you! I'll wake Thomas when he's had his nap.'

It was sunny and cold. Patrick walked briskly down the drive. 'I'm glad you suggested a walk,' he said. 'I was ready to drop off! Where shall we go?'

'Let's go to our house,' Ruth said.

For a moment he looked as if he might refuse.

'I really want to,' Ruth prompted.

'All right,' he said reluctantly. 'It just seems a bit odd.'

They walked in step for a few paces. 'It *is* odd,' Ruth said. 'It's not odd going to look at it, it's odd that we don't live in it.'

'Mmmm,' said Patrick discouragingly. 'Doesn't Thomas love his bouncy thing!'

'Yes,' Ruth said. 'But we don't have a hook for it in our house, and they have a hook in the farmhouse.'

'We can put up a hook!' Patrick said bracingly. 'There's no problem with that!'

Ruth hesitated. The wine she had drunk at lunchtime,

and the example of Miriam's open defiance of her mother, made her feel reckless. She felt ready to force the issue. 'Or we could not bother,' she said. 'We could stay in the farmhouse forever and never live in our own house.'

He checked. 'What?'

'You obviously don't want to go, and your mother obviously wants us to stay there. Shall we decide now that we all live together, and you and I never have a home of our own again?'

'No,' Patrick said instantly. 'No one lives like that. It would look so odd ... like Argentinian peasants or something.'

'It is odd,' Ruth agreed, stretching her strides to keep pace with his.

'And I like our house,' Patrick said as the trim front garden came into view around the curve of the drive. 'I like living here.'

'Yes,' said Ruth.

'The stay in the farmhouse has just dragged on a bit,' Patrick said thoughtfully. 'First you being ill, and then I was worried about you, and then I really wanted to move at Christmas, but the heating was off ... it's just been one thing after another.'

'I can't make us move,' Ruth said simply. They had reached the garden gate, and she swung around to face him. Her face was flushed from the walk, her eyes bright and clear. He felt a sudden straightforward desire for her. In that moment he stopped seeing her as a sick woman, as a mad woman. Suddenly he saw her for what she was: young, sexual, desirable. 'I can't make us move,' Ruth said again. 'It has to be your decision. I've done all I can, and I can't make it happen. If you don't put your foot down, we're going to be there forever.'

She turned from him and went to the front door. 'I don't have a key,' Patrick said.

She took it out of her pocket and opened the door. 'No,' she said. 'This is your mother's key. You have to decide, Patrick, whether this is their house or ours. You have to decide whether we will live here or not.'

He stepped into the hall. The dry, dusty smell of an unused house was like a reproach.

Ruth went ahead of him into the sitting room. 'Let's have a drink,' she said. 'A Christmas drink in our own home.'

He smiled, attracted by the clandestine sense of an assignation. 'I'll see what we have.'

Ruth struck a match and put it to the kindling in the grate. At once the firelight made the room look warm and friendly. She drew the curtains against the red setting sun.

Patrick came back with a bottle of port and a couple of glasses. 'The cupboard's a bit bare,' he said. 'This is all I could find.'

Ruth smiled at him, her face lit by firelight, the room warming up. There was an intimacy about being alone in their house, like a newly married couple when the last of the wedding guests have finally gone, and the bawdy jokes are over, and there is silence.

'It's silly,' Patrick remarked. 'I'd forgotten what a nice house this is.'

He poured the wine and looked around. 'We'll move back, shall we? As soon as the heating is fixed?'

Ruth raised her glass to him. 'And start again,' she said as if it were a toast. 'I'm sorry that it went wrong before, Patrick. I am quite different now.'

He sat beside her on the sofa and kissed her gently. 'It's been a tough year,' he said. 'And I wasn't all the help I should have been. We'll do better next year.'

She turned to him and Patrick put down his glass and kissed her again. With a sense of delightful discovery Patrick slid his hands under her blouse and felt her warm, soft skin. Ruth sighed with relief and welcomed Patrick into her body.

Elizabeth knew.

As they came in the door, pink-cheeked and breathless from walking quickly home up the darkening drive, she took one swift look from one to another and knew that they had been to their own house and made love.

Ruth saw the glance and had an immediate impression of Elizabeth's disapproval. For a moment she thought that the older woman was shocked at her son's sexuality – sneaking out in the afternoon like a teenager – but then she had a sense of something deeper and more serious, something like envy, something like a challenge.

'You were a long time,' Elizabeth said. 'I'm surprised you could see your way home.'

Patrick looked embarrassed. 'It's only dusk,' he said.

'We went to our house,' Ruth said. She looked Elizabeth in the eye. 'We lit the fire in the sitting room and had a glass of port to celebrate Christmas. It was lovely.'

Elizabeth smiled but she looked strained. 'I'm surprised the chimney drew,' she said. 'It's been cold for so long.'

They went into the sitting room. Thomas was on his play mat on the carpet; when he saw his mother he crowed with delight, and his arms and legs waved. Ruth picked him up and turned to her mother-in-law, with her son's head against her cheek.

'We've missed it,' she said firmly. 'We'll move back next week, as soon as the heating is fixed.'

Elizabeth slid a conspiratorial glance at Patrick, but he did not see. He was looking at his wife and son. 'I'll go over tomorrow and put up a hook for his bouncer,' he said.

On Boxing Day it somehow turned into a family walk. They all went to the little house together. Elizabeth and Frederick walked down the drive with them, Ruth pushing Thomas in his pram. 'We'll bring Thomas away when he's had enough,' Frederick said.

'It's too cold for him down there without heating,' Elizabeth remarked. 'Heaven knows how we managed in the old days. The only warm rooms ever were the kitchen and the drawing room. The stairs and the hall were draughty and cold, and the bedrooms were like ice.'

Frederick nodded. 'I used to have chilblains every winter when I was a child,' he said. 'And chapped hands. You hardly ever hear about chilblains now.'

Patrick was half listening. 'It would make quite a nice little film,' he said thoughtfully. 'The medical side of recent progress. People not getting chilblains any more because the houses are warmer, but getting more asthma.'

Elizabeth laughed and slipped her hand in her son's arm. 'Fleas,' she said. 'If you dare to mention them. Now that we have centrally heated houses fleas don't die off in winter. The vet was telling me they breed all the year round. It's a real problem. There's a mini epidemic.'

'And house mites,' Frederick said cheerfully, coming up on the other side of Elizabeth. 'That's the cause of your extra asthma if you ask me. Not enough fresh air.'

Ruth, lagging behind, pushing the pram, saw the three of them, walking in step in the happy unity that seemed so easy for them to achieve. But it was Elizabeth and not Patrick who glanced back towards her and called, 'What about you, Ruth? Are you one of the post-central heating children? Or was your home cold?'

Ruth shook her head. Her aunt's house had never been a home, and she could scarcely remember her childhood home. But then she had a sudden sharp recollection of her home in the States, before the death of her parents. They had rented a small white clapboard house, cool in summer and snug in winter. When Ruth was in bed at night, she could hear the comforting gabble from her parents' television downstairs. The warmth from the furnace in the cellar spread through the house. In autumn her father used to put up storm windows and go up on the roof to check the shingles. Her mother used to make him wear thick working gloves. 'Your hands!' she would exclaim. Ruth remembered her father's hands, long-fingered, soft, with the power to wring music from wood. 'I don't remember,' she said shortly.

They reached the gate. Frederick paused to help her with the pram, while Elizabeth and Patrick opened the front door and went in together.

The sitting room was fusty and dark, with the curtains still closed. The little fire had burned out in the grate. Ruth had not drunk all her port yesterday, and there was a sour, stale smell from the dregs in the glass. The cushions on the floor and the pushed-back sofa showed very clearly to Elizabeth's quick assessing gaze that they had made love on the floor. Ruth felt deeply uncomfortable, as if they had been detected in some secret assignment. The room did not look intimate and seductive as it had looked the day before; it looked sordid.

Elizabeth went over and threw back the curtains. The harsh winter sunlight showed the dust and the red stain inside the wine glasses. Without a word of criticism or condemnation Elizabeth unlocked the sash window and threw it up. The clean winter air flooded in. Ruth picked up the dirty glasses and the bottle and took them to the kitchen. As she left the room she saw Elizabeth stooping to pick up the cushions from the floor, brush them off, and replace them on the sofa. Ruth had a moment of cringing embarrassment that one of them would be stained, that Elizabeth would take off the cover of the cushion for washing; all in that remorselessly civilized way.

In the kitchen Frederick was unpacking the tool kit while Patrick tapped the plaster-board ceiling, looking for the joists.

'Mind you don't hit a cable,' Frederick said. 'Hang on a minute. I've got one of those cable detectors in here.'

'You've got a tool library in there,' Patrick said, smiling. 'Is there any DIY gadget you haven't got?'

'I like a good tool kit,' Frederick said. 'And your mother likes things just so at home. It's very satisfying to do a good job.'

'Aha,' Patrick said as the hollow sound of his tapping changed. 'I think it's here.'

'Tap again?' Frederick said, listening. 'Yes. That sounds like it. Now where d'you want the bouncer, Ruth?'

Ruth gestured to a space between the kitchen table and the back door. 'There?'

'Oh, no,' Elizabeth said. 'He'll reach up and pull off the tablecloth.'

Ruth hesitated. She had never thought of putting a tablecloth on the kitchen table, which was scrubbed pine.

'It should be here,' Elizabeth said, gesturing closer to the back door. 'And then in summer you can have the door open, and he can bounce in the sunshine.'

Elizabeth was right. Ruth found a smile. 'Oh, yes,' she said, trying to sound pleased.

'Shall I have a look at the central heating while I'm here?' Frederick asked. 'I might be able to get it going.'

'It's under guarantee,' Elizabeth warned. 'Don't just thump it with a spanner.'

Frederick raised his eyebrows to Patrick in a mutual silent complaint about the unreasonable and suspicious nature of women. 'I'll just look,' he said, and went to the utility room. A few moments later they heard the boiler click and then flare.

'Extraordinary thing,' Frederick said, coming out of the utility room. 'The clock was disconnected. Can't think how it could have happened. The boiler wasn't firing because it was disconnected from the clock.'

'Must have been loose when they put it in,' Patrick said. He drilled the hole for the bouncer hook, and plaster dust filled the air.

'I suppose so . . .' Frederick said. 'But I can't see why it would suddenly come out. You'd expect it to flicker on and off . . .'

'Oh!' said Elizabeth, waving her hand before her face in protest at the dust. 'Let's get Thomas out of here! Shall we go upstairs and make the beds, Ruth?'

'I'll go,' Ruth said. 'You play with Thomas in the sitting room.' She felt she could not bear to have Elizabeth turning over the cold sheets, just as she had turned over the sofa cushions.

'All right.' Elizabeth lifted Thomas out of the pram and smiled at his welcoming gurgle. 'We'll be happy enough! Call me if you want a hand.'

'Yes,' Ruth said.

There was a companionable male muttering from the kitchen as the men hung the baby bouncer, and then Thomas's delighted giggle from the sitting room as Elizabeth tickled the small outspread palms of his hands. Ruth, going up the stairs alone to the cold bedrooms, felt left out and lonely, but did not know how she could join in.

She made the beds quietly, finding that she was listening to the sounds of the others down below. When the men finished in the kitchen they joined Elizabeth and the baby in the sitting room. She could hear them chatting, Elizabeth advising Patrick not to order more logs or coal until prices came down in the summer. 'We have plenty,' she said. 'I ordered extra because I guessed you might run out. Father will bring a trailer load down for you later in the week.'

Ruth thumped the pillows into place, and shook the duvet.

'I'd offer you a cup of coffee,' Patrick said. 'But we haven't got anything in at all.'

'I cleared it all out when Ruth had her breakdown,' Elizabeth said. 'Better than letting it go to waste. But I kept a complete list of what was in the larder so I can replace it for you to the last tin of beans!'

'We can go shopping . . .' Patrick said.

273

'Not today you can't,' Elizabeth reminded him. 'Boxing Day. I shouldn't think Sainsburys will be open till Tuesday. I can go in then.'

'So you're with us for a few more days?' Frederick asked.

'It looks like it,' Patrick said. 'We'll leave the heating on and come down and air the place. But I don't want to run up the drive every time I want a cup of tea.'

Ruth slammed the bedroom door and came noisily down the stairs. They all looked up at her and smiled. 'Can't you lend us some basics?' she asked Elizabeth. 'A loaf from the freezer? A small jar of coffee? A couple of tea bags? A pint of milk?'

'We don't want to put Mother to any trouble,' Patrick intervened.

'Of course not,' Ruth said determinedly. 'But you're so well organized, Elizabeth, I just assumed you'd have plenty in the house. Don't you have anything to spare?'

Elizabeth hesitated. 'I always have a loaf in the freezer . . .'

'My dear, you know you keep in enough to feed an army!' Frederick exclaimed. 'Let's all go home for lunch and then you two can take your pick of the larder and bring down whatever you want.'

'And anything you haven't got I can pick up at the garage shop,' Ruth said pleasantly.

'Of course,' Elizabeth replied. 'I hope you won't catch me out. I think I can give you everything you need. If you're sure you want to go now. It seems rather a rush . . .'

Ruth nodded, meeting her eyes. 'We were only waiting for the central heating to be mended,' she said levelly. 'And it's on now. We can move back in.'

Fifteen

THAT EVENING Ruth and Patrick curled up before a log fire in their own sitting room after a supper of curried turkey and rice. Elizabeth had given them slices from the Christmas turkey for their supper and Ruth had driven down to the garage shop for a tin of curry powder. Upstairs, Thomas slept in his own cot in his own nursery again.

Frederick had given Patrick a bottle of claret to celebrate their first night back in the little house, and they drank the bright red wine and put the glasses down on the wooden floor, and cracked nuts with a sense of behaving naturally in private at last.

'I'm glad we came home,' Patrick said. 'I thought at the last moment we were going to get stuck until the shops opened on Tuesday.'

Ruth nodded. 'It's always one thing or another,' she said. 'Elizabeth didn't want us to leave.'

Patrick nodded. 'You can see why,' he said fairly. 'She's so close to Thomas you would think he was her own son.'

'No, I wouldn't,' Ruth contradicted. 'I would never think that Thomas was anyone's son but yours and mine.'

Patrick gave her his charming smile and pulled her

against him. 'Manner of speech,' he said against her hair.

'Not my speech,' Ruth said stubbornly as his kisses moved from her warm, smooth head to the line of her neck. She turned her face to him and opened her mouth as he kissed her.

'Bedtime,' Patrick said suddenly. 'In our own bed at last, thank God.'

They went upstairs with their fingers interlinked and made love, in their own bed, with no one but a passing owl to hear.

The end of Patrick's holiday time was like the end of a small reserve of peace. His alarm clock went off early, by accident, and woke Thomas. Instead of the enjoyable well-organized breakfast Ruth had planned, she had to warm Thomas's early-morning bottle and then change his nappy halfway through his feed. Thomas – who liked to have his bottle undisturbed – took noisy exception to this, and his complaint soured his temper for the rest of the morning. Ruth could not put him down and make Patrick's breakfast as she had wished, but had to wedge him under her arm while she filled the kettle and tried to make tea one-handed.

Their early start did not give them more time, it merely increased the confusion. Patrick could not find his cuff links – which he had left up at the farm – and so had to change his shirt for one with buttons at the cuff. It was a pale blue, which meant that he had to choose another tie as well, and the blue tie that matched had been left up at the farmhouse. 'For heaven's sake, as though it mattered!' Ruth snapped. Thomas dropped his bottle and let out a pitiful deprived wail.

'Just *leave* breakfast!' Patrick ordered. 'I'll get a cup of coffee at work. I never said I wanted a cooked breakfast in the first place!'

'But Elizabeth always –' Ruth bit the sentence off.

Patrick came towards her and quietly took Thomas from her. 'Make yourself a cup of tea,' he said gently. 'I'll hold him while you drink it. Mother gets everything ready the night before, and she gets up at the crack of dawn to get everything done. There's no need to try and be like her. We live here now.'

There was a brief silence. Ruth blinked. 'I don't think I'll ever learn to do it like her,' she said.

'I know,' Patrick said frankly. 'And there's no point in us trying to be like them. We'll have to do things our way. I was a fool to wake him this morning anyway. If he'd stayed asleep we would have had loads of time.'

Ruth poured boiling water on two tea-bags in mugs, added milk, and flipped the wet bags into the bin. 'It's not the same.'

'I married you,' Patrick replied stoutly. 'I could have chosen to stay at home and have real tea in a bone-china cup and a cooked breakfast every day of my life.'

'But don't you want both?' Ruth asked.

She saw it – the little flicker of greed that crossed his face, and his instantly smoothing it away. The momentary acknowledgment that yes, indeed, he did want someone to mother his child, and to be his lover, and to cook for him and care for him to the standard of his mother's house.

'No,' Patrick said, as if he meant it.

Ruth smiled. 'Good,' she said, as if she believed it.

*　　*　　*

It seemed to take all morning to get Thomas dressed, and then she had to entertain him in one room after another, as she tried to get the household chores done. He had learned now to reach for something and grasp at it, and his favourite game was to be propped by pillows and offered one object after another to hold and then negligently drop. In the bathroom, while she dutifully cleaned the toilet, the sink, and the bath, Ruth passed him toothbrushes, flannels, and a box of dental floss. Thomas accepted them with pleasure and dropped them all, and looked around for something more. Ruth handed him the little duck from his bath toys, and his sponge. She was leaning over the bath, rinsing the suds away with the shower attachment, when she heard a muffled ominous choke.

She spun around. Thomas had crammed most of the sponge into his mouth but was quite incapable of getting it out again. Yellow sponge bulged from his lips, his eyes were staring, his face flushed as he struggled for air.

'My God!' Ruth said and flew at him. She pulled the sponge from his mouth and Thomas whooped for breath, and then smiled. The incident had not disturbed him at all.

'I could have killed him,' Ruth said. 'Oh, God.'

She snatched him up and held him tight, and they walked downstairs together. Ruth saw her hand on the banister and it trembled so much that she could hardly feel the wood beneath her fingertips. She took Thomas into the sitting room and laid him on his back on the sofa, so that she could look into his inquiring face.

'Oh, God, Thomas,' she said. A sense of her passionate love for him set her trembling again. She took in his clear skin and his wide, innocent eyes. You could still see a little pulse in the top of his head; even his skull was vulnerable. 'Such a little cough!' she said, marvelling at the softness of it. 'What if I hadn't heard?'

Behind her, the front door opened suddenly. 'Hello!' Elizabeth called. 'Anyone at home?'

'In here,' Ruth said. She had a sudden instinct to hide Thomas, as if Elizabeth would know, just by looking at him, that Ruth could have suffocated him.

'I was just passing –' Elizabeth stopped dead. 'Good Lord, Ruth, you're white as a sheet! What's wrong?' At once she looked at Thomas with an expression like terror on her face. She went straight past Ruth and picked him up. Thomas crowed with delight at her touch, and she turned with him in her arms, as if she were rescuing him. 'What happened?' she demanded tightly.

'It was nothing,' Ruth said.

'Nothing?'

Ruth faced her mother-in-law and felt tears coming. 'Did he fall down the stairs?' Elizabeth demanded.

'No,' Ruth said in a low, shaky voice. 'He choked.'

'What on?'

'His bath sponge.' Ruth swallowed down her tears. 'I didn't think,' she said. 'I gave him his sponge to look at and when I turned round he had crammed it all in his mouth. I just pulled it out.'

'All of it?'

Ruth gasped at a new fear. 'I didn't look. I didn't think to look in his mouth. Could he have swallowed some? Could it be stuck in his throat?'

'Look at the sponge!' Elizabeth snapped. 'Fetch it now!'

Ruth ran up the stairs and came down with Thomas's sponge. It was cut in the shape of a little boat. It was complete and intact. The yellow keel made of sponge, the orange superstructure, and the little green sponge funnel on top.

Elizabeth looked it all over carefully. 'Thank God for that,' she said, her voice carefully controlled. 'Why weren't you watching him?'

Ruth answered Elizabeth as if the older woman had every right to cross-question her. She felt so miserably guilty that the hostile interrogation was almost a pleasure. 'I was cleaning the bath,' she said. 'I was just giving him things to look at.'

'You have to have a little box,' Elizabeth said with weary patience. She put Thomas against her shoulder and stroked his back in gentle circular motions. 'A little box with his toys for the day. You swap them around every night so he has different ones every day. You take the box around with you, wherever you go in the house, and when you need a moment to do something, you give him something from the box.'

'Oh,' Ruth said numbly. 'I didn't know.'

It was as if there were too much to learn. Ruth would never grasp it all in time.

Elizabeth nodded, with her lips pressed together. 'He's nearly asleep,' she said. It was true. Thomas, inhaling the familiar scent of his grandmother and held firmly in her arms, with his back patted and her voice in his ear, was drifting off into sleep.

Without asking, Elizabeth went out into the kitchen and put Thomas in his pram. 'He'll sleep now, and you can get your chores done and then supervise him properly when he wakes up,' she said. She glanced out of the French windows to the little garden, where the winter sun was bright. 'He can go out,' she decided, opened the doors and trundled the pram into the garden.

'Thank you,' Ruth said.

Elizabeth tucked the blankets closely around him, then put the waterproof cover on top, and pulled up the hood against the cold air.

'Actually, I was just calling in to see if you wanted any shopping,' she said.

Ruth shook her head. 'I'll go later. I'll take Thomas this afternoon.'

'I'll have Thomas while you shop,' Elizabeth offered. 'It's hard work doing it all with a baby as well.'

Ruth flared briefly. 'I can do it,' she said. 'I am perfectly capable of shopping and caring for my baby at the same time.'

Elizabeth raised an eyebrow. 'I'm glad to hear it,' she said. 'You know where I am if you change your mind. We're both in this afternoon. It will be no trouble if you want to drop him off on your way out.'

Ruth nodded. 'Thank you,' she felt forced to say.

Elizabeth slid past her and out into the hall. 'I shan't say anything to Patrick,' she promised. At once Ruth's mistake seemed infinitely worse if it had to be concealed from her husband. 'He'd only worry.'

'Thank you,' Ruth said again. 'I'll probably tell him myself, anyway.'

Elizabeth nodded. 'As you wish,' she said. 'I'm sure he'll be sympathetic. We're all aware how hard you are trying . . .'

'It was an accident,' Ruth said defensively. 'It must happen thousands of times a day.'

Elizabeth smiled coldly. 'Perhaps,' she said. 'It never happened to either of my children.'

* * *

Ruth took Thomas with her to the shop, but Elizabeth had been right – it was a struggle to cope with shopping and a baby as well. For the first half hour everything went well. Ruth parked in the mother-and-baby space, and put Thomas in the reclining seat on the top of the trolley, and he observed with interest the bright lights of the ceiling and his mother's head coming and going. But after a while he became bored and started to cry.

Ruth was only halfway around the store. She had bought vegetables and fruit and some cheese, but the aisles of cleaning powders and detergents and nursery goods were ahead of her, as well as the bakery and the delicatessen sections.

'Shush, shush,' she said putting her cheek beside Thomas's hot face. 'Soon be finished.'

Thomas got a handful of hair and pulled.

'Ow!' Ruth said and unwound the determined little fingers. At once he yelled louder, his hands reaching out to grasp her again.

'Shush!' Ruth said less tenderly. She turned the heavy trolley and started to push it down the detergent aisle. Thomas's wails grew louder and louder, his face was scarlet, he squeezed real hot tears from screwed-up eyes. A woman glanced sharply at Ruth, as if she were doing something wrong, something to make the baby cry.

Ruth tried to smile unconcernedly, and leaned forward and patted the baby's cheek. 'Not long now,' she tried to say.

Thomas was straining against the safety harness, his little legs kicking irritably. His cry now had a desperate urgent quality as if he were in dreadful danger. The nagging, demanding shriek filled the store, and pulled

282

at Ruth's nerves. She felt every wail as if it were a physical pain.

She abandoned the rest of the shopping list and abruptly headed the trolley to the checkout. A man went past her and looked at her irritably – as if she were disturbing the peace of his afternoon on purpose. Ruth felt enormously, absurdly angry with him, and envious of his carefree stride and his half-empty trolley. Thomas gave one last huge wriggle and then vomited up his entire lunch and his after-lunch bottle over the seat and over the shopping in the trolley.

'Oh, God,' Ruth said.

Thomas screamed. Ruth unbuckled him and snatched him up. He was sobbing convulsively, drenched in sour-smelling vomit.

With one spare hand Ruth pushed the shopping trolley to the checkout. Thomas wept gently against her neck as Ruth bent deep into the trolley to pull out the shopping and stack it on the belt. Some of it was sprayed with Thomas's vomit. The cashier did not hide her distaste, holding the packages with a finger and thumb and wrinkling her nose. She pressed the intercom and asked for someone to come and clean the moving belt, which was now sticky from Thomas's vomit. There was no one to pack. Ruth crammed the shopping into bags, working one-handed with Thomas held against her neck, her shirt and jumper getting steadily wetter with his tears and saliva.

'Sixty-eight pounds ten,' the girl said brightly.

Ruth handed over her card, and then awkwardly signed one-handed. The girl gave her the receipt and the card without a smile, as if it were all Ruth's fault. Her look was disdainful, but also pitying.

Grimly Ruth pushed the trolley to the car, strapped Thomas into his baby seat, and unpacked the shopping into the boot. She pushed the trolley with unnecessary force into the line of waiting trolleys, and drove away.

Thomas fell asleep at once, exhausted by his crying and vomiting. When they got home Ruth did not have the heart to wake him. She lifted him gently out of the car seat, and laid him in his cot. He lay sprawled, with his arms spread wide and his little hands open. His hair was plastered to his little head with sweat; his clothes were saturated with vomit. Ruth smiled at him with immense tenderness. 'Oh, darling, darling boy,' she said gently. 'I'm so sorry. We'll do it better next time.'

She put up the side of the cot and went downstairs to unpack the shopping. Almost at once the telephone rang.

'Is that Mrs Cleary?'

'Yes.'

'This is Saver Store. We have your handbag here, Mrs Cleary.'

'Oh, my God!' Ruth said. She had no recollection of her handbag at all. Then she remembered. She had put it on the roof of the car while loading Thomas and the shopping, and then driven off.

'We found it in the car park.'

'Thank you,' Ruth said. 'Can I collect it tomorrow?'

'I'm afraid we are not allowed to keep lost property of value overnight,' the man said firmly. 'We will have to take it to the police station and you will have to apply and collect it from there.'

'But you know it's mine!' Ruth said irritably.

'Yes, indeed, Mrs Cleary. And if you wish to collect it before four P.M. you can do so, provided you have some means of identity.'

Ruth glanced at the clock on the microwave. 'It's three-thirty now!' she said.

There was an unhelpful silence.

'Oh, all right,' Ruth said. 'I'm coming straight away.'

She hung up and then dialled Elizabeth's number. 'I'm so sorry,' she said without preamble. 'But I've left my handbag at Saver Store, and I have to collect it before four or they pass it on to the police. Thomas has just fallen asleep. Could you possibly pop down and watch him for me for three quarters of an hour? Just so I can go down and fetch it now?'

'Of course,' Elizabeth said pleasantly. She glanced at Frederick, who was pouring tea. 'I can come at once.'

Ruth slung the last of the frozen food into the freezer and pulled on her jacket. As she heard Elizabeth's car pull up she went down the path to greet her. 'Thank you,' she said.

'It's no trouble at all,' Elizabeth said nicely. 'But what a nuisance for you! Has Thomas slept long? Do you want me to wake him?'

'He's fine, he's just gone off,' Ruth said. 'Just listen for him in case he wakes. I'll probably be back before he has even stirred.'

Elizabeth nodded and went into the house. Ruth got into her car and drove back to the shop.

Alone in the house Elizabeth looked around the sitting room. The fire was not laid and the cold ashes and coals in the grate looked unwelcoming and frowsy. She rolled up some newspaper kindling, and laid a little fire and put a match to it. At once the room looked warmer and cheerful. She straightened the cushions on the sofa and drew the curtains. One of the hooks had come undone at the top and the fabric was falling awkwardly. Elizabeth fetched a chair from the kitchen and rehooked the curtain.

She returned the chair to its place by the kitchen table and looked around. The dirty dishes from Ruth's and Thomas's lunch were sitting on top of the dishwasher, which had just finished its cycle. Elizabeth's critical gaze took in everything: the stain on the new worktop, the spattered Aga, the kitchen curtains not tied back with their coordinating loops but left to hang. She glanced into the larder. Thomas was being fed factory-made baby food again; she looked at the rows and rows of expensive jars and frowned at the waste of money. The freezer door was not properly shut. Elizabeth got down on her knees and had to rearrange the boxes to make it fit. Almost unconsciously she moved boxes around until all the meat was together on a meat shelf, and all the vegetables, arranged in order of their sell-by dates, were stacked on the vegetable shelf

The house was silent.

Elizabeth thought she would check on Thomas and went soft-footed up the stairs to his bedroom. She acknowledged to herself that she need not see him. He would cry out when he woke and she could go to him then, but Elizabeth loved to watch Thomas asleep, she liked to sit in the chair in his nursery and sew, or write letters while he slept. She felt that his sweet, peaceful sleep and her patient watching cast a spell around the two of them.

She opened his bedroom door and, smiling, approached the cot.

Thomas, his face stained with tears and his clothes thick with dried vomit, lay on his back, his face pink and his head sweating from the heat of his outdoor clothes.

'Oh, my God,' Elizabeth said. For a moment she thought that he was desperately ill. She picked him up and he stirred and opened his eyes and smiled to see her, then dropped his head down to her shoulder and dozed off again.

He smelled awful. His nappy was dirty and his clothes were impregnated with vomit. He was still sweaty.

Elizabeth's face was like stone. She marched him out of the house and down the garden path and into her car. She strapped him carefully into the baby seat and drove back up the drive to the farmhouse. She unstrapped him and carried him in.

'Look,' she said savagely to Frederick. 'Look at him!'

He came out of the sitting room, folding his paper. 'Brought the little chap back?' he started, but then he saw her face. 'What is it?'

'Look at him,' she said through her teeth. 'I found him like this in his cot. 'God knows how long he's been there. He's obviously been sick all over himself and been left to cry. She didn't even take his coat off after they had been shopping. She just slung him in his cot and left him.'

Frederick's face was shocked. 'What did she say?'

'Nothing! She told me not to disturb him; she said he'd just gone to sleep. I should think she *didn't* want me to disturb him. I should think she was praying that I would just sit downstairs and wait for her to come back!'

Frederick looked grave. 'There may be an explanation,' he said carefully. 'Things do happen, my dear. Maybe the telephone rang and she was called away . . .'

'I have just found my grandson, dirty, sick, and

neglected, in his cot,' Elizabeth said with emphasis. 'There is no excuse for that.'

She turned and went upstairs to the nursery, which had once been Patrick's and now had Thomas's name on a little china nameplate on the door. She sat in the low nursing chair and gently and efficiently stripped off his outdoor suit, and then his little shirt and his trousers. Thomas stirred but hardly woke. She undid his nappy and cleaned him and put on a fresh towelling nappy from the pile that was waiting. She wrapped him in a little blanket and laid him in his cot to finish his sleep. Thomas, dreaming of the fascinating lights of the store and his mother's face swimming in and out of his vision, stretched out again and sank into sleep.

Elizabeth came downstairs and took Thomas's dirty clothes into the kitchen. The weatherproof suit, which was the worst, she laid to one side, and handwashed the rest.

Frederick came in and made her a pot of tea in silence. 'Will you speak to Patrick?'

She nodded. 'They will have to come back here.'

He hesitated. 'It's no way for a young couple to live,' he said. 'They need a bit of privacy.'

'So that she can neglect our grandson and we not know?'

'I think we should listen to her version. She certainly loves him. I don't think she'd neglect him wilfully.'

Elizabeth wrung out the little shirt and trousers and changed the water in the sink. She watched the suds swirl down the drain and then turned and faced her husband. 'Are you saying we should do nothing?' she demanded. 'Not warn Patrick, cover up for her, keep it a secret?'

Frederick thought for a moment and then he shook his head. 'Of course not,' he said. 'The baby comes first. But I am sorry she hasn't made a better go of it.'

'We all are,' Elizabeth said smartly.

Patrick, seated in the editing studio with a producer, trying to find cuts in a programme that was ten minutes too long, was irritated by the note his secretary brought in, which read: 'Your mother rang and said to tell you that you should urgently phone home. At once.'

'Sorry. Just a minute,' Patrick said. He understood that home did not mean the little house, but the farmhouse. He picked up the studio phone and dialled the number. 'It's me,' he said shortly.

The producer watched his face change. He looked shocked, and then incredulous. 'All right,' he said. 'I'll come at once.'

'Trouble?' the producer asked.

Patrick switched on his charming smile. 'I am so sorry,' he said. 'I was enjoying this and it's a good piece. There's a family crisis at home: my son is sick. I have to go. Can you finish it without me and bike a copy over to my house for me to see tonight? I'll phone you first thing in the morning.'

'All right,' the producer said. 'I hope your son is OK.'

Patrick's smile wavered slightly. 'Oh, sure,' he said. 'It's probably nothing.'

He drove home badly, overtaking and cutting in. Partly he was anxious to get home, but also he felt a mixture of rage and distress and, oddly, embarrassment. He felt that Ruth's inability to cope with Thomas reflected badly on him. He felt that his parents deserved

289

a better daughter-in-law, that he should have chosen a better partner. The closeness and sympathy of the days since Christmas dissolved under the acid of his realization that Ruth would never be able to cope.

His mother opened the door to the sound of his step on the threshold. 'Patrick,' she said, and drew him into an embrace, which was consoling and powerful and reassuring.

She led him into the kitchen. Thomas was sitting in his old high chair in his accustomed place by the table. Frederick was opposite, out of reach of the flying spoon that Thomas waved as he waited to be fed. Elizabeth sat down before her grandson and spooned food into his open mouth.

'What's the problem?' Patrick asked, leaning against the door. 'He looks well enough.'

Elizabeth glanced at Frederick and said nothing. Frederick spoke for them both.

'Ruth took him shopping this afternoon and apparently left her handbag in the shop, or something. She phoned Mother and asked her to go down and hold the fort while she drove back to the shop. When Mother got there she found Thomas in his outdoor clothes in his cot. He'd been sick and he was dirty. Mother brought him up here at the double, and here we are. And now she's AWOL. She should have been home by now but she's not reported in. It's a bad business, Patrick.'

Patrick straightened up and turned a little away. He looked out of the kitchen window so they could not see his face. Elizabeth and Frederick exchanged a look.

'He had cried himself to sleep,' she said. 'He was in a dreadful state. And his clothes must have been on him for a while; they were drying out. There's his weather-proof suit. I kept it for you to see.'

Patrick glanced down at the garment, which was drying with large blotches of white stains of vomit. He turned back to the two of them. 'What shall I do?' he asked like a man who has run out of answers. 'What shall I do?'

Ruth was delayed at the store because the security officer who had spoken to her on the telephone could not at first be found. Then, when he came, she had to produce satisfactory proof of identity and fill in a claim form before she could receive her handbag. Then she had to count the money in her purse and confirm that nothing was missing on an itemized receipt. Nothing could be hurried, everything had to be done in order. Ruth bit back her temper and checked her watch. It was five o'clock before she left the shop, and then she was caught in the rush-hour traffic. It was a quarter to six by the time she got home, and she felt flustered and apologetic. She expected to see Patrick's car in the drive alongside Elizabeth's but neither was there, and the house was in darkness.

Inside, the little fire in the sitting room had died away to pale embers, hardly lighting the darkened room. The house was silent except for the soft occasional click of the pipes.

Ruth snapped on the lights in the hall and on the stairs and experienced blinding rage. Elizabeth had *not* come and baby-sat, as had been agreed. Elizabeth had taken Thomas. Even now, Ruth knew, Thomas would be sitting in his high chair in the farmhouse kitchen, eating one of Elizabeth's home-cooked dinners. From the absence of Patrick's car Ruth guessed, rightly, that Patrick would be there too. At half past six exactly Frederick would pour a gin and tonic for each of them, and Elizabeth would take Thomas upstairs for his bath, and Patrick would be invited to sit in the bathroom and watch his son.

The farmhouse, the family, the order, and the serenity seemed infinitely more solid and more attractive than Ruth's house. Elizabeth's mothering of Thomas was more assured, her cooking was better. Ruth opened the sitting-room curtains and looked up the drive towards the farmhouse. There were no headlights coming down the drive as Patrick and Thomas came home to her. Ruth knew that if she did not go and fetch them, or telephone them at once, then Elizabeth would bath Thomas and put him to bed in Patrick's old nursery, and then come downstairs to cook Patrick's supper.

Ruth picked up the telephone and dialled the farmhouse.

Patrick answered. 'Where are you?'

Ruth recoiled from the hostility in his voice. 'Home, of course. What's the matter?'

'I'll come straight down,' he said, and hung up without explanation.

Ruth replaced the receiver on the hook and wandered through to the kitchen. Automatically, she filled the kettle with water and switched it on. She wondered if Elizabeth had complained at being left with Thomas for twice the length of time that Ruth had promised. But it was so unlike Elizabeth to complain that Ruth was certain it could not be that.

She heard Patrick's car in the drive, and his key in the

lock. She went out into the hall to meet him. 'Where's Thomas?'

'At home.'

'Why didn't you bring him?'

He stepped into the light and she saw his face. She had never seen him look like that before: he looked exhausted, drained, and grey. 'He's staying there for tonight,' he said baldly. 'I needed to talk to you alone.'

Ruth thought at once that he had been sacked, or wanted to confess an affair, or some scandalous difficulty at work. 'What's the matter?'

Patrick went into the kitchen and sat at the table. Ruth sat opposite him. In the silence the kettle boiled, and switched itself off.

'Tell me about Thomas today,' Patrick said quietly. 'How was he?'

'He was fine! He was fine! Patrick – please tell me what's going on.'

'I need to know this first,' he said. 'What did you do this afternoon?'

'We went shopping,' Ruth said. 'Then when we came home the shop rang and said I had left my handbag there, so I phoned your mother, and drove down and picked it up, and she took him up to the farmhouse – without telling me,' Ruth added.

Patrick nodded. 'When did you put him in his cot?'

'When we came back from the shops. He fell asleep in the car so I just put him in.' Ruth stretched across the table and held his hands. 'Patrick, stop this. Tell me what is the matter.'

His hands, under her own, were like ice. 'The matter is this: that Mother found him in his cot, covered in sick, sweating from the heat, having cried himself to sleep,' he said dully. 'And she says that this morning you let him choke on a sponge.'

Ruth gasped. 'It was an accident!' she said, outraged. 'And she said she wouldn't tell you!'

Patrick gave her a sharp accusing stare.

'I was going to tell you,' Ruth said quickly. 'It was just an accident. And this afternoon wasn't like that. He was sick in the shop. I just put him in his cot.'

There was a silence.

'Patrick!' Ruth said. 'I just told you! He was sick in the shop and he fell asleep in the car, so I just put him in his cot and let him sleep.'

He did not meet her eyes.

'So it's OK,' Ruth said.

Still he said nothing.

'She's making a fuss about nothing,' Ruth said stoutly.

Patrick got up from the table as if he had heard enough. 'I don't agree,' he said levelly. 'She is very concerned that you left him in his cot like that, and so is the old man. And so am I.'

Ruth got up too. 'But this is absurd!' she said. She put her hand on Patrick's arm. 'There's nothing wrong! We had a completely awful day, but there's nothing really wrong! It was just one of those days – you know – where everything goes wrong, and you feel like throwing him out of the window, you know what it's like!'

Patrick suddenly turned on her. 'No, I don't know!' he exploded. 'I don't know about days when my son chokes and nearly suffocates in the morning and is then abandoned to be sick in his cot all afternoon and his mother wants to throw him out of the window. I don't know about days like that!'

Ruth fell back, shaking her head. 'It wasn't like that . . .' she said.

'Thomas will sleep at the farmhouse tonight.' Patrick gave the order with a strange tone in his voice, as if it were not his decision but some new immutable law. 'And tomorrow you and I will go up there and decide with Mother and Father what to do. We don't think you can be left on your own with him, Ruth.'

'You mean she doesn't.'

The spite in her voice repelled him. 'If you mean my mother, then you are right,' he said. 'My mother does not think you are fit to be in sole charge of my son. And neither does my father. And neither do I.'

'How dare you!' Ruth cried. 'He is *my* son as much as yours, he is *my* son, and I love him, and I care for him, and I would never hurt a hair of his head, and you may not say such a thing! Ever! Ever! Ever!'

'You just said you felt like throwing him out of the window!'

'Everybody does!' Ruth screamed. 'It's called real life! Everybody feels like that sometimes. It doesn't mean I don't love him!'

Patrick turned and went for the front door and Ruth flung herself on him and pulled at his arm and his shoulder, to turn him to face her.

'You can't do this!' she said. 'You can't take him away from me like that!'

His face was bleak. He looked at her and Ruth shrank back from the coldness in his eyes. 'Yes, we can,' he said.

'Patrick,' she whispered. 'Please don't – please don't be like this.'

He shook his head. 'It's you,' he said. 'Not me.'

He opened the door.

'Where are you going?' she asked. Her voice sounded little and thin against the great dark of the country winter night outside.

'I'm going up to the farm,' he said. 'I'm sleeping there tonight. I'll come down and pick you up in the morning.'

She would have stopped him but he turned quickly and went down the path, got into his car, backed it carefully into their drive, and drove off.

In his rear-view mirror he could see the bright oblong of the doorway spilling light into the garden, and Ruth's silhouette, clinging to the doorpost, as if her legs were giving way beneath her.

Sixteen

Ruth did not sleep that night, she sat in the window seat of the sitting room, wrapped in her duvet, with her head leaning against the icy glass, looking out at the night sky and waiting for the first signs of light. She thought that she had never in her life been in a worse situation – not in depression, and not in recovery. Every other situation had been created by accident or by her own folly. For the first time in her life Ruth realized that she had enemies.

She wept a little – that Patrick should leave her so abruptly, that he should have sided with his parents against her, without even considering her version of events. But as the sky grew darker and the wind came up she moved from self-pity into a cold determination. She realized that she had lost Patrick, and lost her marriage. Now she had to fight for her child.

In the farmhouse Patrick got up at two in the morning, after restless sleep with anxious dreams, poured himself a large brandy, and took it back to bed with him. Frederick woke at five, in the solid winter darkness, as black as midnight, sighed at the grief of the day ahead, and went downstairs to make a pot of strong tea.

Only Elizabeth and Thomas, with clear consciences,

slept well. Thomas did not wake until half past seven, and Elizabeth laid him on her bed with his morning bottle while she washed and dressed.

At nine o'clock prompt, Frederick telephoned his solicitor, Simon Sylvester. The call was as brief as Frederick's distress and distaste could make it. Simon Sylvester advised him that the first step in taking a child from its mother was to get a residence order with Patrick and his parents nominated as guardians. Subsequently there would have to be social-worker reports.

'It would help your case no end if the mother was committed,' Simon Sylvester said cheerfully. 'Especially with a record of drinking and drugs. Is she likely to put up a fight?'

'No,' Frederick said, thinking of Ruth's vulnerable desperation. 'No fight in her at all.'

'Parents? Family?'

'No one. The family are American, and the parents are dead.'

'Then she can go inside on your say-so: you're the nearest of kin. She can be locked up by this afternoon and you and your son named as guardians this evening,' Simon said. 'If you've given up on her, that is. If you're throwing her overboard.'

Frederick heard the abrupt dismissal of Ruth without flinching. 'Be on stand-by then,' he said. 'I'll call you at midday.'

At half past nine, Patrick, looking hollow-eyed and grey-skinned, went down the drive to fetch Ruth.

She was waiting, at the sitting-room window bay. For a moment he thought that perhaps she had not gone to bed at all, but had stood there, waiting and hoping for him all night.

When she came out of the house, slammed the front door behind her, and got in the car, he saw that she was alert and wakeful. She had showered and washed her hair, she had changed into a dark cashmere polo-neck sweater, and black jeans. She looked slim, desirable, and challenging.

He drove in silence and she sat beside him in silence. They were both waiting for the other to speak and assessing, by the thousand small signs that intimate couples know, how long the quarrel might extend, how angry it might be, whether there might be a meeting of the eyes, an understanding, a meeting of the fingertips, a reconciling kiss.

Ruth hunched her right shoulder and looked out of the side window. Patrick drove, never taking his eyes off the road, as if it were not his own drive, which he knew well enough to walk in the dark.

When they got out of the car at the farmhouse, the front door opened.

'Dear Ruth,' Elizabeth said gently. 'Come in.'

Ruth followed her into the drawing room, where the fire was lit and the silver coffeepot was on the polished table. Ruth read the signs with a quick glance. This was a best-china occasion; it was intensely serious. Then she saw Thomas in his bouncy cradle-seat.

She did not rush to him and snatch him up. She sat down quietly on the floor beside him, and held up his little duck so he could take it from her and drop it, and have it offered again. There was something very composed about Ruth's gentle play with her son. His eyes went from the toy to her serene face with pleasure.

Elizabeth's silver coffee service and little enamelled spoons seemed suddenly to strike a false note, as Ruth sat cross-legged on the floor, playing quietly with her son as if they were alone together.

Frederick came in. 'Ruth,' he nodded to her, hardly smiling.

'Coffee?' Elizabeth asked.

It seemed that no one wanted coffee.

For a moment no one spoke. It had not been planned in detail. Frederick and Elizabeth and Patrick had merely agreed that some decision must be made, since matters with Thomas could not go on. But they had not descended to conspire against Ruth, and Frederick's consultations with his lawyer were a secret known only to him. Only he knew that the papers to commit Ruth, without her consent, to a mental hospital were being drawn up. Only he knew that Thomas could be a ward of court tonight.

'What's this all about?' Ruth asked. She addressed Elizabeth directly and without hesitation. 'I had an accident with Thomas yesterday morning when he put his sponge in his mouth, and yesterday afternoon I put him into his cot when he had been sick while we were out shopping. He was never left alone, he was never in any danger. When I had to go out, I telephoned you.'

Elizabeth inclined her head but said nothing.

'I am caring for him perfectly well,' Ruth went on, her voice controlled and tight. 'There is no need for concern.'

Still Elizabeth said nothing.

'We are concerned, Ruth,' Frederick said bluntly. 'These things – whether they are exactly as you describe or not – these things have all happened on the first day that Patrick goes back to work and leaves you alone in the little house. If you are not coping with Thomas,

300

Ruth, we will have to insist that you let us help.'

Ruth shot a look at Patrick. He folded his arms and leaned back.

'How help?'

'I'll come down in the morning and take him out for his constitutional in his pram. Or if rain stops play, I'll rock him in the hall or wherever, while you do your chores. Elizabeth will come down in the afternoon to give you a break. Patrick will be home at six every evening. So you have some support.'

Ruth hesitated. 'Is this an offer, or is it an order?'

Frederick cleared his throat. Elizabeth was looking at her well-polished tan shoes. Patrick's eyes were on his father's face. Thomas cooed softly and Ruth offered him another toy.

'You can take it as you wish,' Frederick said. 'It's a description of what is going to happen.'

'Forever?'

'Until we are sure·that you are well enough to care for him on your own.'

'And if I refuse?' she asked.

Patrick stole a quick look at his wife. There was a hardness and a maturity about her that he had never seen before. A sharp brilliance in her look, as if she would face the worst truths in the world, and look them in the eye. She was many miles away now from the grateful ingenue he had married. There was something adult about her now, and rock hard. He was not sure if he liked her, but there was something undeniably erotic in the way she just nodded and moved coldly and intellectually to the next question. He nodded. She was out-manning the men. She had not come as a bereaved mother to weep and call for the return of her baby. She had come out as a lioness to fight until the death.

'I hope you will see that this is for the best,' Frederick said, avoiding the challenge.

She smiled, a scornful, bitter smile, very beautiful on her face. 'But if I do *not* see that? If I refuse?'

Frederick nodded, accepting her challenge and showing his hand with all the deceptive honesty of the skilled poker player. 'Then we keep Thomas here and you are welcome to live here with us again, or visit daily.'

She looked to Patrick again but he was looking at the fire.

'I could take Thomas right away,' she said thoughtfully.

Frederick shook his head. 'We would not permit that,' he said. 'Thomas stays here, either with us or with you with our supervision.' He hesitated. 'Besides,' he said. 'You have nowhere to go, and no money. You have no friends who would take you in, and no family. It would not be fair to you or Thomas, and it's not necessary, Ruth.'

She shot a look at him. 'Not necessary to be free?'

'This is a brief difficult phase in a long, long life,' Frederick said. He spoke solemnly, as if he were weighing her down with the wisdom of his experience. 'In months, maybe in weeks, we will have half forgotten this, and by next year we will hardly remember it at all. Lots of families have difficulties in adjusting to a new baby. There is no reason why our family should be any different. Let us help you, Ruth, and take it in the spirit in which it is meant – because we love our son, and we love our grandson, and we love you.'

There was a silence. Thomas was bored and started to cry in a fretful, inconsequential way. Ruth lifted him out of his bouncy cradle-seat and sat him on her lap. 'Nearly time for his nap,' she said.

'He can go upstairs,' Elizabeth said. 'I'll make his bottle.'

Ruth nodded, and rocked him gently, held firmly under her cheek against the comforting sound of her beating heart. Thomas's downy little head was warm under her chin.

'I have no choice,' Ruth observed.

Her father-in-law nodded. 'That is correct,' he said gently. 'You have no choice.'

Ruth nodded. 'You force me to agree,' she said simply.

Elizabeth came back into the room with the bottle in her hand. 'You agree?'

'Yes.' Ruth nodded dismissively towards Frederick. 'He can come down in the morning and you can come down in the afternoon. The rest of the time Thomas is to be left with me.'

Patrick suddenly realized that he had been sitting with his arms crossed and his shoulders hunched for what felt like all the morning. He released his grip and felt his muscles relax.

'Well done, darling,' he said gently. 'And thank you.'

Ruth looked at him with large dark eyes, which told him nothing. 'I'll put him to sleep in the nursery here,' she said. 'I'll bring the pram up and you can wheel him down when he wakes. I want him brought down to me straight away, as soon as he wakes.'

'I'll do that for you,' Frederick said quietly. He had to suppress a sense of triumph. It had been a long time since he had been faced with a situation of outright and damaging conflict. It had been something of a diplomatic pleasure as well as a duty to bring Ruth into line.

'I'll drive you home,' Patrick offered. 'Dad can come too and collect the pram. That'll save you the walk.'

Again she gave him the dark, unfriendly stare. 'All right,' she said. 'When he's asleep.'

That day Ruth did as they wanted. Frederick pushed the pram down the drive as soon as Thomas had woken, and Ruth greeted them at the garden gate, drew the pram into the house, played with Thomas, and then gave him his lunch. After lunch, which he ate with relish – it was one of the brighter-coloured jars – Ruth took him upstairs to change his nappy and changed all his clothes as well. His morning clothes smelled of Elizabeth's perfume.

At about three o'clock, when Thomas started getting tired again, Ruth put him in his pram and rocked him until his eyelids slowly closed and his one waving foot fell back into the pram. Then she tucked him up and put the pram in the back garden, and started to wash the kitchen floor.

Glancing out of the French windows, she saw Elizabeth, who had entered the garden by the bottom gate, bending over the pram, and gently rocking it with the handle. Ruth opened the back door.

'I should like you to tell me when you arrive,' she said abruptly. 'Don't go straight to the pram like that. He might have been just dozing off and you would have woken him.'

Elizabeth straightened up and nodded. 'I'm sorry,' she apologized. 'I will in future.'

She came into the kitchen, glancing around. 'Would

you like to go out?' she asked. 'Or have a rest? I can finish the chores while Thomas is sleeping.'

'I'm in the middle of washing my kitchen floor. I hardly want to leave it and go out. Would you please go to the sitting room?'

Elizabeth nodded, saying nothing, and went quietly through. Ruth mopped with silent resentment, wrung out the mop, poured away the dirty water, and put the mop and bucket away in the cupboard under the stairs.

She put her head around the sitting-room door. 'I need to do some shopping,' she said abruptly. 'I'll be about an hour.'

Elizabeth was sitting on the sofa, looking at the *Guardian* newspaper. 'Of course,' she said pleasantly. 'If he wakes I'll bring him in and play with him here.'

'He is not to be taken out of this house,' Ruth said flatly. 'When I come back, he is to be here.'

'Of course.' Elizabeth gave her daughter-in-law a tentative smile. 'Of course, Ruth. We're all working together on this.'

Ruth's face was like a wall. 'That's not how I see it,' she said. 'You are not to give him his tea, you are not to bath him. I will do that when I come home.'

'I will change his nappy,' Elizabeth stipulated.

Ruth hesitated. 'All right,' she said and turned and went out of the door.

Elizabeth sat completely still until she heard the car drive away, and then she went through to the kitchen and glanced out of the window at the pram. As the noise of the engine died away down the lane she gave a little sigh, and her shoulders relaxed, as if a burden had slid away. She drew the curtains into the proper tiebacks.

'Poor, dear, unhappy Ruth,' she said softly. 'Such a shame . . .'

Then she went out into the garden to see Thomas.

Ruth was back precisely within the hour, and she unloaded the shopping from the car and left the front door open for Elizabeth to leave.

'I'll see you tomorrow,' Elizabeth said on the doorstep.

Ruth nodded, and shut the door in her face.

Elizabeth gathered the collar of her coat about her ears, and ran down the path to her car. As she drove away from the little house she was smiling.

Thomas was fretful at dinner time and would not eat. He kicked out as he went into his high chair, and his bowl of dinner went flying, landing with a splash of bright tomato red all over the newly washed floor.

Ruth had to heat another bowl of dinner to give to him, and then leave him, squirming crossly in his high chair, starting to cry, as she cleared up the kitchen floor. Just as she thrust the last red-stained lump of kitchen towel in the bin, Thomas's dinner bowl – which should have been fixed with a suction cup on the tray of his high chair – came unstuck and flew across the kitchen to land on the floor again.

'Oh no!' Ruth said. For a moment she thought she would not be able to hold back the tears, but then her face hardened. It was no longer a question of having a bad evening, or washing the floor twice. It was a question of keeping custody of her child, and the danger of Patrick's family's labelling her as insane. In the face of that nightmare Ruth felt she could not afford easy, small emotions. She was facing the worst thing that could

306

possibly happen to her; the spilling of Thomas's dinner was nothing.

She scooped him out of his chair and, leaving the sticky mess on the kitchen floor, took him up the stairs, and laid him gently on his changing mat to get him undressed for his bath.

Thomas, enjoying the change of scene, was all smiles. His face, striped liberally with red tomato sauce, was radiant. When Ruth tickled his bare tummy and gently blew, he gurgled with laughter, and Ruth found herself making soft aeroplane-bombing noises and zooming down to kiss the round of his fat, warm stomach.

She lifted her head when she heard the front door open. Patrick was home. She heard him put down his briefcase, go into the kitchen, exclaim at the state of the floor, and then come up the stairs. Ruth stripped off Thomas's dirty nappy and left it on the changing mat, and carried Thomas, wrapped in a warm towel, to the bathroom.

'Hello,' Patrick said cautiously.

'Hello,' she said.

'How are things?' he asked.

'Fine.'

Ruth ran the bath and then put Thomas carefully in it, one hand behind his back, one firm grip on his arm.

'Anything I can do?' Patrick asked. In the farmhouse he was required to sit on the chair in the bathroom, drink a gin and tonic, and smile occasionally at his son.

'Yes,' Ruth said pleasantly. 'Can you clean up the changing table, there's a dirty nappy there, and then wash the kitchen floor and clean up the kitchen, and then peel some potatoes for supper, and put them on to boil. Make Thomas's bottles and bring them up.'

Patrick blinked. 'The kitchen floor looks like a butcher's shop,' he remarked.

'Doesn't it?' Ruth agreed. 'I've washed it twice already today. That's just one effort. Hurry up, Patrick, or we'll never get supper on.'

'I'll have to change,' he said.

She nodded. Slowly, he went to the bedroom to change into jeans and a sweatshirt. With his two parents on call and Ruth at home all day, he did not see why he should have to wash the kitchen floor on his arrival home after a long day at work. He slipped his feet into comfortable moccasins, and went downstairs.

The kitchen was most unappealing. From the bathroom upstairs he could hear Ruth playing with Thomas, the noise of splashing, and Thomas's delighted giggles. Patrick sighed heavily and fetched the mop.

He had barely finished before Ruth called down the stairs, 'He's ready for his bottle!'

'Coming!' Patrick shouted back.

He made up the feed and carried it up the stairs. Thomas was pink and sweet-smelling from his bath. His pyjamas were a soft white cotton all-in-one sleep suit, which encased his plump little feet and his round, compact body. When he saw his father bringing the bottle, he beamed, stretched out his hand, and babbled.

'He's saying hello!' Ruth exclaimed.

Ruth settled herself in the nursing chair and held Thomas on her lap. Patrick handed her the bottle and drew the curtains against the dark winter night. 'Goodnight, son!' he said cheerfully, and went to the door.

'Nappy,' Ruth reminded him. 'You've forgotten the dirty nappy.'

With a half-suppressed sigh Patrick folded up the disgusting little package and took it downstairs. Ruth cuddled Thomas close and rocked him.

Patrick felt at a disadvantage through the evening. He was expecting Ruth to reproach him for not standing up for her against his parents, but she cooked lamb chops and served them at the table as if she were a perfectly contented wife and mother. The potatoes were disagreeably spotty where Patrick had missed the eyes and markings, and rather hard. Ruth ate them without comment. Patrick left his on the side of his plate, with a martyred air, but then absentmindedly ate them up.

He glanced at the clock on the microwave. 'I have to see the nine-o'clock news,' he said, and got up from the table.

'OK,' Ruth said obligingly. 'We can stack the dishwasher later.'

Patrick said nothing. He had rather thought that Ruth would clear up the kitchen while he watched the news and then bring him a cup of coffee when she had finished. Ruth looked at him as if she could not see these half-formed thoughts behind his eyes.

'Oh, let's do it now,' he said.

They cleared the table in silence, and Ruth wiped down the worktops and put the breakfast things ready. Then they went through to the sitting room. It was nearly time for the ten-o'clock news. Ruth shucked off her shoes and curled up in an armchair to watch. 'Be a darling, and make me a cup of tea,' she asked. 'I'll watch the news and then I'm up to bed. It's been a long horrible day.'

He paused at the doorway. 'I'm sorry about this morning,' he said awkwardly. 'It'll all be all right soon.'

She had her head turned towards the television screen, and she did not turn back to look at him. 'Yes,' she said shortly.

They went to bed together. Patrick expected her to turn on her side and present him with her smooth pale back. But when he put out the light he felt her arms come around him with surprising strength.

He was going to hold her, to pat her back in a consoling manner. But she reared up over him and put her mouth down to his and kissed him, penetratingly, hard.

Patrick felt pierced by lust. He pulled her towards him, and she came astride him at once, her arms wound tightly around his neck, her body hard and heavy along him. As she kissed him he felt her teeth graze his lips, and he groaned with sudden, surprising desire.

Ruth slipped a quick cunning hand down his body and found and grasped his penis. Tumbling deep into desire, Patrick had a sense of adultery, of forbidden pleasure. In the years of their marriage Ruth had never assertively taken the initiative. She had often invited, but she had never forced the issue. This hot, angry sexual woman on top of him was a woman he did not recognize, but he knew, as he instinctively thrust upward, that she was what he wanted.

Ruth's silky nightgown rode up over her thighs, over her back. 'Oh, God!' Patrick said at the touch of her skin. She lowered herself on him with a gasp and then moved, rocking him faster and faster. Patrick, in a blur of sensation, just followed the rapid, demanding movements of her hips, felt himself drawn in, demanded, and finally consumed. She moved her weight so the bone inside the flesh pressed the flesh tantalizingly, delight-fully, irresistibly together.

They lay still for a moment, and then, without a word, Ruth rolled off him. Patrick was still far from thought, whirling in a powerful sexual daze.

'Ruth?' he whispered after a little while.

She did not reply, and he thought she had fallen asleep. He stretched out a hand to caress her, but she rolled away, and all he touched was the warm sheet where she had been. He had a sudden urgent curiosity to know where this wild desire had suddenly come from. How his girl-wife, his orphaned, patronized bride, had suddenly fixed on her own womanhood and her own sensuality, and had found the courage to take him and show him a passion that he had never known before and that was light-years from their usual quiet domestic couplings.

'Ruth?'

On her side, eyes open, Ruth heard him whisper her name, but she lay still. She felt a fierce, wild joy. She had taken Patrick as her mate, at last, after years of waiting for his passion and waiting for her own. She had won him to her, and she would keep him. Not any longer by trying to please him, but by determinedly and excit-ingly pleasing herself.

She waited until she heard the quiet rhythm of his sleeping breath, and then she rolled on her back and stretched with pleasure. 'At least that's one thing she can't do,' she said softly.

Seventeen

FREDERICK WALKED down the drive to Ruth's house. The day was bitterly cold, the sky heavy and grey. 'Looks like snow,' Frederick said to himself.

He rang the doorbell, and Ruth answered. Thomas was already in his pram, well wrapped-up. 'I'll only take him for a short walk, twenty minutes or so,' Frederick said. 'It's freezing.'

Ruth nodded without smiling. He had never seen her before without that slightly nervous, slightly deferential smile. It was an unnerving change; she looked suddenly older, more powerful. For the first time in his life Frederick thought that she was a beautiful woman.

'When you come back you can bring him in,' she said. 'The pram can go in the hall. I'm doing the bedrooms.'

Frederick touched his cap to her in the courteous way he always treated her. She looked at him ironically, but said nothing. 'If you want to go out,' he offered. 'I can stay with him all the morning.'

She shook her head. 'You said an hour,' she said. 'An hour in the morning and two in the afternoon. This is not at my request, nor my convenience. This is what you insist on doing. If you want to change it, then you can go home and I will have him all to myself this morning.'

'We'll stick to our agreement then,' Frederick said. He turned the pram around and went up the drive towards the farmhouse. Ruth could see the puffs of air from his breath as he walked. The pram wheels made dark lines in the whiteness of the frost. She shut the door.

Frederick walked for ten minutes away from the house and then back again. Thomas, rosy-cheeked in the cold air, did not sleep.

'He's still awake,' Frederick said. 'Shall I rock him in the kitchen or the hall?'

'He can come out and play,' Ruth said.

'I can keep him amused while you do your chores,' Frederick offered.

She gave him a cold look. 'Of course. You have forty minutes yet.' She shut the sitting-room door on them both, and Frederick heard her go up the stairs.

Thomas was over-tired by lunchtime and would eat only breakfast cereal; the soothing milky taste was what he wanted. Ruth gave him his bottle in his pram and wheeled him out into the garden. The clouds were clearing and the sun was coming out; the garden was a monochrome of black shadows and blinding white frost on the grass. Ruth rocked Thomas until he turned his head from his bottle and fell asleep, and then she quietly took the bottle from the pram.

Promptly at five to three Elizabeth drove down and parked her car. She walked around to the back garden and saw the pram. She leaned in and put her finger down inside Thomas's little mitten, and touched his cheek to see that he was warm enough. The back door to the kitchen opened.

'I have asked you to come to the front door,' Ruth said. 'I asked you yesterday not to disturb him when he is sleeping.'

Elizabeth straightened up, but she did not look at all reproved. 'I was checking whether he was warm enough,' she said. 'He's fine.'

'I know,' Ruth said. 'I checked him myself five minutes ago.'

Elizabeth laughed her easy laugh. 'Well, we're both happy then,' she said.

Ruth stepped back as her mother-in-law came in the house. 'Now,' Elizabeth offered, 'is there anything I can do for you? You know I hate to sit and do nothing.'

Ruth shook her head, her face blank. 'No,' she said. 'Nothing.'

'Well, I'll have the pleasure of reading the newspaper until Thomas wakes,' Elizabeth said. 'And then I'll change him and play with him until five o'clock. Are you going out?'

A swift expression of deep unhappiness crossed Ruth's face. 'If I have to.'

Elizabeth's smile never wavered. 'Why, you must do whatever you would like to do,' she said. 'Thomas and I will not be in your way. You could rest, or read, or make some phone calls, or cook supper – whatever you would normally do, Ruth!'

There was a short silence. There had been no normality since the arrival of Thomas.

'I'll go for a walk,' Ruth said.

'Wrap up warm!' Elizabeth called.

The front door slammed.

Elizabeth went out to the kitchen and peeped through the window to see the pram. Thomas was still asleep.

Elizabeth opened the larder door and checked the contents. Absentmindedly she opened the freezer door. Someone had disarranged the order of the meat and the vegetables. She reorganized them so that they were in the right places. She glanced around the kitchen. The floor tiles, which she had chosen to reflect light in the rather dark back room, were cloudy. Ruth had not dried them properly, Elizabeth thought. She stacked the kitchen chairs on the table, put the rubbish bin outside, and fetched the mop.

It took a little longer than she had expected. There had been a hardened lump of red baby food on the floor near the Aga, which Ruth had obviously been too idle to get down and scrub. Elizabeth went on her knees to it and got it clean again. Then she restored the kitchen to order and glanced at the clock. Ruth had been gone only twenty minutes; there was still plenty of time. Elizabeth had telephoned Patrick at work that morning to confirm that the new arrangements were working well. Patrick – who had sounded remarkably relaxed, even happy – had said that things were fine at home. But he had mentioned that there seemed to be a lot of chores to do in the evening, peeling the potatoes, for instance. Elizabeth took the bag of potatoes to the sink and peeled and sliced them, and left them in a saucepan of salted water.

She inspected the bag of potatoes with distaste. She believed that food should not be stored in polythene, and always emptied her own potatoes into an earthenware crock. In the absence of anything better, she found an old wickerwork basket, which had once held a large flower display, given for Thomas's birth, and put the potatoes in that.

Then she cleaned the sink, gave the windowsills a quick wipe, and tied back the curtains properly – they had once again been left hanging loose.

A little cry from the garden summoned her. She went out and brought him indoors, decanted him from the pram, changed his nappy with quiet efficiency, and brought him downstairs again to play on the floor before the fire.

The front door slammed. Ruth looked around the door at the picture of her mother-in-law, the flickering fire, the contented baby. 'I think I'll have a bath,' she said, and went upstairs.

She did not come down until two minutes before Elizabeth was due to leave, at 4:58 exactly. Elizabeth rose to her feet and put on her coat as Ruth came in the room.

'Did you enjoy your walk?'

'No,' Ruth said succinctly.

'You'll want me earlier tomorrow,' Elizabeth reminded her. 'You see your therapist tomorrow, don't you?'

'Yes.'

'I'll come at one then, shall I? And don't feel you have to hurry back. I can perfectly well give him his tea.'

'You are not to feed him or to bath him or to take him out of this house,' Ruth said levelly. 'The agreement was that Frederick comes down in the morning and you come down in the afternoon. And he is to stay here.'

Elizabeth looked at the wallpaper above Ruth's bowed head. 'I see no reason for any of us to be rude,' she remarked.

There was a complete silence. Elizabeth savoured the sense of moral victory. In a moment the girl would lift her head and apologize.

But Ruth met her eyes. 'I see every reason to be rude,' she said. 'You have come between me and my husband and between me and my child. You are destroying my happiness and my life.'

'Oh, Ruth!' Elizabeth cried. She reached out her hand but Ruth stood motionless, unresponsive. 'I am trying very, very hard to do the very best for you, and for Patrick, and for Thomas.' She looked imploringly into the young determined face. 'Whatever else you think, you cannot say that I am not trying to make you and Patrick happy together.' Her gesture took in the comfortable sitting room, furnished in the colours she had chosen, the fire she had lit, the curtains she had hemmed. 'All I have ever wanted has been your happiness,' she said gently.

Ruth's expression did not change. 'It's past five.'

Elizabeth turned away from the flinty look in Ruth's face. 'I'll come tomorrow at one,' she said simply, and let herself out.

As soon as the door shut, Ruth shuddered, and pitched herself down on the floor beside Thomas. He half rolled on his side to see her and reached out a plump little hand to her cheek. Ruth lay, smiling into his little face, enjoying his small caress.

'Ma –' Thomas said, enjoying the sound.

Ruth hardly dared breathe.

'Ma –' Thomas said again.

'Yes,' Ruth said firmly. 'I am.'

The next day Elizabeth was on time, as always, but Thomas was not ready for her. He had eaten well at lunchtime, and Ruth had not been able to hurry him.

317

When Elizabeth walked into the kitchen without knocking, Ruth was on her hands and knees picking up dropped food from the floor beneath the high chair and Thomas was spooning a jar of apple purée into his face and around his smiling mouth.

'How lovely to see him eating so well,' Elizabeth said. She picked up the jar and checked the ingredients. There was no added sweetener, which was the only thing in its favour, she thought. 'You run along,' she went on. 'I'll clear up here.'

Ruth hesitated. It was clearly nonsensical to tell Elizabeth not to change Thomas's clothes when his shirt was liberally smeared with dinner and his hair full of apple purée.

'Go on,' Elizabeth urged. 'I can cope.'

Ruth went out into the hall and put on her old black reefer jacket. Elizabeth noted that the new coat – the Christmas present – had not appeared. 'Anything you would like me to do for supper?' Elizabeth asked brightly. 'Then you can be back late; you don't want to have to rush.'

'It will take me half an hour to get to Bath, an hour's appointment, half an hour home again, and maybe ten minutes for delays,' Ruth said. 'I'll be home by half past three. I don't need any help.' She paused. 'And I would rather you did not peel potatoes. Patrick does them when he comes in.'

Elizabeth gave a small sigh, and then picked up Thomas. 'Let's go and wave good-bye to Mummy,' she said cheerfully, and took him to the sitting-room window.

As Ruth's car drove away, Elizabeth looked around the room. The grate had not been cleaned, it was filled with ashes. There was a cup of coffee left on the floor by one of the chairs. The sofa cushions had been put on back to front, there were newspapers on the floor beside Patrick's chair, and the room needed dusting. 'Lots to do!' she said happily to Thomas. 'I don't know what kind of state your mummy would get into if I wasn't here.'

She climbed up the stairs with him against her shoulder. There were wet and soiled clothes in the nursery laundry bag. Elizabeth stripped Thomas, changed his nappy, and put the dirty clothes in the bag. Then she dressed him in the clothes that were her favourites – a strong bright blue for a boy – and took him, and the laundry bag, downstairs again. She just had the washing in the machine, and was tying back the curtains in the kitchen windows, when the telephone rang.

'Hello, Mother,' Patrick said. 'How are things?'

'Fairly well,' she said cautiously. 'She's not getting the laundry done, and the house needs a bit of attention, but she seems to have been all right with Thomas today. He was having lunch when I arrived – just jars, of course.'

'I was calling to say I have to be late,' Patrick said. 'I can't get home before half past seven.'

'What would you like us to do?'

He hesitated. 'I'm not sure. Ideally, I'd like you to have Thomas for the evening, really. His dinner time and then bathtime and bedtime are a lot for Ruth to manage on her own.'

'Of course we can,' she said sweetly. 'I'll take him home now, and Ruth can come up for dinner. You could both come. We'll put Thomas to bed in the nursery, and Frederick can bring him down in the morning.'

319

Again Patrick hesitated. 'Don't you think she would resent it? How is she with you?'

Elizabeth laughed her assured happy laugh. 'Oh, my dear! She's in such a rage with us that none of us can do anything right. But it is the right thing for Thomas and that must be the only thing we are thinking of. I'll take him up to the farmhouse now, shall I?'

'Leave her a note,' Patrick reminded her. 'Tell her that I called and said I would be late, and that I'll come and collect her at seven-thirty, and we'll come on to dinner with you. But we'll bring Thomas back. We can take him home in his carry cot.'

'Oh, don't take him out in the cold night air!'

'No,' Patrick said firmly. 'I know that she won't want him to stay at the farm without us. He'll come home with us. It won't hurt the once.'

'I'll make a steak and Guinness pie,' his mother promised. 'And I guarantee – no black-eyed potatoes!'

'You must teach me how to cook,' Patrick said, smiling. 'I blame you for spoiling me.'

Elizabeth went around the house, checking that everything was right for Ruth's return. She laid the fire in the sitting room and whisked a duster around the more obvious surfaces. She grimaced at the little room. 'Well, Thomas,' she confided. 'It's not how *we* would like it, but I suppose it will have to do until I can come down with Mrs M and do a thoroughly good clean.'

Then she bundled Thomas into his outdoor things, strapped him in his car seat, and carried seat and baby to the car, slamming the front door behind her.

*　　*　　*

Ruth sat in the waiting room at the therapist's house, staring blankly before her. There had been a long break over the Christmas holiday and this was her first visit since then. A very great deal seemed to have happened. Ruth felt that she could not even be sure that Clare Leesome would recognize her. She felt completely changed, as if overnight she had ceased to be a vulnerable young woman and had found inside her someone hard and cold and determined.

Clare looked reassuringly the same. She was wearing a long dark skirt and a deep red soft sweater. 'Hello, Ruth,' she said.

Ruth sat in the chair opposite her.

'And how are things?' Clare asked.

Ruth looked around the room, absorbing the sense of enclosed safety. It struck her that Elizabeth had never been here, never dusted the mantelpiece, never rearranged the books on the desk. The room was a refuge from Elizabeth and from the whole Cleary family.

'They are as bad as they can be,' she said eventually.

Clare waited.

'Thomas had an accident, he choked on a sponge, and then he was sick out shopping and I put him in his cot without changing him because he was asleep. Patrick's mother told Patrick about the accident and that I left him to be sick – and they have insisted that Frederick visits in the morning, and Elizabeth comes in the afternoon.' Ruth's composed bitter voice suddenly shook. 'They don't trust me with him.'

Clare nodded gravely. 'How very, very dreadful for you,' she said.

It was the trigger for Ruth's grief. Ruth choked and then burst into tears. Through her sobs, Clare could hear her voice, as pained as a child, telling of her outrage, her loss, and her terror that they would take Thomas away from her forever.

Clare let her weep until Ruth sat up and pushed her hair away from her flushed face.

'I hadn't cried,' she said. 'I have been so angry.'

Clare nodded. 'I think anyone would feel sad and angry,' she said. 'You are in a very unfair situation. It is perfectly reasonable to be very unhappy and very angry.'

Ruth nodded. 'I don't know what to do,' she said. Her voice was still thin; she looked at Clare like a bewildered child.

'Wipe your face,' Clare said gently.

Ruth looked around. There was a box of tissues on the desk. Clare did not pass them to her but gestured that she should go and fetch them. Ruth got up and walked slowly to the desk, fetched the tissues, and sat down again. She wiped her face; she felt the peace of the room penetrate her.

'I feel better now,' she said, and her voice was steady again.

'What are you doing?' Clare asked.

'I am going along with it,' Ruth said. 'I let them come for their visits and then they go again. I've stopped running around Patrick so much and he is having to do more chores. He's not being treated like he's doing me a favour by coming home any more.'

Clare smiled. 'And how does he like that?' she asked.

Ruth had a sudden recollection of the surprise of her passion in bed with him. 'He doesn't like the washing up,' she said. 'But there are compensations.'

Clare, reading the inward smile, let that comment go.

'And do they say when they will trust you again?'

Ruth shook her head. 'I feel like I am on probation all the time.'

Clare nodded. 'And, of course, no one can survive that sort of inspection,' she said. 'People make mistakes all the time.'

'Yes,' Ruth said eagerly. 'Of course I make mistakes with him. But I would never hurt him on purpose.'

Clare paused. 'But what is the grain of truth in what they are saying?' she asked. 'Would you hurt him by accident? Are you careless? Do you wish you did not have to care for him all the time?'

Ruth sat silent, thinking deeply. She summoned a picture of Thomas, his bright eyes and his smiling face, the dimples of his knuckles and his knees. The plump firmness of his little feet and the perfect straightness of his toes. 'Sometimes I don't want to care for him,' she said honestly. 'When I'm tired or hungry, and I have to see to him first before I can do anything for myself. When he comes first all the time. Sometimes I wish someone would take him away – just for a day or two, so I can get something done without always waiting for him to wake up. And then at other times it is perfectly all right.' She paused. 'I made a mistake with the sponge,' she said. 'It didn't matter. And putting him into his cot to sleep when he had been upset and sick was the right thing to do. Elizabeth made it seem awful, but she wasn't there, and she doesn't know what he was like. He had just that moment fallen asleep and I couldn't face waking him up again.'

Clare waited in case there was anything more. But Ruth just looked up at her and smiled, an innocent, heartfelt smile. 'I love him so much,' she said simply. 'I would lay my life down for him – in an instant, without even thinking about it. To suggest that I would hurt him on purpose is quite impossible.'

Clare smiled back. 'I think you should know that I believe that you are a very good mother,' she said gently. 'I think you are learning all the time how to care for Thomas, and that you are an excellent mother.'

It was like a benediction. Ruth leaned back in her seat and closed her eyes. 'Thank you,' she breathed.

Clare nodded. 'Is there anything more?' she asked.

Ruth shook her head, satisfied. 'I'll hang on,' she said. 'I have nothing to hide. They'll see how good I am with him. They will have to see it.'

Clare thought for a moment. 'And even if they do not see,' she emphasized, thinking of Patrick's careful manipulative phone call, and wondering what his mother and father were hoping and fearing and engineering, 'even if they do not see, then if you are mothering Thomas to the best of your ability and keeping him safe then no one can take him away from you.'

Ruth looked at her for a moment, not as a patient in need of help but as a woman looks at another woman when she has finally understood the odds that are stacked against her. 'No,' she said. 'You don't know them. If they really want to take him away from me, they'll do it. They know lawyers and doctors, they even have judges as personal friends. If they want something they get it. I just have to hang on and hope that they will be satisfied with this.'

The traffic was bad on the return journey and Ruth did not get back to the little house until the early winter dark had fallen. She looked for the light from the windows as she turned in to the drive, but they were dark. Only the porch light was on, to light her way to the closed front door. She felt a sensation of growing terror. They had done it. They had done what she had feared they might do. They had taken Thomas. The house was deserted, and her child was gone. She turned the car carelessly in the driveway and scraped the wing. There was an expensive sound of crumpling metal and the screech of paint against the gatepost. Ruth tore open the driver's door and ran up the front path to the house.

She fumbled with the keys and flung the door open, but she knew before she stepped into the dark and silent hall that the house was empty. Thomas was not there.

For a dreadful moment she was certain that he had been injured: some accident, and Elizabeth had rushed him in her car to the hospital. 'Oh, God,' Ruth moaned, envisaging too clearly his face crumpled by some dreadful fall, his hair matted with blood, a twisted limb, a broken arm . . . 'Oh, God.'

She turned and ran from the house, out to the car again, and tore the car door open. She reversed back out into the lane, still on the same steering lock so she hit the gatepost again. This time she did not even hear the noise or feel the impact. She slammed on her headlights and stepped hard on the accelerator and stormed up the drive to the farmhouse. Frederick would know what had happened, and where they were.

In the turning circle she braked and a spray of sharp gravel flew up from her wheels. There were two cars parked outside the house: Frederick's and Elizabeth's. Ruth's mind was working furiously. If Elizabeth's car was here, then she was probably here, Thomas was probably here – unless they had gone to the hospital in an ambulance.

Ruth ran across the gravel to the front door, pushed it open without knocking, and went into the hall. The sitting-room door opened.

'I thought I heard your car,' Frederick said calmly. 'How nice –'

She pushed him in the chest, hard and angrily, forcing him back. She brushed past him and saw, at the fireside, Thomas, lying on his back on Patrick's old nursery play mat with Patrick's old nursery toys around him.

For a moment she simply stared at him, as if she could not believe that the horror story of her imagining was not real, as if she could not believe that this was truly her son, and his grandmother on her knees on the floor beside him, showing him things, and tickling his palms to make him laugh.

'What the hell are you doing?' Ruth cried harshly.

Elizabeth looked up. 'What's the matter?'

'What the hell, what the bloody hell are you doing with my son?'

Ruth strode across the room and snatched up Thomas. He was startled and let out a little cry. Frederick at once stepped forward and then froze, very alert.

'Ruth,' Elizabeth said soothingly, 'Ruth, calm down.'

'I told you,' Ruth gabbled, spitting in her anger. 'I told you he was not to be taken out of my house. I ordered you to leave him there!'

Elizabeth stretched out her hand. 'I know, I know you did.'

'I thought he was *dead*!' Ruth screamed at her. 'I got home, I thought he was dead! I came up here to see what had happened, what dreadful, dreadful thing had happened, and here you are, having tea, playing on the floor . . .' Ruth suddenly collapsed into sobs. Frederick instantly moved, and took Thomas from her. The baby let out another wail and Frederick slipped from the room with him. Ruth's knees gave way beneath her and she slumped to the floor.

'Hush, Ruth,' Elizabeth said gently. 'Calm down, dear.'

Ruth's harsh sobs were turning into rasping breaths. She could not breathe, she could not get air. Elizabeth stood behind her, listening to her labouring for oxygen. Frederick came back into the room, without Thomas, and silently held up a key to show that Thomas was safely locked in the nursery. Elizabeth nodded and mimed a telephone, and mouthed the word 'doctor'. He nodded at once and withdrew.

'Shhh, Ruth, ssshhh,' Elizabeth said. 'Breathe, dear, don't get in such a state.'

Ruth did not even hear her. She was struggling in a battle against her closing throat and her constricting chest; her harsh rasping gasps filled the pretty room.

Elizabeth could hear Frederick's low, urgent voice in the hall but Ruth heard nothing, fighting in a world of growing darkness and growing panic and growing pain.

'Drink this,' Frederick said firmly. He put a cold glass in her hand and held it to her lips. Ruth gagged on the brandy and spat most of it back. Frederick held it to her mouth again and she choked and swallowed, and choked again. He knelt down beside her and gently cupped his hands over her mouth and nose. 'Breathe gently,' he said. 'You'll be all right, breathe gently.'

Slowly Ruth's breathing steadied as she stopped hyperventilating. Frederick gave her another swallow of brandy, then he helped her onto the sofa, lifted her legs up. Elizabeth propped a pillow behind her head. 'There,' she said, and her voice was full of pity.

'The doctor is coming to see you,' Frederick said gently to Ruth. Her skin was pale and thick, like wax, he thought. 'Just lie here. Have another sip of brandy.'

Elizabeth slipped from the room and out to the hall, waiting for the sound of the doctor's car. She did not want to be near Ruth. She could hardly bear to see that ugly distorted face. Ruth did not fit in the pretty room, in the ordered life. Elizabeth heard Frederick's soothing murmur and the more distant whimper from the nursery, where Thomas was locked in, safely away from the anger and the tears. Then she heard the sound of the doctor's car.

She opened the front door as he was coming up the steps. 'She had some kind of hysterical fit,' she said softly. 'She took it into her head that Thomas was dead and she came racing up here screaming and crying. Then she had a fit. Frederick is with her; she's on the sofa.'

He nodded, briefly pressed her hand, and went into the sitting room.

Frederick was sitting in the chair at Ruth's head, talking to her gently, very softly, giving her little sips from the glass of brandy. Dr MacFadden took in the scene and came towards Ruth.

'Hello,' he said gently.

Vaguely she looked up at him.

'D'you know who I am?' he asked.

She looked blank. It felt as if his voice were coming from a long way away, as if it could be nothing to do with her, as if she had tumbled down a long slope into a place where nothing mattered very much any more.

'I'm tired,' she said. Her voice rasped, her throat was sore from screaming and that dreadful struggle for air.

'Would you like to sleep?' he asked. 'Shall we get you into bed, and I could give you an injection and you could get some rest? You look all in.'

She nodded. William MacFadden nodded to Frederick and the two men supported her and took her from the room. Elizabeth led the way upstairs and into the guest bedroom. The bed was made up; Elizabeth twitched off the covers.

'Just slip her shoes off and get her in,' the doctor advised gently.

They laid her on the bed with a detached respect, as if she were a corpse. Elizabeth took off the shoes and noticed a ladder in Ruth's tights. She pulled the cover over her.

'My bag,' William MacFadden said quietly to Frederick, and then turned back to the bed. 'Can you hear me, Ruth? Can you hear me?'

She turned her head on the pillow and looked at him. He thought he had never seen such a weary, tragic face. 'Yes,' she said softly.

'I'm going to give you an injection so you get a good night's sleep,' he said, speaking clearly and strongly. 'In the morning I'll come and see how you are. You'll stay here for tonight.'

Her mouth formed a word. 'Thomas.'

He turned to Elizabeth. 'What's she saying?'

Ruth tried again: 'Thomas.'

'I don't know,' Elizabeth said.

Frederick came in with the bag and William took out a hypodermic syringe, wiped Ruth's bare vulnerable inside arm with antiseptic, and injected Valium into a pale blue vein.

'Thomas,' Ruth whispered. 'I want Thomas.' And then she was asleep.

Eighteen

PATRICK CAME HOME at half past seven and opened the front door with a cheerful call. 'I saw the little house was in darkness, so I guessed you were all up here.'

His mother shook her head, and Patrick instantly caught her gravity. 'What is it?'

'It's Ruth. She had some kind of hysterical fit,' she said. 'She came up here, thinking Thomas was dead. I don't know exactly what she thought. We called the doctor and he sedated her, and now she is asleep upstairs. He's coming to see her again tomorrow.'

He looked aghast. 'What on earth was wrong?'

Elizabeth shrugged. 'She went to see her therapist and then she stormed back in this terrible state.'

He looked from her to his father. 'I am sorry,' he said helplessly. 'I am sorry. You've both tried so hard . . . I am sorry.'

'All part of the job,' Frederick said with gruff sympathy. 'And at least Thomas is all right.'

'He's in his cot asleep,' Elizabeth said. 'D'you want to see him?'

Patrick nodded. 'I'll go up,' he said.

'Stiff gin and tonic when you come down, old man,'

his father said. 'Doubles tonight. Bring the colour back into our cheeks.'

'Supper in half an hour,' Elizabeth said, going towards the kitchen.

Patrick mounted the stairs slowly and opened the door to his old nursery. His mother had redecorated it for Thomas in the same wallpaper and colours that he remembered from his earliest childhood. The wallpaper was a cream background with small Winnie the Pooh bears floating, holding on to balloons, and smaller Piglets floating beside them. There was a frieze picture of more characters from the stories. The room was warm, with yellow linen curtains drawn against the dark night. It smelled faintly of clean laundry, baby powder, and, as he approached the cot, the warm, sweet smell of sleeping baby.

Patrick paused, looking down at the little moon face of his son. A sense of great despair and unhappiness swept over him as he looked at those upcurved, untroubled eyelids and the little pout of the mouth.

'I don't know what to do,' Patrick confided to the still room. 'I don't know what to do for the best.'

Before he went downstairs he glanced in at Ruth. She was sweating from the bedclothes piled on top of her clothes. She was lying on her back and breathing noisily, through her mouth. Hesitantly, he took off the blankets and left her with just a sheet and a counterpane. He touched her as he might touch an infected animal, warily and with distaste. The slim, demanding, erotic woman of just two nights before seemed like a dream. Ruth was sick again, he thought, and he hated sickly women.

They ate in silence. No one was very hungry. Patrick drank a good deal of red wine, and when Elizabeth went

332

to bed early, the two men had a whisky together. Patrick slept in his old single bedroom. He did not share the guest bed with Ruth; he felt that it would be like sleeping next to a corpse.

The click of the automatic central heating switching on jolted Ruth into wakefulness, and she lay for a moment in complete confusion. Her throat was sore and her mouth dry and foul; she was fully dressed and in a room she did not at once recognize. She sat up, swallowed, and then remembered that Thomas was all right, and that she had been so very afraid for him, so painfully, agonizingly, afraid.

She swung off the bed and went tiptoeing out of her room to the nursery. Thomas was in the cot, still sleeping. She could see the gentle rise and fall of his chest, and hear his soft breath and his little occasional snuffle. One hand opened, in a dream, and closed again. She watched him for several minutes, drinking in the reassurance that he was clean, dry, well, at peace, and then she turned and went back to her bedroom.

She had no clean clothes, she had no toiletries, she could not brush her hair or clean her teeth. She felt dirty and at a disadvantage, but she splashed water on her face and combed her hair with her fingers. The smooth bob fell into place but hung very limp and plain. She rubbed her teeth with a wet finger and rinsed her mouth. Then she went downstairs.

Frederick was in the kitchen in his dressing gown, sitting at the kitchen table with a pot of tea and his newspaper. He rose when he saw her, and she saw a swift uneasy look cross his face.

'I'm all right,' she said abruptly.

He nodded and sat down again. 'Would you like a cup of tea?'

She took a cup and saucer from the cupboard. 'Yes, please.'

There was an awkward silence.

'I'll make up a bottle for Thomas,' Ruth said. 'He'll probably wake soon.'

'I can do it,' Frederick offered.

'I will.' Ruth turned her back to him and busied herself with measuring scoops and boiled water from the kettle.

'The doctor is coming back to see you this morning,' Frederick remarked.

Ruth kept her face turned away. She had only the dimmest memory of yesterday evening. At Frederick's prompting she recalled the face of William MacFadden and her slide into silence and sleep.

'All right,' she said. She glanced at Frederick. 'I was frightened yesterday because the house was in darkness. Elizabeth promised me that they would be there when I came home. I had no idea what was going on.'

'I left a note,' Elizabeth said abruptly from the doorway. She was in her dressing gown, but her hair was smooth and her face was wide awake, her eyes clear. Beside her Ruth felt frowsy and unkempt. 'Patrick rang to tell me that he would be home late, and that I was to bring Thomas here so that the evening would not be too much for you.' She stepped forward and rested her well-manicured hand on Frederick's shoulder. 'Did you not see my note? On the hall table?'

Ruth shook her head. 'I didn't see it.' She thought for a moment. 'There was nothing on the hall table,' she said certainly. 'There was no note there, nothing.'

Elizabeth met her gaze but did not reply.

There was a distant wail from upstairs as Thomas woke for his early-morning feed. Both women reached for the bottle but Elizabeth let Ruth take it. She stepped back as the younger woman went out and nodded to Frederick. 'Stay within earshot,' she said softly.

He nodded, and followed Ruth up the stairs to the nursery. Briskly, Elizabeth began to lay the dining-room table for breakfast.

William MacFadden came to visit during his break from morning surgery, at eleven o'clock. Patrick had fetched Ruth's clothes from the little house, and she was dressed in a clean shirt and blue jeans. She looked young and pretty and well.

'You look a lot better,' he said approvingly.

Patrick took Thomas from her and went to the bedroom door. 'I'll be in the nursery if you need me,' he said.

Ruth let them go. 'I'm better,' she said to William. 'I'm fine.'

'No after effects?'

She shook her head.

'I wonder if you should go on a course of mild sedatives,' William suggested. 'You do seem a little high-strung, something to make you a little more relaxed?'

Ruth looked at him. 'No,' she said shortly. 'I've had enough of your pills.'

He felt that she was blaming him, and disliked her for it. 'It was a nasty panic attack you had,' he said smoothly. 'Distressing.'

'My baby had disappeared from his home,' Ruth said bitingly. 'I had no idea where he was or what was happening. Of course I was afraid.'

'You must have known he would be safe with your mother-in-law . . .' Dr MacFadden interrupted.

Ruth shot him a hard look. 'No, I did not,' she said.

He raised his eyebrows as if he did not want to comment, or even consider what she said. 'Is there anything I can do for you? Would you like to see me at the surgery? You could have an evening appointment so we are not at all rushed? I could refer you to a therapist?'

'No, thank you,' Ruth said.

He paused for a moment longer, but the list of patients who needed to see him was on his mind, and he did not know what should be done for Ruth.

'Very well, then,' he said. 'I'll see myself out.'

Elizabeth and Frederick were waiting for him in the hall.

'How is she?' Elizabeth asked.

'Irritable,' he replied. 'But in control.'

Patrick walked with him to the car. 'Should we have her committed?' he asked frankly. 'Get this sorted out once and for all?'

Dr MacFadden recoiled. 'She's not psychotic!'

'I don't know what she is!' Frederick gestured to Ruth's new car. The front wing, which had suffered a double blow, was crumpled beyond repair. 'That's the second car she's gone through in as many months. She can't seem to manage anything.'

'Is she at risk?'

The two men looked at the car.

'Obviously,' Frederick said.

Dr MacFadden took a deep breath. 'If you want her

committed for an assessment of her mental health, then I would sign the forms,' he promised.

'Good man,' Frederick said quietly. 'I think we'd all be happier.'

Upstairs Ruth went to find Patrick. 'I should like to go home now,' she said.

Patrick was dressing Thomas and had one hand inexpertly laid on Thomas's stomach while spreading cream on his bottom with the other.

'Oh!' he said.

Ruth nodded. 'As soon as Thomas is dressed. I have a whole load of things I want to get done today.'

'I rather thought we'd stay here, till you're completely better.'

'There's nothing in the least wrong with me,' Ruth said simply. 'I came home last night to a dark house and my baby missing and I was terribly upset. If he had been there, as he should have been, then everything would have been all right. If you want to make sure that I am not upset, then you should let me look after my own baby.'

'Hush . . .' Patrick said, glancing at the open door.

'Elizabeth had no right to take him out of the house without my permission,' Ruth said as clearly as before. 'And she has no right to tidy my deep freeze, or peel potatoes, or tie back my bloody kitchen curtains!'

'Everything all right up there?' Frederick called up the stairs. 'Time for a cup of coffee?'

'We're just going!' Ruth called back. 'I'll have coffee at home, thank you.'

She stepped forward and slipped Thomas's vest over

337

his head, and pulled his shirt on top. Thomas let out a wail of protest while she captured each foot, put on his socks and his felt slippers. She picked him up and carried him downstairs.

'If you're sure . . .' Elizabeth said. She glanced at Patrick, coming down the stairs behind Ruth. He shrugged.

'Frederick will pop down at midday,' Elizabeth suggested. 'And I'll come down this afternoon.'

'On one condition,' Ruth specified. They were all wary of her.

'What is that?' Frederick asked.

'That Thomas is never, never to be taken out of my house, without my express permission.'

Elizabeth prompted Patrick with a glance.

'But, Ruth, that was my idea, not Mother's,' he said. 'I rang and said I would be late. It was my idea that we should all come up here for dinner, to save you the bother of coping with Thomas on your own and cooking dinner.'

'I am a wife and mother,' Ruth said, laying claim to titles she would have despised a year earlier. 'I am a wife and mother and I have a job to do. I have to care for Thomas and I have to manage our house. If I can't do it, I'll get help. I'll hire help. But I won't have people continually interfering. Thomas is to stay at home.'

There was a silence; they all looked down the hall towards Frederick. 'For a trial period of one week,' he said carefully. 'And if there is another upset, or any cause for concern at all, then we will reconsider.'

Ruth, holding Thomas under her chin, met his gaze. 'What d'you mean?'

'If there is another upset, then you will have to seek treatment,' Frederick said frankly.

338

For a moment he thought she had not heard him, her face was so blank. 'Treatment?' she said. 'I'm not ill.'

'That is not for you to judge,' Frederick said simply. 'You are not qualified to judge. Neither am I; none of us are. But if things do not get better we'll call in the experts.'

'You want me to go back to Springfield House?' she asked incredulously.

Frederick shook his head. 'A closed hospital,' he said quietly.

Ruth's breath came out in a little hiss. 'You're planning to have me committed,' she said slowly. 'You're planning to call me a loony and send me to a loony bin.'

Elizabeth and Patrick recoiled at the words but Frederick never wavered. 'If that's how you want to describe it,' he said steadily. 'I have the power to do it, Ruth. Any close family member, with a doctor's agreement, can do it.'

She nodded, saying nothing. Her eyes met his, but he saw from the dark dilation of her pupils that she saw nothing. 'I know,' she said softly. 'I know you have the power.'

They were all silent for a moment, as if they were all aghast at how far they had come.

'I don't want to do it,' Frederick said gently.

She nodded again. 'I believe you,' she said. 'I believe that you would do it very reluctantly and sadly.'

'I will only do it if it is my duty: to keep Thomas safe, and to keep you safe.'

She focused her shocked eyes on his face. 'And those are your only criteria?' She glanced towards Elizabeth. 'Thomas's safety? Not what anyone else says about me? Not whether I'm good enough – or not?'

339

'No,' he said steadily. 'Your safety and Thomas's safety are the only criteria.'

She breathed out again, and moved slowly down the hall. 'Very well,' she said. 'I understand what I am facing.'

Slowly she walked past him to the front door. He opened the door for her and she walked past him, without a word of thanks, without turning her head. Patrick followed her and got into his car, while Ruth put Thomas into the baby seat in her car.

'What was this?' Frederick asked, pointing to the crumpled wing.

For a moment she looked blank, then she said abruptly: 'It doesn't matter. It doesn't matter at all,' and she got in the car, started the engine, and drove steadily away.

Elizabeth caught a glimpse of her son's set face as he too drove past. He raised a hand to them, and followed Ruth's car down the drive.

In the little house things were incongruously normal. The heating was on and the house, thanks to Elizabeth's tidying, looked smart and welcoming. Ruth was taking off Thomas's coat in the hall when Patrick came in.

'There's no note,' she said abruptly.

Patrick looked at the hall table, where his mother said she had left a note for Ruth. It was empty.

'There must be,' he said.

Ruth looked at him but said nothing. 'Are you going to work now?'

'If you can manage.' Patrick glanced at his watch. 'I won't be late tonight, especially if I can get in now.'

'I can manage.'

He paused at the front door. 'Are you sure?' he asked.

She nodded, her face blank. 'Your father is supervising me this morning, and she's coming this afternoon, and you'll be home by six. I won't ever have more than an hour on my own with my son, if that's what you want.'

'You know it's not what we want!' he exclaimed, but broke off. 'We'll talk tonight,' he promised, hoping that they would not have to talk. 'We'll have a good long talk tonight.'

He kissed her gently on the side of her face. To his surprise she turned and kissed him back, on the mouth. He tasted the slightly sweet warmth of her breath. There was a promise in the kiss; Patrick felt desire.

'It's not me that needs to get back to normality,' Ruth said quietly. 'Think about it, Patrick. It might be the rest of you.'

When Elizabeth came down at two o'clock she rang the front doorbell, as she had been told to do. Ruth, who had dropped the latch to prevent Elizabeth's walking in, took her time opening the door, and when she saw Elizabeth she turned and went back to the kitchen, where Thomas was sitting in his high chair, watching his mother, and hammering a spoon on the tray.

'As you know, there was no note,' Ruth said over her shoulder. She was frying mince on the stove. Elizabeth watched as the little droplets of hot grease spattered on top of the Aga and Ruth did not wipe them up.

'I beg your pardon?'

'There was no note to tell me where Thomas was. You said you had left a note but you did not.'

341

Elizabeth suppressed a small sigh, put down her handbag and went back out to the hall. In a few minutes she came back in holding a folded sheet of paper. 'It had fallen down behind the hall table,' she said. 'But I am surprised you did not see it on the floor.'

Ruth peremptorily took it and read it. It was very clear and very reassuring. She handed it back to Elizabeth without comment.

'Has he had a sleep today?' Elizabeth asked.

'No,' Ruth said. She took the frying pan over to the sink and drained the fat off the meat, letting it run down the drain. Elizabeth bit her lip to suppress the advice that Ruth would get blocked drains if she poured melted fat down them.

'I will sponge his face and hands and change him and rock him in the garden then,' Elizabeth offered. 'It's quite warm in the sun.'

Ruth nodded. 'I'm going down to the village to get some tomato purée,' she said. 'Remember that he is to be here when I come back. Whatever Patrick says. Whatever anyone says.'

Elizabeth nodded, and lifted Thomas out of his high chair. Ruth once again had not fastened his safety straps.

Nineteen

THE FOLLOWING DAY was Saturday, and Patrick did not go in to work. They had a cautious weekend together. Patrick suggested Sunday lunch at the farm, but Ruth gave him a look that was a clear refusal. Instead, he took Thomas up to the farmhouse after lunch and brought him back in the evening. Ruth slept away the afternoon.

When the routine of the week started again, nothing changed. Elizabeth and Ruth spoke less and less at arrival and departure, but Elizabeth did not touch things in Ruth's kitchen, or do her chores. Ruth waited, without much hope, for someone, Frederick or Patrick, to acknowledge that the house was well run, that the child was well and happy, and that she no longer need be supervised.

When Thursday came, and Ruth had an appointment with her therapist, she found that Patrick had taken the afternoon off work and was going to drive her in to Bath and back out again in the evening. 'Or we could stop for a drink if you like,' he suggested.

'Why?'

'Because of last week,' he said shortly.

'I was upset last week because Elizabeth took Thomas

343

out of the house without my permission and without telling me where they had gone,' Ruth repeated steadily.

'She left a note,' he said.

'She *says* she left a note.'

He looked at her with open dislike. 'I hardly think that my mother is likely to lie,' he said.

Ruth got into Patrick's car and slammed the door. 'Oh, don't you,' she said under her breath.

Her session with Clare Leesome was uneasy. Towards the end, Clare asked her: 'Are you feeling angry, Ruth?' and saw from the swift, direct look that Ruth was too furious to speak: even to her.

'Not particularly,' Ruth said unhelpfully.

At the end of the session Ruth said, 'I don't think I will come again. I think I should finish now.'

Clare's face showed nothing but interest and concern. 'Do you think so?' she asked.

'Yes,' Ruth said. 'As long as I am coming here, then they have something on me. It reminds them that I was ill. They say "visiting your therapist" as if I was completely mad. They can use it against me.'

Clare nodded. 'You could see me and not tell them,' she suggested.

Ruth thought for a moment and shook her head. 'She would find out,' she said. 'She reads my diary, she would check the milometer on the car, she knows everything.'

Clare privately thought that it was unlikely that anyone would go that far, but she said nothing. 'I think your main concern should be whether you feel you have finished working with me,' she said gently. 'Not what anyone else may think about you.'

Ruth stood up. 'Nothing matters more than that I keep Thomas,' she said flatly. 'Seeing you is jeopardizing

344

that. So I'm going to stop seeing you. If things ever get better, I may telephone and ask to come back.' She picked up her handbag. 'Thank you,' she said shortly. 'You've been very helpful.'

'I cannot ask you to stay,' Clare said quickly. 'But it is not a choice between seeing me and keeping Thomas. Anyone would understand that it is a sign of good health for you to work through your feelings with a therapist. No one would take a child away from a mother who was a progressing patient.'

Ruth shook her head, and went to the door. 'They will if they want to,' she said flatly. 'So thank you. Good-bye.'

'I've stopped seeing my therapist,' Ruth said baldly, when they got home. Thomas was in his high chair eating squares of toasted cheese. Elizabeth poured Patrick a cup of tea.

Elizabeth and Patrick exchanged a swift alarmed look. 'Why?' Patrick asked.

'Because I don't need a therapist any more. I am completely cured of depression,' Ruth said briskly.

Elizabeth hesitated. 'But you are still – sometimes – very unhappy, Ruth,' she said cautiously.

'Oh, yes,' Ruth said with open dislike. 'I'm very, very unhappy, and I am very angry with the situation that you, the three of you, have put me in. But none of that needs therapy. What is needed is that the situation change.'

Elizabeth turned and unfastened the curtains from the tiebacks and drew them against the darkening sky.

'It will change,' Patrick said reassuringly. 'Everything

will change as soon as you are completely relaxed and on top of things.'

'And when do you think that will be?' Ruth challenged him, but she was looking towards Elizabeth. 'Next month? February?'

'Oh, for sure,' Patrick said. 'February.'

But February came and went and still Frederick arrived for an hour every morning and Elizabeth for two hours every afternoon. It was very cold and misty, and they played with Thomas in the sitting room while Ruth tidied the rest of the house, or did the ironing, or cooked Patrick's supper. There was not enough for her to do to fill three hours every day. Elizabeth suggested that she make matching cushion covers for the sofa, and promised her some wonderful material, and the loan of her sewing machine. Ruth looked blank. 'We have cushions already,' she said.

Ruth's antagonism solidified and settled in the four weeks in which it became apparent that nothing would ever change. Thomas had been adopted into his grand-parents' routine and Ruth had to go along with the rhythm of their lives, however empty it left her own.

As the weather improved in March, Frederick took Thomas for longer walks up the drive. One day they were caught by a sudden shower of rain and he took shelter in the farmhouse, telephoned Ruth to say that they were in the dry, and he would bring Thomas back as soon as the shower lifted. Thomas stayed for lunch at the farmhouse that day, and Elizabeth brought him back in the afternoon. Frederick's hour in the morning imperceptibly extended to two, and Elizabeth lingered on in the afternoons. Ruth found that she was gradually excluded from Thomas's play times and wakeful times. He woke her in the early mornings, at about seven o'clock, and she had the task of trying to dress a protesting and growing baby, and feed him his breakfast. But when he had eaten and was sponged clean and all smiles, it was Frederick who took him out for a walk and pointed out catkins and the early snowdrops. When Frederick brought him home he was either asleep or grouchy and hungry and Ruth had the task of feeding him, changing his nappy, and laying him down for his nap. When Elizabeth arrived, he was generally still in the garden sleeping, and when he woke he was all smiles. Elizabeth had the relaxed afternoon playtime; when she left at between four and five o'clock, he was starting to get tired and hungry again. From five till bathtime was his worst period of the day. Hungry but refusing to eat, tired but it was too early for his bath and bed. The two or three hours until Patrick came home were the most onerous and least satisfactory of the day, and Ruth coped with them alone and unaided, after a boring, lonely day on her own.

'If she would only ask for help,' Elizabeth sighed to Frederick. She had telephoned to check the arrangements for tomorrow and had heard Thomas wailing lustily in the background and banging his spoon on his plate. 'I can manage that baby with one hand tied behind my back.'

'She only has him for a couple of hours,' Frederick said. 'You would have thought she could have managed that.'

Elizabeth did not explain that Ruth's couple of hours were always the busiest and most stressful hours of the day. She just smiled. 'I would have hoped so,' she said.

During the days Ruth did not have enough to do. She wrote a couple of proposals for programmes for Radio Westerly, but they rejected one without even discussing it, and the other she lost heart in, and threw away. She started to practise cookery and bought herself a couple of books of menus. When the weather grew warmer in March, she tried to take an interest in the garden.

But always, over her shoulder, was the knowledge that her mother-in-law knew far better what should be done. Elizabeth would pop into the kitchen while Ruth was kneading pastry, with flour spilled on the floor and smeared against her jumper where she had leaned against the worktop, and she would smile and say, 'Gracious! What are you making! Enough to feed an army?' and go back to Thomas, leaving Ruth to realize that she had got the quantities wrong, and that a huge lump of pastry would go to waste.

When Ruth was weeding on her hands and knees on the damp lawn, Thomas sleeping in his pram beside her, Elizabeth arrived through the back gate, leaned over the pram to see her grandson, and then turned to Ruth.

'Those aren't weeds, darling,' she said helpfully. 'They're dwarf asters. You'd better put them back in again.'

Ruth looked at the huge pile of plants she had spent an hour digging up.

'Oh, dear,' said Elizabeth. 'And those are daffodil bulbs, which shouldn't have been disturbed. I don't think you'll get a lot to flower now.'

'I'll put them back,' Ruth said grimly.

'Let me help. Thomas is still asleep,' Elizabeth offered. 'I'll get some gloves.'

'I'll do it,' Ruth said.

Elizabeth laughed. 'You do like to learn the hard way!' she exclaimed and went inside the house, leaving Ruth to the cold soil and the muddy lawn, and the pile of wilting plants. Ruth could see the kitchen curtains move as Elizabeth tied them back in the right way.

Ruth no longer protested at Elizabeth's tidying of her house. It was easier to find things in the freezer when they were all on labelled shelves. It was more convenient with small things at the front of the larder. The curtains did look prettier tied back. The only habit Elizabeth still maintained that Ruth still hated was the casual way that she entered the house through the garden gate, checked on the baby, and then came in through the back door with a casual 'Hello!'

If Ruth locked the back door – which meant locking the pram outside – Elizabeth checked Thomas in the pram and then strolled around to the front door and tried it. If it was locked, she might ring the bell or she might open it with her own key. She had no sense at all that the little house was not her own property, that she should await an invitation to enter. When Ruth complained to Patrick, he merely shrugged and said, 'Well, they *do* own it legally, darling.' When she asked Elizabeth to use the front door, and to leave the pram in the back garden alone, Elizabeth just laughed and said, 'But I do so love to see him asleep.'

Ruth did not complain to Frederick. In the months that passed after his warning that he would take Thomas away from her and commit her to an asylum, she took great care not to offend Frederick, and to deny Elizabeth nothing. She never forgot that she was living at home, and caring for her son, with their permission.

In March and April the daffodils came out. As Elizabeth had predicted, Ruth had spoiled the show in the back garden, but the ones at the farmhouse were superb. Elizabeth brought armfuls down every day and filled the little house with them. She walked across the fields on every fine day, and came in the back gate. Ruth would watch her from one of the bedroom windows, her light step, her carefree proprietorial glance at their fields, at their hedges, at their drive, and then at their little house. Ruth's hands would tighten as she watched Elizabeth come into the garden, and then, every time, every single time, Elizabeth would lean over the pram, rocking the handle slightly with her hand, and whisper to Thomas as he lay asleep.

One time Ruth ran downstairs and flung open the kitchen door as Elizabeth turned to the house. 'I've asked you a thousand times to leave the pram alone!' she snapped.

Elizabeth was quite unmoved. 'I just like to say hello,' she said.

'Why do you have to speak to him?' Ruth demanded. 'You do it every time.'

Elizabeth walked past her, fetched a vase, and filled it with water for the flowers. 'I just say hello,' she said pleasantly. It was as if she did not care what her daughter-in-law thought, as if Ruth's anger and resentment were as much a part of an otherwise agreeable world as clouds and late frosts.

'The grass will need cutting as soon as the daffodils

have died back,' Elizabeth said. 'And the daffodils will need a little feed. I'll ask Frederick to bring down the mower, and I have some fertilizer ready to do our daffodils.'

'We can buy our own mower,' Ruth said at once.

Elizabeth laughed again. 'Don't be so absurd!' she said. 'We hardly use it, it's just a little electric mower for the front lawn around the roses, but it will do your patch of lawn. Frederick can mow it for you when he comes down.'

'I will do it,' Ruth said stubbornly.

Elizabeth turned. 'Are you quite well, Ruth?' she asked with concern. 'You seem rather irritable. Should you have a little rest this afternoon?'

Ruth looked from her mother-in-law's radiant face to the bright yellow trumpets of the daffodils and back to Elizabeth's unwavering smile. 'I'm going shopping,' she said sulkily.

'Don't hurry back!' Elizabeth called. 'We'll be fine!'

Frederick brought down the mower in his car the next day. 'This is not to be used until I've put a trip switch on the cable,' he said. 'I had no idea that I'd ever used it without one. With a trip switch, if you slice the cable by accident, then the power cuts out automatically and you don't get a shock.'

'Would it be a bad shock?' Ruth asked.

'Oh! Quite lethal!' Frederick said cheerfully. 'You'd get the full 240 volts! That'd make your hair stand on end! A number of people die every year. But the trip switch will do it. I'll pop into Bath and buy one this afternoon when Elizabeth is with you.'

'She doesn't have to come down,' Ruth said. 'You could go to Bath together.'

He looked away. 'It's how she likes it,' he said briefly. 'We're in a nice routine now.'

'But when will it change?' Ruth pressed him. 'You can't want to come down every morning and afternoon, and all through the summer as well! When will it change?'

He picked up the mower and went towards the little shed at the side of the garden. 'When he goes to school, I suppose,' he threw over his shoulder. 'When he's off our hands, a bit.'

'School?' Ruth repeated blankly.

Thomas, who had been kicking his feet in his pram, struggled to sit up and gave a little shout. Frederick instantly came out of the garden shed and took hold of the pram. 'We'll go up the lane and see if we can see some birds' nests,' he promised. He reached behind the baby and propped him up, so that he could see the passing scenery. He tipped his hat to Ruth. 'See you later, my dear,' he said.

'Do you and Patrick and Elizabeth think that we are going on like this forever?' Ruth demanded. 'Until Thomas is old enough to go to school? For four years?'

Frederick manoeuvred the pram out through the back gate and gave her a smile. 'Why not?' he asked. 'It suits us all so very well.'

Ruth put a hand out to delay him. 'Am I never to have my baby to myself?'

His smile was kind. 'Steady the Buffs,' he said comfortably. 'Let's not get dramatic. We're doing very nicely as we are.'

Ruth's hand dropped from his sleeve, and she stepped

back and watched him go up the drive, pushing Thomas's pram, and chatting to him. She thought that she would stand thus, by the garden gate, watching her son taken away from her, every day for four years. Then, when he was old enough to go to school, it would not be the school of her choice; and she would not be waiting for him at the school gate every afternoon. He would be sent to a school that Patrick and his parents preferred, and several times a week they would collect him. Most likely, it would be Patrick's old school, where his mother and father were still friends with the staff. When Thomas was seven – or at the very latest eleven years old – they would send him to go to boarding school, Patrick's old school, and she would not see him at all, from one holiday to another. He would never be her little boy, just as he had never been her baby.

Up the lane, every now and then Frederick would stop the pram and hold a leaf for Thomas to see, or incline the pram so that the baby could peep into the hedge. Ruth felt as if they might never come back to her, as if Thomas was slowly, slowly going away, and that nothing she could do, neither rage nor docility, would regain him. As Frederick said, it was a routine that suited them all very well. Ruth could see that nothing would change it.

She turned away from the garden gate and went into the garden. In one corner was the new garden shed, where Patrick kept his new tool kit – a moving-in present from his father. She took out a large reel of extension cable, and took it to the kitchen. Carefully, she took the screwdriver and removed the set of sockets from the end of it, leaving the cables bare. Two cables she wrapped in insulating tape. One – the brown live-power cable – she held with the pliers and cut and stripped the insulation away to expose a good length of copper wires. Then she put the cable and the tool box out of sight, in the cupboard under the stairs.

When Frederick brought Thomas home she smiled and thanked him for taking Thomas for his walk, lifted the baby from the pram, and showed Frederick out of the house. She gave Thomas his lunch and laid him down to sleep – not in his pram, but in his cot. Thomas watched the mobile hanging from his nursery ceiling, and fell asleep.

When his eyes closed and his breathing was steady and regular, she went down to the garden, plugged in Frederick's mower, and mowed two and a half rows, taking great care with the cable. She stopped mowing the grass at the point where the pram was usually left for Thomas's afternoon nap, and then she unplugged the mower and took it back to the shed. She wheeled the empty pram out into the garden, placing it where the cut grass abruptly ended, and bundled the blankets, so it looked as if a baby were asleep inside.

Ruth stepped back to admire the illusion of a sleeping baby in the pram, then she went back into the house and fetched the extension cable from under the stairs. She took the stripped live wire, twisted it around the shiny chrome frame of the pram, and then spooled the cable out, running it back towards the house, in through the back door, and plugged it into the socket at the kitchen worktop, but left it switched off. She went back out to the garden and looked again at the pram. The cable was almost completely hidden by the long uncut grass and by the drooping leaves of the dying daffodils. Ruth picked up handfuls of leaves and mown grass and scattered them along the line of the cable until it could not be seen from any angle.

She went to the garden shed and unwound the bright orange cable of the electric mower. She took down a pair of garden shears from the hook Frederick had made for them. Two yards from the end of the cable of the mower she snipped it cleanly in half and examined the cut. It was a good clean cut, as a mower running at full speed would make.

She left it in the shed and went back out to the garden, checking the run of the cable once again, and the connection with the pram. She went into the house and switched on. She realized she was holding her breath, waiting for something to happen, as if she would be able to see the lethal 240 volts snaking down the cable to the pram. She took up Frederick's gift to Patrick of the live-wire tester and went out to the pram. Half thinking that none of this was real, and certain that none of it would work, she laid the metal end of the little screwdriver on the pram. At once the red bulb in the handle lit up. The pram was live.

Ruth went back to the house and flicked off the switch. It was five minutes to two. Elizabeth would arrive at any moment.

'It's up to her,' Ruth said. Her mouth was curiously stiff, as if her body, like her consciousness, was slowly solidifying, freezing into horror at what she was doing. 'It's not up to me, it's completely up to her.'

The garden gate banged. Through the window Ruth saw Elizabeth walk in the garden gate without invitation, as she always did, looking around her with pleasure, as she always did, at her garden and her little house. She strolled up to the pram, put both hands on the pram

355

handle, and leaned in, as she had been asked – so many times – not to do.

'There you are, then,' Ruth remarked inconsequentially, and switched on.

There was a sudden movement as Elizabeth was flung several feet backwards from the pram. Her legs kicked, her arms flailed, and then she was still: completely still.

With dreamlike slowness Ruth unplugged the extension cable and wound it up towards the pram. The live wire had seared a small dark mark on the metal. Ruth rubbed it with her finger. It hardly showed. She took the cable to the garden shed, and tried to replace the set of sockets on the end. Her hands were useless: they were trembling too much, and her fingers were slack and uncontrollable. She pushed the wires into the sockets and left them till later. She took the electric mower out of the shed and put it precisely at the end of the cut grass, where the pram had been. She wheeled the pram into the house. There were a few tiny grass clippings that had come in on the wheels. Ruth got down on her hands and knees and cleaned the wheels of the pram, and wiped the floor from hall to back door, to catch every single spot of green.

She went back out to the garden. Elizabeth was lying where she had fallen; Ruth did not even look at her. She put the severed mower cable under the still blade of the mower, and ran the rest of the cable into the house and plugged it in.

She looked around the kitchen. Everything was back in its place, where it should be. Only then did she walk cautiously out to the garden and look into Elizabeth's face, as she lay on her back in the grass.

Elizabeth gazed up at Ruth, her eyes open. Ruth

recoiled with an exclamation of horror. Elizabeth had seen this, had seen all of it, had lain there, watching. Ruth stepped back, but Elizabeth did not rise up from the grass and come, accusingly, after her. She lay as she had fallen, her hands clenched as they had been wrenched from the pram handle, her palms scalded. Ruth stepped a little closer again. Elizabeth's open eyes were sightless. The woman was dead. Ruth stared down into Elizabeth's blanched face as if, at the end, there might have been some reconciliation. She paused for no more than a moment, then she screamed, as loudly as she could, and raced back into the house. She snatched up the phone and telephoned 999. The operator was calm, Ruth babbled about an accident, her mother-in-law cutting the grass, and managed to give the address. Then she telephoned Frederick at the farmhouse. The phone rang and rang before he answered.

'Ruth!' he said. 'I was just getting the car out to go to Bath . . .'

'Come at once! Oh, come at once!' She was weeping, hysterical.

'Is it Thomas? What have you done?'

At that one question Ruth felt a leap of extraordinary, liberating joy. Frederick's first thought had been that she might have hurt her child. 'No! No!' she said, her voice high and light. 'It's Mother! It's Mother!'

He slammed down the phone and she pictured him running to the car. In moments he was pulling up at the front door and running up the path.

'She got the mower out before I could stop her!' Ruth exclaimed. 'I was upstairs and I came running downstairs as soon as I heard the noise of the mower. But when I got out there it was – '

She broke off, Frederick brushed past her into the garden, flung himself down beside his dead wife. Ruth, very still, watched from the kitchen window as he gathered her into his arms and held her very close. Then Ruth sighed and turned away. Very carefully and tidily, she started to tie back the kitchen curtains as they ought to be.

There had to be an inquest. Ruth gave her evidence in a thin, shocked voice, and Frederick and Patrick sat on either side of her and held her hands.

The funeral was a few days later, the village church filled with mourners and bright with spring flowers, as Elizabeth would have wanted. The arrangements were not quite as she would have done them, but Ruth was learning from one of the flower rota ladies how they should be done.

The lunch was provided by a catering company, although Ruth had wanted to do it all herself. She had supervised the layout of the buffet, and it was Ruth who had insisted that they change the paper napkins for proper linen ones.

When everyone had gone home, Ruth and Patrick did not want to leave Frederick alone in the echoing house. 'We'll stay tonight,' Ruth decided. 'I'll make a quiche and salad, and we'll all have an early night.'

Next morning Elizabeth's cleaning lady, Mrs M, came in as usual, and had to come to Ruth for instructions. Together they cleared and cleaned the dining room of the remains of the buffet, and dusted and vacuumed the drawing room. Together they put fresh sheets on the upstairs beds, while Thomas struggled along the floor, practising crawling. Ruth sent Patrick down to the little house to pack their clothes for a stay of several days. 'We can't leave your father on his own,' she said. 'And I have so much to do here.'

When Patrick came back there was a light lunch on the table, and Ruth and Frederick were having a glass of sherry while Mrs M fed Thomas in the kitchen.

'I should go in to work this afternoon,' Patrick said hesitantly. 'Unless you need me here?'

Ruth shook her head. 'Will you be home at six?' she asked.

Patrick nodded.

'Dinner at eight then,' she said.

Patrick kissed her cheek and felt her breath warm against his ear.

He came home on time and heard Thomas splashing in the bath while his grandfather supervised. Ruth came out of the kitchen wearing his mother's apron, carrying two glasses of gin and tonic with ice and lime.

'Will you take one up to Frederick?' she asked. 'He's standing in for you!'

Patrick took the two iced glasses without a word. This was a new Ruth; he did not want to comment until he had the measure of her.

'I'll come up in a moment,' she promised. 'I just have to turn the joint. We're having roast beef tonight.'

Frederick and Patrick together persuaded Thomas out of the bath and into his pyjamas, then Ruth appeared with his night-time bottle and rocked him to sleep. When she came down again, it was ten to eight and dinner was ready. Frederick carved the meat. It was perfectly done.

Twenty

THEY AGREED to stay for a fortnight, until Frederick should be able to cope on his own. But when Patrick mentioned at breakfast one morning that they should return to the little house, Ruth shrugged.

'It seems so convenient,' she said. 'If Father wants us, that is?'

Frederick smiled, spooning homemade marmalade onto his plate. 'No doubt about that,' he said. 'But I'll understand if you want to get back. I'll have to adapt, that's all.'

'No, why?' Ruth interrupted charmingly. 'There's so much to do here, Patrick, you don't know the half of it. There's the garden to see to, and the house, and the baking, and the flowers. I don't think I can possibly manage it, coming up every day.'

'I don't mind at all,' Patrick said uncertainly. 'I thought you'd want to go home, that's all, to our house.'

She poured him another cup of fresh coffee. 'I never really liked it,' she said dismissively.

'It is a bit cramped,' Frederick acknowledged.

'And I can't possibly run two houses . . .'

'Do you want to stay here?' Patrick demanded.

She slid him a look from under half-closed eyelids. 'If

Father wants us,' she said. 'I should have thought it was the ideal solution.'

'But what about . . .' Patrick broke off. 'You know, not crowding each other – a bit of privacy.'

'I had a thought about that,' Frederick said. 'It struck me that Ruth might be thinking along these lines, and I was wondering about moving into your old bedroom, Patrick, at the end of the corridor. You two could have the master bedroom with the bathroom beside it, make a little suite for yourself in there.'

'Yes,' Ruth said simply. 'That's what I thought too. I know an architect who can come and have a look at it, whenever we like. And we need to redecorate upstairs anyway; it really is getting rather shabby. We could do it all at once.'

'Not more decorating,' Patrick groaned in mock horror.

Ruth did not even smile. 'I know exactly what I want,' she said. 'I know exactly how I want everything done, and I have a box of the most beautiful curtain material just crying out to be used.'

THE END

Fallen Skies

Philippa Gregory

'It is both uncompromising and brave'
ELIZABETH BUCHAN, *Daily Telegraph*

Lily Valance wants to forget the war. She's determined to
enjoy the world of the 1920s, with its music, singing,
laughter and pleasure. When she meets Captain Stephen
Winters, a decorated hero back from the Front, she's drawn
to his wealth and status. In Lily, he sees his salvation – from
the past, from the nightmares, from the guilt at surviving
where so many were lost.

But it's a dream that cannot last. Lily has no intention of
leaving her singing career. The hidden tensions behind the
respectable facade of the Winters household come to a
head. Stephen's nightmares merge ever closer with reality
and the truth of what took place in the mud and darkness
brings him and all who love him to a terrible reckoning . . .

'Superbly crafted . . . a fine book.' *Daily Mail*

ISBN 0 00 647336 9

A Respectable Trade

Philippa Gregory

As seen on BBC TV

'The great roar and sweep of history is successfully braided into the intimate daily detail of this compelling and intelligent book'   PENNY PERRICK, *The Times*

Bristol in 1787 is booming, a city where power beckons those who dare to take risks. Josiah Cole, a small dockside trader, is prepared to gamble everything to join the big players of the city. But he needs capital and a well-connected wife.

Marriage to Frances Scott is a mutually convenient solution. Trading her social contacts for Josiah's protection, Frances finds her life and fortune dependent upon the respectable trade of sugar, rum and slaves.

Into her new world comes Mehuru, once a priest in the ancient African kingdom of Yoruba. From opposite ends of the earth, despite the enmity of slavery, Mehuru and Frances confront each other and their need for love and liberty.

'Filled with authenticity.'   *Today*

ISBN 0 00 649970 8